DREAM
OF
DING
VILLAGE

DREAM
OF
DING
VILLAGE

Yan Lianke

Translated by
Cindy Carter

Grove Press
New York

First published in Great Britain in 2011 by Corsair,
an imprint of Constable & Robinson

Printed in the United States of America

ISBN-13: 978-0-8021-1932-2

Grove Press
an imprint of Grove/Atlantic, Inc.
841 Broadway
New York, NY 10003
Distributed by Publishers Group West
www.groveatlantic.com

11 12 13 14   10 9 8 7 6 5 4 3 2 1

DREAM
OF
DING
VILLAGE

VOLUME 1

The Cupbearer's Dream

In my dream, behold, a vine was before me; and in the vine there were three branches and it was as though it budded, and her blossoms shot forth; and the clusters thereof brought forth ripe grapes: And Pharaoh's cup was in my hand; and I took the grapes, and pressed them into Pharaoh's cup, and I gave the cup into Pharaoh's hand.

The Baker's Dream

I also was in my dream, and, behold, I had three white baskets on my head; and in the uppermost basket there was all manner of bakemeats for Pharaoh, and the birds did eat them out of the basket upon my head.

The Pharaoh's Dream

Pharaoh dreamed: and, behold, he stood by the river. And, behold, there came up out of the river seven well-favoured kine and fat-fleshed, and they fed in a meadow. And behold, seven other kine came up after them out of the river, ill-favoured and lean-fleshed; and stood by the other kine upon the brink of the river. And the ill-favoured and lean-fleshed kine did eat up the seven well-favoured and fat kine. So Pharaoh awoke. And he slept and dreamed the second time; and behold, seven ears of corn came up upon one stalk, rank and good. And behold, seven thin ears and blasted with the east wind sprung up after them. And the seven thin ears devoured the seven rank and full ears. And Pharaoh awoke, and behold, it was a dream.

VOLUME 2

二

CHAPTER ONE

1

The dusk settles over a day in late autumn. The sun sets above the East Henan plain, a blood-red ball turning the earth and sky a deep shade of crimson. As red unfurls, slowly the dusk turns to evening. Autumn grows deeper; the cold more intense. The village streets are all empty and silent.

Dogs are in their dens.

Chickens at roost in their coops.

The cows have returned early from the fields and are snug in their sheds.

The silence is intense. Yet even in the absence of voices or sound, Ding Village lives on. Choked by death, it will not die. In the silent shades of autumn, the village has withered, along with its people. They shrink and wither in tandem with the days, like corpses buried underground.

The grass upon the plain has turned brittle and dry. The trees are all bare; the crops have withered. The villagers are shrunken inside their homes, never to emerge again.

Ever since the blood came. Ever since the blood ran red.

Dusk had spread across the plain by the time my grandpa Ding Shuiyang returned from the city. He arrived on the long-distance coach that travels between Wei county and the distant city of Kaifeng, the bus dropping him at the edge of the main road like a fallen leaf.

The concrete road linking Ding Village with the outside world was built ten years ago, when everyone in the village was caught up in the blood-selling boom. As Grandpa stood at the roadside looking towards the village, a gust of wind seemed to clear his head and restore order to his muddled thoughts. Things he hadn't understood before began to fall into place. For the first time since he'd left the village early that morning to meet with the county cadres, the fog seemed to lift. There, standing at the roadside that linked Ding Village to the rest of the world, realization dawned on him. The realization that with clouds come the rain. That late autumn begets winter's chill. That those who had sold their blood ten years ago would now have the fever. And that those with the fever would die, as surely as the falling leaves.

The fever hid in blood; Grandpa hid in dreams.

The fever loved its blood; Grandpa loved his dreams.

Grandpa dreamed most every night. For the last three nights, he'd had the same dream: *the cities he'd visited – Kaifeng and Wei county, with their underground networks of pipes like cobwebs – running thick with blood. And from the cracks and curvatures of pipes, from the l-bends and the u-bends, blood spurts like water. A fountain of brackish rain sprays the air; a bright-red assault on the senses. And there, upon the plain, he saw the wells and rivers all turned red, rancid with the stench of blood. In every city and every township, doctors wept as the fever spread. But on the streets of Ding Village, one lone doctor sat and laughed. Bathed in golden sunlight, the village was silent and peaceful, its residents behind locked doors. But, day by day, the doctor in his white lab coat, his physician's bag at his feet, would sit perched upon a rock beneath the scholar trees and laugh. Ha-ha-ha-ha-ha. The sunshine would be filled with the sound of laughter. A big loud belly-laugh, ringing out as clear as a bell, strong enough to shake the trees and make the yellow leaves rain down, as surely as the autumn breeze . . .*

And when the dream had ended, the county bigwigs – the higher-ups – summoned Grandpa for a meeting. Since Ding Village no longer had a mayor, it was left to Grandpa to go instead. He returned to the village with an understanding of certain facts, like a series of links in a chain.

The first thing Grandpa had learned was that the fever wasn't really a fever at all. Its proper medical name was Acquired Immune Deficiency Syndrome, or AIDS. The second thing was that those who had sold their blood so many years ago, and who had come down with a fever within a fortnight of selling it, would now have AIDS. The third thing was that the first symptoms of AIDS wouldn't appear until eight, nine, or even ten years later. Most people, mistaking the symptoms for a common cold, would take medicine to bring down their fever and before long, they would be back to normal. But a few months later, the disease would flare up again, and the symptoms would be much worse: weakness, skin sores, ulcers on the mouth and tongue, dehydration and weight loss. By then, you had only a few months to live. You might manage to hang on for six months, maybe even eight or nine, but very few made it through a year. In the end, everyone who got sick died.

They died like falling leaves.

Their light extinguished, gone from this world.

The fourth thing was something Grandpa already knew: that for the past two years, people in the village had been dying. Not a month went by without at least one death, and nearly every family had lost someone. After more than forty deaths in the space of two years, the graves in the village cemetery were as dense as sheaves of wheat in a farmer's field. Some of those who got sick thought that it was hepatitis, while others called it 'a shadow on the lungs'. Still others, with perfectly healthy livers and lungs, lost their appetites and couldn't stomach food. A fortnight or so later, thin and coughing or vomiting blood, they died. *Died like falling leaves, their light gone from this world* . . . Afterwards, the other villagers would claim they had died of gastritis or hepatitis, of tuberculosis, or of a disease of the stomach or liver or lungs. But, in fact, it was the fever. Every one of them had died of AIDS.

The fifth thing Grandpa learned was that AIDS had originally been a foreigners' disease, a big-city disease rumoured to affect only deviant people. But now China had it, too. It was spreading across the countryside, and those who were getting sick were normal, upstanding people. The sickness came in waves, like swarms of locusts descending over a field and destroying the vegetation. If one person got sick, the only certainty was that many more would soon follow.

The sixth thing was that if you got AIDS, you died. AIDS was a new, incurable disease, and no amount of money could save you. But the sickness had only just begun: that was the seventh thing. The real explosion wouldn't come until the next year, or the year after next. That's when people would start dying like moths to a flame. Right now they were dying like dogs, and everyone knows that in this world, people care a lot more about dogs than they do about moths.

The eighth thing was about me, buried behind the brick wall of the elementary school. I was only twelve, in my fifth year at the school, when I died. I died from eating a poisoned tomato I found on the way home from school. Six months earlier, somebody had poisoned our family's chickens. Not long after that, my mother's pig had died after eating a poisoned chunk of radish. It was just a few months later that I found the tomato sitting on a rock by the side of the road. Someone must have put it there, knowing I'd see it on my way home from school. As soon as I'd eaten it, my belly started to ache, like somebody was stabbing my insides with scissors. Before I could walk more than a few steps, I fell down in the middle of the road. By the time my dad found me and carried me home in his arms, I was frothing at the mouth. By the time he laid me on my bed, I was already dead.

I died not from the fever, not from AIDS, but because my dad had run a blood-collection station in Ding Village ten years earlier. He bought blood from the villagers and resold it for a profit. I died because my dad was the biggest blood merchant not just in Ding Village but in Two-Li Village, Willow Hamlet, Yellow Creek and dozens of other villages for miles around. He wasn't just a blood merchant: he was a blood kingpin.

The day I died, my dad didn't even cry. He sat at my bedside and smoked a cigarette. Then he went out into the village with my uncle, his younger brother. My dad carried a pointed shovel; my uncle had a chopping knife with a gleaming blade. They stood at the village crossroads, cursing and screaming at the top of their lungs.

'Come and show your faces, if you've got the guts!' shrieked my uncle, Ding Liang. 'Don't think you can hide, you poisoning bastards! Come out and see if I don't chop you in two!'

'So you're jealous of me, is that it?' shouted my father, Ding Hui, planting his shovel in the ground. 'Can't stand it that I'm rich and didn't get the fever? Well, fuck you and all your ancestors! First you kill my chickens, then my pigs, and now you think you can get away with poisoning my boy?'

Shouting and cursing, the brothers stood at the crossroads from noon until the sky grew dark, but not a single villager came out. No one wanted to answer to my uncle, or face up to my father.

In the end, all they could do was bury me.

They put me in the ground and buried me.

By tradition, I was too young to be buried in the ancestral grave, so Grandpa carried my little corpse to the elementary school, where he lived as a caretaker. He made me a narrow wooden coffin, filled it with my schoolbooks, notebooks, pencils and pens, and buried it outside the schoolyard, behind the back wall of his house.

Grandpa had always fancied himself as a scholar. He'd gone to school, spent a lifetime as the school caretaker and bell-ringer, and was known throughout the village as Professor Ding. So it was only natural that he'd want to bury me with my books: a favourite storybook, a collection of folk tales, a few volumes of Chinese myths and legends, and a Chinese and an English dictionary.

After I was gone, Grandpa would sometimes stand at my grave and wonder if the villagers would try to kill anyone else in our family. Would they poison his granddaughter, my younger sister Yingzi? Or his only remaining grandson, my uncle's boy Little Jun? He began to think about making my father and my uncle go to every house in the village and kowtow. Make them kneel in the dirt, knock their heads upon the ground three times and beg the villagers not to poison any more of our family. Beg them not to leave us without descendants to carry on the Ding family name.

At about the same time Grandpa was mulling this over, my uncle came down with the fever.

Grandpa knew that it was retribution. Uncle was sick because he'd once worked for my father, buying blood from the villagers and reselling it at a profit. When Grandpa found out that Uncle was sick, he changed his mind about asking him to kowtow to all the villagers, and instead decided to have my father do it alone.

The ninth thing my grandpa learned was that within a year, perhaps two, the fever would spread across the plain. It would burst upon us like a flood, engulfing Ding Village, Willow Hamlet, Yellow Creek, Two-Li Village and countless others in its path. Like the Yellow River bursting its banks, it would surge through dozens, maybe hundreds of villages. And when that happened, people would die like ants. The dead would litter the ground like fallen leaves. In time, most of the villagers would die, and Ding Village would vanish for ever. Like leaves upon a dying tree, the villagers would wither and fall to the ground, to be swept away by the wind.

The tenth thing Grandpa learned was that the higher-ups wanted to quarantine all the sick people in the village so that they wouldn't spread the fever to the healthy ones, to those who hadn't sold blood.

'Professor Ding,' the cadres said. 'Your son was the biggest blood merchant in the village, so it's only fair that you step up now. You have to use your influence to convince everyone who is sick to move into the village school.'

When he heard this, my Grandpa was silent for a very long time. Even now, it makes him uncomfortable, makes him think thoughts that are better left unspoken. When Grandpa thought about my death, he wanted to force my father, the blood kingpin, to go down on his knees and kowtow to every family in the village. And when that was done, my father could throw himself into a well, swallow some poison, or hang himself. Any method would do, as long as he died. And the sooner, the better, so that everyone in the village could witness his death.

It was a shocking thought to imagine my father grovelling before the villagers and then being made to commit suicide, a thought Grandpa hadn't thought himself capable of. But when the shock had passed, Grandpa began walking into the village in the direction of our house.

He was really going to do it. He was going to ask my father to apologize to everyone and then to kill himself.

Because the sooner my father died, the better.

2

What happened to Ding Village was unthinkable: in less than two years, this tiny village of fewer than 200 households and 800 people had lost more than 40 people to the fever. Over the last year, there had been an average of two or three deaths per month. Hardly a week went by without someone dying. The oldest were in their fifties and the youngest just a few years old. In each case, the sickness started with a fever lasting several weeks, which is how the disease got its nickname 'the fever'. It had spread until it had the village by the throat, and now there seemed no end to the stranglehold. No end to the dying, and no end of tears.

The village coffin makers had worn through several sets of tools and had to keep replacing their hatchets and saws. But the season of death had only just begun. In the months to come, the dead would number like the autumn grain, and graves would be as common as sheaves of wheat.

Death settled over Ding Village like deep, black night, blanketing the neighbouring hamlets and villages. The news that passed back and forth along the streets each day was just as dark. If it wasn't that another person had come down with the fever, it was that someone had lost a family member in the middle of the night. News even spread that a woman whose husband had died from the fever was planning to remarry into a distant mountain village, as far away as possible from this fever-ridden, god-forsaken plain.

The days were slow and tortuous. Death hovered in the doorways, buzzing from house to house like a mosquito spreading disease. Wherever it touched, you could be sure that three or four months later, someone else would be found dead in his or her bed.

So many people were dying, so many were dead. In one household, a family might weep for a day before burying their relative in a black wooden coffin that had cost their life savings. In another household, there might be sighs instead of tears, a family gathering around the corpse in silent vigil before the burial.

The three elderly village carpenters worked all day long building coffins. Two of them came down with backaches from overwork. The paulownia trees used to make the coffins were all chopped down. There was no timber left in the village.

Old Mister Wang, the maker of funeral wreaths, was kept busy cutting and snipping paper flowers, until his hands were covered in blisters that dried into hard, yellow calluses.

The villagers became indolent and indifferent to everyday life. With death camped on their doorsteps, no one could be bothered to till the fields or do any planting. No one bothered to leave the village to look for seasonal work. The villagers spent their days at home, their doors and windows shut to stop the fever from coming in.

But that's what they were waiting for, waiting for the fever to rush in and kill them. Day by day they waited and watched. Some said that the government was planning to send trucks and soldiers to round up people with the fever and bury them alive in the Gobi Desert, like they used to do with plague victims long ago. Although everyone knew that this was just a rumour, somewhere in their hearts they believed it. They locked their doors and windows, stayed at home and waited for the fever to come, and for more people to die.

As the villagers died off, so did the village.

The earth grew barren. No one turned the soil.

The fields grew dry. No one watered the crops.

In some of the homes that had been touched by death, the families had stopped doing the housework. They no longer washed the pots and pans. From one meal to the next, they cooked rice in the same unwashed pot and ate with the same dirty bowls and chopsticks.

If you hadn't seen someone in the village for weeks, you didn't ask where he or she had gone. You just assumed they were dead. If you happened to run into them a few days later, perhaps while drawing water at the well, you'd just stop and stare in shock. There would be a long silence as you stared at each other in amazement. Then you'd say: 'My God, you're still alive.' And he might answer, 'I was in bed with a headache. I thought it was the fever, but as it turns out, it wasn't.' After some relieved laughter, you would brush past each other, you with your shoulder pole and wooden buckets filled with water, he continuing his way to the well with empty ones.

That's what our village had become.

Ding Village in the days of fever, the days of agony and waiting.

After making up his mind to talk to my father, Grandpa left the school and trudged down the road to the village. It was sunset, and the light had already begun to fade. When Grandpa reached the centre of the village, he saw Ma Xianglin sitting outside his house repairing his three-stringed fiddle. Ma Xianglin was an amateur singer and storyteller. And Ma Xianglin had the fever. The instrument he used to accompany his singing hadn't been played in many years; its lacquered surface was chipped and peeling. Ma Xianglin had built his family's three-bedroom brick house by selling his blood. Now, as he sat beneath the tiled eaves of the house he'd bought and paid for, he took up his fiddle and began to sing hoarsely, in a voice as rough as tree bark:

The sun that sets in the western hills
and rises from the eastern sea
brings another day of joy,
or another day of misery . . .

The grain you sell for pocket change
brings another day of plenty,
or another day of want . . .

Listening to Ma Xianglin sing, you would never guess that he was sick. But Grandpa could see that the colour of death was on him. As he drew closer, he noticed a greenish tinge to Ma Xianglin's skin. Then there were the sores, pustules that had hardened into dark red scabs, dotting his face like shrivelled, sun-dried peas. When Ma Xianglin caught sight of Grandpa, he put down his fiddle and smiled. It was the sickly, hopeful, overeager smile of a beggar hoping for food.

'Professor Ding,' called Ma Xianglin in his sing-song voice. 'I heard you had a meeting with the higher-ups.'

Grandpa couldn't help but stare. 'Xianglin, since when did you lose so much weight?'

'I haven't lost weight. I can still eat two steamed buns at one sitting . . . so what did they say?' Ma Xianglin asked impatiently. 'Have they found a cure?'

Grandpa thought for a moment. 'Sure. They said the new medicine will be here any day now. One shot and you'll be cured.'

Xianglin grinned. 'When do we get the new medicines?'

'It won't be long.'

'How long is not long?'

'Not long. No more than a few days.'

'How many days, exactly?'

'If we don't get the medicines in a few days, I'll go back and ask them.' Grandpa turned and continued towards my father's house.

Turning into a narrow alleyway, Grandpa noticed white funeral scrolls pasted on the lintels of every house. Some of the scrolls were old and yellowed; others new and blindingly white. With all that white paper fluttering in the breeze, the alley looked like it had been hit by a snowstorm. Further down the alley, Grandpa passed the house of a family whose son had died of the fever just before his thirtieth birthday. The funeral couplet pasted on the lintels read: *Since you have gone, the house is empty, it has been three seasons now / Extinguish the lamps, let the twilight come, we must endure the setting sun.* Then there was the Li family, whose daughter-in-law had died of the fever not long after marrying their son. She had been infected with the disease in her hometown and passed it on to her husband and newborn child. Hoping that their son and grandchild would take a turn for the better, the family had pasted up this couplet: *The moon has sunk, the stars are dim, the family home is dark / but there is hope that come tomorrow, the sun will shine again.*

At the next house there were two white scrolls, one on either side of the door, with no calligraphy at all. Curious as to why anyone would bother to paste up blank funeral scrolls, Grandpa took a closer look. It was only when he ran his fingers over the scrolls that he discovered two more layers of paper underneath. At least three people in this house had died from the fever. The family, either too tired or too superstitious to write yet another funeral couplet, had simply pasted up the new scrolls and left them blank.

As Grandpa stood in the doorway staring at the empty scrolls, he heard Ma Xianglin, who had followed him down the alley, shouting after him.

'Professor Ding! Since the new medicine will be here soon, why not celebrate?' Grandpa turned around slowly.

'Tell everyone to come to the school, and I'll put on a concert for the whole village. You know how well I sing, and people need an excuse to get out of their houses,' said Ma Xianglin.

'The school is the perfect place for a concert.' Ma Xianglin took a few steps forward.

'If you ask, everyone will listen. Just like they did when you asked them to sell their blood. And it was your son Ding Hui they sold it to, even though everyone knew he used the same needles and cotton swabs again and again. Not to bring up the past . . . but every time I sold my blood, I went to your son, reused needles or not. I sold him everything I had, and now when I run into him on the street, he can't even be bothered to say hello. Of course, that's all in the past, no point bringing it up now. All I ask is that you tell everyone to come to the school so I can sing them a few songs. I don't mean to harp on the past, Professor, really I don't. Just let me sing a few folk songs so I won't feel so depressed. Otherwise, I'm afraid I won't live long enough to see those new medicines.'

Ma Xianglin, now standing a few paces away, stared into Grandpa's eyes. A beggar hoping for food. Over Ma Xianglin's shoulder, Grandpa saw several other villagers gazing at him expectantly. There was Li Sanren, the former village mayor; Zhao Xiuqin, a local loudmouth known for her delicious cooking; and Zhao Dequan, a simple, honest farmer. Grandpa knew them well, and knew that they all had the fever. He knew exactly what they had come to ask.

'The new medicine will be here any day now,' he announced loudly. 'Xianglin, when do you want to give your concert?'

The old musician beamed. 'Tonight. Or if that's too soon, tomorrow night. Tell the villagers I'll sing anything they like, for as long as they want to listen.'

3

After parting from Ma Xianglin with promises, Grandpa continued walking towards our house. My family lived on New Street, south of the village. Built during the blood boom,

New Street was the newest street in the village. If you got rich from buying or selling blood, you moved your family from the village centre to New Street and built a brand new two-storey house, which was as high as local building regulations allowed. Each lot was about one *mu*, one-sixth of an acre, with a house at one end and brick walls enclosing the other three sides. Every house was covered in white ceramic tiles, and the walls were built from machine-made red brick. Red and white: the colours of joy and sorrow. All year round, the neighbourhood gave off the smell of newness and wealth. There was also a tinge of gold and a whiff of sulphur. The whole street smelled of sulphur, brick and mortar.

In the midst of all this stood our house. Night and day, the stench of sulphur filled our nostrils, stung our eyes and provoked people to envy. Everyone wanted a house on New Street, and those who couldn't afford one were willing to sell their blood to get it.

That's how they got the fever.

In all, about two-dozen families lived on New Street. At the head of every household was a blood merchant, or 'bloodhead'. The bloodheads made more money than anybody else and that's why they could afford to live on New Street. They moved south of the village, and built new houses. It was the bloodheads who made New Street what it was.

My father was the first blood merchant in the village and he soon became the richest. That is the reason why our house, which was built at the very centre of New Street, was three-storeys high, even though the local building regulations limited each house to only two. If anyone else had tried to do the same, the government would have put a stop to it. But when my father added a third storey, no one seemed to mind.

We didn't set out to build a three-storey home, not at first. When everyone else was living in thatched, mud-brick cottages, my father built a single-storey house of brick and tiles. When everyone else started building brick-and-tile houses, my father tore down ours and built a new two-storey in its place. When everyone else started building two-storey houses, my father added a third storey. When other people tried to add a third storey or build a three-storey home from the ground up, the government stepped in, saying that regulations limited model villages to buildings of no more than two storys.

But our house had three storeys: one more than anyone else.

Like most people in the village, we had a pig pen and a chicken coop in our courtyard. But they seemed out of place, they didn't match the architecture of our house. Even the pigeon cages beneath the eaves seemed out of place. In designing our house, my father had tried to copy the fancy western-style homes that he'd seen in the big city of Kaifeng. He ordered pink-and-white marble tiles for the floors and paved the courtyard with square slabs of concrete. Instead of a tried and true outdoor squat toilet of the sort that Chinese people had been using successfully for hundreds, even thousands of years, we had an indoor toilet made of white porcelain. But my parents, unable to adapt to shitting while sitting down, ended up building a squat latrine behind the house, anyway.

We also had a washing machine and a laundry room, but my mother preferred to take her basin out into the courtyard to do the washing there.

The toilet and the washing machine were just for show. Ditto for the freezer and the refrigerator, the dining room and dining table. We had these things in our house, but only to show that we could afford them. None of us actually used them.

When Grandpa arrived at our house that evening, he found the front gate locked and the whole family out in the courtyard having their dinner of steamed buns, rice soup and a stew of glass noodles, turnip and cabbage. Confetti-sized bits of red pepper clung to the cabbage, making it look like someone had shredded a Chinese New Year's calendar into the stew. Seated on low stools around a small table in the centre of the courtyard, my parents and sister were in the middle of eating their dinner when they heard a knock at the gate and saw that it was Grandpa.

My little sister let him in and closed the gate. My mother pulled up another stool and ladled out an extra bowl of soup. Grandpa picked up his chopsticks, but instead of eating, he stared at my father as if he were a stranger. There was no warmth in Grandpa's eyes.

My father gazed back at Grandpa just as coldly. Two complete strangers.

'Dad, why aren't you eating?' he asked, finally.

'Son, there's something weighing on my mind and I've got to say it.'

'Can't it wait until we've eaten?'

'No, I won't be able to eat a bite or sleep a wink until I say this.'

My father set down his bowl, laid his chopsticks across the rim and cast a sideways glance at Grandpa. 'All right, go ahead.'

'I had a meeting in the county today . . .' Grandpa began.

'And they told you that the fever is AIDS, and that AIDS is a new and incurable disease, right?' my father interrupted.

'You might as well eat your dinner, Dad, because you're not telling me anything I don't already know. Two out of three people in the village know it. It's just the sick ones who don't, and most of them are just pretending not to know.' He looked at Grandpa with disdain. It was the sort of glance a student might give a teacher setting an exam on some subject his students had long since mastered. Then, ignoring Grandpa, he took up his bowl and chopsticks and buried himself in his meal.

Grandpa was a teacher, sort of. He had spent his whole life working in the school and ringing the school bell. Now, in his sixtieth year, he was still the designated caretaker and bell-ringer. Sometimes, when one of the teachers got sick or couldn't teach for some reason, he was called in to take their place. On these occasions, he might spend half a day teaching the opening stanzas of the *Three-Character Classic*, which he would write out in painstaking, platter-sized characters on the blackboard.

Dad had once been a student in Grandpa's class, but he no longer deferred to him as a former teacher. Grandpa could see the disrespect in his son's eyes. As he watched my father take up his bowl and continue eating, Grandpa gently set down his own bowl and chopsticks on the table.

After a long silence, he said: 'Son, it's not like I'm asking you to commit suicide. I just think you should kowtow in front of the villagers and apologize for what you've done.'

My father glared at him. 'Why should I?'

'Because you were a bloodhead.'

'So was everyone who lives on this street.'

'They were just following your lead. No one made as much blood money as you.'

My father slammed down his bowl, spilling soup all over the table. He threw down his chopsticks. They rolled across the tabletop and clattered to the ground.

'Dad,' he said, glaring at Grandpa. 'If you ever raise this subject again, you're no father to me. And you can forget about me supporting you in your old age, or even going to your funeral.'

Grandpa sat woodenly, staring down at the table. Finally, he spoke.

'Son, I'm begging you . . . get down on your knees and apologize to the villagers. How can you refuse an old man?' he said softly.

'Dad, I think you should leave,' my father was nearly shouting. 'Because if you say another word, you're no father to me.'

'Hui, it's not that much to ask. One little apology and we can put this all behind us.'

'Get out,' my father screamed. 'You're not my father and I'm not your son!'

Grandpa paused for a moment to take in my father's words. 'More than forty people in this village have died,' he said as he stood up to leave. 'That makes forty apologies, forty kowtows. Or is that too exhausting for you? Would it kill you to apologize?'

Grandpa suddenly looked weary, as if the effort of making this speech had exhausted him. He glanced at my mother, then at my little sister Yingzi.

'Yingzi, come to school tomorrow and I'll help you make up those missed classes. Your regular teacher isn't coming back, so I'll be teaching language class from now on.'

When Grandpa left, no one bothered to see him to the door. He slowly shuffled out, his back hunched and his head bowed, like an old mountain goat after a long day's trek.

CHAPTER TWO

1

There are only three streets in our village. One runs east to west, the other two run north to south. Before New Street, the village streets formed a perfect cross, the same shape as the Chinese ideograph meaning 'ten'. After New Street was added, the village looked more like a cross with a horizontal line underneath, the same as the Chinese ideograph meaning 'earth'.

After his fight with my dad, Grandpa left New Street and went to my uncle's house, where he brooded for a while before walking the mile back to the elementary school. The school had originally been part of a village temple dedicated to Guan Yu, the god of wealth. Guan Yu's shrine had occupied the main hall and the classrooms were in an adjacent wing. For decades the villagers had come to the temple to burn incense and pray for wealth, but when they started getting rich from selling blood, they tore down the temple. They didn't believe in Guan Yu any more: they believed in selling blood.

After the villagers converted to blood-selling, they built a new school on several acres of uncultivated land, just south of the village. They built a red-brick wall and a two-storey schoolhouse facing east. They installed plate glass in all the windows and wooden signs on all the classroom doors: 'Grade One, Class One'; 'Grade Two, Class One', 'Grade Three, Class One', although because the village was so small, there was never more than one class per grade. A basketball hoop was put up in the schoolyard, and a wooden placard reading Ding Village Elementary School was hung from the main gate. And that was it: Ding Village had a brand new school. Grandpa moved in as the permanent caretaker. And besides Grandpa, there were two other teachers, one to teach mathematics and one for language. Both were young and had been hired from outside the village. The only thing was . . . when they found out that Ding Village had the fever, they both stopped teaching and never came back.

No way were they coming back.

No way in hell.

And so Grandpa found himself alone in the school. He was caretaker to the doors and plate-glass windows. He looked after the desks, chairs and blackboards. Grandpa was the school watchman in the wretched days of fever that swept the village and the plain.

Even now, years later, the place still had that new-school sulphur smell. On certain late autumn nights, the fumes from the school were even stronger than those from New Street. But Grandpa always found the smell of sulphur to be calming. It set his mind at ease, and made him think of days gone by.

On this particular autumn evening, dusk had come and gone and the school was bathed in silence. The blanketing silence of the plain, a quiet that seeped into the schoolhouse and billowed out again like fog. Grandpa sat on the base of the basketball hoop in the centre of the schoolyard and raised his head to the sky, enjoying the feeling of the moist autumn air on his face. It was only then that he realized he was hungry. Because of his trip to the county, he'd hardly eaten that day. His hunger set his nerves on edge and made his heart feel tight in his chest. With each pang of hunger, each tug of his nerves, Grandpa's shoulders trembled.

His mind drifted back to springtime many years earlier. One by one, the events appeared before his eyes as if it were yesterday. Like freshly budding leaves, the images unfurled and rose up before him, as crystal clear as the full moon in the sky.

Grandpa saw each detail of that spring with perfect clarity, and he *knew*.

A sudden gust of wind set the leaves rustling in the trees, reminding him of a long-forgotten spring. And with that spring came the county Director of Education, with two cadres in tow, to mobilize the villagers to sell their blood. It was only halfway into the spring, but the village had already settled into the warmth and comforts of the season, the fresh spring air and pleasant fragrances wafting through the streets. Until, that is, until the Director of Education blew in to meet with Li Sanren, the village mayor, and informed him that the higher-ups had decided to organize a blood-selling drive among the villagers.

'You want them to do what?' Mayor Li's jaw had dropped in shock.

'Good Lord. Who ever heard of asking people to sell their blood?'

Three days later, when the mayor had still not held a meeting to mobilize the villagers to sell their blood, the county director made another visit to Ding Village. While the director pleaded his case, Mayor Li squatted on the ground and chain-smoked in silence.

A fortnight later, the director returned again. This time, he hadn't come to lobby the mayor about the blood drive, but to sack him.

After forty years as the mayor of Ding Village, Li Sanren was fired from his post.

Following a brief announcement, a village meeting was held. Li Sanren sat through the meeting slack-jawed, too shocked to speak. Not that it mattered, because the county director did most of the talking. After taking control of the meeting, he made a personal appeal to the villagers to sell their blood. He talked at length about the past, the future, the development of a 'plasma economy' and the need for a 'strong and prosperous China'.

When he had finished his spiel, the director stared at the silent villagers.

'Well, did you hear what I said? Speak up!' he barked. 'I'm not here just to hear the sound of my own voice, you know.

What's wrong with you people? Did you leave your ears at home? Has the cat got your tongues?'

His shouting frightened the poultry. Far from the meeting site, chickens fluttered and squawked. His barking frightened the hounds. A dog that had been lying on the ground beside its owner stood up on its haunches, hackles raised, and began snarling at the director. This in turn frightened the dog's owner, who aimed a kick at the animal's belly and shouted: 'Shut up, for God's sake! Shut up! You'll bark at anyone!'

The dog ran off whimpering and with its tail between its legs.

The county director threw down the files he had been holding and slumped in his chair, defeated. A short while later, he left the meeting hall and went to the school in search of my Grandpa.

Although Grandpa wasn't officially a teacher at the school, he might as well have been. He was certainly the oldest person there. As a boy, he could recite the *Three-Character Classic*, rattle off the *Book of Family Names* and calculate birth-dates and fortunes according to the old Yuan dynasty lunar calendar. After the Communist revolution, there was a big drive to stamp out illiteracy in the countryside. The higher-ups opened a small school in the village temple and Grandpa became a teacher there. The first thing he did was to teach his students to read all of the surnames in the *Book of Family Names*. Next he taught them how to trace the *Three-Character Classic* in the dirt with sticks. After the higher-ups decided to gather all the students from Ding Village, Willow Hamlet, Yellow Creek and Two-Li Village into the temple school, they sent a qualified teacher to replace Grandpa, who began teaching the new curriculum: the *Revised Three-Character Classic*, Chinese poetry and civics ('Our country is the People's Republic of China and our capital is in Beijing.') It was after Grandpa stopped teaching that he took on the role of caretaker. He rang the school bell, looked after the grounds and made sure that no one stole anything from the temple.

And so it went on for decades. While the other teachers were rewarded with salaries, Grandpa received his compensation in the form of excrement and urine from the school toilets, which was used to fertilize our family's fields. Year after year, decade after decade, Grandpa took care of the school and was treated as a teacher, at least by the villagers. Yet when it came to paying salaries, the school didn't treat Grandpa as a teacher. Only when it suited them: when they were short-staffed or needed someone to teach a class. Then they were only too glad to call him in as a substitute.

That afternoon, when the county director arrived at the school, Grandpa was out sweeping the courtyard. When he learned that the director had come to see him personally, he flushed with excitement, tossed aside his broom and hurried to greet him. At the sight of the director standing at the school gate, grandpa's face turned an even deeper shade of autumn.

'Hello, chief! Come on in and sit down.'

'No time for a sit down,' the director answered. 'Professor Ding . . . every committee in the province has been ordered to go into the villages and get the peasantry to sell blood. My department has been assigned fifty villages. That is why I'm here today. I called a meeting to mobilize the villagers, but before I could say more than a few words, I ran into a bit of a snag.'

'Sell blood, did you say?'

'You're respected throughout the village, and everyone looks up to you. Since Ding Village doesn't have a mayor right now, it is time for you to step up,' said the director.

'My God . . . you want them to sell blood?'

'The Department of Education has been ordered to mobilize fifty villages as blood plasma resource centres. Ding Village is one of them. If you won't take the lead in this, who will?'

'But good heavens, you're asking people to sell their blood?'

'Professor Ding, you're an educated man. Surely you must know that the body's blood is like a natural spring: the more you take, the more it flows.'

Grandpa stood before the director, the colour draining from his face.

What had been autumn crimson was now as barren as a winter plain.

'Professor Ding,' the director continued. 'May I remind you that you're a caretaker and bell-ringer at this school, not a teacher. But every time you were nominated as a model teacher, I gave my seal of approval. And as a model teacher, you received award certificates and cash bonuses. Now I'm giving you one small assignment and you refuse to carry it out. Are you trying to show me disrespect?'

Grandpa stood at the school gate in silence. He remembered how every year, when it came time to nominate a model teacher, the maths teacher and the language teacher would vie for the honour. So intense was the competition between them that there could be no consensus, so the school always nominated Grandpa instead. After the county director had approved the nomination, Grandpa was summoned to receive his award certificate and cash bonus. Although the bonuses never amounted to much, just enough to buy two sacks of chemical fertilizer, he still had the bright-red certificates of merit hanging on his walls.

'Other provinces have developed at least seventy or eighty villages as blood plasma resource centres. If I can't even come up with forty or fifty, I'm going to lose my job,' the director pleaded.

Grandpa made no answer. By now, students were leaning out of their classrooms to stare at Grandpa and the director, their heads filling the doorways and windowsills of the school.

The two instructors who had never been chosen as model teachers were watching from the sidelines, with odd expressions on their faces. Both seemed eager to have a few words with the director, but he didn't even acknowledge their presence.

The only person the director was interested in was Grandpa.

'Professor Ding, I'm not asking for much. Just talk to the villagers and explain that selling blood is no big deal. Tell them that blood is like a natural spring: the more you take, the more it flows. That's all you need to say, just a few words on behalf of myself and the Department of Education. Won't you do this for me?'

'All right,' Grandpa mumbled at last. 'I'll give it a try.'

'Just a few words, that's all I ask.'

Grandpa rang the bell, signalling everyone to gather in the village square for another meeting. The Director of Education reminded him to keep his speech short and to stay focused on the topic: the body's blood is like a natural spring; the more you take, the more it flows, etc.

Grandpa stood beneath the scholar tree in the centre of the village and gazed at the assembled villagers for a very long time before he spoke:

'Follow me to the riverbed,' he said. 'I want to show you something.'

Dutifully, the villagers followed Grandpa to the riverbed east of the village. Despite the recent rains, the riverbed was dry. Ding Village had the misfortune to be situated along an ancient path of the Yellow River, and when the river had changed course, Ding Village and the surrounding villages and hamlets were left high and dry. It had been this way for as long as anyone could remember. For hundreds, even thousands of years. Nowadays, the only water in these parts came from the spring rains.

With a shovel in his hand, Grandpa led the procession. The Director of Education and two county cadres followed close behind. The villagers brought up the rear.

When Grandpa reached the riverbed, he searched around for a moist patch of sand, rubbed it between his hands and began to dig a small hole. Before long, the hole was half-filled with water. Grandpa produced a chipped ceramic bowl and began ladling the water from the hole and pouring it on to the sand. Again and again he ladled, pouring one bowl of water after another on to the sand. Just as if it seemed that the hole had gone dry, Grandpa paused. In a matter of moments, the water began to seep in, and the hole was once again full of water.

The more water he took, the more it flowed. It was just like the director had said.

Grandpa threw down the bowl on the sand and dusted off his hands.

'Did you see that?' he asked, glancing around at the villagers. 'Water never runs dry. The more you take, the more it flows.'

He raised his voice. 'It's the same with blood. Blood always replenishes itself. The more you take, the more it flows.'

Grandpa shifted his gaze to the county director. 'They're waiting for me at the school,' he explained. 'If I'm not there to ring the bell, the kids won't know when class is over.'

The director, who couldn't care less whether or not the students knew when to leave class, looked first at Grandpa and then at the villagers. 'Do you understand now?' he barked. 'Water never runs dry, and you can never sell too much blood. Blood is like spring water. That's just basic science.

'You can get rich or stay poor,' the director continued, kicking at the bowl lying in the sand. 'It's up to you. You can travel the golden road to wealth and prosperity, or you can stay on the same dirt path and live like paupers. Ding Village is the poorest village in the province. You haven't got two coins to rub together. Rich or poor, it's your decision. Go home and think about that.'

'Think it over,' he continued. 'Other places in the province are selling blood like crazy. In other villages, they're putting up rows of multi-storey buildings. But decades after liberation, after decades of socialism and Communist Party leadership, all Ding Village has to show for itself is a bunch of thatched huts.'

When the director had said his piece, he left. So did Grandpa.

The villagers dispersed, each to their homes. They had a lot to think about.

Rich or poor, it was their decision.

As dusk fell, a bleak chill settled over the dry riverbed. Rays of setting sun washed over the sandy soil, leaving pools of red and russet, patches like congealed blood. The fresh green smell of vegetation wafted in from distant fields of wheat and flowed across the sand like water, leaving invisible ripples on the shore.

My father, who had stayed behind after the others had left, lingered on the riverbed beside the hole that Grandpa had dug. He stared into that hole for a very long time. Finally he bent down, cupped his hands and began to drink the water, splashing it on his face and laughing.

He plunged his hands into the hole and started to dig, transforming the half-dry pit into a living spring. Water gurgled up past the rim of the hole and overflowed onto the dry sand. A broken chopstick, caught up in the eddy, was carried away like a willow twig.

My twenty-three-year-old father sat back on his heels and laughed.

2

It was after midnight when Grandpa went to bed. Images of blood-selling filled his dreams. He saw plainly the course of the fever: its causes and effects. He felt the pulse and flow of the blood-selling business and blood-wealth. Cause and effect were clear: what you plant in spring, you harvest in the autumn. You reap what you sow.

Grandpa slept in a squat, two-room brick building next to the school gate. The only furnishings in the inner room were a bed and desk. The outer room contained a simple stove, stools, bowls and chopsticks, a basin and a chopping block. If there was one thing Grandpa knew, it was the importance of keeping those two rooms shipshape. Each night before bedtime, he stacked stools against the wall, arranged bowls and chopsticks on the chopping block and stowed pails of drinking water beneath the stove. In the inner room, he swept up bits of broken chalk and placed them in a box on the top-right-hand corner of the desk. He gathered piles of old textbooks and homework notebooks and stacked them in desk drawers. If Grandpa could keep his house in order, with a place for everything and everything in its place, then he could keep his dreams neat and orderly as well. And in the morning, when the sun rose and Grandpa opened his eyes, the dreams of the night before would stay with him, as vividly real as stalks of wheat in a field or beans upon a vine. Not a word forgotten, not a detail lost.

Each night before bedtime, Grandpa put his house in order. And, each night, his dreams were as neat and orderly as the homework of a diligent student.

In his dreams, he saw so clearly the events that had led to the blood-selling.

In his dreams, he finally understood.

With a clanging of hammers, they drove in the stakes of Ding Village's first blood-collection station, a dark-green canvas tent that sprang from the soil like a fresh green turnip. Red lettering on a wooden signpost outside the tent identified it as the County Hospital Blood Bank. But on the first day, not a single villager came to sell blood. It was the same on the second day. On the third day, the county Director of Education showed up at the gate of the school in his Jeep. He had a few things to say to Grandpa.

'Professor Ding, the county governor is going to fire me if I don't get this blood station up and running. What do you suggest we do?

'I'm not trying to put you in an awkward position, Professor Ding. Tomorrow I've arranged for trucks to take some people from Ding Village on a tour of Cai county. It is the richest county in Henan; a model for the whole province. All I need you to do is recruit one person from each household to join the tour.

'In addition to giving each person a travel subsidy of ten yuan per day, we'll also be passing through the provincial capital, so everyone will have the chance to see the sights and do some shopping.

'I'm sorry, Professor, but if you don't help me organize this trip, you needn't bother ringing the bell at this school any more, because Ding Village won't have a school.'

With this, the Director of Education climbed back into his Jeep and set off for the next village on his list. The vehicle sped into the distance, the engine purring softly, unlike the noisy tractors that rumbled across the plain. Grandpa stood at the school gate and gazed at the clouds of exhaust that the Jeep left in its wake. His face had turned pale. He had always heard that Cai county, located in another region of Henan, was destitute. How on earth had it become a model of wealth for the entire province?

After the county director breezed out of the village, Grandpa had no choice but to go door to door and try to recruit one member of each household to gather bright and early at the village marketplace and wait for the trucks that would take them to Cai county.

'Does everyone really get ten yuan per day?' the villagers asked.

'That's what the director said,' answered Grandpa. 'And he's as good as his word.'

'And on the way home, do we really get to tour the capital?'

'If that's what the director said,' sighed Grandpa, 'I'm sure he's as good as his word.'

So it was that people and events were set in motion. The trip seeded the way for the people of Ding Village to begin selling their blood, as farmers fertilize their fields each spring in preparation for the autumn harvest. Whenever Grandpa saw that tour of Cai county in his dreams, his eyes would fill with tears and he would toss and turn in bed and sigh.

Cai county was more than 100 miles from Ding Village. Although the villagers had made an early start, it was nearly noon by the time they reached their destination, Cottonwood Village. Crossing the county line was like driving into some sort of paradise. The villagers were startled to see both sides of the main road lined by modern, two-storey homes of red brick and tile. The rows of houses were as neat and symmetrical as if someone had drawn them on paper with a ruler. There were flowers in every doorway, trees in every courtyard and broad avenues of poured concrete. On the outer wall of each house hung a square, red-bordered plaque with three, four or five shiny gold stars. The five-star plaques were reserved for those who had excelled at selling blood, the so-called 'Five-Star Outstanding Blood Donor Households'. The four-star plaques were given to the runners-up, and the three-star plaques to households whose blood contributions had been average.

The county director escorted his visitors on a house-to-house tour of Cottonwood. No one from Ding Village had imagined that another village could look so much like a big city. Even the streets had grand-sounding names such as Sunshine Boulevard, Harmony Avenue, Prosperity Lane and Happiness Road. Each door had a placard with the street name and house number clearly marked. Pigsties and chicken coops that had once cluttered courtyards were now concentrated in the centre of the village and surrounded by a low wall of clean red brick.

Inside the houses, even the household appliances and furnishings seemed standardized: refrigerators were to the left of the entry hall, televisions in the living room opposite the sofa, and washing machines in the bathroom next to the kitchen. Door and window frames were shiny new aluminum alloy; chests, wardrobes and cabinets were red lacquer adorned with gold leaf. The beds were heaped with silk and satin quilts and woollen blankets, and every room smelled nice.

During the tour, the Director of Education took the lead. My father followed close behind, with the people of Ding Village at the rear.

Outside on the street, they ran into a group of laughing, chattering village women loaded down with bundles of fresh vegetables and bags of fish and meat. When the villagers asked the women if they'd been out shopping, the women answered that there was no need to shop, because the village committee gave away food for free. All you had to do was go to the committee headquarters and collect what you needed for the day. If you wanted spinach or cabbage or chives, you just took some from the shelf. If you wanted pork, you got a chunk from the butcher's block. If you wanted fish, you caught one from the public pond.

The visitors from Ding Village gaped at the women in disbelief, their suspicion as thick as city walls. 'Seriously?' asked my father. 'Surely that can't be true.' His words seemed to offend the women, who stared coldly at my father and the other Ding villagers and then turned to leave without another word. They had better things to do than stand around talking to a bunch of country bumpkins. As the women walked away, they turned back to cast nasty looks at my father.

For a moment, he stood dumbstruck in the middle of that immaculate and well-planned street. Then, catching sight of another middle-aged woman loaded down with fish and vegetables, he ran over, blocking her path. 'Hey,' he said breathlessly. 'Did you really get all that food for free?'

The woman gave my father an incredulous look.

'I mean, who pays for all this fish and meat? Where does the money come from?'

By way of an answer, the woman pushed up her sleeve, revealing a patch of needle-marks on her forearm. They were about the same size and colour of small red sesame seeds. 'If you're here for a tour, then you must already know,' she said, with a sidelong glance at my father. 'We're the model blood-selling village for the whole county, for the entire province. Don't you know that everyone here sells blood?'

My father stared at the tiny pinpricks on the woman's arm. Just as the silence began to grow awkward, he looked up. 'Do they hurt?'

The woman laughed. 'Oh, they itch a little when it rains, but they're no worse than ant bites.'

'Don't you get light-headed, selling blood every day?'

The woman looked at my father in surprise. 'Who says we sell every day? It's more like once every ten days or a fortnight.

If you don't sell at least that often, your veins start to feel swollen. It's like being full of milk and not being able to nurse your baby.'

Having satisfied their curiosity, the villagers allowed the woman to continue on her way. They watched as she carried her groceries through the door of her house at 25 Bright Lane.

After that, the villagers split up into small groups to explore Cottonwood. They wandered through the alleyways, gawked at the two-storey homes that lined every street and inspected the chicken coops and pigsties in the village centre. They visited the red-tiled, green-roofed kindergarten and admired the spotless new elementary school. They went wherever they wanted, asked whatever questions they wished and marvelled at this seeming utopia – a model for county, district and province – that had been made possible by selling blood.

The district and county blood stations were located at the village crossroads. Each looked just like a hospital, with a Red Cross insignia over the entrance and doctors in white lab coats bustling in and out. The doctors spent the entire day drawing blood, testing blood and classifying it into types. Eventually, the plasma was collected into larger bags and bottles that were disinfected, sealed and processed before being shipped somewhere else.

After my father had visited the blood-collection stations, he accompanied a group of young Cottonwood locals to a social club on Longevity Boulevard, the widest avenue in the village. The club was crowded with young men ranging in age from their teens to their mid-thirties. All of them seemed to be in high spirits, their faces ruddy with the glow of good health. Some played poker or chess, while others sat around cracking melon seeds between their teeth as they watched television or read books. My father was surprised to see some of the men playing ping-pong: back then, ping-pong tables were a rarity usually found only in schools or big-city gymnasiums.

That year, the weather was unseasonably warm. Although it was only mid-spring, the men of Cottonwood had finished the spring planting and had nothing to do but amuse themselves at their club. Caught up in the excitement of card games, chess matches and ping-pong contests, they rolled up their shirtsleeves, waved their arms about and shouted encouragement or good-natured profanity. My father noticed that each of these healthy young men, like the middle-aged women he had encountered on the street, had forearms pocked with needle marks. Each bare arm revealed a patch of tiny dots like dark-red sesame seeds left to dry in the sun.

After a while, my father left the club and rejoined his friends from Ding Village. They stood together along the broad concrete expanse of Longevity Boulevard, basking in the sunshine and enjoying the warmth and fragrance of Cottonwood. They rolled up their sleeves, exposing their forearms to the hot midday sun. Side by side, their tanned and naked arms resembled a row of plump carrots on display at a greengrocer's stall. The heat beat down upon their skin, filling the air with the vaguely unpleasant smell of sweaty bodies. Mixed and muddied with other scents, it floated down the avenue like silt through river water.

The visitors from Ding Village looked down at their smooth, unscarred arms and exclaimed: 'What fools we've been, to waste all this!' They patted their untapped veins and muttered: 'What the hell, let's sell our blood. What do we have to lose?'

They slapped their arms and pinched their veins until the skin was black and blue, as mottled as a chunk of fat-streaked pork, and thought: 'Screw you, Cottonwood . . . you think you're better than us? You think that only your blood is worth its weight in gold?'

3

And so the inhabitants of Ding Village began to sell their blood. What started as a trickle soon became a stream. Before long, it had turned into a blood boom.

In this village of 800 people, a dozen blood-collection stations sprang up almost overnight. Nearly every governmental organization got in on the act: the county hospital, the village hospital, the Chinese Red Cross, the veterinary hospital, the livestock breeding centre, the Department of Propaganda, the Department of Education, the Department of Village Administration, the Department of Party Organization, the Chamber of Commerce, the police force and even the local PLA military garrison had blood banks. All it took was a hand-lettered wooden sign, some medical equipment, a couple of nurses and an accountant.

Blood banks opened in the village market, at the village crossroads and in the empty rooms of private homes. They even opened in converted cowsheds. The owners would simply scrub down the floors and walls, lay wooden planks over the trough to make a table and hang blood-collection vials from the rafters. With this and some basic equipment – needles, syringes, plastic tubes, bottles of rubbing alcohol and more vials – they were ready to begin buying and selling blood.

Throughout the village, blood-filled plastic tubing hung like vines, and bottles of plasma like plump red grapes. Everywhere you looked there were broken glass vials and syringes, discarded cotton balls, used needles and splashes of congealed blood. Bottles for collecting and sorting blood plasma dangled from rafters and littered the surfaces of benches and tables. All day long, the air was filled with the stench of fresh blood.

The trees of the village – Chinese mahogany, elm and paulownia – absorbed this same air, and their leaves and bark began to take on a faint red hue. In the past, the leaves of the scholar trees had been soft and thin, pale yellow with greenish-brown threads. But this year, the new leaves were tinged with pink and veins of brownish-purple. The veterinary hospital, which had set up its blood bank beneath a scholar tree at the west end of the village, collected so much blood that the leaves of that tree soon turned reddish-orange, its leaves much riper and plumper than in previous years.

The village dogs, alerted by the scent of blood, spent all day long sniffing the air and scratching at the doors of the blood banks. Sometimes a dog would manage to run in and grab a few wads of blood-soaked cotton in its jaws before being kicked out. Afterwards, the dog would trot back to its hideaway to gnaw and swallow its prize.

The village was filled with doctors and nurses in white lab coats. They seemed to work without rest, their foreheads soaked with perspiration, rushing back and forth like shoppers at a temple fair. They spent their days drawing blood, handing out wads of sterile cotton and telling people to keep the cotton pressed to their arms for at least five minutes.

'Press for five minutes . . . press for five minutes . . .' The doctors and nurses repeated this phrase so often that it became their mantra.

Doctors advised the villagers to drink sugar-water after having their blood drawn. Soon all of the local shops had sold out of sugar, and people had to order supplies from other counties and provinces.

Doctors counselled the villagers to take several days of bed rest after having blood drawn. So, on sunny days, the streets, alleyways, courtyards and doorways were crowded with villagers lounging on rattan chairs, wooden beds and cots.

Doctors encouraged residents from neighbouring villages and hamlets to come to Ding Village to sell blood. Soon the streets of Ding Village were crowded to overflowing with a never-ending stream of visitors. Ding Village added two new restaurants to cater for the traffic, and two stalls that sold salt, sugar, sundries and other blood-enhancing foodstuffs and tonics.

Ding Village hustled and bustled, flourished and thrived.

Ding Village quickly became Wei county's model blood-selling village. That same year, the county director sold his Jeep and bought a brand-new luxury sedan. He returned to the village in style, sauntering around the streets in his chauffeur-driven sedan and stopping to inspect every blood station along the way. He stopped off at my parents' house, where he ate two bowls of egg-and-mushroom noodles, then he dropped by at the school to shake my Grandpa's hand and give him a few words of unexpected praise.

'Professor Ding,' he said, warmly clasping Grandpa's hand. 'You're the saviour of Ding Village. You liberated it from poverty and made it rich!'

But Ding Village's blood boom was short-lived.

Cracks began to appear. The hustle and bustle receded. Things began to quiet down.

Then my father took the stage.

4

The people of Ding Village sold blood on a rotation system based on age, blood type, physical health and other factors. Nearly every villager from the age of eighteen to fifty was issued a blood-donation card, about the size of a small business card, printed on cheap brown paper. The front of the card listed your name, age, blood type and any chronic diseases or ailments. On the back was a chart that recorded the dates and quantity of each blood sale. Your card stipulated how often you were allowed to sell your blood. Fortunately for the villagers, most were allowed to sell blood once a month. Some villagers between the ages of eighteen and twenty-five – by virtue of their youth and good health – were even allowed to sell one vial of blood every fortnight. A few were limited to once every two or three months.

For this reason, the blood banks were forced to become mobile blood units: they set up camp in Ding Village one month, then moved on to Willow Hamlet, Yellow Creek or Two-Li Village the next.

After the business went mobile, selling blood in Ding Village became much less convenient. No longer could a villager show up at the local blood bank with a bowl of food and an extended arm, eat his meal as the blood dripped from his veins into a collection bottle slung from his belt, and walk out with full belly and a fistful of cash. Nor could a villager stop at the blood bank on her way home from the fields and leave with a nice crisp 100-yuan note (emblazoned with the smiling face of Chairman Mao), which she held up to the sunlight to check that it wasn't counterfeit.

Until, one day, my father made a trip to the city and returned home with a load of needles, syringes, plastic tubing, sterile cotton wipes and glass vials. He dumped his purchases on the bed, fetched a wooden plank from the pigsty and fashioned it into a hand-lettered sign that read: 'Ding Family Blood Bank'. Then he walked out to the scholar tree in the centre of the village, clanged a rock against the metal bell and shouted loudly enough for the whole village to hear:

'If you want to sell blood, come see Ding Hui at the Ding Family Blood Bank . . . the others only pay eighty per vial, but I'll give you eighty-five!'

Sure enough, after my father had repeated this announcement several times, the villagers began to emerge from their homes. By noon, our family's house was surrounded by people clamouring to sell their blood.

That was the day the Ding Family Blood Bank was born.

Within six months, Ding Village had given birth to a dozen more private blood banks. Because the owners were too inexperienced to know where to sell the blood they had collected, they sold it to my father instead. He then resold it at a considerable markup to the blood-collection trucks that loitered outside the village late at night. Once again, blood-selling took Ding Village and the surrounding villages by storm. Ten years later, when sickness descended on the plain and those who had sold their blood discovered they had the fever, death became commonplace. People died like moths to a flame.

They died like falling leaves.
Their light extinguished, gone from this world.

CHAPTER THREE

1

It is late autumn, the dawn of a new day. The sun rises above the East Henan plain. A blood-red ball turning the earth and sky a deep shade of crimson. As red unfurls, so follows morning. Another day begins.

Grandpa woke with the sunrise to begin his rounds, and was now spreading the news about Ma Xianglin's performance at the school that evening.

'Anyone home?' he called, poking his head in the door of the first house. 'There's a *zhuizi* concert at the school tonight, to celebrate the new medicine. You should come along . . . it's better than being shut up at home.'

'There's really new medicine?' came a voice from inside.

'I've been a teacher all my life,' Grandpa laughed. 'Have you ever known me to lie?'

At the next house, Grandpa pushed open the front door. 'Hey . . . don't stay inside all day worrying. Join us at the school tonight for a *zhuizi* performance.'

'Who's playing?' asked the man inside. 'Is it Ma Xianglin?'

'Who else?' answered Grandpa. 'You must have noticed he's been getting sicker. If we all show up for his concert tonight, it might cheer him up a bit, give him the strength to last until the new medicine gets here.'

'There's really new medicine?'

'I've been a teacher all my life . . . have you ever known me to lie?'

And so it went, house after house.

When Grandpa reached New Street, he saw my parents and sister walking home. They had just returned from their field and my mother held several bundles of vegetables in her arms. When they caught sight of Grandpa, the whole family froze in their tracks, as if they'd run into someone they would rather not meet. Grandpa stood in the middle of the street, an awkward smile on his face.

'Yingzi,' he called to his granddaughter. 'Come to the school tonight and listen to some songs and stories. It'll be more fun than staying home and watching television.'

Before Yingzi could reply, my mother grabbed her by the elbow and hustled her into the house, brushing past Grandpa without a word.

After they had gone, my dad and Grandpa were left alone on the street, locked in a father-son stalemate. The sun overhead cast a harsh light on the walls and tiled rooftops of New Street. From the fields outside the village came the faintest autumn chill, mingled with the delicate fragrance of freshly turned soil. When Grandpa raised his head to find the source of this scent, he saw Zhao Xiuqin's husband Wang Baoshan in the distance, working his private plot of land. Not long earlier, Wang Baoshan had decided to let the field go fallow. Since his wife had the fever, he'd said, what was the point in ploughing or planting? Pretty soon, he wouldn't have any family left to feed. But now that he'd heard the news about the new medicine, he was back outside, working in his field.

Turning the soil helps to keep it moist.

There's still time to plant some winter cabbage.

Even if we don't plant this year, it makes sense to keep the soil in shape.

There's always next year.

Grandpa watched Wang Baoshan at work, ploughing his field and turning the soil. He turned back to my father with a smile. 'You should come to Ma Xianglin's concert tonight, too.'

'Why should I?'

'Because the whole village will be there. It's a good opportunity. You can kneel on stage and kowtow, tell everyone you're sorry and that will be the end of it. One little apology, and we can put this whole mess behind us.'

'Dad, have you lost your mind?' asked my father, staring in disbelief. 'No one in this village tells me what to do, least of all you. And no one else is asking for an apology.'

Grandpa looked carefully at his son's face. It was as thunderously angry as a poster of a household god, those fierce deities that the villagers plastered on their doors to ward off evil spirits.

'Do you take me for a fool, Hui?' he snorted. 'You think I don't know that when you drew blood, you used the same cotton swabs on three or four different people? God only knows how many times you reused those needles.'

The look he received in return was pure hatred. 'Old man, if you weren't my own father, I'd slap you across the face.' With this, my father brushed past Grandpa and followed my mother into the house.

'Hui!' Grandpa shouted at his son's retreating back, 'All right, I won't make you kowtow in front of the whole village. But can't you at least say a few words of apology?'

My father didn't even bother to turn around. He had heard enough.

'You're not even willing to apologize?' Grandpa pleaded, chasing after him. 'Is that what you're telling me, son?'

As my father reached the courtyard gate, he paused. 'Don't waste your time hating me,' he spoke loudly and clearly. 'Because before the end of this year, I'm moving my family out of the village and you'll never see any of us again.'

My father ducked into the courtyard and slammed the gate behind him, leaving Grandpa standing like an old wooden hitching post on a new and more fashionable street.

But Grandpa had the final say: 'Mark my words, Hui . . . you'll come to no good end. You just remember that!'

Later that day, after the sun had set and the moon had risen, the villagers gathered at the school for music, songs and storytelling.

Using electrical cables from the classrooms, Grandpa and some of the village men rigged up several 100-watt bulbs and hung them from the basketball hoop, flooding the schoolyard with incandescent light. They placed wooden doors on piles of bricks to construct a makeshift stage. To this, they added a high stool for Ma Xianglin to sit on as he performed, and a slightly lower stool with a teapot and mug, in case he got thirsty. Once everything was in order, the performance could begin.

Villagers crowded into the basketball court in front of the stage, both the sick and the healthy sitting cross-legged on the ground, eager to join in the fun and see what all the fuss was about.

Nearly 300 villagers had turned out to see the concert. They filled the basketball court and the schoolyard like a flock of crows in a field. The sick sat towards the front, near the stage. Those who were healthy, still untouched by the fever, sat at the back.

The season was nearly over, and a late autumn chill had crept into the still night air. In Two-Li Village, Willow Hamlet, Yellow Creek and other nearby villages, they felt it too. The late autumn chill had spread through the county, the province, and all across the plain.

Some of the villagers who had come to see Ma Xianglin perform wore padded cotton jackets or had them draped over their shoulders. For those with the fever, catching cold was of vital concern: already more than a few people in the village had caught a cold and died. Even the tiniest cold could be life-threatening for someone with a weakened immune system, and the sick villagers sat huddled in their padded coats as if it was the middle of winter. The schoolyard was a jumble of laughing, chattering people. They talked about the new medicine and the fact that the fever could now be cured with a single injection. They talked about their good fortune and traded words of consolation, each as fragile as the wings of a cicada.

By now, the moon had risen over the schoolhouse. Ma Xianglin sat on the stage, perched on a stool clutching his fiddle. His face had a greenish tinge, the colour of death. The villagers realized that Ma Xianglin's illness had reached a critical stage, and that he didn't have much longer to live. If the new medicines didn't get there soon, he would probably be dead within a couple of weeks.

And yet if he could spend each day like this, playing his fiddle and singing his cares away, maybe he could alter his fate. Maybe the difference between life and death really was that simple. Maybe he would manage to hang on for a few more weeks, or even a few more months. As long as he was willing to sing, and the villagers were willing to listen.

Grandpa emerged from his rooms with a thermos of hot water and two empty bowls. 'Anyone thirsty?' he called to the people gathered in front of the stage. He even bent down to ask several of the elderly villagers if they wanted anything to drink. When everyone had assured him that they were fine and not at all thirsty, Grandpa placed the thermos and bowls in a corner of the stage and turned to the ailing Ma Xianglin.

'Shall we get started?' Grandpa asked loudly. 'The moon's already risen.'

'Let's begin,' answered Ma Xianglin in his sing-song voice.

With these words, Ma Xianglin was miraculously transformed. He began tuning his fiddle and confidently testing the strings (the instrument was already in perfect tune, and he knew it). Everyone knew that his white hair, scabby skin and purplish lips and gums were bad omens, signs that death was near. But as Ma Xianglin started to play, his face regained some colour, a glow that seemed to come from deep within. He smiled at the villagers and then, composing his expression, drew the bow across the strings of his fiddle. He looked as cheerful as a rosy-cheeked young man preparing for his wedding. Even the sores on his face glowed red beneath the stage-lights, like tiny spots of brightness.

The blood seemed to have returned to Ma Xianglin's darkened lips, turning them red again. Eyes half-closed, he bobbed his head in time with the music, playing only for himself, as if the audience didn't even exist. The fingers of his left hand moved up and down the neck of his instrument; now slowly, now more quickly. With his right hand, he drew his bow back and forth between the strings; now quickly, now slowly again. The sound that emerged was like water flowing across parched desert sands. Clear and cool, but with an undercurrent of stifling heat; hot and prickly, but with a promise of something fresh and clean. After nodding a few times, Ma Xianglin announced that he would open with 'Words on Leaving Home', a ballad known to all the villagers. He cleared his throat and began to sing:

A son left home to journey far away
His mother saw him to the village gates
Her words fell light upon his ears
But proved worth their weight in gold

Oh son, she said, my son
The world out there is not like home
Remember to dress warmly
When the weather's cold
And keep your pantry stocked
So that you never starve

When you meet an old gent
Respect him as you would your father
When you meet an old woman
Address her as you would your mother

Call the older ladies 'Auntie'
And the younger ladies 'Ma'am'
Treat young women as your sisters
And young men like brothers of your clan . . .

When Ma Xianglin had finished singing the song, he launched into another about Mu Guiying, the famous female general of the Song dynasty. He sang about Cheng Yaojin, a salt merchant who had led a peasant uprising during the Sui dynasty. He recounted the adventures of the 'Three Knights-Errant and the Five Sworn Brothers' and other well-known heroes from Chinese history.

As Ma Xianglin basked in the glory of being on stage, the villagers became conscious of small details they had forgotten about him. For one thing, Ma Xianglin had never had a talent for remembering lyrics. As a young man, he'd failed to master the big book of lyrics and librettos that all students of Hunan folk opera were required to memorize. Although he had been an enthusiastic student, his inability to memorize lyrics and his tendency to play and sing off-key had led his operatic master to dismiss him from the theatre troupe. Thus deprived of a professional career, Ma Xianglin had spent a lifetime singing and playing his three-stringed fiddle in the confines of his family's courtyard. This night, before an audience of 300 people, was no different: Ma Xianglin had still not mastered that big book of lyrics and librettos. Unable to remember all the words, he simply sang the passages he could remember. Fortunately, those he remembered were the best ones.

Ma Xianglin performed well-loved songs, extracts from his favourite plays and bits from operas. Not only was it his first time performing for the villagers, it was the first time he'd played on a real stage. It was his first proper performance, and perhaps his last. For all these reasons, and because Grandpa had gone to so much trouble to arrange the concert, Ma Xianglin put forth all the passion and concentration he could muster. He stood straight and tall, his head held high. He sang with half-closed eyes, seeing no one, completely immersed in his music. As the fingers of his left hand danced up and down the strings of his fiddle, he drew the bow in his right hand back and forth. Although his voice was a bit raspy, its coarseness was like a pinch of salt in a pot of pork-bone soup: it only made the broth seem tastier.

He sang in the local dialect and his audience could understand every word. He sang about generals and rebels, robbers and heroes, and real-life characters from Chinese history, all of whose names were known to most of the villagers, at least the older ones, and whose faces often decorated colourful Chinese New Year posters. Although these characters had lived hundreds, even thousands of years ago, their adventures were as familiar to the villagers as if they'd happened yesterday. For those who knew the stories already, hearing Ma Xianglin perform was like eating from only the finest dishes at the banquet. For teenagers and children who didn't know the background to the stories, watching Ma Xianglin's gestures and expressions was enough.

As Ma Xianglin bobbed his head in time to the music, his forehead began to perspire, giving his face an even ruddier glow. Beads of sweat flew from his face, spattering the people sitting nearest. The rhythmic tapping of his feet on the willow planks of the stage sounded like someone striking a wooden fish-drum over and over. When he reached a particularly exciting passage, he would begin stomping on the boards with his right foot, like he was pounding a gigantic drum.

Although the schoolyard was filled with music and song, the evening was eerily silent. No one in the audience made a sound. The moon and stars above were milky-white; they cast a stark, radiant light over the plain. From distant fields of wheat, now blanketed in pale-green seedlings, came the whisper of new life, a sound as imperceptible as a cloud of feathers drifting through the air. In fields that had been allowed to go fallow – for some of the villagers, there seemed little point in planting this season – rows of withered stalks gleamed pale beneath the moonlight, giving off a whiff of futility and decay. Closer still, from the ancient path of the Yellow River, the smell of sand: as if the grains had been heated over a fire and then doused with water. The scents converged in the schoolyard, mingling with the cool night air and touching the proceedings with a different kind of atmosphere, something peaceful and hypnotic, set to the strains of Ma Xianglin's music.

Ma Xianglin smiled and nodded, bobbing his head in time to the beat. Like a maestro giving the performance of his career, he was so immersed in his singing that he scarcely noticed when his voice grew hoarse. The villagers were equally rapt. Watching Ma Xianglin's impassioned performance, it was easy to forget that they were just like him: that they too had the fever and that any day might be their last. His passion was infectious. It was so easy to forget about everything. To think about nothing but the music, losing themselves in Ma Xianglin's singing, the sound of his three-stringed fiddle and the rhythmic tapping of his feet on the boards of the stage.

That was all there was. Nothing else mattered.

A strange deathly silence had settled over the schoolyard. An audience of nearly 300 people, as quiet as an audience of one, listening to Ma Xianglin's voice:

> *With sword in hand,*
> *Xue Rengui marched west*
> *For days and nights and hundreds of miles*
> *His men and mounts withstood the test*
> *Exhausted and outnumbered,*
> *Through hamlets, villages and towns*
> *They felled a mighty army*
> *And struck their enemies down.*

Suddenly, the schoolyard was not as silent as before. It started with whispers, which turned into loud conversations. Some of the villagers began turning to look behind them. Although it wasn't clear what they were looking at, others followed suit. In the midst of all this looking and pointing, whispering and talking, Zhao Xiuqin and her husband Wang Baoshan stood up from the audience and shouted: 'Professor Ding . . . Professor Ding!'

The music and singing came to an abrupt halt. Grandpa rose from his place near the front of the stage. 'What's wrong?'

'Are there really new medicines that can cure the fever?' Zhao Xiuqin asked loudly, looking at Grandpa. 'And don't lie to me like you've been lying to the whole village.'

'I've been a teacher all my life,' answered Grandpa. 'Have you ever known me to tell a lie?'

'But your son Ding Hui is sitting back there,' Wang Baoshan took up his wife's argument, 'and he says there is no such thing. He says he's never heard of these new medicines that are supposed to cure the fever.' He turned to look towards the back of the schoolyard.

As if on cue, everyone in the audience swivelled their heads to look.

There, standing at back of the crowd with my sister Yingzi, was my dad. No one had imagined that he would actually show up at the concert. But he hadn't wanted to be left out, so had come to join in the fun, to listen to the music and stories just like the rest of the villagers. And while he was there listening, he had apparently told someone that there weren't any new medicines that could cure the fever.

That was what had caused the ruckus, and the trouble that followed.

By now, all of the villagers were staring at my dad. They waited for him to speak, as if his words might hold the cure they had been hoping for.

Ma Xianglin was no longer singing. He stood on stage, watching the events below. The silence that followed was deafening. The sort of silence one hears after the fuse has been lit on a bundle of dynamite or a keg of gunpowder. The villagers seemed to be holding their breath, as if the slightest exhalation might set off an explosion. They stared at Dad and Grandpa and waited to see what would happen. They waited for the explosion, and the aftermath.

My dad spoke first. 'What's the point in lying?' he shouted over the heads of the crowd. 'Why don't you just tell them the truth? There aren't any new medicines.'

Once again, all eyes turned to Grandpa.

Grandpa said nothing.

He stood stiffly, staring back at the villagers. Then, skirting the edge of the audience, he began walking towards my dad. He moved slowly and deliberately, threading in and out of the crowd, struggling under the weight of its gaze, until he had reached the back of the schoolyard and was standing face to face with his son. In the yellow glare of the light bulbs, Grandpa's face was a mottled blue and purple; his eyes, two angry red orbs bulging from their sockets. As he glared at his son, he clenched his fists unconsciously and chewed at his lower lip, raking it with his teeth.

Dad stared back at Grandpa, his face impassive, daring him to do his worst. Father and son stared at each other coldly, stubbornly, neither willing to back down. With so many villagers watching, the schoolyard seemed to have as many pairs of eyes as trees in a forest; the atmosphere was as dense as the sandstorms that blew across the plain. The looks that passed between father and son were cold as ice, as sharp as daggers. Looks that could kill.

The moments stretched on. Grandpa was still clenching his fists, perspiration dripping down his back. The corner of his mouth began to twitch as if being tugged by an invisible string. There was another involuntary twitch, and then, with a loud cry, Grandpa attacked. Arms outstretched, he lunged forward and grabbed my dad by the neck, throwing him off balance. Before anyone could react, Grandpa had wrestled Dad to the ground and had both hands wrapped around his throat, and was choking him.

'How would you know there aren't any new medicines?' Grandpa shouted. 'How would you know? . . . I'll teach you to buy people's blood! I'll teach you a lesson you won't forget!'

Still shouting and cursing, Grandpa dug his thumbs into my dad's throat, expertly cutting off his airway. Dad lay sprawled on the ground where he had fallen, flailing his legs and trying to push Grandpa away, but Grandpa was now straddling his chest, thumbs pressing down hard on his Adam's apple. With a sickening crunch, Dad's windpipe collapsed, and his eyes rolled back in his head, bulging from their sockets. His kicking slowed; his feet pedlled the ground a few times and then stopped. His hands grew weak, then fell away from Grandpa's chest.

It happened quickly, like a thunderstorm from a clear blue sky. Moments before, there hadn't been a cloud in sight, then Grandpa had begun to strangle the life out of his son. There was no going back. This couldn't be undone. And yet Grandpa was my father's father, and Father was my grandpa's son: flesh of his flesh, blood of his blood. It wasn't supposed to be like this, father and son trying to kill each other, fighting to the death. But that is exactly what it was: a death match.

Watching from the sidelines, my sister Yingzi was in tears, crying out first for her daddy, then for her grandpa.

Everyone else seemed to be in shock. Maybe it was shock, or maybe it was something else. None of the villagers clustered around the two men had made any attempt to stop the fight. No one had spoken. It was the rapt silence of a crowd watching two bulls lock horns, the silence of spectators at a bullfight or a cockfight, the suspenseful waiting to see which side would win.

The whole village waited to see whether or not Grandpa would strangle the life out of his son.

'Daddy, Daddy, no . . . !' My sister's screams broke the silence. 'Stop it, Grandpa, stop it!'

Grandpa reacted to Yingzi's cries as though he'd been struck with a blow to the back of the head. He loosened his grip on my father's throat. His hands went slack, and then he just . . . let go.

It ended as quickly as it began. A passing thunderstorm; a sudden shower.

Like a man awakening from a bad dream, Grandpa shook his head and struggled to his feet. He seemed confused by the crowd of people, dazed by the glare of lights overhead. As he stared at his son sprawled on the ground, he muttered to himself in a voice too low for anyone to hear: 'All I asked you to do was apologize . . . Would it have killed you to say you're sorry?'

My dad lay on the ground, struggling to catch his breath. He lay there for a long time before he finally managed to sit up. His breathing was ragged, his skin mottled red and white. He looked like someone who had scaled a mountainside and finally reached the top, exhausted. Dad loosened his collar to get some air and unzipped his grey autumn jacket, revealing two thumb prints that stood out on his neck like angry red burns. His eyes watered, but he didn't even bother to wipe away the tears. Nor did he speak; he couldn't have if he'd tried. The noise coming from his throat sounded like the wheezing of an asthmatic.

After a while, the wheezing subsided and my dad rose to his feet. He glared at Grandpa – a cold, hate-filled look – then reached out and slapped my sister across the face.

'I told you we shouldn't have come here,' he roared. 'But you insisted! You should have listened to me! Next time you'll listen!'

Dad glowered at Grandpa – oh, if looks could kill – before turning his gaze on the villagers, the same people who had stood by and watched him being strangled by his own father. Not one of them had tried to stop the fight, not one of them had stepped in to save him. Dad wheeled around, grabbed Yingzi by the hand and stomped off, dragging my weeping sister behind him.

Grandpa watched my father walk away until he was just a blur in the distance, a shrunken figure at the school gate.

Then, his face covered in perspiration, Grandpa began retracing his steps to the stage, stopping only when he stood face to face with Ma Xianglin. The musician seemed not to have moved at all: he was rooted to the same spot on the stage. Grandpa turned to the villagers, likewise frozen in their places. He gazed at them for a moment before falling to his knees with a thump. In a voice loud enough for everyone to hear, Grandpa proclaimed, 'As you can see, I'm not a young man. I kneel before you now, in my sixtieth year, to apologize to everyone on behalf of my oldest son, Ding Hui. I know a lot of you got infected from selling him your blood, and he is to blame for that. But please remember that my youngest boy has the fever too, and my twelve-year-old grandson died after being poisoned. Seeing as how it is come to this, I hope you can find it in your hearts to forgive us.'

Leaning forward, my grandfather knocked his head against the boards of the stage. 'Please accept my apology. I beg you not to hold a grudge against our family.'

Thwack. Grandpa struck his head upon the stage a second time. 'I know I let everyone down. I was the one who told you that blood is like a natural spring, that the more you take, the more it flows.'

Thwack. The third and final kowtow. 'I also want to apologize for helping the government organize the trip to Cai county. The trip that started everyone selling their blood, and sold you into the sickness you are suffering from today.'

After the first apology, several of the villagers jumped on the stage and tried to lift Grandpa up. 'There's no need for this,' they told him. 'There's really no need.' But Grandpa managed to shake them off and perform the final two kowtows, thus completing the ritual. When he was finished, he rose to his feet like a man who had fulfilled a vow, or made good on a long-overdue promise.

Grandpa gazed at the large crowd of villagers like a teacher surveying a classroom full of students. They looked back at him expectantly, as if waiting for him to announce the start of class.

'Beginning tomorrow,' Grandpa announced in his most professorial tone, 'anyone who is sick can come and live in the village school. Now, I know the village hasn't had a cadre in years, but if you're willing to put your trust in me, I promise that I'll take care of you. You'll be fed and housed at the school. I'll make an appointment with the higher-ups to ask for a food subsidy. Just say the word and I'll get you anything you need. And if you don't think I'm working hard enough on your behalf, you can go to my sons' houses and poison their pigs, their chickens, and any children they have left.'

'I might as well tell you the truth,' Grandpa continued. 'The higher-ups never said there were any new medicines that could cure the fever. What they told me is that the fever is really AIDS, and that it's a contagious disease, like the plague. Even the government doesn't have a cure. It's a new disease, and once you get infected, it's fatal. If you're not afraid of passing it on to your families, you can stay at home with them. But if you're worried about infecting them, you are welcome to come and live at the school, and leave your families at home where they will be safe.'

Grandpa paused for a moment and scanned the crowd of villagers. Just as he was about to continue his speech, there was a thudding sound behind him, like a wooden pillar crashing on stage. Grandpa turned around to see that Ma Xianglin had toppled from his stool, his neck twisted at an unnatural angle, his face as white as a funeral scroll. His fiddle lay on the ground beside him, its strings still vibrating from the fall.

When Grandpa had announced that there weren't any new medicines, Ma Xianglin had collapsed. Tiny streams of blood trickled from his mouth and nostrils.

The schoolyard filled with the stench of blood. Ma Xianglin was gone. He had died on the only stage where he had sung.

3

Grandpa helped Ma Xianglin's wife make the burial arrangements. He even commissioned an out-of-town artist to paint a portrait of the musician. The artist, of course, knew nothing about the fever that had hit Ding Village, and Grandpa didn't bother to tell him. The funeral portrait was a scroll painting showing Ma Xianglin with his eyes closed, immersed in his music, giving the performance of a lifetime to an enormous audience. Thousands of people watched in fascination, listened in rapture as Ma Xianglin sang his songs and played his fiddle. The portrait was crowded with faces. People perched on the wall of the schoolyard or high up in the branches of trees. It was quite a crowd, a sea of humanity. It resembled a temple fair, with vendors plying the crowds, selling sweet potatoes and candied apples on sticks. The portrait looked like a fun place to be.

At the funeral, they rolled up the scroll and placed it in Ma Xianglin's coffin, alongside his beloved fiddle.

That was how they buried Ma Xianglin, with his favourite instrument and his finest moment.

Then they nailed down the coffin and put him in the ground.

VOLUME 3

CHAPTER ONE

1

After Ma Xianglin's funeral, the sick began flocking to the village school. Some came just for their meals; others moved in for good.

Winter came, and with it the cold, and the first snowstorm. It fell with a fury, as thick as goose down, carpeting everything in white. The world turned white almost overnight. The plain became a sheet of crisp white paper upon which the villages were sketched, with people and animals dotting the landscape.

As the weather grew colder, sick villagers with nowhere else to go were only too glad to move into the village school. What had once been an elementary school and before that, a temple dedicated to Guan Yu, the Chinese god of good fortune, now became a hospice for people with the fever. The coal, firewood and kindling formerly used to heat classrooms now warmed makeshift dormitories, drawing even more sick villagers to the school.

One day, during a visit to the school, Li Sanren, the former village mayor, whose fever had become quite serious, decided he didn't want to go home. Li Sanren had been living at home with his wife. Although she cooked his meals, made his bed, washed his clothes and boiled his medicinal herbs, he found her standard of care lacking.

'Professor Ding,' he said, a smile lighting up his sickly face, 'what do you say I come and live here, at the school?'

And that's exactly what he did. Li Sanren went home and fetched his bedroll, said goodbye to his wife and moved into his new lodgings at the school. Life in the schoolhouse was, if anything, better than his life at home: the walls were thicker, not nearly so draughty, and there was always plenty of firewood. Some of his meals he took with Grandpa; others he cooked for himself in a small upstairs room.

Winter settled in.

The early days of winter brought another death to the village, this time a woman who had been infected despite never having sold a drop of blood. Wu Xiangzhi was only thirty when she died, and barely twenty-one when she'd married Ding Yuejin, a relative of ours. Wu Xiangzhi was a delicate thing, a timid sort of girl who fainted at the sight of blood. For this reason, her husband had always pampered her.

'I'd rather die than let my wife sell blood,' he'd say. 'I'd sooner sell all the blood in my veins than let my woman get involved in such a dirty trade.' Yet the husband who had sold his blood was still alive and well, while his wife was dead in her grave. Several years earlier they had lost a baby daughter to the fever, the infant who Wu Xiangzhi had nursed. The villagers could scarcely believe it. Was this the way the fever spread, was this how whole families got infected?

Fear and uncertainty brought more people flooding into the school. Soon, nearly every villager with the fever was living in the elementary school. My uncle Ding Liang was one of the last to arrive.

The day his wife dropped him off at the school gate, it was snowing. The couple stood awkwardly, shuffling their feet in the snow. 'You'd better go,' my uncle said at last. 'There are too many sick people here. If I haven't infected you, someone else might.'

But my aunt continued to stand there, snowflakes falling on her hair.

'You go on home,' Uncle told her. 'Don't worry about me. I'll be okay. My dad's here.'

Obediently, my aunt turned and began to walk away. Uncle watched her disappear into the snowstorm. She was quite far away when he shouted, 'Don't forget to visit! Come and see me every day!' My aunt nodded her head, confirming that she'd heard him, but still Uncle made no move to enter the schoolyard. He stood at the gate, gazing after his wife. It was the gaze of a lover, the gaze of a man who feared he might never see his wife again. Uncle loved his wife. He loved her as he loved this life.

Uncle had been experiencing the symptoms of the fever for some time, but the initial discomfort had passed. Although he hadn't the strength to lift a pail of water, he had regained his appetite and could eat a whole steamed bun and half a bowl of soup at one sitting. Several months earlier, when the disease had first taken hold, he'd assumed it was a common cold or fever. After a brief respite during which he had seemed to recover, his skin had begun to itch. One morning Uncle woke to find his face, crotch and trunk covered in nasty-looking sores. The itching was intolerable, so bad that it made him want to bash his head against a wall. He began suffering from unexplained sore throats, bouts of nausea and an inability to eat, even when he knew he was hungry. He seemed to vomit up twice as much food as he managed to swallow. By then, Uncle realized what was happening: he had the fever. Worried about infecting his wife Tingting or his son, my cousin Little Jun, Uncle decided to move out of his bedroom and into a separate room of the house.

'Someday soon, I'll be dead,' he told my aunt. 'Once I'm gone, I want you to take Jun and leave Ding Village. Get married to someone living far away, as far away as possible from this awful place.'

Yet his conversation with my dad was a different story. 'Brother,' he said, 'Tingting and Jun went into the city for tests and they came up negative. When I'm dead, you've got to make sure they don't leave the village. If Tingting ever remarried, I'd roll over in my grave. My soul would never rest in peace.'

Yes, Uncle loved his wife, almost as much as he loved his life.

One day, thinking about his illness, and the fact that he would soon die, the tears began to fall. 'Why are you crying?' my aunt asked.

'It's not dying I'm afraid of,' Uncle sniffled. 'I just hate the thought of leaving you alone. Promise me that when I'm gone, you'll get remarried and take our son away from this village.'

His conversation with my grandpa was a different tune. 'Dad,' he said, 'you know Tingting listens to you, and you know she trusts you. Since no one in this world will ever love her as much as me, and no one will ever treat her better, you've got to convince her to stay in the village and never get remarried.'

But Grandpa wasn't ready to make this promise. 'If you stay alive, son,' Grandpa reasoned, 'she'll have no cause to get remarried. There's an exception to every rule, right? Folks get diagnosed with terminal cancer all the time, but some of them survive for ten more years.'

Hoping that he might prove an exception to the rule, Uncle went on with his life, taking second helpings at meals and drinking double shots of sorghum whisky for dessert. As a twenty-nine-year old man in his prime with an attractive twenty-eight-year old wife, his biggest worry now was his sex life. His wife refused to let him touch her, or even hold her hand. What was the point of defying the odds, of going on living, if your life had no meaning? He wished he had someone to talk to, but when it came to sex, he had no idea how to broach the subject.

Oh yes, Uncle loved his wife. He loved her, but he also loved his life.

It was unfortunate that after leaving her husband standing at the school gate, my aunt forgot to turn back and look at him. Uncle kept watching, waiting for her to turn around, but she never did. He bit his lip so hard it bled, but he wasn't going to cry.

Still biting his lip, Uncle kicked at a pebble on the ground.

The little village school grew crowded. Nowadays, the people roaming the halls were not elementary school students but grown men and women, mostly between the ages of thirty and forty-five. Following Grandpa's instructions, the sexes were segregated: men's dorms in the classrooms on the second floor, and women's dorms on the first floor. Some brought proper beds from home, while others slept on doors or wooden planks. The less-fortunate simply pushed a few desks together and slept on top of them. The tap in the schoolyard was constantly running, and there was always a line of people waiting in front of it. Near the tap, there were two small storage rooms piled with broken desks, chairs and classroom equipment. One had been converted into a kitchen for the residents. As soon as one person had cleared a space near the door and set up a stove, another installed a wooden board for kneading dough beneath the windowsill, and so on, until the little room was so cluttered you could hardly put a foot down.

The clean white snow in the schoolyard was trampled into mud.

Spaces beneath stairwells overflowed with jars, crockery, and sacks of rice and grain.

Grandpa bustled around the school, giving instructions to the residents and overseeing what got moved and where. He made sure that the classrooms were cleared of essential items. Blackboards, chalk, textbooks and homework notebooks left behind by students were collected and locked safely in a storage room.

Though students had stopped coming to class, the school remained in use. There were people who needed it. Grandpa, his brow moist with youthful perspiration, busied himself looking after everyone's needs. Having something to do made him feel younger and more energetic. Even his hunched back seemed straighter. Although his hair was still white, it looked shinier and healthier, not as grizzled as before.

In a second-grade classroom, residents pushed desks against the wall and arranged chairs in the centre of the room to form a meeting hall. One of the residents, a man who couldn't cook very well, made a suggestion: 'As most of us are sick and are going to die soon, why should we have to cook for ourselves? Wouldn't it make more sense to eat our meals together?'

After some quick calculations, the residents agreed that cooking separately was a waste of time and money. By eating together, they could save on firewood and conserve their food stores. The most critical matter now was the promised government food subsidy. The higher-ups had promised to provide high-quality rice and enriched flour to everyone with the fever who agreed to be quarantined in the school. The reasoning was that this way, sick villagers wouldn't have to cook for themselves, and they could also save money on food and rent.

Grandpa called everyone to a meeting in the converted classroom. This seemed appropriate because he was, after all, a teacher. Well, a sort-of teacher. Many of the residents were illiterate, unable to read or write more than a few characters, but those who were able to read had been taught by Grandpa in his days as a substitute teacher. They were, in a sense, his students. Now they were grown men and women, but they were living in the school, a place where Grandpa had always been in charge of things. All of them were sick, and some might die any day now. Grandpa was the only one at the school who didn't have the fever, and he wasn't afraid of catching it. It was only natural that they would look to him as a leader. Well, a sort-of leader.

The residents filed into the classroom and began taking their seats. Among them were Ding Yuejin, Zhao Xiuqin, Ding Zhuangzi, Li Sanren, Zhao Dequan and a sprinkling of other villagers, a few dozen in all. The classroom was crowded. There were people everywhere, sitting or standing, some leaning on walls. Everyone seemed relaxed and smiling, just happy to be together. Like students waiting for the start of class, they waited quietly for Grandpa to begin the meeting.

Standing at the front of the classroom on a dais made from three layers of bricks, Grandpa gazed at the villagers like a teacher surveying his class. 'Settle down,' he said. 'Everyone take a seat.' When those who had been leaning against walls or windowsills had sat down, Grandpa addressed the group in a practised voice.

'First, I've spent my life working in this school, and I suppose you could say I'm halfway to being a teacher. Now that you're living in this school, you'll listen to me and do as I say. If anyone has a problem with that, please raise your hand.'

Grandpa eyed the assembled residents and waited. Several grown-up villagers began snickering in their seats like school-children. Grandpa shot them a stern glance.

'Okay, since no one raised their hand, that's settled. Number one on the agenda: until we receive the government food subsidy, we'll have to pool our staple food supplies. Ding Yuejin will be in charge of keeping accounts. Your contributions of flour, rice and grain will be sorted for quality and recorded in your account. If you contribute more than your monthly quota, your contribution for the following month will be reduced. Likewise, if you contribute less than your quota one month, you'll be expected to make up for it the next.

'Two: although you won't be charged for the water you use, we'll take up a collection for the electricity bill each month. I don't want to see anyone leaving the lights on all night long. You should try to conserve electricity, just like you would at home.

'Three: the women will handle the cooking, and the men will do maintenance and other chores around the school. The very sick will have lighter workloads, and those who are healthy will be expected to take up the slack. I'm putting Zhao Xiuqin in charge of the cooking. You ladies can take turns cooking every day, or every three days, or whatever schedule suits you best.

'Four: I'm in my sixties now, and like most of you, my days are numbered. None of us knows how much time we've got left, so let's be honest with each other. Once we're dead, other people in this village still have to go on living. One of these days we'll be gone from this school, and the kids will be back in their classes. So let's agree that starting today, you won't go running back home willy-nilly, kissing your wives and kids and spreading the disease to your families.

'Another thing: now that you're living in this school, I trust that everyone will respect school property. That goes for everything, including chairs, desks, windows and walls. Don't go thinking that because these things don't belong to you, you can do with them what you like. Please treat this school with the same respect you'd treat your home.

'Five: the reason we're here is not just to avoid infecting other people, but to make your lives more pleasant, and to enjoy the time you have left. You can play chess or watch television, read or sleep. If you want some special activity or a particular kind of meal, all you have to do is ask. Whatever you want to do, you can do. Whatever you want to eat, you can eat. I want to say one thing to everybody here: I know that the fever feels like the end of the world, but if the world's going to end anyway, your final days ought to be your happiest ones.'

Here, Grandpa paused and turned to look out of the window at the snowstorm. The snowflakes were as large as pear blossoms, and just as white. As they fell, they transformed the trampled, muddy schoolyard into a clean white expanse.

A rush of cold air came through the door, mingling with the classroom stench of sickness, like clean fresh water swirling into a muddy stream. Outside in the schoolyard, a spotted dog that had most likely followed its owner to the school sat beneath the basketball hoop. It seemed to be staring at the classroom windows, hoping to find its master inside. Now covered in snow, it looked like a little lost sheep.

Grandpa turned his attention back to the classroom. Surveying the crowd of villagers, a sea of sickly faces dotted with dark scabs, he asked, 'Does anyone have anything to say? If not, let's get busy cooking. Today is our first meal together, so no matter who cooks, let's make sure it's a good one. Since we're cooking for everyone, you can use the big steel woks we bought for out-of-town students. Stoves are in the student kitchens on the west side of the basketball court.'

And with that, the meeting was adjourned.

Amid much laughter and excited chattering, the villagers clustered around the stove in the middle of the classroom.

Others returned to their sleeping quarters to set up beds and unpack their bedrolls and belongings.

Grandpa left the classroom and went outside into the storm, snowflakes clinging to his face like droplets of water. Each gust of wind sent more snow hurling into his face, which was still glowing with the warmth of the classroom. Grandpa felt pleased with the points he'd made in his speech, the rules he had laid out for life in the school.

As the snow melted quickly on his warm skin, it streamed down his face like tears.

A white world. The schoolyard, a vast white plain that crunched beneath his feet as he walked.

'Dad!' Grandpa turned around to see that his son had caught up with him.

'Will I be sleeping in the big dormitory with the others?'

'Why not stay with me?' Grandpa suggested. 'It's a smaller room, much warmer.'

'Sure,' Uncle agreed, sounding relieved. 'But Dad, why did you have to go and put Ding Yuejin in charge of the accounts?'

'He was the village accountant. He's got experience.'

'Still, you would have been better off with me in charge.'

'How so?' asked Grandpa.

'I'm your son. No matter what, you know you can trust me.'

'I know I can trust him, too.'

Uncle laughed. 'I suppose it doesn't matter who you choose. We're all going to die soon anyway, so it's not like anyone's got a motive to steal.'

They trudged towards Grandpa's rooms beside the school gate, and were soon swallowed up in the snowstorm.

Their voices carried on the air.

Their outlines melted into snow.

2

After the snow had melted, the sick villagers found that life in the school was better than they had imagined. Even paradise couldn't measure up to this. When Grandpa shouted that the food was ready, everyone would gather around with their bowls in their hands. You could pick and choose whatever you wanted to eat, and take as much food as you liked. There were many dishes to choose from: savoury or sweet, hearty or light, thick soups or thin, vegetarian stir-fry, fish or meat. When you had finished eating, you rinsed your bowl in the sink and returned it to your assigned shelf, or stored it in one of the many bags that hung everywhere, even from the branches of trees. When someone found a herbal remedy said to cure the fever, the herbs were boiled in a large cauldron and ladled into bowls for everyone to drink. When someone got a treat from home – dumplings, say, or steamed pork buns – they would be divided among the whole group.

Apart from meals and medicine, there wasn't much to do. You could bask in the sun or watch television, or round up a foursome for a few hands of poker. Some immersed themselves in two-man games of Chinese chess or Go.

There was nothing to think about, nothing to worry about. You could take long walks in the courtyard or stay in bed all day if you liked. No one would bother you or boss you around. You were as free as a dandelion in a field.

If you got homesick, you could visit your family in the village. If you missed your crops, you could go and check on your fields. If there was something you needed, you could send a message to your family and they would bring it to the school.

For a few weeks, life in the school seemed a paradise beyond compare. But this paradise didn't last for long.

There was a thief in the school. Like a rat, the thief seemed to be able to get into every nook and cranny. It started when half a sack of rice went missing from the kitchen. Then a whole bag of soybeans disappeared from a corner by the stove. Not long after that, Li Sanren complained that the forty yuan he had stashed under his pillow was gone. The next victim was Ding Xiaoming's young wife, Yang Lingling. Ding Xiaoming was a cousin of ours on our father's side. His grandpa and my grandpa were brothers, which made him a first cousin to my father and my uncle. Lingling, who was still in her early twenties, had found out that she had the fever soon after marrying into our village. It turns out that a few years earlier, while living with her parents in her hometown, she had sold her blood. Although she never blamed anyone for giving her the disease, she spent every day silent and worried. She never smiled. The day her husband learned she had the fever, he smacked her hard across the face and shouted: 'The first time we met, I asked if you'd ever sold blood and you swore up and down that you hadn't! What do you have to say for yourself now?'

The beating left Lingling's face swollen, and her spirit bruised. It made her never want to smile again. It made her not want to go on living. Especially after her husband dropped her off at the school to live with the other sick people.

A week after she arrived at the school, Lingling discovered that the brand new, red silk padded jacket she'd hung from her bedpost had disappeared. One evening, when she went to put it on, it just wasn't there.

The thefts in the school were escalating like an infestation of rats. Something had to be done. Grandpa called everyone to another meeting in the large classroom.

'At this point,' Grandpa began in a loud voice, 'most of you are nearing the end of your lives. Why on earth would you steal money or grain or a brand-new silk jacket? What good is money if you're not alive to spend it? What good is grain once you're in your grave? You've got stoves and plenty of firewood to keep you warm . . . why would any of you need to steal someone else's things?

'Starting today,' Grandpa continued, 'no one leaves this school to go back home. I want to make sure that the things that were stolen stay right here. That's number one. Number two: I'm not going to conduct an investigation into who was responsible, but I expect the thief to return the stolen goods. You can wait until tonight and put them back when it's dark. I want the grain returned to the kitchen, the money given back to its rightful owner and the jacket hanging on the bedpost where you found it.'

The setting sun inched across the courtyard, filling the classroom with its crimson rays. The winter wind began to howl; a sudden gust sent ash from the classroom stove scattering in all directions. While Grandpa was speaking, the villagers gazed suspiciously at one another, searching each face – some clearly sick, some healthier – for signs of larceny. But stare as they might, it was impossible to tell who was the thief among them.

From the middle of the crowd, my uncle shouted: 'Search! Search!' Several of the younger men took up his cry: 'Search! Search the rooms!'

Grandpa tried to restore calm. 'There's no need to search,' he said from the podium. 'All I ask is that the things be returned tonight. If you're too embarrassed to face the owners, you can just leave the items in the courtyard after everyone's gone to bed.'

With that, Grandpa ended the meeting and dismissed the villagers. There was much grumbling as they left the classroom, mostly from the men, who wondered what sort of greedy bastard would steal half a bag of grain when he was on the verge of dying anyway.

On the way out, Uncle caught up with his cousin's wife.

'Lingling,' he told her, 'you really should have put your clothes in a safer place.'

'It was just a jacket. Where else was I supposed to hang it?'

'I've got an extra sweater you can borrow, if you like.'

'No, thanks. I'm okay. I'm wearing two sweaters already.'

That night, some of the residents were chatting or watching television as usual. Others were in the kitchens and classrooms boiling their own concoctions of herbal remedies. In every classroom, storage room, corridor and stairwell, there were small makeshift stoves and clay pots bubbling with medicinal herbs, the dregs of which the villagers drank as a cure for the fever. Day and night, the pungent, bitter smell filled the school, drifting out of the yard and across the plain. It was as though the little school was a pharmaceutical factory manufacturing herbal remedies.

Once everyone had taken his or her medicine, it was time for bed. One by one, the residents fell asleep. The schoolyard was as silent as the plain, the plain as silent as a desert. All that could be heard was the whistle of the winter wind outside.

In Grandpa's rooms, Uncle was lying in his bed beneath the window. When he had first moved in, he'd had to clear away piles of old homework notebooks just to make room for his bed. Now that his wife Tingting had left the village and moved back in with her mother, Uncle was worried.

'Hey, Dad,' he said, 'did you ever talk to Tingting about that thing I asked?'

'What thing?'

'About not letting her get remarried after I die.'

'Go to sleep, son.'

There was no more conversation after that. The gloomy winter night made the darkness inside the little room seem thick and oppressive, the air sticky like glue. The hour was late, the night as deep and dark as a well. In the eerie silence, Uncle heard what sounded like footsteps outside. He waited for a moment, listening carefully, then rolled over in his bed and asked, 'Dad, which one of the villagers is the thief, do you suppose?'

In the silence while he waited for Grandpa to answer, Uncle thought he heard footsteps again. Someone was out there, he was sure of it.

'Dad!' he hissed. 'Are you awake?'

Still no answer.

As there was no sound from Grandpa, Uncle slowly sat up. He thought he might as well go out into the courtyard and try to get a look at the thief. Silently, he crept out of bed and draped his coat over his shoulders. He was nearly out of the door when Grandpa rolled over in his bed.

'Where are you going?'

'Oh, I thought you were asleep.'

'I asked where you were going.'

'Tingting went back to her mother today, so I'm in no mood to sleep.'

With an effort, Grandpa sat up in his bed. 'Honestly, boy, I don't know what's the matter with you.'

'Dad, there's something you don't know. The truth is, Tingting was engaged to someone else before she married me. His family lives in the same village as her mother. That's the reason why I'm so worried.'

Grandpa peered up at his son but said nothing. In the darkness, he couldn't see Uncle's face, just a shadowy figure looming close to the door. He might just as well be looking at a charred pillar of wood.

After a while, Grandpa asked, 'Did you take your medicine today?'

'Don't bother, Dad. I know there's no cure for what I've got.'

'Even so, there's no harm in trying.'

'Forget it. If the fever can't be cured, it can't be cured. I just hope I can manage to give it to Tingting, so she can't get remarried after I'm gone. Then I'll be able to rest in peace.'

Grandpa recoiled, too stunned to speak.

Uncle opened the door, pulling on his coat as he left, and stepped outside. In the empty schoolyard, pale moonlight covered the ground like a thin layer of ice. Uncle trod carefully, like a man crossing a frozen lake, trying not to break the glassy surface. After a few tentative steps, he stopped and glanced over at the two-storey schoolhouse to the west. The upstairs and downstairs classrooms had been turned into dormitories for the sick, each housing between five and eight adult men and women. The school was now a hospice for people with the fever.

But it was also home to a thief.

Inside the school, everyone was asleep. Uncle could hear people snoring, the sound echoing through the courtyard like a deep rumble travelling through pipes. As Uncle walked towards the darkened building, he thought he saw something, or someone, huddled in the shadows. It looked like the thief, bending down to leave the bag of rice he'd stolen. Uncle quickened his pace.

As he drew closer, he saw that it was a person squatting on the ground. Not just any person, but his cousin's wife, Lingling, who had married into the village just six months earlier.

'Who's there?'

'Me. Is that you, Ding Liang?'

'Lingling? What are you doing out here in the middle of the night?'

'I wanted to find out which of your villagers was the thief. I wanted to see who stole my new silk jacket.'

Uncle laughed. 'It seems that you and I think alike. I was hoping to get a look at the thief, too, and find out who stole your jacket.' Uncle squatted on the ground next to Lingling, who moved over to make room for him. Crouched side by side in the shadows, they looked like two sacks of grain leaning against the wall of the building.

The moon cast its light on a stray cat that was chasing after a mouse in the far corner of the schoolyard. The two creatures scurried across the basketball court, their claws scrabbling on the sand-covered ground.

'Lingling,' Uncle said. 'Are you afraid?'

'I used to be afraid of everything,' she answered. 'I couldn't even watch someone kill a chicken without my knees going weak. When I started selling blood, I got braver. Now that I know I've got this disease, nothing scares me any more.'

'Why did you sell your blood in the first place?'

'So I could buy a bottle of nice shampoo. There was a girl in our village who used a certain kind of shampoo that made her hair as smooth as silk. I wanted to try it, too, but it was expensive. The girl told me that she had paid for the shampoo by selling blood, so I decided to do the same.'

When Lingling had finished, Uncle stared up at the sky for a long time. It looked like a pool of deep blue water.

'I didn't know that,' he said at last.

'Why did *you* do it?'

'My older brother was a bloodhead. I saw all these other people going to him to sell their blood, so finally I did, too.'

Lingling gazed at Uncle thoughtfully. 'Everyone says your brother's a cheat. They say he drew a pint and a half of blood for every pint he paid for.'

This made Uncle laugh. He flashed Lingling a smile and nudged her elbow.

'Seeing that someone stole your jacket,' he said, shifting away from the topic of blood, 'have you thought about getting your own back by stealing from someone else?'

'No,' she answered. 'A person has to consider her reputation.'

'If we're going to die soon, why should we care about our reputation? You lived a respectable life, but when your husband heard you had the fever, he beat you, didn't he? Not only did he stop caring, not only did he stop loving you, but he had to slap you around a bit before he kicked you out.'

Uncle was quiet for a moment. 'If it were me,' he continued, 'I wouldn't have told him in the first place. I'd have given him the fever. It would have served him right.'

Lingling stared at Uncle, scandalized. She shifted her body a little further away from his, as though he were a stranger to be avoided, or a thief she didn't want to get too close to.

'Did you pass the disease to your wife?' she asked.

'No, but I will, eventually.'

Uncle was squatting on the concrete, his back and head leaning against the brick wall. The cold from the bricks seeped through his padded coat and on to his skin. He suddenly felt a chill run down his spine, as if someone were pouring freezing water down his back. He lowered his head, and two streams of tears rolled down his cheeks.

Lingling could not see his tears, but she heard the rasp in his voice.

'Do you hate your wife?' she asked, lowering her head to look at him.

'She was always good to me,' Uncle answered, wiping away tears, 'until she found out I was sick.' Emboldened by the darkness, he turned to face his cousin's wife. 'I want to tell you something, Lingling, and I don't care if you laugh at me.

I'm not embarrassed. Ever since I got sick, my wife won't let me touch her. Can you believe that? I'm not even thirty years old, and my own wife won't let me come near her.'

Lingling lowered her head again, as if she were trying to touch it on the ground. For a very long time, she did not speak. My uncle couldn't see her face but she was blushing hotly, the blood burning in her cheeks. After what seemed like a long time – when her hot skin had regained its coolness – only then did Lingling dare to raise her head and look at Uncle.

'It's the same for all of us, Ding Liang,' she said gently. 'I'm not afraid to tell you, either . . . After my husband found out I was sick, he never touched me again. I was only twenty-four, and only married a few months. We were newlyweds.'

At long last, Lingling and my uncle turned to face each other.

They gazed into one another's eyes, their faces very close.

Although the moon had already passed overhead, the schoolyard glowed like the frozen surface of a pond, like light reflected in a pane of glass. Even in the shadows where they were sitting, Lingling and Uncle could see each other's faces clearly. They could see every little detail.

It occurred to Uncle that Lingling's face was like an apple, a plump ripe apple ready for picking. The brown patches on her face were like markings on an apple, signs of the sweetness beneath the skin. Some people thought that apples with spots were more desirable, more full of flavour. Uncle gazed at Lingling hungrily. Breathing in the scent of her skin, he thought he could detect a faint whiff of the virginal – the clean, unsullied water of a mountain spring. But Lingling also had the tinge of a newlywed, like a dash of cold water added to a pot of water just as it is about to boil over.

Uncle cleared his throat and summoned his courage. 'Lingling,' he announced boldly. 'I want to ask you something.'

'Ask me what?'

'Oh, to hell with it,' he blurted out. 'You and I should be together.'

'But . . . how can we?' She sounded frightened.

'Listen, both of us have been married, and both of us are going to die soon. If we want to be together, we should be. We ought to be able to do anything we please.'

Once again, Lingling seemed scandalized. She stared at my uncle in amazement, as if seeing him for the first time.

The night was getting colder. The temperature had dropped to freezing. Uncle's face took on a bluish tinge; the brown spots on his face looked like pebbles buried in the frozen earth. Lingling gazed at him, and Uncle gazed back at her. In the end, unable to suffer the intensity of his desire, she had to turn away. Uncle's eyes were like two dark caves that threatened to swallow her whole. Lingling lowered her head again.

'Ding Liang,' she spoke quietly, 'I think you've forgotten that I'm married to your cousin.'

'If he treated you well, the thought never would have crossed my mind,' Uncle answered. 'But your husband hasn't been good to you, has he? He even beat you. No matter how badly my wife treated me, I never raised a hand to her.'

'But for better or worse, you and my husband are family. He thinks of you as an older brother.'

'Family, older brother, younger brother . . . what does any of that matter now? You and I are going to die soon.'

'If anyone ever found out, they'd skin us alive.'

'So let them. We're not going to be alive much longer, anyway.'

'I'm serious. If word got out, they'd kill us.'

'Like I said, we're all going to die soon. If people find out, at least you and I can die together.'

Lingling raised her head to look at Uncle. She gave him a searching look, as if she were trying to gauge whether or not he really was the person he said he was, a person who was going to die soon. His face, normally so pale in the daylight, looked different in the shadows, little more than a dark blur. The condensation from his breath was white against the darkness. When he spoke, it warmed her face like steam rising from a kettle.

'When we're dead,' she said, 'will we be buried together?'

'I hope so,' he answered.

'My husband told me that even after he was dead, he didn't want to be buried next to me.'

'I hope they bury me next to you,' Uncle said, moving his body closer.

He attempted an embrace, first taking hold of Lingling's hand, then wrapping his arms around her. He held her as if she were a lost lamb that he'd found after years of searching. He held her tightly, as though fearing she might change her mind and try to run away again. Stroking his chest with her fingers, she allowed him to hold her.

The night was nearly over. Soon it would be light again, just another day. From across the plain came the sounds of morning stirring after a long night's rest. This was the hour when snowdrifts, hidden in the shadows, hardened into ice. Snowflakes turned to hail, rattling through the sky like tiny grains of rice. They pattered on to the rooftops and covered the schoolyard, landing on Lingling and Uncle, as they sat huddled together, still wrapped in one another's arms.

They sat like that for a long time. Then, without a word, they both stood up. They made their way silently to a small room next to the kitchen. It was a storage room used for food supplies and other odds and ends. Somehow, tacitly, it was the room they had decided on.

The room was warm, and they in turn filled the room with warmth.

There, in that storage room, they recaptured what it meant to be alive.

3

Ding Village basked in the warmth of a brilliant sun. In every direction, flowers had burst into bloom almost overnight, sweeping into the village like a tide. Luxuriant blossoms lined every street, filled every courtyard, carpeted the fields outside the village gates. Even the dried-up channel marking the ancient path of the Yellow River was a profusion of flowers: chrysanthemums, plum blossoms, peonies, roses, wild orchids, winter jasmine, dandelions, dog-tails and several kinds of flowering grasses usually only found on mountaintops. There were shades of red and yellow, purple and pink, orange and lavender and white; purplish-red and reddish-purple, greenish-blue and bluish-green, aqua tinged with jade. There were flowers of every shape and colour, strange varieties you couldn't begin to name – some as big as serving bowls, others small as buttons. They grew from the walls and roofs of pigsties, over chicken coops and cow pens, their pungent scent wafting through the streets, washing over Ding Village like a flood, a perfumed tide . . .

Unable to fathom how hundreds of flowers could have bloomed so suddenly, Grandpa prowled the streets suspiciously, looking for signs. As he crossed the village from east to west, he noticed that the faces of the villagers – elders, adults and children alike – were all smiling. They bustled back and forth along the flower-lined streets, some balancing cloth-covered wicker baskets swinging from bamboo shoulder poles, others lugging sacks tied with rope and bulging with mysterious contents. Even tiny boys and girls of no more than a few years old seemed to be carrying heavy bundles. When Grandpa tried to ask what they were doing, no one stopped to answer him. Everyone appeared to be in a terrible hurry, rushing to and from their homes, not walking so much as running, racing from place to place.

Grandpa began to follow a group of villagers, trailing them through flower-filled streets. It wasn't until he reached the west end of the village that he saw what all the fuss was about: the surrounding fields were quite literally awash with flowers, a vast sea of them, an endless expanse of petals rippling in the breeze. It was magnificent. Even the sky above seemed tinged with their colours: blushing, feminine pinks and faintly erotic yellows. The villagers clustered in groups, hard at work in their families' fields. The men wielded pickaxes, and seemed to be digging up the soil around the roots of flowering plants and trees. It was as if they were rushing to break the soil and get their crops of sweet potatoes or peanuts planted before the winter set in.

Grandpa also caught sight of Li Sanren, the former mayor of Ding Village, out in his family's field. Usually so sombre and silent, he was smiling broadly as he worked alongside the other villagers. His forehead was covered in perspiration, his backside jutting out as he dug his shovel into the ground. Every so often, he would bend over, pick up a flowering plant he had unearthed and shake clods of dirt from its roots before tossing it aside and moving on to the next one. After he had uprooted and shaken a few dozen, he would squat down next to his wife and children to gather the clods of dirt from the ground and toss them into two wicker baskets. When the baskets were full, he covered them with bed sheets, lifted them on a shoulder pole and headed for home. Staggering under the weight of those baskets, Li Sanren seemed in danger of falling, but he soldiered on, forcing himself to keep walking . . .

Once upon a time, Li Sanren had been the mayor of Ding Village. Just a few years younger than Grandpa, he was a former military man who had been posted to the pleasant city of Hangzhou, known throughout China as 'the paradise of the south'. In a fenced-off army barracks outside the city, he had served his country, received commendations for his service and become an official member of the Chinese Communist Party. But when the time came for him to be promoted, he had a sudden realization. After much soul-searching and nail-biting, he penned a letter to his commanding officers. It read like a blood oath: in it, he vowed to return to his hometown and help transform Ding Village into 'a paradise of the north'.

And so he left the army.

Over the next few decades, Li Sanren worked day and night helping the villagers to plant and harvest, irrigate their fields and collect manure for use as fertilizer. When the higher-ups said to turn the soil, he did. When they said to plant wheat seedlings or cotton, he did. But years passed like days, and soon decades had gone by. Other than an increase in population, the village was unchanged, exactly the way it was when he'd started. In all those years, Ding Village had not managed to add a single new tile-roofed house. It had not acquired a single new piece of machinery or farm equipment. Even the number of pull-tractors was exactly the same. The surrounding villages of Willow Hamlet, Yellow Creek and Two-Li Village were also still quite poor, but Ding Village was skeletally poor by comparison. A village of skin and bones.

One day, a villager walked up to Li Sanren and spat in his face. 'Li Sanren, you've got some nerve, calling yourself our leader,' the man complained. 'In all the years you've been village mayor and party secretary, my family hasn't had one square meal. We can't even afford to have dumplings at New Year!'

In the end, Li Sanren was removed from office. As soon as the blood-selling began, he was sacked. He became silent and taciturn, hardly speaking to the other villagers. His face turned ashen and grey, as if someone had slapped him with the sole of a dirty shoe.

The higher-ups, taking notice of my dad's success in the blood trade, asked him to become the mayor of Ding Village. They hoped he'd help the village set up a few more blood-collection stations and foster a few more successful blood merchants, instead of spending his time collecting blood for his own business. Realizing that more bloodheads meant more competition for him, and less money for his family, Dad turned down the job, leaving Ding Village without a mayor. The post would remain empty for many years. Even today, the village doesn't have a mayor.

When the higher-ups called on the people of Ding Village to sell more blood, Li Sanren stubbornly refused to participate. He wanted no part of it. 'I didn't spend all those years as mayor,' he argued, 'to see it come to this . . . folks out there selling their own blood.'

But Li Sanren's wife, after visiting the fancy new tile-roofed houses of her friends and neighbours who'd sold their blood, took to cursing her husband in public. 'Li Sanren, you call yourself a man? You're not even man enough to sell blood. With you as mayor all those years, it's no wonder that the women in this village can't even afford sanitary pads! It's all your fault. You're nothing better than a eunuch, a coward who's too scared to sell a pint of blood, much less half a pint, or a drop, even! What kind of man gets scared by a few drops of his own blood?'

That day, Li Sanren was squatting outside the door of his house, eating his dinner. He allowed his wife to curse him, suffering her insults and abuse without comment.

When she had finished her tirade, he threw his empty bowl on the ground and walked off without a word. She supposed he had got sick of listening to her and had just gone out for a walk. But later, as she was washing up the dishes and getting ready to feed the pigs, Li Sanren walked into the kitchen clutching a 100-yuan bill. One of his sleeves was rolled up to the elbow, and he was flexing and pinching the exposed arm. His face was unusually pale, covered with nervous perspiration. He crossed the kitchen, placed the bill on a corner of the stove and turned to his wife.

'There,' he said tearfully. 'You see? I sold my blood.'

She paused from her washing up and stared at her husband's pale face.

'Well, that's more like it,' she said, laughing. 'Now you're a real man.'

She looked at him. 'Do you want some sugar-water?'

'No,' he answered, his eyes filled with tears. 'I spent half my life working for the revolution, and now I've been reduced to selling my blood.'

Soon Li Sanren was selling his blood regularly. At first it was just once a month, then every twenty days, then every ten. Towards the end, if he had gone too long without selling blood, his veins would begin to feel swollen. It was as if they were bursting with blood. If the blood wasn't siphoned out it would begin to seep from his pores.

As the number of villagers selling their blood increased, so did the number of bloodheads. There was a lot of competition. Bloodheads began going door to door with their equipment, collecting plasma as if it were scrap metal or worn-out shoes. You didn't even have to leave your house. Every day you would hear them calling – 'Blood collector! Anyone selling blood?' – like pedlars hawking their wares.

Blood merchants even went out into the fields to collect blood from farmers working their land.

'Hey, there!' the bloodhead would shout. 'Got any blood to sell?'

'Go away,' the farmer would reply, 'I just sold some.'

But the bloodhead wouldn't go away.

'That's some fine-looking wheat you've got there. The sprouts are nice and dark.'

The farmer would beam with pride. 'Can you guess how much chemical fertilizer I used?'

The bloodhead would then kneel down for a closer look, as if admiring the newly sprouted wheat. 'I don't know how much you used, but I know you probably paid for it by selling blood. A pint of blood will buy you two bags of chemical fertilizer. On this little plot, one bag should be enough for a bumper harvest.'

'Of course, farming's the main thing,' the bloodhead would say casually. 'Some people quit farming when they start selling blood, or even abandon their land. Of course, blood always replenishes itself, but a person can only live so long. Even if you live to be a hundred, you can't keep selling blood past a certain age. But a plot of land like this . . . you can farm it for a hundred, even a thousand years, and it'll keep producing great harvests. Blood-selling is different. You can't do that for hundreds or thousands of years. Am I right?'

Now they were speaking the same language. Setting his work aside, the farmer would walk to the edge of his field to talk to this friendly stranger, a bloodhead from another village. After chatting for a while, the farmer would impulsively roll up his sleeve and hold out his arm. 'Tell you what,' he'd say, 'seeing as how we've hit it off so well, what do you say I sell you a pint?'

After the farmer had sold another pint of his blood, and the merchant had paid for it, the two would part like old friends.

Having established this comfortable rapport, the blood merchant would visit often. Every few weeks, he'd arrive at the field with his syringes and tubes, to chat for a while and extract another pint of blood from the farmer's veins. That was how it worked.

One day, Li Sanren was out in his field, using a pickaxe to turn the soil in the corners where his plow couldn't reach. The wheat harvest was over, and it was time to plant the autumn corn. Autumn planting was different from summer planting: it was more of a race against time. If a farmer could manage to get his seed corn into the ground just one day early, it might ripen several days ahead of schedule, allowing him to harvest it before the winds and rain set in. Li Sanren knew how important it was to plant his seed corn within the next couple of days.

Turning the soil at the edges of his plot was back-breaking work that had to be done manually. Now that Li Sanren was selling blood two or three times a month, his face had turned sallow, as if his skin were coated with a thin layer of wax. When he'd been the mayor, he could swing a pickaxe as easily as if it were the handle of a hoe, but now it felt like trying to heft a boulder.

Although it was autumn, the summer heat had not yet passed. If you looked to the horizon, the scorching sun made it look like the whole plain was ablaze. As Li Sanren swung his pickaxe, breaking up the clods of dirt, sweat poured down his face like rainwater. He was barefoot, stripped to the waist, his back glistening with moisture as if he'd just taken a swim. His sweat made the red sesame-sized needle marks on his bare arms itch and swell to the size of mosquito bites. He was nearing the end of his strength. The previous year, he'd turned the soil on the borders of his plot in only half a day. But this year, after six months of selling blood, he'd been working for two days straight and the job was only half-finished.

The sun was high in the sky. Smoke rose from the chimneys of Ding Village and wafted through the air like plumes of white silk. By now, my grandmother had been dead nearly three months. She had trodden on a basin that my dad left lying on the ground and had ended up covered in Type-A blood. When she saw all the blood, she collapsed from fright. From then on, she suffered from panic attacks and an irregular heartbeat. Eventually, the strain on her heart proved to be too much: it stopped beating entirely, and she died. After her death, my dad and my uncle swore tearfully that they'd stop buying and collecting blood, that they'd give up the trade altogether. But now, only three months later, they were at it again, making the rounds with their three-wheeled cart.

On this particular day, Dad and Uncle were cycling home from a remote village, far from the main road, where they'd gone to collect blood. Their three-wheeled cart was crammed with bottles and bags full of blood plasma. It was high season for farmers, who couldn't spare the time to leave their fields and get to the nearest blood station. But my dad had signed a contract promising to deliver a certain amount to the blood-collection trucks each day.

Because he had a quota to fill, my dad had no choice but to go out to the remote villages and into the fields. He had no choice but to stand in the fields and call for the farmers to come and sell their blood.

On their way back to the village, Dad and Uncle saw Li Sanren turning the soil in his field. Uncle stopped the cart at the edge of the field.

'Hey, you! Got any blood to sell?'

Li Sanren raised his head and stared at Uncle a moment before continuing his work.

'Oi!' Uncle called again. 'You selling or not?'

'You Dings,' Li Sanren spat, 'you won't be satisfied until you've milked this village dry.'

Uncle, who was still only eighteen at the time, cursed under his breath. 'Fuck you, you old bastard. We show up at your field with cash in hand and still you won't sell.'

Dad joined Uncle at the edge of the field. After observing Li Sanren for a while, he stepped down and began walking across the spongy soil. It was like walking over a field of cotton, each step releasing a burst of rich, sweet scent. When he was standing face to face with Li Sanren, Dad greeted him politely.

'Hello, Mr Mayor, sir.'

Li Sanren stared at my father in shock, his pickaxe frozen in mid-air. It had been nearly two years since anyone had called him mayor, much less 'sir'. Although Li Sanren said nothing, he put down his pickaxe and listened to what my dad had to say.

'Mr Mayor, sir, a few days ago I attended a meeting to talk about my experience in the blood trade with some of the county cadres. Both the county governor and the director of education in charge of rural development and poverty alleviation criticized Ding Village for not selling enough blood. They were also displeased that we don't have a village cadre to help organize blood-collection efforts. They asked if I'd be willing to step in and become mayor.'

Here, my father paused and peered at the former mayor, as if trying to gauge his reaction. Li Sanren peered back at him.

'Of course, I'd never take the job,' Dad assured him. 'I told them there's only one person in this village qualified to be mayor, and that's you.'

Li Sanren stared, his eyes widening.

'My family founded this village,' Dad continued, 'and although you and I might not share the same name, I'll be the first to say that no one has worked harder for this village than you. As long as you're alive, no one will ever take your place. As long as you're here, there's no one more qualified to lead this village.'

When he had finished speaking, my father turned and began retracing his steps across the field. Grasshoppers and insects leaped out from the newly turned soil, landing on his shoes and running up his body. He jiggled his arms and legs, trying to shake them off. As he reached the edge of the field, he heard Li Sanren calling from behind him.

'Ding Hui, come back! I suppose I can risk selling one more pint.'

'Your face looks a bit jaundiced,' Dad noted. 'Maybe you ought to wait a few more days.'

'When you've lived through everything I have,' Li Sanren said stoically, 'there's nothing scary about selling a little blood. And damn, what's a few drops of blood, if it'll help my country?'

When Li Sanren was lying comfortably in the shade of a tree beside his field, head pillowed on the handle of his pickaxe, Dad hung an empty plasma bag from a branch above him. Uncle plunged a needle into Li Sanren's vein, and his blood began to flow through the plastic tubing – about as wide as a chopstick – and slowly fill the bag.

The print on the bag said '500 cc', but it held 600 when full. If you tapped lightly on the bag while you were drawing blood, you might manage to draw as much as 700 cc without the donor even realizing.

Naturally, Dad tapped on the bag as he drew Li Sanren's blood, claiming that this was necessary to prevent the blood from coagulating. All the while, he kept up a steady stream of conversation.

'Besides you, no one in this village is qualified to be mayor.'

'I've had enough,' sighed Li Sanren. 'I spent half my life working for this village.'

'But you're not even fifty. You're too young to retire.'

'If I do make a comeback, Ding Hui, I hope you'll be my second-in-charge.'

'I already told the county governor and the director of education that if you don't come out of retirement and take command, they could beat me to death and I still wouldn't accept the post.'

'How much blood have you taken?'

'Don't worry. It's almost full.'

Soon the bag was full to bursting. When Uncle took it down from the tree, it jiggled like a distended hot-water bottle.

From the shadowy field rose the thick, sweet stench of blood. A smell like freshly picked red berries boiling in a pot of water. After uncle had removed the needle from the crook of Li Sanren's arm and begun packing up his equipment, my father handed the former mayor a crisp 100-yuan note.

'Do you need change?' Li Sanren asked.

'Well, the price of plasma is down,' answered Dad. 'It's only eighty yuan per bag now.'

'Then I'll give you twenty back.'

'No, Mr Mayor,' Dad said, grasping him by the hand, 'please don't insult me. It's just a few yuan. Even if it were fifty yuan, I still couldn't take it.'

Li Sanren sheepishly accepted the money. His face was unnaturally pale. His pallor, and the beads of sweat pouring down his face, made him look like a wax figure that had been left out in the rain. He tried to stand up and walk back to his field, but before he had taken more than a few steps, he began to sway and had to squat down on the ground, leaning on the handle of his pickaxe.

'Ding Hui!' he cried. 'I'm feeling dizzy. It's like everything is spinning.'

'I didn't make you sell your blood,' Dad chided. 'But you insisted. Want us to turn you upside down and get your blood flowing again?'

'Might as well try,' Li Sanren agreed.

He lay back down on the ground and allowed Dad and Uncle to grasp his legs and lift him into the air until he was hanging upside down. They let him dangle there for a while, gently shaking his legs to get the blood moving towards his head, as though he were a pair of just-washed trousers they were trying to shake the excess water from.

When they had finished shaking him, they lowered him to the ground. 'Feeling any better?'

Li Sanren stood up slowly, took a few steps and smiled. 'Much better. When you've lived through everything I have, there's nothing scary about selling a little blood.'

Dad and Uncle got into their three-wheeled cart and began pedalling away.

Still unsteady on his feet and leaning on his pickaxe for support, Li Sanren headed back to his field to continue his work. Watching him, Dad and Uncle were worried he might collapse again, but fortunately he didn't. When he reached the centre of his field, Li Sanren turned back and shouted, 'Don't forget, Ding Hui! If I become mayor again, I want you as my second-in-command!'

Dad and Uncle turned to smile at him and continued on their way. When they reached the entrance to the village, they noticed that there seemed to be a lot of villagers lying about in the sunshine, on every small slope or bit of slanted ground. They had their feet elevated and heads pointed downhill, as was their practice when they'd just given blood and felt dizzy. Other villagers had taken wooden doors from their courtyards and propped them up on two differently sized stools, to form a slanted platform on which they could recline. Some of the younger men stood on their heads with their heels resting against walls, a pastime known as 'irrigating the brain'. Dad and Uncle realized that while they had been away collecting blood in another village, a different crew of bloodheads had come to Ding Village to poach their customers. They stopped in the street and stared around them. Dad was too shocked to speak; Uncle too angry not to.

'You motherfuckers!' Uncle shouted. 'You fucking mother-fuckers!'

It wasn't clear who he was cursing, the villagers or the bloodheads.

Li Sanren was not yet fifty when he started selling his blood. Once he started selling, there was no going back. In the blood trade, there were beginnings but no endings. By the time Li Sanren realized he had the fever, he was nearly sixty. Because of his age, the disease seemed to hit him harder than it did anyone else, leaving him too weak to speak. It was an ending, of sorts. It was an ending to all his years of hoping that he might become mayor again. After ten years, Ding Village still had no local cadre, and the higher-ups had never bothered to appoint a new mayor.

Li Sanren had aged rapidly. Nearing sixty, he looked more like a man in his seventies. It seemed likely that he would die soon, perhaps even in a matter of months. His illness had reached a critical stage. He walked slowly, painfully, as if his feet were weighted down with boulders. 'I don't see why you can't live in the school like all the others,' his wife complained, 'instead of staying home and making me wait on you all day long.' And so the former mayor moved into the school to live with the other sick villagers. After that, he rarely ever spoke. He spent his days alone, taking slow solitary walks in the schoolyard, watching but never interacting with the others. Each night, he climbed into the bed he'd made in a corner of the classroom and went to sleep. It was as if he spent every day waiting to die. But on this particular day, the sun had come out, and it was dazzling . . .

Ding Village was alive with flowers, blanketing the earth with colour and filling the sky with their perfume. The villagers waded through this sea of flowers, some digging in the ground with spades and shovels, others carrying loads on their shoulders or backs. Too winded by their exertions to speak, they worked steadily and silently; faces glistening with sweat and wreathed in smiles, they bustled here and there, back and forth. From his position at the entrance to the village, Grandpa could see Li Sanren emerging from the fields, carrying two baskets on a bamboo shoulder pole. Because the baskets were draped with sheets, Grandpa could not see what was in them, but judging from the way they sagged towards the ground, the contents must have been incredibly heavy. With every step he took, the shoulder pole creaked and groaned under the weight of those baskets. Now that his illness was full-blown, Li Sanren certainly didn't have much longer to live, but he seemed happy somehow, his face beaming as he shouldered his heavy burden. As he drew nearer, Grandpa rushed up and asked what he was carrying, but like the other villagers, Li Sanren smiled and said nothing. He paused for a moment to shift the weight of the pole to his other shoulder, then brushed past grandpa and continued on his way. He seemed to be heading home. Just then, Li Sanren's five- or six-year-old grandson appeared out of nowhere, clutching a large bundle – it seemed to be something wrapped in clothing – in his arms. Shouting 'Grandpa! Grandpa!' as he ran, the little boy tried to catch up with Li Sanren. As he passed my grandfather, the little boy tripped over a winter-jasmine bush that had sprung up in the middle of the road, and went tumbling head over heels. The bundle flew from his arms, its contents falling into the road with much clinking and clanging. Turning to see what had caused such a racket, my grandfather froze in amazement. Joyous amazement. Never in his life could he have imagined what was contained in that bundle: there were glittering gold bars, shiny gold coins, and golden nuggets the size of plump peanuts. Beneath the surface of the flower-filled plain, there was gold growing in the soil. It had been there all along. Sitting in the middle of the road and staring at the gold that had slipped from his grasp, Li Sanren's little grandson began to cry. Thinking that he ought to help the boy, Grandpa walked over and stretched out his arm . . . and in that moment . . .

The dream ended. Grandpa was awake.

It was Li Sanren, standing beside his bed, who had woken him.

4

Grandpa realized he must have been asleep. At least, it seemed like he had been asleep. He had a hazy recollection of Li

Sanren tiptoeing into his room and standing beside his bed for a while, before whispering, 'Shuiyang . . . Ding Shuiyang?' That was what had woken him.

Grandpa noticed that his arm was lying on top of his quilt, rather than tucked warmly underneath. It was the same outstretched arm he had offered to Li Sanren's little grandson. He could remember the scene vividly, he could still see it . . . he could see . . .

. . . a vast expanse of flowers on the plain, a sea of flowers covering Ding Village, the surrounding fields and the distant riverbed where once the Yellow River flowed. A rainbow of sparkling colours, and underneath, the glitter of gold . . . gold bricks, gold tiles, gold bars, gold nuggets, gold lumps and bits of gold as tiny and as numerous as grains of wheat or sand . . . Grandpa shut his eyes, trying to picture the flowers and the gold that grew beneath them, hoping to recapture the scene . . .

But the scene had faded. It was gone.

Hearing his name being whispered again, Grandpa rolled over in bed with a smile, ready to tell Li Sanren about the dream he had been having. But as soon as he saw the stricken look on Li Sanren's face, the words died on his lips.

'Sanren, what's happened?' Grandpa asked, sitting up in his bed.

'That goddamned thief . . .' Li Sanren's voice was choked with anger. 'He has no respect for anything. There's nothing that bastard won't steal.'

'What have you lost?'

'The one thing I couldn't afford to lose.'

'What on earth did you lose?' Grandpa asked impatiently, throwing on his clothes. 'Honestly, Sanren, when you were the mayor, no one could out-talk you. These days, you can't even form a coherent sentence.'

Li Sanren searched Grandpa's face. After a moment of hesitation, he spoke. 'I might as well tell you the truth, Shuiyang. After I left office, I kept the official seal of the village party committee. I thought that since the village didn't have a mayor or a party secretary, I ought to hold on to it for safekeeping. All these years, I've never let it out of my sight. Last night before I went to sleep, I hid the seal and a bit of cash under my pillow. When I woke up this morning, they were gone.

'I don't care about the cash,' Li Sanren continued earnestly. 'But I can't afford to lose that seal. I've got to get it back, no matter what. It hasn't left my sight in ten years, but when I looked this morning, it was gone.'

The sky was growing light, filling the room with pale sunshine. Noticing that Uncle had not returned, and that his bed had not been slept in, Grandpa's face darkened into a scowl. For a moment, he seemed to forget all about the stolen seal. Then, catching sight of Li Sanren's shrunken, emaciated body and desperate expression, Grandpa asked: 'How much money is missing?'

'I don't care about the money, but I have to get that seal back.'

'How much did you lose?' Grandpa insisted.

'Like I said, the money doesn't matter. But I have to find the seal.'

Grandpa stared at Li Sanren. He'd never seen him like this before, so agitated. After a moment, Grandpa asked quietly: 'How do you suggest we find it?'

'Search the school.' Li Sanren's voice was cold. 'Shuiyang, you've been a teacher all your life, and you always taught your students not to steal. Now you've invited all these sick villagers to live in the school, and they're thieving right under your nose.'

Without replying, Grandpa left the room. Li Sanren followed him out into the courtyard.

Already, the eastern horizon was a pool of golden light . . . *a sea of golden flowers, covering the earth and sky, linking every plot and every field . . . flowers piled as high as mountain ranges, stretching into the distance . . . flowers tumbling into the schoolyard, drowning the school in petals . . .*

94

The two-storey schoolhouse was quiet. All the residents were still asleep. On early winter mornings like this, it was warmer to stay huddled under the blankets.

Outside in the schoolyard, a magpie was singing from high in the branches of the paulownia tree. The magpie's song was said to be a good omen, the herald of a joyous event. It could only mean that something wonderful had happened in the schoolyard: someone in the school must have cause to celebrate.

Hanging from a low branch of the tree was a square of sheet metal, a makeshift gong that functioned as a school bell. Removing a metal bar from a fork in the tree, Grandpa struck it against the gong, setting off a loud clanging. It was the signal for all the residents to assemble immediately in the schoolyard.

The metal sheet, long unused, was corroded with rust. As Grandpa struck it with the steel bar, flakes of rust fell from its surface. Since students had stopped coming to class, the 'school bell' had been out of use, reduced to an ornament, much like the flagpole that rose from a cement platform on the east side of the schoolyard. In the past, every school day had begun with the requisite flag-raising ceremony. Now the flagpole stood empty, a forgotten relic of days gone by.

But now, once more, the school was filled with a familiar sound: the clanging and banging of a gong echoing through the schoolyard like musket fire.

Residents wrapped in coats began appearing at the second-storey windows. 'What's going on?' they shouted.

In the same tone of voice that he had used during his days as the village mayor, Li Sanren shouted back. 'Assembly! Everyone gather in the yard for assembly!'

'Did you catch the thief?' someone asked.

'Come down for assembly,' Li Sanren hollered back, 'and you'll find out!'

Villagers began to emerge from the schoolhouse, some rubbing the sleep from their eyes, others pulling on or buttoning up clothes. They streamed into the schoolyard, filling the assembly ground between the paulownia tree and the basketball court. Uncle and Lingling were there, too. In the confusion, no one had seen them slip out of the storeroom and blend in with the crowd. Both were still adjusting their clothing, their faces glowing with such radiance that, if you didn't know better, you'd never guess they were sick. They stood some distance apart, like two people who barely knew each other (and certainly hadn't just spent the night together).

The sun was already up, bursting from the eastern horizon to signal the start of a new day: a fine day to catch a thief.

'At this point, most of you are very sick,' Grandpa began. 'You're here today, but could be gone tomorrow. Yet at a time like this, you're still stealing . . . stealing from each other. Last night, someone stole money from Li Sanren.'

'I don't care about the money,' Li Sanren interrupted loudly. 'But the thief also took the official seal of the Ding Village party committee. For ten years, I've never let that seal out of my sight, and last night it was stolen.'

'So I have no choice but to search the school,' Grandpa said. Then, raising his voice: 'Who will volunteer to help Li Sanren and I conduct a room-to-room search?'

Grandpa swept his gaze over the crowd of villagers. Before his eyes had even reached the other side, Uncle had elbowed his way to the front. 'I'll help search,' he said excitedly. 'After all, I'm a victim, too. That thief has got some nerve, stealing my cousin's wife's new jacket.'

At this, Lingling blushed as red as the sunrise. She watched as, stepping from the crowd like a conquering hero, Uncle took his place at Grandpa's side.

After they had found two more volunteers, they set about searching the school from room to room and from top to bottom.

The search turned up two thieves. One was Zhao Xiuqin, the woman who cooked most of their meals. Zhao Xiuqin's disease was in its maturity. The spots on her face had hardened into lumps, swollen to the size of cooked peas. The bumpy rash that covered her wrists and hands was different: clusters of bright-red bumps, the same shade as the sun over the plain.

As soon as one bump disappeared, another rose to take its place. They crowded together jostling for space, itching so intolerably that she couldn't help scratching them. Her constant scratching had caused the bumps to become infected; now festering sores, they gave off a foul, salty odour that she did her best to hide from the others.

Ordinarily, after six months of illness and multiple outbreaks of this kind of rash, a person would be nearing death. But Zhao Xiuqin was no ordinary person. She had suffered more outbreaks than most, and she was still very much alive.

Her husband Wang Baoshan, ten years her senior, had sold his blood and borrowed money to pay for her dowry. After she had spent the dowry helping her younger brother find a wife, Zhao Xiuqin turned to selling her own blood to help her husband repay the debt. Now, a decade later, she had the disease while her husband remained uninfected.

Six months earlier, when her fever first flared, she had spent days slumped on the ground of their courtyard, kicking her heels against the dirt and cursing her fate. 'It isn't fair,' she moaned. 'It just isn't fair . . .'

When her husband tried to lift her from the ground, she scratched his face with her fingernails, drawing blood. 'You did this to me, you bastard!' she screamed. 'It's all your fault!'

For days she was inconsolable. She cursed and cried and stomped her feet, sending up clouds of dust. Then, just like that, the tantrums and the crying stopped. She resumed her usual household duties: cooking, feeding the chickens and bringing her husband his meals.

Now that she was living in the school, she was cooking not for her husband but for every sick person in the village. Not only was she cooking for them, she was stealing from them, too.

Zhao Xiuqin's bed was in the corner of a first-grade classroom on the ground floor. Grandpa and Li Sanren moved from classroom to classroom, overturning beds, tearing off quilts and rifling through boxes and bundles of clothing. When they reached Zhao Xiuqin's bed, she was not there. She had begun cooking well before sunrise. Day in and day out, from morning to night, she worked tirelessly and without complaint: cooking meals, washing bowls, scrubbing pots and doing whatever needed to be done. Besides that, she was an excellent cook.

That day, as the search party reached her bed, she was in the kitchen making breakfast. As Grandpa tore off her quilt and began searching under the bed, Li Sanren shook her pillow. He found it suspiciously heavy, as if it were filled with lead. When he ripped open the seams, a stream of white rice spilled onto the floor. Grains of rice cascaded to the floor, for everyone to see.

They were astounded, their faces frozen in shock. Never would they have imagined that the woman who cooked their meals was also the thief who'd been stealing their food supplies. A member of the search party was sent to the kitchen to fetch Zhao Xiuqin.

Meanwhile, on the second floor of the schoolhouse, my uncle was pulling another thief from his bed. Again, the identity of the thief came as a surprise: Zhao Dequan, a mild-mannered fifty-year-old farmer who had never raised his voice to anyone in his life.

While everyone else had assembled down in the schoolyard, Zhao Dequan had remained in bed. For the last few days, he'd been feeling weaker than usual, and hardly had the strength to walk unaided. The other residents, fearing that he wouldn't live more than a few days, didn't have the heart to disturb him. By the time Uncle and the others reached Zhao Dequan's bedside, all the other upstairs classrooms had already been searched. They found Zhao lying on top of his quilt, resting. The sunlight streaming through the window made his face look red and parched, like a shrivelled corpse left out in the sun.

It shocked everyone to think that Zhao Dequan had been stealing. Zhao was a simple, guileless farmer who had spent his life working the land. When it came to selling his crops or doing business, he never bothered to read the scales, haggle over prices or quibble about who was owed what. Eight or ten years earlier, during the mad boom of buying and selling, he had sold his blood without once thinking to ask how much he ought to be paid for it. He took whatever amount the bloodheads offered, and allowed them to draw as much blood from his veins as they pleased.

When my father asked how much blood he should draw, Zhao Dequan had answered: 'Take as much as you want. If my face turns yellow, then it's time to stop.'

Naturally, my father chose the largest plasma bag and filled it near to bursting. By the time the needle was removed from Zhao's arm, his face was jaundiced and his forehead beaded with perspiration. Dad gave him a few extra yuan for the additional blood he'd taken.

'Ding Hui,' Zhao said as he accepted the cash, 'of all the blood merchants, you're the one who treats me best.'

From then on, he kept coming back to sell his blood to my father.

Naturally, Zhao was the last person Uncle would have labelled a thief, and the last person anyone would have suspected of stealing the red silk jacket that had been part of Lingling's bridal trousseau. In the bright sunlight that streamed through the classroom window, his features were mummified, corpse-like. His eyes, covered with a whitish film, were like the eyes of a dead fish. As he watched the members of the search party bustling back and forth, searching the beds around him, his dead-fish eyes gleamed with undisguised envy. It was the envy that a very sick man feels for those not quite as sick as he is. He envied them their energy, and the life left in them. His eyes were filled with tears and he heaved a heavy sigh. A long, drawn-out sigh.

Noticing Zhao's despondence, a few of the residents tried to cheer him up with the standard jokes and wisecracks. 'Hey, the sooner you die,' one man grinned, 'the sooner you get to be reborn!' None of them imagined that they were talking to a thief, a man who had stolen a pretty piece of clothing from a pretty young bride.

The search group had finished the classroom and were about to leave without even bothering to search Zhao's belongings when Uncle, for some reason, paused at the door and turned to stare at Zhao Dequan. For some reason he couldn't have explained, even to himself, he marched over to the foot of Zhao's bed, yanked back the covers and pulled out a cloth-wrapped bundle. When he unwrapped it, he found that it contained Lingling's stolen bridal jacket.

Zhao Xiuqin was called from her kitchen.

Zhao Dequan was roused from his bed.

The thieves shared the same surname. They were a disgrace to the name of Zhao, and had brought shame upon Zhaos living everywhere.

The sun was rising and the schoolyard was beginning to warm up. A clean, fresh scent wafted in from distant fields. The birds were singing in the trees. Several dozen angry villagers crowded the courtyard, calling for Zhao Xiuqin to come out and face them, as if they'd known all along that she was a thief. There was no sense that they were wronging her, or accusing her unjustly. She was the one who had wronged them: she had let down the whole village.

After milling around the paulownia tree for a while, several people decided to go to the kitchen and fetch her. But if they had expected her to come out with her head hung low in shame, guilt written across her face, they were quite mistaken. There was not a hint of contrition in her expression as she emerged from the kitchen, wiping her hands on her apron. She seemed more annoyed than alarmed at being called away from work so abruptly. Confidently, even defiantly, she walked through the schoolyard and stood before the crowd like a storybook hero facing down a horde of enemies.

Grandpa stared at the pillow full of rice that was propped against the tree trunk, then turned his gaze to the cook.

'Xiuqin, is it true?' he asked. 'Did you steal rice from the kitchen?'

'No. What's going on?'

'I've heard the rumours that you used to steal crops from

other people's fields, but I never thought you'd steal grain from people in the same situation as you, people who are dying.' Sadly, Grandpa looked down at the ground, now covered in rice that had spilled from the pillow. Zhao Xiuqin followed his eyes. When she saw the pillow, she froze, speechless.

A second later, she rushed forward and was clutching the pillow to her chest like it was a child someone was trying to snatch away from her. She squatted on the ground in front of Grandpa, cradling the pillow in her arms and stomping her feet upon the dusty ground.

'You searched my things!' she howled. 'You heartless ingrate bastards . . . you searched my things and didn't even tell me!

'You've all got the fever, but you have no conscience, no gratitude . . . how could you search my bed without even asking me? Why should I have to wait on a bunch of sick people, when I could be home taking care of my own family? Every day I get up early to make you breakfast, and when you've eaten your fill, you just toss your bowls down and leave. Why should I get stuck washing your dirty dishes? It's always me who has to go to the well and draw all the cooking and drinking water, but you don't even try to conserve water . . . you waste a whole basin washing one little bowl. I'm as sick as any of the rest of you, and none of us is going to make it through the year. Seeing as how we're all going to die soon, why should I be your unpaid slave? After all I do for you, is a little bit of extra rice each month too much to ask? If I were doing the same work anywhere else, I'd be getting that, plus at least a few hundred yuan per month. But have I ever asked to be paid for my work here, have I ever asked for so much as a penny? You're always saying what a great cook I am, and how much you love my food. But why should I spend all day slaving in the kitchen for nothing, waiting on you hand and foot? All I wanted was a measly little bag of rice.'

All the while Zhao Xiuqin was shouting and accusing, she never shed a single tear. If there was a sob in her voice, it was the cry of a person who has been grievously wronged. When she had finished her tirade, she wiped her eyes as if she had been crying and looked around at the villagers.

'Does your family need the rice that badly?' Grandpa asked.

Zhao Xiuqin stared at him. 'They have nothing. They haven't got a stick of firewood or a blade of kindling to rub together.'

'Then you should have told me!' Grandpa shouted angrily. 'I would have given you some of mine to give to them.'

'I wasn't going to beg from you. That would have been even worse. All I wanted was my due.'

This time, it was Grandpa's turn to be speechless. There was nothing he could say. The crowd of villagers also seemed to have lost their tongues. The tables had turned: now they were the ones who had wronged Zhao Xiuqin, rather than the other way around. At that moment, Uncle and several of the village men appeared, leading Zhao Dequan down the stairs of the schoolhouse.

Zhao Dequan displayed none of the cook's courage or forcefulness. Although he was a man, he was neither as gutsy – nor as brave – as Zhao Xiuqin. With his pale, jaundiced face sweating profusely, despite the slight mid-winter chill, he looked like a prisoner being led to an execution ground. His small, shuffling steps made him appear to be moving backward rather than forward.

As he reached the bottom of the staircase, Zhao Dequan raised his head and caught sight of the villagers gathered in the schoolyard. He turned to say something to my uncle, and Uncle answered something back. When Zhao Dequan turned around again, his face seemed to have turned even more deathly pale. It was obvious to everyone that he was in the final stages of the disease, nearing the end of his life. His weight-loss had left him stick-thin. The coat that had once fitted him like a glove hung from his shrunken frame; his trousers were two gigantic buckets that pooled around his ankles and flapped against his legs when he walked. With his twig-brittle bones and leaf-thin skin, he seemed not to walk so much as flutter . . . no longer a man, but a phantom. In this way, he floated into their midst, and stood before the crowd with his head hung low, like a student who had been caught cheating during an exam and had been called before the entire class.

Small beads of perspiration stood out on his forehead; his skin alternating between a sickly yellow and an even more sickly white. The villagers, who had been so focused on Zhao Xiuqin now turned their attention to Zhao Dequan. It was impossible to believe that this wisp of a man, this phantom, could have stolen Lingling's red silk jacket. She could hardly believe it herself. She stared in confusion at Zhao Dequan, then at Uncle, who was holding her jacket.

'I found this at the foot of his bed, beneath the covers,' Uncle said, as he handed her the jacket.

Slowly, painfully, Zhao Dequan squatted on the ground and hung his head in shame. It was as though he had just witnessed the passing not of a jacket, but of his life's honour. His face looked sallower than before: as if made of wax, with the eyes of a dead fish. He stared fixedly at the tips of his toes, shrinking in on himself like a whipped dog cowering in a corner.

'Dequan,' Grandpa said. 'Did you really take the jacket?'

Zhao Dequan huddled on the ground and did not speak.

'I'm asking . . . are you the one who took it?'

Zhao Dequan shrunk into himself and was silent.

'If it wasn't you, you've got to speak up.'

Zhao Dequan glanced at Grandpa from the corner of his eye, but stayed as silent as an empty well, his body withered like a dying leaf.

Uncle spoke up. 'I'm the one who found the jacket under your covers. Are you claiming it is a false accusation?' Zhao Dequan bowed his head even lower and remained silent.

Grandpa shot a stony look at Uncle. 'Shut your mouth, boy. You've said enough.'

Uncle shut his mouth and glowered darkly.

By now, the sun had broken away from the horizon, and

having reached a certain height, was spilling its liquid gold into the schoolyard. The villagers looked from Grandpa to Zhao Dequan and back again, waiting to see how the drama would end.

'Zhao Dequan, I'm disappointed in you,' Grandpa said. 'Your own son is getting married soon, and here you are, stealing a jacket that Lingling got as a wedding present.'

At these words, Zhao Dequan seemed to grow even more nervous. Beads of sweat dripped from his forehead on to the ground.

The villagers were silent. In the midst of this silence, Zhao Xiuqin suddenly stood up and began walking towards the kitchen, still clutching her pillowcase filled with rice.

'Where are you going?' Grandpa asked.

'I left the pot boiling on the stove,' she answered. 'If it burns, we'll have nothing to eat for breakfast.'

Li Sanren sensed an opportunity. 'Er, Xiuqin,' he said casually. 'You don't happen to have the village seal, do you?'

'No,' she answered sullenly. 'The way you act, you'd think it was made of gold.'

Li Sanren pondered this for a moment, then squatted down beside Zhao Dequan.

'Dequan . . . my brother, my old friend,' he said, in his sweetest, most reassuring voice. 'We're both men in our fifties. If you did take the seal from under my pillow, you know . . . well, just give it back.'

Slowly, solemnly, Zhao Dequan shook his head.

'You're sure you didn't take it?' Li Sanren tried one more time.

Zhao nodded.

Li Sanren stood up, a defeated man. A thin layer of nervous perspiration now coated his forehead, as if he had caught the sweats from Zhao Dequan. With a desperate, hopeful look, he turned to the crowd of villagers. 'Whoever took the money can keep it,' he announced loudly. 'But I hope you will return the village seal. In ten years, I have never let that seal out of my sight. I used to keep it in a locked box at home and carry it on my person whenever I went out. Last night, before I went to bed, I put the money and the seal under my pillow. When I woke up this morning, they were gone.

'Like I said, I don't care about the money.' Li Sanren raised his voice even louder. 'But you must give me back the seal!'

The incident blew over quietly. Nothing more was said of it.

The days passed quickly, one fading into the next, and soon the school was calm and quiet once more. One day, Lingling was making her way towards the women's toilets. The men's toilets were outdoors, just east of the schoolhouse. The women's, also outdoors, were to the west. Walking briskly in her red silk jacket, Lingling appeared like a flaming miniature sun moving through the school, passing the residents who were out in the schoolyard enjoying the sunshine. A touch of warmth to ease the suffering and help them endure what little remained of their lives. As Lingling passed a row of villagers, relaxing and dozing lazily, Zhao Dequan followed her with his eyes. Then he stood up and began following her with his feet.

The toilets were a makeshift affair, just a row of outdoor squats surrounded by a high wall. When Lingling emerged, Zhao Dequan was waiting for her. For a few seconds, the two stared at each other. Then with a look of disdain, Lingling began to walk away, but Zhao Dequan stepped forward into her path.

'Lingling, would you be willing to . . .' His voice was no more than a whisper. 'Do you think you could sell me your jacket?'

Zhao Dequan attempted a smile, but it was a sickly thing, a skeletal sort of smile. 'I'm not embarrassed to ask, because I know I don't have much time left. I doubt I'll last the winter.'

His smile faded. 'The thing is, when my wife and I got married, I promised her that one day I would buy her a red silk jacket, just like yours. Now my son is about to be married and I'm dying, but she has never forgotten my promise. Before I die, I want to do this one thing . . . to give my wife the jacket I promised her.'

Lingling stared at him for a moment, and then began to walk away.

'I'll give you fifty yuan for it!' he shouted, as she brushed past him.

'All right, eighty!' Lingling kept walking.

'How about a hundred?'

Lingling turned around. 'Why don't you go into the city and get your own?'

5

Yes, the incident blew over quietly. Nothing more was said. After all, not much had been stolen – a bit of rice, some pocket change, a jacket and the village seal – and the thieves responsible had been caught. Before he died, Zhao Dequan had simply wanted to give his wife the red silk jacket he had promised her as a wedding gift. Now that their son was grown and about to be married, the shadow of his promise weighed on him heavily. It is a terrible thing to be dying of the fever and know you still owe your wife the promise of a red silk bridal jacket. It was this thought that had made him do the deed. As for Zhao Xiuqin, her theft was justified. After slaving away in the kitchen night and day without pay, she had only taken what was rightfully hers.

In light of these events, Grandpa laid down some new regulations. One: as Zhao Dequan had returned the jacket to Lingling, he would not be punished. Two: if Zhao Xiuqin and her two assistants were willing to continue their cooking duties, they would be exempt from the required monthly contributions of rice, flour and cereal grains. Although they would not be paid for their work, they would eat for free. Three: from now on, any resident caught stealing would be banished from the school. Anyone greedy or dishonest, or simply light-fingered, could go home and die in their own bed.

Since everyone was living on borrowed time, it seemed pointless to quibble any further. Li Sanren, who still hadn't managed to locate the missing village seal, was finding it hard to let go of the matter, although he pretended otherwise. 'I'm done searching,' he'd say. 'Besides, what's the point? Ding Village doesn't even have a village party committee any more.' But as soon as the classrooms were empty, he would sneak inside to search the beds, peek under blankets and rifle through people's belongings. He even conducted a search of the holes in the walls where rats lived, digging through their rank nests and among their droppings.

He never found the seal.

The loss tormented him. Sometimes when he was sitting alone, he would heave a long, deep sigh, as if his mind were a vast plain of regrets. Then came a day when Li Sanren could not be found in his usual haunts. He was not out in the schoolyard, enjoying the sunshine, nor was he searching the classrooms or sitting by some sunny upstairs window. He was huddled in his bed beneath the covers, where he had been all day. He had burrowed into his quilt the night before, and remained there at dawn and all through the morning. When he had still not emerged at lunchtime, Grandpa sent Uncle to fetch him.

Uncle stood at the door of the classroom, banging his chopsticks against his bowl and shouting. 'Li Sanren, get up! It's time for lunch!'

Receiving no reply, he tried a different tactic.

'Mr Mayor, aren't you hungry?'

When there was still no answer, Uncle went over to Li Sanren's bed and gave him a little push. It was like trying to nudge a pillar of stone.

Still holding his bowl and chopsticks, Uncle frantically threw off the bedclothes and saw that Li Sanren's face was green. A dark, putrid green. Li Sanren was dead.

He had been dead for some time. He might have passed away before midnight, or during the early hours of the morning. There was a small, dark pool beside his pillow, where he had coughed up blood. It was blackened and congealed, like mud. A puddle of congealed mud.

No one had expected Li Sanren to die so soon. Most thought that Zhao Dequan would be the first to go. Yet here was Li Sanren, cold in his bed, while Zhao Dequan was still alive. Despite the pool of blood, Li Sanren's features were relaxed, indicating that he hadn't suffered much before he died. Perhaps he'd simply spat up some blood and then passed quietly away. He might have died with regrets, though. His eyes were open and his mouth agape, like he'd been trying to say something, but had died before he could get the words out.

Uncle stood at Li Sanren's bedside for what seemed a long time, his face drained of colour and his chopsticks frozen in mid-air. It wasn't fear that left him pale, but the cold hard fact of knowing that someday soon he, too, would die. After a while, Uncle put down his bowl and chopsticks and bent forward to see if Li Sanren was breathing. When he placed his fingers gingerly under the man's nose, Uncle could feel no breath, just a cold chill emanating from his nostrils. Straightening up, Uncle crossed the classroom, opened a window and leaned out. Down below, some of the residents were milling around on their way to lunch.

'Hey!' Uncle shouted. 'Li Sanren is dead!'

Everyone looked up. 'What did you say?' someone shouted back.

'Li Sanren is dead. His body is already cold.'

The villagers stared at one another in shock. No longer in a hurry to get to lunch, they climbed the stairs to the second-floor classroom to see if Li Sanren was really dead. Five or six of them took turns waving their hands in front of his nostrils to check if he was breathing.

Grandpa came into the classroom, looking very pale and upset. After checking to see if Li Sanren was breathing, he turned to the villagers.

'Someone go and tell his family. They'll need to get the coffin and the funeral clothes made.'

'Why not wait until we've had lunch?' someone suggested. 'Otherwise, the food will get cold.'

After thinking about this for a moment, Grandpa pulled up the covers, covering Li Sanren's face, then led everyone downstairs to eat. During lunch, no one spoke about Li Sanren. Everyone ate their lunch as usual, those that had heard the news and those who hadn't.

It was a calm, windless day. The sun was shining brightly, the schoolyard warm and peaceful. Some of the residents sat on the ground, others stood as they ate their lunch of steamed bread, stew and a cracked-corn porridge that was Zhao Xiuqin's special recipe. Some sat on benches they'd brought from the classrooms, while others simply took off their shoes and sat on those. Chewing on the bread and slurping their soup, they talked about things in the village and repeated the same jokes – some funny, others not – that they'd been telling for years. Some joined in the conversation; others did not. It was a typical lunch, the same as any other, as if nothing unusual had happened.

Lingling squatted next to Uncle as they ate. 'Did old Mayor Li die or something?' she asked.

'What are you talking about?' Uncle said, giving her a strange look. 'He just said he wasn't feeling well enough to come down for lunch.'

'I wish whoever stole his seal would give it back. Then he wouldn't be so sad all the time.'

'You got your jacket back, that's what matters. You shouldn't worry so much about other people.'

Grandpa looked around at the villagers as they tucked into their lunches. Others, already finished, carried on animated conversations. When most of the residents had finished eating, he stood up and made an announcement.

'Li Sanren has decided he doesn't want to live at the school anymore,' he said. Then, turning to the cook, he said, 'Xiuqin. From now on, you'll be preparing one less meal.'

There was a shocked silence as the villagers digested Grandpa's words. They seemed to understand what he was saying, but at the same time, they weren't quite sure. They gazed around at each other, no one daring to ask the question that was on everyone's minds. The schoolyard was deathly silent, quiet enough to hear people breathing. Or holding their breath.

A single feather, carried on a gust of wind, seemed to slice through the silence. At that moment, Ding Zuizui, sitting near the kitchen door, cleared his throat and announced that he wanted to tell everyone a joke.

'Once upon a time,' he began, 'there was a clever county official who could handle any task that was put in front of him with the greatest of ease. One day, the county magistrate – hoping to test him – brought him to the outskirts of the capital city. Pointing to a pretty young girl walking down a path beside a vegetable patch, the magistrate said: "Go over and talk to that girl. If she lets you kiss her on the lips, I'll hand over my official seal and let you do my job for three full days. If she doesn't, I get to give you fifty lashes with a cane. Is it a deal?" After thinking it over, the clever county official walked over to the girl. After he had spoken no more than a few sentences, she raised her face to his, opened her mouth wide and allowed him to kiss her full on the lips. After that, the clever official was given the seal and got to be acting county magistrate for three days. Now, what do you suppose the clever official said to the girl?' Ding Zuizui asked the villagers, who had stopped eating and were listening with great interest.

He took a few sips of his soup, letting the suspense build for a while before answering.

'After he pulled her aside, he said, "Why were you stealing leeks from my family's vegetable patch?" "I wasn't stealing leeks," she said, "I just happened to be walking by. Are you calling me a thief?" "But I saw you picking leeks and eating them," the clever official said. "Can you prove you weren't stealing?" "I was not. If you don't believe me, just look in my mouth," said the girl, opening her mouth. "Can you see any leeks in there?" "Of course I can't," answered the official, "because you swallowed them." The girl got angry. "What am I supposed to do, cut open my belly and show you?" "That won't be necessary," the official told her. "Leeks have a strong scent. Just let me smell your breath, and I'll be able to tell right away." So the girl opened her mouth and raised her head to let him sniff her breath, and of course, that's when he kissed her. Naturally, the county magistrate had no choice but to turn over the great seal of state to the clever official. Within three days, the official had used the power of his office to relocate all of his friends and family from the countryside to the city, where he gave them high-ranking positions in county government or business. And they all got rich and lived happily ever after.'

Ding Zuizui, nicknamed 'the Mouth', had arrived at the elementary school only a few days earlier. After finding out that he had the fever, he had announced to his whole family that he was moving into the school to enjoy his 'last few days of paradise'. The day his family dropped him off, he had been laughing and chattering. From then on, there was always laughter in the school, and a seemingly endless supply of stories and jokes.

Grandpa's announcement that Li Sanren was leaving the school and moving back home had given the residents a scare. But after hearing the Mouth tell his joke, they had recovered from their fright and were now in high spirits, smiling and laughing. Some laughed primly, through pursed lips. Others threw back their heads and roared with laughter. A few laughed so hard they actually fell off their stools, dropping their bowls and spilling soup down the fronts of their shirts.

6

On the day of Li Sanren's funeral, just two days after his death, his wife didn't cry. She did, however, ask Grandpa what was the matter with her husband's corpse. Why did the old devil's eyes keep popping open, and why wouldn't his mouth stay shut? Had something been bothering him when he died, and was it troubling his soul?

Grandpa went with her to the funeral tent to take a look, and sure enough, Li Sanren was lying there with open eyes and gaping mouth. His eyes seemed bigger in death than they had ever been in his life; his eyeballs, rolled back into their sockets, were as white as a widow's funeral cap. Grandpa thought for a moment and then, without a word to Sanren's wife or any of the others, left the village by himself. He wasn't exactly sure where he was going, but he knew what he had to do.

Many hours later, he returned with a freshly carved seal inscribed 'Communist Party Committee, Ding Village.' It was round and new, and looked very official. He had also brought a small round tin of the sticky red paste used for inking seals. Grandpa put these items in the casket himself, hoping to dispel the loss that had clouded Li Sanren's final days. After he had placed the village seal in his right hand, and the tin of ink in his left, Grandpa told the former mayor: 'Look, Sanren, I finally found your seal. No one stole it. It was in the school the whole time. It just fell through a crack in the floorboards.' Grandpa placed a hand over Li Sanren's eyes and gently closed them. This time they stayed shut. He did the same with Li Sanren's mouth, making sure his lips stayed pressed together.

Li Sanren's eyes were finally closed, his lips pressed shut. With his features in repose, he looked very different. Although his body in its casket was emaciated and wasted, his face was peaceful, even serene. It was the face of a man who had suffered no losses, no disappointments, no regrets. It was the face of perfect serenity.

CHAPTER TWO

1

Let me tell you a bit about my family, about my grandpa and my dad. Let me tell you about the dreams my grandpa had about my dad, and about our family. Dreams for them, and about them; dreams that were miles long and fathoms deep.

My dad had decided to move our family out of the village. Ding Village had become a cheerless and desolate place. A wasteland. It had lost its humanity. Most of the sick villagers had moved into the elementary school, and those who hadn't now spent their days indoors at home. The streets were deserted; it was rare to see anyone moving about, or to hear the sound of voices. At some point, the villagers had stopped pasting funeral scrolls on the lintels of their doors. Death had become so commonplace, such an everyday event, that people couldn't be bothered to go around pasting up funeral scrolls, buying fancy caskets or planning elaborate funerals. Some people stopped going to funerals altogether. When a person died, it was like turning out a light. Like extinguishing a lamp or watching a leaf drop from a tree in autumn. The village was a silent and lonely place. As quiet and solitary as a grave. Already, several families had left New Street and moved to the county capital. One family moved even further, to the city of Kaifeng.

They were leaving in droves, abandoning the village and the fancy new houses they'd built. Ding Village was emptying out. Becoming a wasteland. Losing its humanity.

After his own father had tried to strangle him, my dad made up his mind to leave. He was going to move his family out of the village, once and for all. But when he sat down to do the calculations, Dad came up short. If he wanted to move his family to the county capital or to Kaifeng, he realized, he'd need a lot more cash. These money troubles kept him awake at night. Early one morning, after a sleepless night spent tossing and turning in his bed, my dad went out into the courtyard and then out into the village. He walked through quiet streets until he came to the western end of the village, where he stood and watched the sun rise. As a new day broke across the plain, it brought with it the bitter scent of medicinal herbs. Dad knew that the smell must be coming from the elementary school, where the residents would already be awake and boiling up their morning doses of herbal remedies. But it was only when he caught sight of the smoke rising from the schoolhouse – those little white plumes of smoke from so many fires and pots of boiling herbs – that his heart began to pound in his chest. It beat against his ribcage as if someone were inside there, poking around and pulling at strings.

Staring at the smoke rising from the school, which now seemed not so white but tinged with silver and gold, it had dawned on him, that with so many deaths in the village, with so many people sick and dying, the higher-ups would have to take action, do something to show their concern.

The government would have to do something for the people of Ding Village. It couldn't just ignore them. It couldn't stay silent, blindly doing nothing.

Because who ever heard of a government that saw and heard nothing, said and did nothing, took no action and showed no concern?

2

My father was a man born to greatness. He had come into this world to do great things. It was destiny that had made him a son of Ding Shuiyang, a son of Ding Village, and later, a father to me.

In the beginning, he had found himself in charge of the blood of Ding Village, and the blood of other villages for miles around. Not just in charge of their blood, but of their fate. In the end, he would find himself in charge of their coffins and graves. Father never imagined that in this lifetime, he would end up responsible for so many things, but he felt compelled to try. It was in this spirit of trial and error that he went to visit a county cadre he knew, not knowing whether or not the meeting would be a success. He was like a man pushing open a door, hoping that the sun would shine in. My father travelled to the capital of Wei county.

Over the last ten years, the capital had grown affluent, unbelievably so. My father had an appointment with the highest-ranking official he knew: the former County Director of Education in charge of rural development and poverty alleviation, who had since been promoted to Deputy Provincial Governor. He was also the chairman of the Wei county task force on HIV and AIDS. He and my father had had many dealings and negotiations in the past.

'Dozens of people have already died,' the deputy governor said to my father. 'Why didn't you come to me sooner? Don't you know how much I care about Ding Village? You and your father, Professor Ding, should know that Ding Village will always have a special place in my heart.'

'The county government,' he added, 'is providing free coffins to anyone who dies of the fever. Hasn't anyone in Ding Village heard about this policy? Didn't anyone explain it to you?'

In the course of their conversation, the deputy governor and my father spoke of many things.

'There's nothing we can do for those who have already died,' said the deputy governor. 'But anyone who's dying of the fever now can submit an application to the county, and as long as their paperwork is in order, they will each receive one black coffin, free of charge.'

'Now go back to Ding Village and tell them what I told you,' said the deputy governor, as the meeting ended. 'By the way, I still miss those spicy mustard greens you grow in the village. Next time you visit, remember to bring some of them with you, the tender ones.'

3

Grandpa knew that he was dreaming, because he was seeing the sort of things you only see in dreams. He didn't want to go on dreaming, didn't want to see these things, but the dreamscape was so peculiar, and the scene so very odd, he couldn't help himself. Unable to resist, he stepped through the door . . .

. . . And found himself in a large concrete yard, with buildings all around.

The buildings were all factories, and they were busy making coffins. It was a coffin-manufacturing plant.

Other than that, Grandpa didn't know where he was. He knew that he was in a dream, but he had no idea where the dream had transported him. He remembered crossing a flat, desolate plain until he reached the ancient, dried-up path of the Yellow River. Then he was on silted ground, standing in a basin that stretched as far as the eye could see. All around him were sand dunes that rose to the height of small hills that tapered off into gullies and ravines. Through the dunes, he had caught sight of the coffin factory.

The factory was surrounded by a barbed-wire fence. The ground inside the fence was covered with rows of finished black coffins. Because the coffins were of varying sizes, shapes and thicknesses, they seemed to have been classified into different grades. Chalk markings on the surface of each coffin indicated whether it was 'Grade A', 'Grade B' or 'Grade C'.

It must have been about noon, because the sun had reached its highest point over the plain. Dazzling rays of sunshine streamed through the air like so many golden threads.

Through the rusted chain-link fence, Grandpa saw shimmering waves of sunlight playing over the sandy ground, rolling over the sand dunes like floodwaters.

Grandpa stood gazing at the sea of finished coffins, their polished black surfaces gleaming in the midday sun. There were thousands upon thousands, lined up neatly on a stretch of concrete so vast it could have contained an entire village. The head of each casket was adorned with an over-sized Chinese character – one of the traditional ideographs signalling respect for the dead – written in thick gold brush strokes. Each character was the size of a large basin; each brush stoke as thick as a man's arm. Sunlight reflected from the golden surface, dazzling his eyes.

Grandpa knew that this was a government factory, manufacturing coffins for people dying of the fever.

He noticed two large signs, enormous versions of the village funeral scrolls, on either side of the factory gate. They read: 'We cherish the lives of those taken ill. / May your journey to heaven be peaceful.' As he'd reached the gate, Grandpa had paused to talk to the security guard. 'What sort of place is this?' he'd asked, and had been told it was a coffin factory. 'Who built it?' 'The county government,' answered the man. When Grandpa had asked if he could go in and take a look around, the guard had said, 'Of course. We'd never turn away anyone who wants to tour our facility.'

And so, entering the gate, Grandpa had come upon thousands of polished black coffins. They stretched before him like a dark oily lake, each with golden ideographs glittering on the surface like leaping fish.

As Grandpa moved further into the complex, he heard the rumble of machinery, as loud as thunder. Following the sound, he came upon a cement path that wound its way around a large sand dune. As he rounded the dune, he saw in the distance two long rows of workshops. Dozens of carpenters and joiners, painters and varnishers, carvers and engravers bustled in and out of the workshops. It appeared to be an assembly line of sorts. There was a large piece of machinery

117

spitting out unfinished planks of wood, which were then assembled into coffins, carved with characters, carried outdoors and placed on racks, where they were painted black and varnished. When the paint and varnish had dried, someone would touch up the characters at the head of each coffin with gold paint. After this process was complete, another worker would classify the finished coffins according to quality and mark them 'Grade A', 'Grade B' or 'Grade C'.

The assembly line moved at a feverish pace. The carpenters and joiners, painters and varnishers, carvers and engravers, even the quality inspectors, were drenched in sweat, joining and painting and carving and checking as fast as they could. None could spare a moment to speak to Grandpa; they simply glanced up at him and went back to their work. Leaving the assembly line, Grandpa moved on to the next workshop. Along the way, he saw a middle-aged man who seemed to be in charge of grading the coffins from A to C.

'How can you possibly rank coffins?' Grandpa asked.

'There's a rank to everything,' the man answered. 'Some people get the wheat, others have to settle for the chaff.'

He walked away, leaving Grandpa standing dumbstruck.

When Grandpa entered the next workshop, a building constructed of pine boards and steel frames, he saw that the coffins being manufactured here were very different from the ones outside. Examining a dozen shiny black caskets, he noticed that three were made from four-inch-thick planks of paulownia wood, and two were constructed of even thicker planks of red pine. The latter was an extremely expensive timber, prized for its resistance to moisture, insects and rot, but it was rare in these parts. But it wasn't just the materials that set apart these caskets. It was the craftsmanship. Unlike the simple ideographs at the head of the other coffins, these had characters bordered by elaborate carvings of dragons and phoenixes. The sides of each casket boasted intricately wrought carvings of souls rising from the earth, ascending to the heavens and being welcomed into the Buddhist western paradise. With their gaudy carvings and gold adornments, the caskets looked like miniature pleasure palaces.

Further on, Grandpa came upon an even larger casket propped on two benches. Four engravers, one on each side of the casket, were embellishing the panels with scenes of ascending souls and heavenly greetings, as well as even more elaborate depictions of heavenly and earthly paradises. A team of artists was highlighting the scenes with generous amounts of silver and gold, giving the casket an even more sumptuous appearance. Yet another engraver had the casket lid propped against a wall, and was carving scenes of joyous feasts and glorious homecomings populated with an impressive multitude of children, grandchildren and other descendants and relations. The smiling children, handsome men, beautiful women and dignified elders were incredibly life-life, each tiny figure carved to perfection, down to the smallest detail. The dancing girls and maidservants that attended the occupant of the casket on the occasion of his glorious homecoming were lithe and sensuous, beautiful beyond description, like the palace women of some bygone imperial dynasty. The artisans displayed a solemn, almost pious, devotion to their work, as if the casket were not destined to be buried underground but placed on display in a museum.

When Grandpa stepped forward for a closer look at the work of the five engravers, he was astonished to see that the casket was constructed entirely of cedar. Not only that, but cedar of the finest sort; each panel was a separate, seamless plank of wood. Grandpa stood silently before the casket, gazing in breathless wonder at the carvings of golden dragons and silver phoenixes, palatial gardens and pleasure palaces, villages and hamlets, luxuriant fields, flowing rivers and towering mountain ranges. One panel featured a carving of a heavenly banquet table complete with packets of Great China brand cigarettes, expensive bottles of Maotai liquor, whole roasted chickens and plates of the rarest fish to ever swim the Yellow River. There were mahjong tiles and decks of poker cards laid out, should the occupant of the casket fancy a game of chance, and nubile servant girls and stout retainers standing by, should he prefer to be fanned or massaged.

Even more oddly, the artisans who had carved this masterpiece, this vision of paradise, had filled it with a television set, washing machine, refrigerator and an array of gadgets and household appliances that my grandfather had never laid eyes on. Next to this wealth of modern conveniences was a traditional Chinese building, above whose half-moon door someone had inscribed the words 'People's Bank of China'.

The engravers' meticulous attention to detail and total devotion to their work made it seem as if they were crafting not a funeral casket, but an image of the Buddha. Fine beads of sweat clung to their foreheads; their eyes, distended from the constant strain on their vision, bulged slightly from their sockets. They wielded carving tools of various shapes: some were long, thin blades, while others were crescent-shaped or slightly angled, or looked very much like the razors used for scraping callouses off the bottom of one's feet. The movement of their blades sent pale golden curlicues of cedar drifting through the air and fluttering to the ground. The floor was covered with a thick carpet of cedar shavings, as numerous as grains on a threshing room floor or petals in late spring. The fragrant scent of cedar swirled through the room and into the air outside. Grandpa wondered for whom the casket was being made. None of the sick villagers he knew could afford such a lavish casket, this burial fit for a king. Taking advantage of a brief lull in which one of the engravers stopped to sharpen his blade, Grandpa said: 'It's a beautiful casket.'

'That's our finest model, the Dragon,' answered the man, looking up at Grandpa.

'Oh, it has a name?' Grandpa glanced over at the casket made of pine. 'What's that one over there called, the one where people are being greeted into paradise?'

'The Phoenix.'

'And the paulownia, with the carvings just on the ends?'

'The Lion King.'

'Oh, I see,' said Grandpa, although he didn't. 'Who's the Dragon casket being made for?'

The engraver raised his head impatiently and stared at Grandpa as if he'd asked a question he shouldn't have. After loitering in silence for a little while longer, Grandpa decided to leave. As he exited the workshop, leaving behind those exotic caskets, he saw that the sun had already shifted to the west of the sand dunes. Despite the winter sunshine, there was now a distinct chill in the air. No longer did the black lacquered coffins – with their assigned ranks of A, B and C – seem like a dark and shining lake. They were more like a battle formation, a battalion of coffins.

A large truck parked to one side was loaded with a mountain of black coffins. Several workers were carefully balancing the last few on top. Down below, a supervisor shouted instructions to the men who were loading the truck, telling them to make sure the coffins didn't bump or scrape each other, and watching to see that they wrapped each one in straw matting before it was loaded on to the truck. The supervisor, dressed in a short blue-padded coat with a collar of fake fur, gesticulated wildly as he barked orders to his men. His speech was crude and loud. Grandpa thought his voice oddly familiar, the sort of voice that he might hear at home in Ding Village.

Curious to find out who was speaking, Grandpa turned around to look. Sure enough, it was a familiar voice from home. The supervisor was none other than my father, Ding Hui. After a moment of shock, Grandpa began wading through the sea of coffins towards his son. By now, the men had finished loading the coffins on to the truck and securing them with rope. They and my father hopped into the truck just as the driver started the engine. With a burst of exhaust, the truck rumbled through the factory gate, leaving my grandfather far behind.

Grandpa stood on the exact spot where the truck had just been parked. As he watched it disappear, he shouted his son's name. 'Hui . . . Come back, son! Hui . . . !'

*

121

Then Grandpa was awake.

When he woke from his dream, Grandpa was surprised to see my father standing at the foot of his bed, whispering, 'Dad? Dad?'

He told Grandpa about his visit to the county, and explained how the director of education in charge of rural development and poverty alleviation had been promoted to deputy governor in charge of the county task force on HIV and AIDS. He told him how the deputy governor had asked him to pass on his warmest wishes to Grandpa, and how he'd also promised to provide every fever patient in Ding Village with a bottle of cooking oil and a string of firecrackers so that they could enjoy Chinese New Year in style.

Grandpa sat dazed on the edge of his bed, staring at my father and remembering his dream. He felt as if he were still in the coffin factory, still immersed in a dream.

4

Chinese New Year came and went.

There was the usual big celebration on the first day of the lunar year, and the usual smaller celebration on the fifth day.

Then something unusual happened. Something unexpected.

Over New Year, many people had gone to visit relatives living outside the village. In the course of these visits, they had learned that the Wei county government was providing free black-lacquered coffins to the families of people dying of the fever. They also learned that these coffins were being manufactured in a special factory somewhere on the outskirts of the county capital. They lived in the same county, they had the same disease . . . So why, the residents of Ding Village wondered, should they settle for a cheap bottle of cooking oil and a few firecrackers, when other people were getting coffins worth hundreds of yuan?

It was a good question. They decided to ask my dad. He'd negotiated the deal, so he seemed like the one to ask.

A few weeks after New Year, Zhao Xiuqin and Ding Yuejin went to see my dad. When they arrived, just after breakfast, my dad was digging up the soil in a corner of our courtyard. It was the same corner where our chicken coop and pig pen used to stand; that is, until the villagers poisoned our chickens and pig. Now that he had no animals left to feed, Dad had decided to tear down the walls, dig up the soil and turn it into a vegetable patch where he could plant spicy mustard greens. Beside a mound of broken bricks, the newly turned soil was dark and muddy, a rich black muck created from years of chicken and pig droppings. You couldn't ask for a better place to plant mustard greens. The soil had the warm familiar stink of a well-fertilized field or vegetable garden. Having stripped off his cotton jacket, my dad was hard at work turning the soil when Zhao Xiuqin, Ding Yuejin and some other villagers arrived at his gate, clamouring to know why sick people in other villages got fancy coffins, when all they got was a bottle of lousy cooking oil.

Leaving aside his work, my dad went over to meet them at the gate. 'If it hadn't been for all my hard work,' he told them, 'you wouldn't even have cooking oil.'

Then he told them that there was one village of only 200 people that had lost half its population in less than a year. By comparison, Ding Village was lucky. Did they really want to make a big fuss about coffins, when there were people who needed them more?

Then he told them about another village where 300 of the 500 residents had the fever. Did they really want to take coffins from people like that?

The villagers couldn't argue.

Seeing that they had nothing more to say, my dad left them standing at the gate and resumed his digging. Winter would soon end; spring was on its way: when it came to planting spicy mustard greens, all you had to do was wait for the first day of spring, scatter the seeds on the ground, and water them every two days. Within a week, you would have sprouts. Within a fortnight, you'd have tiny little pale, blue-green plants that filled the air with their pungent scent.

Just about the time my dad was planting his mustard greens, there was another death in the village. The man who had died was not yet thirty, and his family couldn't afford to pay for his coffin. This was a topic of much conversation and gossip among the villagers. Finally, one of the man's relatives came to see my father.

'Ding Hui,' he said. 'We're all brothers here. Can't you ask the higher-ups to give us a coffin?'

'If I could have got coffins,' my father said awkwardly, 'don't you think I would have asked for them? I managed to get you cooking oil and firecrackers for New Year, didn't I?'

Realising that my father would do no more for him, the man left.

Soon, the mustard greens my father had planted were coming up strong, filling our courtyard with their pungent scent. The butterflies came. They landed briefly then fluttered away. So did the bees. Mustard greens were far too spicy to attract the butterflies and not nearly sweet enough to tempt the bees.

But in the end, our little vegetable patch would prove to be seductive.

Before long, our family would enjoy all the sweet delights of spring.

VOLUME 4

四

CHAPTER ONE

1

New Year passed. One by one, the days of the first lunar month went by. The first, the fifth, the fifteenth . . . each day had been and gone, but nothing much had changed. The sun shone warm, the winds blew cold. Medicinal herbs were boiled and drunk. People sickened, died and were buried.

The burials were a reminder of the good old days in the school, days of talk and laughter. The sick living together as a community, in good company and good cheer. Since the sick villagers had gone home for New Year, to their lonely rooms and silent courtyards, the mild cases had become serious, the serious cases terminal, and the terminal cases had passed away. Everyone wanted to resume their communal life in the school, but after the spat with my dad about coffins – during which some nasty things were said – they were embarrassed to face Grandpa. After all, the man they had cursed was still Grandpa's son, his flesh and blood.

One day after breakfast, Zhao Dequan, Ding Yuejin, Jia Genzhu, Ding Zhuxi, Zhao Xiuqin and some of the others were outside, enjoying the sunshine. The sun hung overhead, warming the village. Uncle and Lingling were there as well, standing apart from the group, gazing into one another's eyes like lovers. Or like thieves, thieves of love.

Their stolen moment was interrupted by someone saying: 'Who is going to tell Professor Ding that we want to move back into the school?'

Uncle laughed and turned to face the others. 'I'll go,' he volunteered. There was a round of murmurs as everyone agreed that, of course, Uncle was the perfect man for the job.

'But who's going to go with me?'

Before anyone could answer, Uncle said: 'How about you, Lingling?'

Lingling seemed hesitant, but Zhao Xiuqin urged her. 'Yes, Lingling, you go. You're not that sick, and your legs are still strong.'

And so Uncle and Lingling left the village together and walked towards the school.

It wasn't a long walk. The fields on both sides of the road were a sea of green, and the mossy scent of newly sprouted wheat drifted through the sunlit air. The weather was clear and cloudless, the air above the plain fresh and intoxicating. Beneath the empty sky, the distant villages of Willow Hamlet, Yellow Creek and Two-Li crouched like shadows on the horizon. Lingling and Uncle were on the outskirts of the village. Although they were not far from the nearest houses there seemed to be no one else around. At this hour, most people were gathered in the village centre, eating and sunning themselves. Walking shoulder to shoulder with Lingling, uncle glanced around carefully before taking her hand.

Lingling looked back at the village in alarm.

'Don't worry,' said Uncle. 'We're alone.'

'Did you miss me?' she asked, smiling.

'Why, didn't you miss me?'

'No.' Lingling's face turned serious.

'I don't believe you.'

'I've been worried I'm getting sicker. I might die any day now.'

Peering at her face, Uncle saw that Lingling's colour wasn't as good as it had been before New Year. There an undertone to her normally rosy skin, something putrid and dark beneath the surface, like dirty water soaking through red cloth. A dozen more spots had appeared on her forehead, shiny reddish-brown lumps capped with white. Uncle examined Lingling's wrist and the back of her hand, but found no new blemishes there. Her skin retained something of the glow of youth: the glow of a new bride, a woman in her early twenties.

'You'll be fine,' Uncle assured her. 'It's nothing to worry about.'

'How would you know?'

'I've been sick for almost a year, so I'm practically a doctor myself.' Then, smiling: 'Now, let's take a look at those hips of yours.'

Lingling stood and stared at Uncle.

'Come on, Lingling, I missed you so much I could hardly stand it.' Gazing at Lingling's hips, uncle began trying to pull her into a grassy field by the side of the road. The field must have lain fallow for some time, because the grass was knee-high in places, even higher in others. Now in late winter, the grass was dry and brittle, but you could tell how luxuriant it had once been. The withered grass gave off a mildewed scent that somehow seemed moister than fresh green grass or newly sprouted wheat.

When Lingling refused to go into the field with him, Uncle pleaded. 'Didn't you miss me at all?'

'I did,' she admitted, which only made Uncle tug at her hand harder.

'But what's the point,' she asked, 'when there's no reason to go on living?'

'There is no point, but every day you're alive, you have to find some reason to go on living.'

Finally, Uncle managed to coax Lingling off the road. Hand in hand, they walked into the field, trampling the grass beneath their feet. When they came to a patch where the grass grew higher, they lay down together, flattening the grass with their bodies.

There, in the tall grass, they did what men and women do.

They did it with a frenzy. They were mad for each other, their sickness forgotten, as if they'd never been unwell. In the sunlight that played across their bodies, Uncle saw that the spots on Lingling's skin were swollen with blood, glowing like plump red agates. The lumps on her buttocks and back were bright-red dots, like twinkling lights along a big city street. In her excitement, Lingling's face took on a rosy hue, a faint red glow that drove away the shadows underneath. In that moment, Uncle discovered that Lingling had not just youth, but beauty: her large eyes, moist and dark; the bridge of her nose as straight and tall as a chopstick standing at attention. When they had first lain down in the tall grass, sheltered from the wind and prying eyes, she had seemed as withered and dry as the grass around her, but now she was radiant. The spots that covered her body only seemed to highlight the tenderness of her youth, the pale softness of her skin. Looking at her, Uncle was once again sent into a frenzy. He was mad for her. She rose to his desire, embracing his lust like the tender young grass on the plain welcomes the warmth of spring.

When the frenzy was over, there was sweat, and there were tears. Lingling and Uncle lay on their backs, side by side on the grass, squinting up at the sun.

'I wish we could get married,' Uncle said.

'I doubt I'll live through the year.'

'I'd marry you even if you only had a month to live.'

'What about your wife?'

'Who cares about her?'

Lingling rolled away from Uncle and sat up. After a moment, she said: 'Forget it. We'll both be dead soon, anyway.'

Mulling this over, Uncle had to agree: divorce and remarriage didn't seem worth the trouble. They stood up, looked down at the trampled patch of grass they had made, and laughed. Then they continued towards the school, trying to mask their smiles.

When they arrived, they found Grandpa tidying up the large classroom where the residents had held their meetings. He was wiping the blackboard with a damp rag, erasing crude chalk drawings of dogs, pigs and other animals with the names of various villagers written underneath. When Grandpa saw

Uncle grinning at the door of the classroom, he asked: 'Did you draw these?'

Uncle ignored the question. 'Everyone wants to move back into the school, Dad.'

'No.' Grandpa shook his head. 'It's time for the kids to start classes again.'

'But what use is school when all the adults are dying?' said Uncle.

'After the adults are dead, the kids will still be here,' replied Grandpa.

'But who's going to raise them when their parents are gone?' Lingling asked, searching Grandpa's face. She was suddenly struck by how much he looked like her husband's father, the father-in-law she'd never met. Although her father-in-law was long dead by the time she married into the family, she'd seen his photograph propped on the long table that served as an ancestral shrine. He was a thin, wiry man who gazed wistfully at the camera, as if he were reluctant to leave this world. Because of the family resemblance, and perhaps because of her relationship with Grandpa's son, Lingling now looked upon Grandpa as a sort of substitute father-in-law.

'If their parents can live longer by moving into the school,' she reasoned, 'isn't that a few less days that the kids will be orphans, a few less days of grief?'

Grandpa hung the rag from a nail on the blackboard and dusted the chalk from his hands. 'All right,' he agreed. 'Tell everyone they can move back.'

Uncle and Lingling went back to the village to tell the others the good news. Once they had left the schoolyard behind them, they held hands. As they passed the grassy field, they glanced at each other and smiled. Then, without a word, they left the road and walked into the field together, hand in hand.

Hidden by the grass, they sat.

Hidden in the grass, they lay.

The sun shone down upon their naked skin.

2

Before the villagers could move back into the school, there was the matter of food supplies to be dealt with. Each resident was still required to donate a certain amount of wheat flour, corn meal, rice, beans and legumes each month. The first collection was taken up in the centre of the village, with Ding Yuejin serving as accountant. After he had weighed the grain, separated the coarse from the fine and noted any donations that were over or under, he had each villager place his or her contribution into communal sacks. As the cook, Zhao Xiuqin was exempt from the food quota, but she was on hand to help collect donations. As she was tying one of the sacks with rope, she discovered that someone had stuffed bricks in with the flour. There were four bricks of 5lbs each, which meant that someone had shorted the group by 20lbs of flour. Rummaging in another sack of flour, she found not bricks, but stones the size of large serving bowls. And in a sack of rice, she unearthed not bricks or stones but tiles weighing several pounds each.

Zhao Xiuqin angrily tossed the stones, bricks and tiles into the middle of the street, where they formed a large, dusty heap. The stones were as big as a man's head. Taken together, the contents of the flour-dusted heap must have weighed at least 100lbs. So far, the food contributions totalled four and a half sacks of flour, two and a half sacks of rice, a few sacks of corn meal and slightly more than one bag of beans. The stones, bricks and tiles were enough to fill more than a whole sack. The villagers gathered around the pile, shaking their heads and voicing their disapproval.

'My goodness, what an awful thing to do. With everyone so sick, this is no time to be cheating.'

'We're all going to die anyway! Who'd pull such a rotten stunt?'

Holding up a flour-coated brick, Zhao Xiuqin shouted: 'Too much of a coward to come forward, are you? Everyone was supposed to give fifty pounds of flour, but these bricks must weigh at least twenty pounds! You rotten, cheating bastard . . . because you shorted us, when we run out of food to eat, everyone's going to think I stole it!'

Raising the brick higher, the cook began to pace back and forth in front of the sacks of food. 'Take a look! You all said I was the village thief, but the worst I ever did was take a scallion from a field, or dig up a turnip to feed my husband and son. Or pick a cucumber to quench my thirst on a hot day. But someone puts twenty pounds of bricks in a bag of flour, or a couple of stones in with the rice, and you don't call that thieving?' She tossed down the brick in disgust and turned her attention to one of the flour-covered stones. Before she got sick, Zhao Xiuqin could easily have lifted several such stones, or carried a heavy load of them in baskets on a shoulder pole, but the fever had made her weak. It took several tries before she managed to lift the stone from the ground. Pacing back and forth in front of the villagers, cradling the stone in her arms like an infant, she raised her voice.

'See how heavy this stone is? I can hardly lift it! I want to know what stupid idiot thinks this is edible. I'd like to see you carry this home and cook it up in a pot!' Zhao Xiuqin dropped the stone to the ground with a thud, then assumed a very male posture: one foot on the stone, the other on the ground, fists on hips and arms outstretched.

'So this is what you're cooking at home every day, rocks instead of rice? Your kids are swallowing stones and shitting pebbles? You're serving your old folks bricks and broken tiles?'

At last, exhausted by her pacing and cursing, Zhao Xiuqin plopped down on one of the sacks of grain. The food collection had begun just after lunch. By now, the sun had solidified its position in the sky, and was smothering the village in warmth. At this time of year, as winter lingered into spring, most people still wore padded coats or jackets draped over their shoulders. Some of the older villagers were dressed in sheepskin jackets to ward off the chill. Despite the lingering cold, the scholar trees had begun to bloom; translucent green and yellow buds glistened on their branches like droplets of water. On this day, the whole of Ding Village had turned out to watch the food collection. This, in itself, was an exciting event. Finding stones in among the sacks of food was even more thrilling. The village hadn't seen this much excitement in years, not since the fever had arrived. Young and old alike left their houses to come and stare, to crowd around the pile of stones and bricks and curse the cheating scoundrel who had done it.

And, of course, to watch Zhao Xiuqin curse the cheating scoundrel who had done it.

Jia Genzhu, a young man who had become ill only recently, wanted to live in the school more than anyone. Once he was living in the school, his mother wouldn't have to spend her days crying in secret, and his wife wouldn't have to worry about him infecting her or their child. That was why he had donated only the whitest rice and the finest flour. He'd felt a bit put out when he'd seen the quality of the other donations: coarser grain and rice that wasn't quite so white. Now, staring at the pile of stones and bricks, he felt positively cheated. 'Fuck it!' he cursed. 'Fuck this! Give me back my food . . . I'm not moving into the school!'

'Fine,' said Uncle. 'But if you want a refund, you'll forfeit ten pounds of flour.'

'Why is that?' Jia Genzhu asked, staring in disbelief.

'Because if everyone asks for their food back, we'll come up short. We can't very well refund bricks and stones, can we?'

Jia Genzhu thought this over. 'Oh, well. I suppose I might as well move into the school.'

The other people who had donated food crowded around the pile of rubble, grumbling as they examined the flour-covered bricks and stones. The sun was now sneaking west, flooding the village streets with red. A late-winter wind whistled across the plain, leaving a chill in the air. The villagers had to stamp their feet and rub their hands to keep warm.

At that moment, my grandfather arrived on the scene. He had grown impatient waiting for everyone to arrive at the school, so he had come out to meet them. When the villagers explained to him what had happened, he stared at the pile of bricks and stones.

'So if we don't find out who did this, you're not going to move into the school?' asked Grandpa.

There was a chorus of protest. Everyone seemed to agree that living in the school was better than sitting around at home, waiting to die.

'Well, then,' said Grandpa impatiently. 'Let's go.'

But no one made a move to leave. They stared at the pile of rocks and bricks as if it represented a great personal loss. They seemed rooted to the spot, unable to move.

'If you're not moving into the school, you might as well go back to your homes,' Grandpa said at last. The villagers remained silent.

'But if you are,' he added hopefully, 'let's get a cart and bring this food to the school.'

Sitting and standing, hands tucked in their sleeves or stuck in their pockets, the villagers traded silent glances. There seemed to be an unspoken agreement that they shouldn't leave things this way. That this never should have happened in the first place. As the deadlock wore on, the setting sun fell towards the western horizon like a dying comet, giving off one final burst of heat.

Seeing that no one else was going to move or speak, Grandpa turned to Ding Yuejin. 'How heavy are these bricks and stones?'

'I'm not sure,' Yuejin said. 'Why don't we weigh them?'

Jia Genzhu and Zhao Dequan loaded the stones, bricks and tiles into baskets so that Ding Yuejin could weigh them with his scale. When each basket had been weighed, the total came out to just over 100lbs. Grandpa then asked how many people were moving into the school, and how much extra each person would have to pitch in to make up for the shortfall. Before Grandpa could finish his sentence, Jia Genzhu interrupted. 'Professor Ding, there is no way that I am going to pitch in more than I already have. If you don't believe me, just ask Ding Yuejin . . . I gave only the best-quality rice and flour.

Every grain of rice was perfectly white, as big as baby teeth, and the flour as fine as foam on a river.'

When Jia Genzhu had finished speaking, Zhao Dequan, who had parked his backside on a sack of flour and was muttering under his breath, spoke up. 'I'm, uh . . . I'm not going to pitch in, either.'

The others joined in, protesting that they, too, had already given enough.

Grandpa stood for a few moments, thinking to himself. Then, without a word of explanation, he left the villagers and began walking east. He walked east until he came to New Street. The villagers had no idea where Grandpa had gone or what he was up to, but they waited for him anyway, milling around the village centre like drought victims hoping for rain. A short while later, as the sun finally set, Grandpa returned. With him was my dad, pushing a bicycle laden with two large sacks of flour. As father and son trudged towards the village square, they were greeted by silence and stares of disbelief from the villagers. The silence was broken only by the clanging of my dad's bicycle chain. As they drew closer, the villagers saw that the sacks on his bicycle contained expensive Grade-A flour from the state-owned mill. Only the finest-quality flour would do for our family, the same as people in the city ate.

When he and Grandpa had first set out from the house with the bags of flour, my dad had worn a look of disgust: the disdain he felt for the villagers was written all over his face. But as he approached the crossroads, where the villagers could see him, he put on a broad magnanimous smile, all lips and teeth. Glancing around at the crowd, he noticed Ding Yuejin, Jia Genzhu, Zhao Xiuqin and several of the others who had come to his house to argue about coffins.

'What's a measly hundred pounds of flour among old friends and neighbours?', said Dad. 'With everyone so sick, it's hardly worth quibbling over. Am I right?'

With a glance at the large pile of bricks and stones, my dad unloaded the two sacks from the back of his bicycle and placed them next to the other sacks of donated food. Dusting the flour from the back seat of his bicycle, he proclaimed: 'That's a hundred pounds of the highest quality flour. The same kind as they use in the city. Please accept it as a small token of my regard.'

As he wheeled his bike around and prepared to leave, he said in a harsher tone of voice: 'I want you to remember this, and remember that I've never treated you unfairly or done anything to let you down. If anyone in this village has been treated unfairly, it's me.'

With that parting shot, Dad hopped on his bike and pedalled off.

That seemed to settle the matter. The more the villagers thought about it, the more they felt they'd been unfair to my dad, and unfair to the whole Ding family. For a while, their suspicions about my dad were laid to rest. It would be some time before they began to suspect him again.

Later that night, everything had returned to normal. The villagers were back in the school, fast asleep in their beds. Uncle was sleeping in Grandpa's quarters, just as before.

After they turned out the lights, Uncle and Grandpa lay in their beds talking. 'Shit,' said Uncle.

'What?' asked Grandpa.

'I put one little rock in a bag of rice, and my brother ends up donating two sacks of flour.'

Grandpa sat up in bed and stared at his youngest son.

'So, Dad, who do you think put the bricks into the flour?'

Grandpa didn't answer.

'I bet it was Ding Yuejin,' said Uncle. 'He was weighing the flour, so he's the only one who could have put in twenty pounds of bricks without anyone noticing. And another thing . . . just before New Year, when his wife died, I heard he bought a load of bricks to build her grave.'

As Uncle was speaking, there were noises outside the window: a muffled cough, the shuffling of feet, footsteps fading into the distance. Uncle paused to listen for a moment before continuing his conversation. A while later, telling Grandpa he was going out to the toilets, Uncle pulled on his clothes, left the room and followed in the direction of the footsteps.

3

A few weeks later, the school was in an uproar: someone had locked Uncle and Lingling in the grain-storage room next to the kitchen. Grandpa had been roused from his bed, and the residents of the school were gathered around the storeroom door, waiting. Everyone had got dressed and turned out to watch the excitement, the drama of forbidden lovers caught in the act.

The night was cool and bright; moonlight spilled like water into the schoolyard. The crowd milled outside the storeroom, shouting for someone to unlock the door and let Lingling and Uncle out, but no one seemed to know where to find the key.

Locked inside the storeroom, Uncle heard the scuffle of footsteps outside. A stampede moving closer, then silence. He had the feeling that the crowd had crept up to the window and was listening for sounds inside. 'Come on, have a heart!' he yelled through the window. 'We're all dying . . . none of us has much time left. How can you do this to us?'

Zhao Xiuqin stepped from the crowd, opened the kitchen door and turned on the light so that it shone on the adjacent storeroom. The lock on the storeroom door was brand new, its black-painted surface still shiny. 'Ding Liang,' she shouted. 'I knew something was going on between you and Lingling, but I never breathed a word to anyone. My lips are sealed as tight as this door. But it's not my padlock on there. Someone must have brought the lock from home so they could catch you two together.'

There was a moment of silence before Uncle spoke again. 'So what if they did?' He sounded peevish. 'You could take me out and shoot me and I wouldn't care. A lot of us have died already. I cheat death every day . . . what do I care if I get caught cheating with someone else's wife?'

The crowd darkening the door fell silent. There was really nothing they could say. Whoever had locked Uncle and Lingling in the storeroom had made a mistake. A big mistake. Uncle and Lingling's stolen pleasures now seemed justified. Legitimate, even. The residents crowded outside the storeroom stared at one another and wondered what they ought to do next.

Zhao Dequan, one of the older and wiser villagers, peered at the faces gathered under the lamplight. 'Will someone please open the door?' he pleaded.

Jia Genzhu shot him a look. 'But who has the key?'

Zhao Dequan squatted back down on the ground, as silent and immobile as an old wooden post.

Ding Yuejin stepped forward, examined the padlock and turned back to the crowd. 'Who locked this door?' he demanded. 'We're all going to die any day now, and you're running around like the morality police? If they can have one more day of happiness, why can't you just let them enjoy it?'

'Seriously,' he continued, 'Ding Liang is a better man than his brother. He doesn't deserve this. Unlock the door.'

Jia Genzhu had also come forward and was examining the lock. 'Someone please open this door,' he begged. 'Ding Liang and Lingling are only in their twenties, and as long as they're alive, they still have to be able to face people. Whatever happens, we can't let this get back to the village or their families. They'd be ruined.'

A few of the other residents made the same appeal, but no one seemed to know who had locked the door or who had the key. By now, Lingling was huddled in a corner of the storeroom, crying. Her sobs seeped through the cracks in the walls like a draught of chill air. Everyone felt sorry for her: she'd married into the village young, and been struck with the fever almost before the honeymoon was over. They couldn't be sure if she'd rushed into marriage knowing she was sick, or if she'd found out she was sick only after the wedding, but either way, she'd brought disaster on her husband and in-laws. No matter what the story was, she'd shattered the family's peace like a pane of glass, and left them to pick up the pieces. It was no wonder she'd become a pariah in her own household, given the cold shoulder – and even colder words – by her husband and his relatives.

Now Lingling was worse then sick, she was an adulteress. If her husband ever found out, there would be hell to pay. The fact that her lover was Ding Liang, her husband's first cousin, made the situation even worse. For Lingling, there was nothing for it but to weep. Everyone who heard her desperate sobs was moved to pity. Meanwhile, Uncle was rattling the doors and windows of the storeroom, trying to find a way out. Grandpa had heard the noise and emerged from his rooms to see what was the matter. It was only then that he realized all those times his son had left in the middle of the night, saying he was going to talk to someone or drop in for a game of chess, he had been secretly meeting Lingling.

When the villagers saw Grandpa storming towards them, they quickly stepped aside to clear him a path. The crowd fell silent, waiting to see how Grandpa would handle the situation. The only sound was my uncle's plaintive voice from inside the storeroom. 'Dad? Dad . . . is that you?'

'You're going to be the death of me,' Grandpa growled as he reached the door. 'You and that brother of yours.'

'Open the door first, Dad, then we'll talk.'

Grandpa said nothing.

'Just open the door. We can talk about this later.'

Turning back to the crowd, Grandpa asked that whoever had the key to come forward and unlock the door. There was an uncomfortable silence. The residents looked around at each other, not knowing who had locked the door or who held the key. By now, Lingling had stopped crying and was standing next to Uncle, waiting for someone to unlock the door and let them out. But no one came forward with the key, or admitted to having seen anyone lock the storeroom door.

Outside the school, the late winter chill was rising, coming over the schoolyard wall like water over a levee. In the silence, you could hear the cold air sweeping across the plain. There were the occasional croaks and chirps that one hears on bitter winter nights, but it was impossible to tell where the insect sounds were coming from. Perhaps it was from the ancient path of the Yellow River, or from some far corner of the plain. As the silence deepened, the sounds became clearer.

'Someone please give me the key,' Grandpa said. 'If you like, I'll kneel down right now and apologize on behalf of Lingling and my son. Come what may, we're all neighbours, and none of you has long to live.'

'Dad!' Uncle shouted from inside the storeroom. 'Just smash the lock!'

The villagers began hunting for things they could use to break the lock. Rocks, hammers, cleavers from the kitchen, whatever was handy. But just as they were about to try to force the lock, everyone stopped in their tracks.

There was no point in breaking the lock or forcing open the door. Lingling's husband was coming through the school gate. Ding Xiaoming, my uncle's cousin, was walking into the schoolyard.

Unlike his wife, Ding Xiaoming didn't have the fever. He didn't get the fever because he hadn't ever sold his blood. His own father had sold blood, but the fever had killed him years ago, putting an early end to his suffering. Ding Xiaoming was still young, strong and healthy, and now he was bounding through the schoolyard, heading straight for the storeroom.

Someone shouted: 'Look! Isn't that Lingling's husband?'

Of course, everyone turned their heads to look.

It *was* Lingling's husband, and he was bounding towards them like a panther. Taking huge leaps like a tiger on the hunt. Grandpa saw him, too, and the colour drained from his face. Grandpa, of course, knew Ding Xiaoming well: the man was his nephew. Xiaoming's father had been Grandpa's brother, younger by just two years. After the blood-selling started, the two families had become estranged by wealth: my father had built a two-storey house with a white-tiled exterior and my uncle had built a house with a tiled roof. Xiaoming's family, on the other hand, was still living in a mud-brick house with a thatched roof. After Xiaoming's father suddenly passed away, things got even worse. One day, his mother had pointed to my uncle's house and said: 'That's not a tile-roofed house. It's the village blood bank!' Then, pointing to our house: 'Those walls aren't white tiles. They're made with our bones!' Once these words reached my father and uncle's ears, the families kept their distance, meeting only at the gravesides of their common ancestors.

After the fever hit and I was poisoned, word of my death spread quickly throughout the village. When Xiaoming's mother heard the news, she said: 'It's retribution, that's what it is, divine retribution.' Of course, this got back to my mother, who rushed over to their house and caused such a scene that our families broke off all contact.

After that, our two families were as strangers. Not like relatives at all. And now, because of my uncle's illicit affair with Lingling, Ding Xiaoming was rushing into the school like a tiger. Before he even reached the crowd, the villagers had cleared a path for him, scurrying to get out of his way. It was hard to see his face in the moonlight, but he was obviously enraged. As he marched towards the storeroom, the villagers edged away from him. In the dim light coming through the kitchen door, their faces seemed drained of colour. Even the dark spots that were the mark of their disease seemed to have faded into nothingness, their faces bloodless and pale.

Before the door, Grandpa stood frozen. Everyone stood frozen. Even the insect sounds on the plain seemed to have died out; everyone was silent.

The crowd stared as Ding Xiaoming advanced towards the storeroom. What no one had expected, what no one had anticipated, was that Xiaoming would have the key to the padlock. But he was the one who had had it all along. Taking up a stance before the door, Xiaoming produced a small silver key and tried to insert it into the lock. But the padlock wouldn't open, because he'd got the key in upside down.

Then he turned the key the other way around. The padlock sprang open.

The door opening was like the cruel onslaught of a storm on a summer's day. There was a burst of noise – a clash and clang, as the door burst open – but it only lasted for a second. The moment the door was open, Xiaoming grabbed his wife by the hand and pulled her out. It was as if she'd been waiting on the other side of the door for him to reach in and grab her.

Xiaoming was a strong man. He was not what you would call tall, but he was stocky, a few stone overweight. He seized his wife by the collar and began dragging her away like a tiger carrying off its prey. Lingling's face was frightened and pale, her hair dishevelled. Her feet barely touched the ground, as if she were being lifted up and dragged along by her hair. Xiaoming was silent, his face livid. He brushed past Grandpa without a word, and retraced his steps through the crowd. As the villagers edged away to give him room, they caught a glimpse of Lingling – her face a ghastly shade of white, flashing by like lightning. Grandpa said nothing when Xiaoming passed him; he was still in shock. But as he turned to watch Xiaoming stalking through the crowd, dragging his wife behind him, Grandpa took a few steps forward, as if to follow him.

'Xiaoming!' Grandpa shouted.

Lingling's husband stopped and turned around.

'Lingling is very sick,' Grandpa pleaded. 'Can't you show her some mercy?'

Xiaoming did not reply straight away, but nor did he stay silent for long. He squinted into the light, trying to see Grandpa's face, then spat on the ground. Taking a few steps forward, he spat again, this time at Grandpa's feet.

'Mind your own business,' he said coldly. 'And control that son of yours!'

With that, Xiaoming turned and left, dragging his wife behind him.

It wasn't right. All the residents milling about the school-yard were in agreement. It wasn't right that things had turned out this way. Such a promising drama really deserved a better ending. Disappointed, they gazed after Xiaoming as he dragged his wife across the schoolyard and out through the front gate. Long after he had disappeared, they remained motionless, as if unsure about what had just happened.

Maybe they were confused. Or maybe they simply didn't want to leave the schoolyard and the site of the drama. So they just stood blankly and stared. Stupidly. People with nothing better to do.

Then they remembered my uncle. It took two to commit adultery, and although the woman had gone, the man was still there. The villagers turned around to look, but discovered that while they had been watching Xiaoming drag away his wife, my uncle had slipped out unnoticed. They saw him sitting on the threshold of the storeroom, with his head hung low and his hands on his knees, like a guilty child who couldn't bear to go into the house and face his parents, a naughty boy who was starting to get hungry, but was too afraid to go in for dinner. To their disappointment, he was fully dressed. He was even wearing his padded coat, the buttons done up neatly to the neck.

The villagers looked eagerly from Grandpa to Uncle, from father to son, wondering what would happen next.

Grandpa made the first move. Taking a step forward, he lifted his leg and aimed a good swift kick at his son. 'Go to your room! Haven't you humiliated yourself enough for one day?'

Uncle stood up and began walking back to Grandpa's rooms. As he passed the crowd of villagers, they saw that he was smiling, a little smirk he couldn't manage to hide. 'All right, you've had your fun, your little joke,' he told them. 'But whatever you do, please don't tell my wife. I know I'm going to die soon anyway, but I'm afraid of what she'd do if she found out.'

Uncle was almost halfway across the schoolyard when he turned back and shouted: 'Seriously, everyone, I'm begging you . . . don't let my wife find out about this!'

CHAPTER TWO

1

The next day, Ding Yuejin and Jia Genzhu paid a visit to Grandpa. They had plotted their visit well in advance . . .

The day began the same as any other. The sun came up over the plain, banishing the last dregs of winter and flooding the schoolyard with warmth. The first signs of spring had appeared. The cottonwoods and paulownia were tinged with green: dark, furry buds and bell-shaped blossoms that couldn't have been there the day before. They seemed to have appeared overnight, as if Uncle and Lingling's night of stolen passion had ushered in the spring.

A fresh scent drifted through the school, the faint perfume of grass and tiny plants that had begun to sprout from the crevices between the school walls. Translucent, pale yellow and green leaves shimmered in the sunlight like golden offerings. Spring had tiptoed in with hardly a whisper. Because of the stolen pleasures that had taken place in the schoolyard, the season had arrived there first, banishing the cold and wintry atmosphere and setting life in motion.

The residents of the school were still asleep, weary after a long night of excitement and drama. Most of the other villagers had risen with the sunrise, throwing open their pig pens and chicken coops to the promise of the first day of spring. But though the sun had been up for hours, the residents in the school were only just entering the land of dreams. The snorers had just begun their rumbling. The sleep-talkers had just begun their whisperings.

145

While all around them people slept, Jia Genzhu and Ding Yuejin got down to business. They slept in the same second-floor classroom on the east side of the schoolhouse. Jia Genzhu had risen first, awakened by the sunlight spilling through the window and on to his bed, warming his face. As soon as he opened his eyes, he went over to the window, saw that the day was already growing late, and hurried to the bed opposite to shake Ding Yuejin awake.

Ding Yuejin sat up groggily. After his head had cleared, he remembered the day's important errand, dressed quickly and left the classroom with Jia Genzhu.

The two men went downstairs and crossed the schoolyard, heading for the little building next to the gate. When they reached Grandpa's quarters, they peeked in through his window before knocking on the door. Almost as soon as they knocked, they heard a voice behind them, and turned to find Grandpa standing there.

Uncle was still fast asleep in bed, exhausted from his eventful evening. He had fallen asleep almost immediately after a brief fight with Grandpa, an argument they'd carried out in whispers.

'I'm disappointed, son,' Grandpa had told him. 'I never thought you'd do something so shameful.'

Uncle hadn't answered.

'If you go on like this,' Grandpa continued, 'you'll come to no good end.'

'What does that mean, no good end? The fever is going to kill me anyway.'

'What about your wife? Do you think you're being fair to Tingting?'

'You want to talk about fair? She wasn't even a virgin when we got married, and she never even apologized for it.'

'Well then, do you think you're being fair to your son?'

'I'm tired, Dad. I need to sleep.'

'How can you sleep?'

Uncle stayed quiet and tried to concentrate on falling asleep.

'What if Tingting or your in-laws find out?' Grandpa asked.

146

'How are they going to find out?' Uncle rolled over and tried to fall asleep. Moments later, he was snoring quietly. His exertions of the previous evening – and, of course, being caught in the act – had sapped him of his strength. Like an exhausted runner who has just finished a marathon, Uncle needed his rest.

But Grandpa, torn between anger and worry, could find no rest. He sat up in bed, wide-awake, listening to his son's irregular snoring and wishing he could strangle him in his bed. He would have strangled him, too, if only he had the strength.

Fully dressed, wrapped in his quilt, Grandpa allowed his mind to wander. He thought of many things yet found himself thinking about nothing at all. The idle droning in his head continued far into the night. By the time the sky grew light, his mind was a blank, a vast and desolate blank. He wanted to hate his son, but couldn't; he wanted to pity him, but couldn't do that, either. He hadn't enough of either emotion.

As the first rays of morning filtered through the window, Grandpa's eyelids were heavy but he was no closer to sleep. He rose from his bed and moved towards the door. On his way out, he passed Uncle's bed. It would be so easy to lean down and strangle him. Grandpa leaned down, but only to pick up a corner of the quilt that had fallen to the floor and place it over his son's shoulders. As he did so, he noticed several new spots on Uncle's shoulder, four or five swollen red lumps the size of large peas.

Grandpa ran his fingers over the lumps, examining them carefully.

Then he left the room, left the school and went out for a walk in the fields.

When Grandpa returned, he found Ding Yuejin and Jia Genzhu knocking on his door. Coming up behind them, he asked: 'What's the matter, boys?'

The matter turned out to be something unexpected, something Grandpa hadn't foreseen. It was as unexpected as the sun rising in the west and setting in the east, or waking up one morning to find that a mountain had risen from the plain.

As unforeseen as a field of ripe summer wheat in the dead of winter; or waters raging through an ancient riverbed that had lain dry for centuries.

When they heard Grandpa's voice, the young men wheeled around to find him standing behind them, just a few feet away. Grandpa looked haggard and exhausted, the whites of his eyes covered with spidery red veins. Caught off guard, the two young men glanced at each other and tried to decide what to say.

Ding Yuejin spoke first. 'Uncle, have you been up all night?'

'I couldn't sleep,' Grandpa answered with a rueful laugh.

Jia Genzhu gave Ding Yuejin a meaningful look, then cleared his throat. 'Professor Ding, there is something we want to discuss with you.'

'Sure. Go ahead.'

Genzhu tilted his head towards the gate. 'Let's talk over there.'

'Anywhere is just the same to me.'

'We wouldn't want to wake Ding Liang,' Yuejin explained.

They retreated to the school gate, taking up a position under the eaves of an adjacent building. The two young men stared at each other, as if trying to decide who should speak first. Finally, Genzhu nodded at Yuejin. 'Go ahead.'

'No, it's better if you start.'

Genzhu allowed his eyes to rest on Grandpa's face for a few moments. Then, setting his mouth in a straight line and licking his lips, he spoke. 'Professor, Yuejin and I aren't going to be alive much longer. We've been thinking it over, and there's something we need to get off our chests.'

Grandpa waited.

'We're the ones who locked Ding Liang and Lingling in the storage room,' Genzhu admitted with a smile.

Grandpa's expression changed: he turned pale and looked confused, even a little frightened. Caught between anger and fear, he seemed like a man about to lose his grip and fall tumbling to the ground. He looked to Ding Yuejin, expecting that he, at least, would hang his head or look apologetic. But there was no hint of contrition in the young man's face. Head held high, Yuejin wore the same smile as Genzhu, the same shameless grin that Grandpa had so often seen on the face of his own son, Ding Liang. The two young men said nothing, as if they were waiting to see how Grandpa would react.

Grandpa, astonished by their attitude, simply stared.

'We might as well tell you the whole truth,' Genzhu continued. 'After we locked them in, we sent someone to give Lingling's husband the key.'

Yuejin added, 'Genzhu wanted to give your daughter-in-law a key, too, until I stopped him.'

Genzhu shot his friend a look. 'I didn't do it for your sake, Professor. I was thinking of you, not your son.'

'Uncle, there's something else we want to discuss with you. We know you don't want your son's wife to find out about his affair. So we've come to you with a proposition. Nothing bad will happen as long as you agree to it. Everything will be fine, once you agree.'

'Agree to what?' Grandpa asked.

'Genzhu, you tell him.'

'It doesn't matter who says it.'

'Still though, you tell him.'

'All right, I will.' Genzhu turned to face Grandpa. 'Now, Professor, don't get angry when you hear this. We were afraid you might, which is why we came to talk to you in person. We know that you are a reasonable man, and we can discuss this calmly. If it were anyone else, say Li Sanren when he was alive and still the village mayor and party secretary, we would have just gone ahead and done it without even asking.'

'What on earth are you two boys trying to say?'

'What we're saying,' answered Genzhu, 'is you don't need to be in charge of things at the school any more, or take care of the sick villagers. From now on, Yuejin and I will handle all that.'

'That's right,' Yuejin chimed in. 'Just consider us the new school principals, the leaders of all these sick people. Act like we're the village mayor and party secretary, and do whatever we say. Because if you listen to us, so will everyone else.'

Grandpa laughed. 'Oh, so that's all you came to tell me?'

'That's all,' answered Genzhu, straight-faced. 'We want you to call a meeting and announce that from now on, the two of us are in charge of everything at the school, including the government food subsidies. We also hear that Ding Hui has the official village seal. We want you to get it from him and hand it over to us. You can consider us your new mayor and party secretary.'

Grandpa stared at them in silence.

'All you need to do is make the announcement,' said Yuejin.

'And if you don't,' Genzhu added, 'we'll tell Tingting all about your son's affair, and it'll break up his marriage and destroy the whole family.'

'Don't worry, Professor. With the two of us in charge of the school and the village, what could possibly go wrong?'

'And we promise to do a better job than you did,' said Genzhu. 'Everyone knows Ding Hui has been selling off the coffins he got free from the government. We hear he's trying to raise money to move his family out of the village, either to Kaifeng or the county capital. And Ding Liang not only cheated on his wife, he did it with his own cousin's wife! With kids like that, you think you're still qualified to manage this village or this school?'

'Professor, we're asking you to do this for your own good, and for the good of your family. But if you don't,' Genzhu sneered, 'we'll tell your daughter-in-law how we caught her husband sleeping with Lingling. Then you'll find yourself in a real mess, and your family will be ruined.'

The two seemed to have worked out their good-cop bad-cop routine in advance, trading lines like a straight man and a fall guy in an amateur comedy show. It was the sort of thing Ma Xianglin might have performed on stage, when he was still alive. Now Grandpa was the audience, watching and listening under the hot sun. His face had turned pale and beads of perspiration had formed on his forehead. In that moment, Grandpa seemed terribly old. Every hair on his head had gone white. His silvery-white head bobbed up and down beneath the eaves of the building, like one of the mylar balloons they sold in the city. Were it not tethered to his neck, it might have floated up into the air, or landed on a metal spike atop the schoolyard gate.

When the two young men had finished speaking, Grandpa stared at them, slack-jawed and wide-eyed as he had been throughout the entire conversation. Here was his kinsman and nephew Ding Yuejin, and Jia Genzhu from the village. He'd known both of these boys since the day they were born – he'd even taught them in school – but now they were strangers, textbook illustrations he couldn't make sense of, two mathematical problems that didn't compute.

High up in the branches of the paulownia trees, the sparrows were singing, their song falling through the silent schoolyard like rain. The three men stood quietly beneath the eaves, searching one another's faces. Theirs was a stubborn silence, a deathly silence that no one wanted to be the first to break. At last, Jia Genzhu, who had always been impatient, even as a boy, cleared his throat. 'Well, Professor? Do you understand what we're telling you?'

2

Grandpa stepped aside, just as he had been told to do. He made the announcement during lunch. Without going into too much detail, Grandpa said that he was getting old, and that his two sons were a disappointment and a disgrace. Seeing as how they had made him lose face in front of everyone, it didn't seem right that he remain in charge of the school or the sick residents, much less the entire village. Better that he step aside and turn things over to Jia Genzhu and Ding Yuejin. With their youth and enthusiasm, Grandpa said, it was better that they be in charge.

The residents of the school squatted on the sunny ground outside the kitchen and storeroom, eating their lunch. Recalling how Uncle and Lingling had been trapped in the storeroom, caught in flagrante delicto, they had to agree that Grandpa seemed to have lost his mandate. How could he manage other people's lives when he couldn't even control his own kids? Some in the crowd began craning their necks, looking around for Uncle. They noticed him squatting against the east wall of the kitchen, as far away from the storeroom as possible. When he saw them staring, he flashed them a rascally grin, as if getting caught with Lingling was not a big deal. As if his father losing his mandate and handing over power to Jia Genzhu and Ding Yuejin was not a big deal. It was hard to tell if his grin was fake – maybe he was just putting up a front – or if he really wasn't at all embarrassed about the previous night's scandal. As the villagers puzzled over the meaning of his smile, someone near the kitchen shouted: 'Hey, Ding Liang! Did you score some last night?'

My uncle shouted back a reply. 'When you're dying, every day counts. You've got to score wherever you can.'

Ding Yuejin and Jia Genzhu didn't hear this exchange, nor did they see Uncle's grin. While Grandpa was making his announcement, they set their bowls on the ground and listened attentively. As soon as he was finished, they unfurled a large red poster and began pasting it to the trunk of a cottonwood tree opposite the kitchen door.

Solemnly, silently, Ding Yuejin and Jia Genzhu plastered their poster to the tree, then stood back to admire their work. The residents, crowding around the tree for a closer look, saw that it was a list of rules and regulations:

1. **Every month, all residents of the school must contribute a certain quota to the communal food supply. Anyone who tries to cheat or comes up short can go fuck their grandmother, and may their whole family die of the fever.**

2. All government donations of grain, rice, cooking oil and medicine will be administered by the school. Anyone who gets greedy or takes more than their share can go fuck their ancestors, and may all their descendants die of the fever.

3. Jia Genzhu and Ding Yuejin will be in charge of distributing coffins donated by the government, whenever we get them. Anyone who doesn't follow orders will not receive a coffin, plus we will tell the whole village to go fuck that person's ancestors and curse their descendants.

4. No one is allowed to embezzle school property or take it for their personal use without the express permission of Jia Genzhu and Ding Yuejin. Thieves and embezzlers will die a horrible death and their graves will be plundered.

5. All matters, big or small, pertaining to the common welfare must first be approved by Jia Genzhu and Ding Yuejin. Any business conducted without their written permission or without a stamp from the village party committee will be considered null and void. Anyone who disobeys will die young, lose their parents and have their kids crippled in car accidents.

6. Extra-marital sex, hanky-panky and lewd behavior will not be tolerated in the school. Anyone caught engaging in immoral acts or corrupting public values will be marched through the village with a sign around their neck and a tall paper hat, and have fever-infected blood poured all over them.

7. Anyone who disagrees or does not comply with the above regulations will be cursed for life, have nightmares about dying and pass the fever to all their family, friends

and relatives. Plus, he or she will be sent home immediately and never allowed back in the school. If said person does try to come back, his (or her) fever will become full-blown.

The villagers milled around the tree, reading the new rules and regulations. Some read aloud, others silently, but all wore smug smiles, as if they'd just given someone a good, well-deserved cursing. Everyone agreed that the rules were very well written, acceptable and satisfying. They turned to look at Jia Genzhu and Ding Yuejin, who were squatting against a wall, finishing their lunch. Both men wore stern expressions, their faces dark as thunderclouds. They had drawn up the rules and regulations, inaugurated a new regime, and that was how it was going to be.

But as it turned out, life under the new regime was not so simple. There would be many other dodgy schemes and fishy goings-on in both the village and the school.

Ding Village had changed, and life would never be the same.

3

Jia Genzhu's little brother, Genbao, was getting married. This was not a dodgy scheme but a joyous event. Though Genbao had the fever, his family and neighbours – the whole village, in fact – had colluded to keep it secret and help him find a wife. When talking to outsiders, they would go on and on about how healthy he was, and what a great appetite he had, and how he could polish off two plates of food, two bowls of soup and three steamed buns at a single sitting. Genzhu had finally managed to convince a young, healthy, uninfected woman from another village to marry him. Now that the happy event was approaching, the family needed ten large tables for the wedding banquet, but all the banquet tables in the village had been used for making coffins. Unable to borrow the tables they needed, Jia Genzhu and his brother decided to take some desks from the school.

Jia Genzhu had spent the better part of the morning moving desks from the classrooms and loading them on to carts. As he was getting ready to leave, Grandpa stopped him at the gate and said that the desks were for student use only, and no one was allowed to move them. If Genbao wanted to take the desks out of the school, he'd have to do it over Grandpa's dead body.

The yellow painted desks were brand new, stacked six to a cart. Grandpa began unloading desks from one of the carts, while twenty-two-year-old Genbao loaded them back on again. This had led to an argument, and all the residents had come out to watch.

Jia Genzhu and Ding Yuejin were there, as well.

The two men had been in charge of the school for three days. In that time, they had never eaten more than their fair share at mealtimes, nor had they taken any more communal medicine than was their due, but they had already made two trips into the nearest town to ask local cadres for help on behalf of the residents of the school. So far, they had managed to negotiate a subsidy of 10lbs of flour and 10lbs of rice for each sick villager, plus a one-third reduction in their household land taxes, collected after the harvest. It was an unexpected boon: not only were they getting free food, they were saving money on their taxes. At the very least, it would save them the trouble of arguing with tax collectors, come harvest time. It was in this happy atmosphere that Grandpa had to go and pick a fight with Jia Genzhu's little brother.

'No one is allowed to take the desks out of the school,' Grandpa told Genbao.

'But Professor Ding,' said the young man, 'I've got the fever, too, don't you know?'

'If you've got the fever, what are you doing marrying that girl?'

'What do you expect me to do, stay a bachelor until I die?'

When Grandpa blocked the gate so that Genbao couldn't take out his cart, the crowd tried to reason with him.

'What's wrong with borrowing a few desks?' one man asked Grandpa. 'It's not like he won't give them back.'

'With everyone in the village dying, it's no easy thing to find a wife,' said another. 'Professor Ding, you're not trying to get back at Genzhu for taking over the school, are you?'

Grandpa maintained his position at the gate and said nothing. A warm sun shone high in the sky. At this time of day, most of the residents had stripped out of their padded coats and jackets. Some wore sweatshirts or old woollen sweaters; one man was wearing only a cotton shirt with a jacket draped over his shoulders. The season was too chilly for a single layer, too warm for a padded coat, and too apt to change, so wearing layers was a good solution. Grandpa wore a yellow sweatshirt of indeterminate age that made his skin look sickly. Beads of perspiration stood out on his sallow forehead like water oozing from a yellow loess plain. He had wedged his body in between the school gates, one hand gripping each side, his feet rooted to the ground like wooden stakes. Staring at their faces, Grandpa addressed the crowd:

'If anyone here can guarantee that after you die, your children won't come here to learn to read and write, I'll let Genbao walk off with these desks right now.'

No one answered.

'Can you guarantee me that?' Grandpa asked, raising his voice.

Everyone was silent, not moving a muscle. The atmosphere grew chill. As they were standing in the schoolyard, wondering what to do, Jia Genzhu appeared. His step was unhurried, but his face was dark with suppressed rage. The crowd parted to let him pass. When he was standing face to face with Grandpa, he said: 'Professor, did you forget what we talked about three days ago?' His voice was cold and menacing.

'As long as I'm still the custodian of this school,' Grandpa answered evenly, 'no one is allowed to take those desks.'

'And you've done a fine job as custodian,' Jia Genzhu conceded. 'But doesn't this school belong to the village? Isn't it called Ding Village Elementary?'

Grandpa couldn't deny such an obvious fact. 'Of course it is,' he answered.

Jia Genzhu had the voice of reason – not to mention the official seal of the Ding Village party committee – on his side. Taking a piece of paper and the village seal from his pocket, Genzhu squatted down and spread the paper on his knees. Then he put the seal to his mouth, blew on it to moisten the ink, and placed a round, bright-red mark upon the paper. Handing the paper to Grandpa, he said: 'Is that proof enough? Now will you let him through?'

Seeing that Grandpa was not about to budge from the gate, Jia Genzhu squatted down again and scrawled the following line in pencil on the paper: 'After a thorough investigation into the matter, we hereby grant permission for Jia Genbao to remove twelve desks from the Ding Village Elementary School premises.' After signing his name with a flourish over the official red seal, he stood up and waved the paper in Grandpa's face. 'Got anything else you want to say?'

Grandpa briefly glanced at the paper, taking in the pencilled words and the official-looking red seal, then squinted suspiciously at Jia Genzhu. It was the sort of look one might give a little boy prone to telling fibs, a look of mingled pity and disdain. Everyone in the crowd, including Jia Genzhu, picked up on it, but they seemed to feel that this time, it was Grandpa who was in the wrong. After all, it wasn't the end of the world, just a few desks. And didn't he have a signed and sealed document, with words like 'after a thorough investigation' and 'we hereby grant permission', saying it was okay to release school property? Besides, it didn't seem right to treat Genbao so badly on the eve of his wedding.

Uncle squeezed through the crowd to plead the boy's case. 'Dad, it's not like the desks belong to us. Why bother yourself?'

'Shut your mouth,' Grandpa snapped. 'If it weren't for you, I wouldn't be in this mess.'

Uncle smiled and said nothing. Still smiling, he melted back into the crowd, adding: 'All right, all right, I'll stay out of it. I suppose it's none of my business.'

Zhao Xiuqin was the next to step forward. 'Professor Ding, you can't be that short-sighted. I don't see your name written on any of these desks.'

'How would you know, Xiuqin?' Grandpa retorted. 'You wouldn't even recognize your own name.'

Zhao Xiuqin's mouth fell open, but no sound emerged. For once, she was speechless.

Now it was Ding Yuejin who elbowed his way through the crowd, pushing people aside. 'Professor, I gave Genbao permission to take those desks. Get out of the way and let him through.'

'Oh, just because you gave permission, that makes it okay?' Grandpa pushed his face so close to Yuejin's that it seemed he might swallow him up.

Yuejin, unafraid of Grandpa, stared right back at him. 'Jia Genzhu and I both gave permission,' he declared loudly. 'We talked it over and decided to let his brother take the desks.'

Grandpa stiffened and stared up at the sky, ignoring Jia Genzhu and Ding Yuejin. Then, with a quick glance at the crowd of villagers, he raised his chin and said: 'If you want to get past this gate, you'll have to drive right over me.'

Grandpa yanked the metal gates on either side of him shut, so that his body was trapped in the middle. It was as if he were soldered to the gate, and no amount of pushing, pulling or punching on the part of Genzhu or Yuejin was going to separate him from it.

The situation had reached a deadlock. The atmosphere had turned to ice. No one in the crowd said a word. They looked from Jia Genzhu to Ding Yuejin to Grandpa, waiting to see how the three men would break the impasse. By now, everyone realized that Grandpa's refusal to let the desks leave the school had nothing to do with desks, or with the affair between Uncle and Lingling. It was a struggle for control of the school . . . and everything in it.

And so, silently, they waited. A black mood prevailed over the three men. Despite the early spring sunshine, the atmosphere sent a chill through everyone in the schoolyard.

The signed and sealed document trembled in Jia Genzhu's hand. Ever so slightly, but the tremor was there. His face was the colour of storm clouds, his lips taut as strung wire. He eyed Grandpa warily, as if the old man were an ageing bull that hadn't lost its strength to fight. An old ox who simply refused to die.

Unlike Jia Genzhu, Ding Yuejin showed no sign of anger. His was the helpless expression of a man whose face has just been spat in. For better or worse, Grandpa was still his uncle, and his former teacher, besides. There was very little Yuejin could do in this situation. Instead, he looked to Genzhu, hoping that the other man would do something to get Grandpa to step away from the gate and allow Genbao to leave with the desks. Since it was Jia Genzhu's brother getting married, and his family who wanted the desks for the wedding banquet, it seemed up to Genzhu to resolve the situation. Everyone knew that Genzhu's twenty-two-year-old brother had the fever, but since he had never sold his blood, it wasn't clear how he'd become infected. The only reason Genbao had been able to find a wife – that is, to trick a girl from another village into marrying him – was that the entire population of Ding Village had conspired to hide the truth about his infection from outsiders. Genbao's fiancée, two years his junior, was a pretty, well-educated young woman who had taken the university entrance exam and failed. She'd failed by just a few marks. A few more marks and she would have passed the exam, entered university and never had to marry Jia Genbao. But she hadn't passed, and now she was marrying into Ding Village, marrying into the fever.

'But mother,' the girl had complained, 'they say everyone in Ding Village has the fever.'

'The villagers swore to me that Genbao doesn't have it,' her mother had answered. 'Since he's not infected, what are you so worried about?

'I sent you to school for ten years,' she reminded her daughter, 'and you didn't even pass the university exam. I haven't fed and clothed you for twenty years to see it all go to waste. You think I'm going to let you live at home until you die an old maid?'

The girl had burst into tears.

Eventually, tearfully, she had promised to marry into Ding Village. The wedding was to take place in a matter of days. Once he was married, Genbao would be a real man, a man who might have descendants to carry on his family name. Because he had the fever, he probably wouldn't live long enough to get to know his own children, but at least he wouldn't die with so many regrets. He had been eagerly awaiting his wedding, happily making preparations, and now the only thing left was to find a few tables for the wedding banquet. Genbao never imagined that a few days before his wedding, he'd find Grandpa blocking his path.

Grandpa wasn't just standing in the way of the desks, he was standing in the way of his happiness. A thin, frail young man, Genbao was still in the early stage of his disease. The initial fever hadn't faded yet, and it had left him weak and listless. Because he was so small and sick, and because Grandpa was so many years his senior, Genbao could do nothing but look pitiful and hope his big brother would come to his rescue. Genzhu had promised that as long as he was alive and in charge of the school and the village, he would see to it that his family's future was secure. This included paying for his younger brother's wedding, making funeral arrangements for his elderly parents and adding a few extra rooms to the house, something they'd hoped to do during the blood boom but had never been able to afford. Yet here was Grandpa, blocking the gate and refusing to let Genbao borrow a few crummy desks. It was pitiful to see the way Genbao looked at his older brother, as if hoping he'd say something to make Grandpa get out of the way and let them leave with the desks he needed for his wedding banquet.

With a half-hopeful, half-embarrassed expression, Genbao stared up at his big brother, waiting for him to speak. After a few moments, Genzhu said calmly, 'Genbao, take these desks back to wherever you found them.'

Genbao stared at his brother in confusion.

'Do as I say. Put them back where you found them.'

Sadly, reluctantly, Genbao turned his cart around and began trudging back to the schoolhouse. The wheeled cart, groaning under the weight of so many desks, left a trail of dust in its wake. As they watched the cart move slowly across the school-yard, the faces of the residents registered disappointment and dismay. They couldn't understand why Genzhu had backed down, or why the confrontation had come to such an abysmal ending. The sun had shifted to the centre of the schoolyard, and the atmosphere was thick with the scent of early spring. Grass and trees sprouting on the plain filled the air with moisture, like dampness rising from a river.

Grandpa, too, was surprised that things had ended this way. He certainly hadn't expected Jia Genzhu to be so reasonable, or to give in so easily. He suddenly felt guilty, as if he'd wronged Genzhu somehow, or ruined his little brother's wedding. Gazing towards the schoolhouse at the frail young man unloading desks from his cart, Grandpa turned to Genzhu. 'I'll help you borrow some tables. I can't believe there isn't a single banquet table left in this village.'

'That won't be necessary,' Genzhu answered icily. His words were cold, enunciated, deliberate. As he brushed past Grandpa at the gate, his face was hard and angry, the veins on his neck standing out like pale blue willow branches. Everyone in the crowd saw it: the coldness he directed towards Grandpa as he passed through the gate and began walking towards the village. He didn't seem to be in any hurry. Clutching his walking stick, a tree stump with the branches removed, he limped slowly across the plain.

4

Events were beginning to form rings. First one ring, then another, interconnected like links in a chain.

Jia Genzhu's return to the village was followed closely by my aunt's departure: my aunt Tingting sweeping out of the village and down the road like a whirlwind, making straight for the elementary school. With her mouth twitching, and dragging my cousin Xiao Jun by the hand, she walked so quickly that he had to run to keep up with her, his little feet pounding the dirt.

The plain was an expanse of tender young wheat shimmering in the sunlight. In untilled fields where vegetation grew wild, tiny plants pushed their heads through the soil, reaching up to get a better look at the world. Across the plain, in Two-Li Village and Yellow Creek, those well enough to work were out in the fields, irrigating or tending to their crops. Their figures stood out beneath the distant sky like scarecrows swaying in the wind. And now, blowing in from the village, was another small figure, dragging a child behind her. It was a scene not unlike that night in the school, when Ding Xiaoming had pulled his wife from the storeroom and marched her back home.

It was midday, the hour when the villagers would normally be eating or preparing lunch. But on this day, no one in Ding Village was cooking, much less eating. Housewives who would usually be stoking fires had doused them. Cold water was poured into pots to stop them from boiling. Bowls were left empty on the sideboard. No one knew quite what had happened, but there was a sense that something big was about to take place. A crowd of men and women, young and old, adults and tiny children rolled along behind my aunt like a cavalry, leaving clouds of dust in their wake.

A man standing in a doorway shouted to his wife who had just joined the crowd: 'Haven't you meddled enough already? Get back home!' His wife detached herself from the mob and slunk into the house.

An old woman in the village square grumbled. 'Haven't enough people died already? Now you're going to march over there and hound those poor people to death?' Her son and grandson stayed where they were and didn't join in the fun.

But other mothers snatched the bowls from their children's hands and urged them on. 'Go on, go and see what all the fuss is about . . . Hurry up, you don't want to miss out on the fun.' Their sons and daughters scampered off and followed the crowd towards the school.

Ding Village hadn't seen this much excitement in years. Not since the fever arrived had there been so much drama. It promised to be even more exciting than Ma Xianglin's big performance. This was something bigger and better: a real-life drama, not someone reading lines on a stage.

At this time of day, the school was quiet. Zhao Xiuqin and her two assistants were cooking in the kitchen. Most of the residents were in their rooms. The schoolyard was as silent and deserted as winter on the Central Plain. That is, until my aunt came rolling through the gate with her son in tow, followed by a large mob of villagers and their cavalcade of footsteps. As they pushed open the school gate, there was a metallic screech loud enough to make the roots of your teeth ache.

Grandpa and Uncle were the first people in the school to hear the noise. They were sitting in Grandpa's quarters, arguing about what had just happened, and about whether or not Grandpa was right to have treated Jia Genbao the way he had.

'Dad, you ought to remember that Genbao has the fever, too.'

'All the more reason not to trick that poor girl into marrying him.'

'It's not like she's from Ding Village. She's not one of ours . . . why should you care?'

'You're no better than he is,' Grandpa said angrily, and got up to leave.

But trouble had arrived at the school. Trouble had arrived on his doorstep. As Grandpa stepped into the main room, he saw Uncle's wife standing at the door.

When their eyes met, they both froze in their tracks, like two speeding drivers screeching to a halt just before impact. Only silently.

Grandpa saw that Tingting's normally rosy complexion was slightly off colour. He immediately understood what had happened, and understood what was about to happen. Uncle, cowering behind him, must have understood it too, because he shrank back into the inner room and shut the door behind him.

Grandpa turned around and hollered, 'Liang! Come out and apologize to your wife!'

Not a peep, not a sound from inside the room. It might as well have been empty.

Grandpa was enraged. 'You miserable excuse for a son! Get your arse out here and tell your wife you're sorry!'

This time, not only did Uncle refuse to come out, he barred and locked the door.

Grandpa walked over to the sturdy willow door and began kicking at it, pounding it with his feet. When it wouldn't open, he picked up a wooden stool and raised it over his head, ready to smash in the door. But at that moment, something caused him to reverse his course. It was Tingting, stepping over the threshold and telling him gently: 'Dad, stop.'

With those two words, his rage seemed to dissipate, like floodwaters receding, or the disappearing tail of a cyclone. He turned to see Tingting standing in the middle of the room, the anger fading from her face, her colour returning to normal. When she was calm and composed, she glanced at the locked and bolted door, tucked an errant strand of hair behind her ear and said: 'Don't bother calling him, Dad. He's too much of a coward to answer.'

Grandpa stood motionless, still holding the stool over his head.

'It's probably better this way,' Tingting continued evenly. 'I've never done anything to let your family down. I can get divorced, move back to my hometown, and not have to worry about him infecting me or Xiao Jun.'

Grandpa lowered the stool slowly, very slowly, until it hung limply at his side, like a puppet tethered by a string.

There was an awkward pause. Tingting blushed a deep crimson, licked her dry lips and said, 'I'm taking Xiao Jun with me. If you want to see your grandson, you're welcome to visit him at my parents' house. But if Ding Liang shows up, I'll have my brothers break his legs.'

Then Tingting turned and left the room. She left before Grandpa had a chance to answer.

Uncle's wife was gone.

5

After Jia Genzhu returned from the village, he and Ding Yuejin closeted themselves in an empty classroom. When they emerged a while later, they went off in search of Ding Shuiyang, otherwise known as Professor Ding. To me, he was always just Grandpa.

Tingting was gone by the time they arrived at Grandpa's rooms, but the crowd of onlookers had not dispersed.

'Move along now, go home,' Genzhu told them. 'There's nothing to see here.'

The villagers, who hadn't heard about the school coup, seemed confused by Jia Genzhu's authoritative tone: he spoke like he was a party official.

Ding Yuejin, standing at Genzhu's side, took it upon himself to explain. 'You heard the man. From now on, he'll be making the decisions around here. Genzhu and I are in charge of the school.'

And with that, the two men walked into Grandpa's rooms. 'Professor, we've got something else we'd like to discuss with you,' said Ding Yuejin, with a smile.

Jia Genzhu, unsmiling, handed Grandpa a piece of note-paper bearing the official village seal. It was very much like the piece of paper he'd handed him earlier at the gate, but the words were different, the message more alarming. It read:

After a thorough investigation into the matter, we hereby revoke Ding Shuiyang's credentials as a teacher and caretaker of stuff at the Ding Village Elementary School. From this day forward, Comrade Ding Shuiyang is not

an employee of Ding Village Elementary School, and may not meddle in any matter to do with the school.

Below this, Ding Yuejin and Jia Genzhu had affixed their signatures and the date. Grandpa skimmed the order once, glanced up in disbelief, then read it again more carefully, his wrinkled face twitching with annoyance. He thought about crumpling the paper into a ball and throwing it in their faces, until he noticed several young men standing behind them: Jia Hongli, Jia Sangen, Ding Sanzi and Ding Xiaoyue. All were close relatives of either Genzhu or Yuejin, young men in their late twenties or early thirties who had recently come down with the fever. Some stood with arms crossed, others leaned against the doorway, sneering at Grandpa as if he were a personal enemy who they had cornered at last.

'You're trying to get rid of me?' asked Grandpa.

'It's clear that you're not fit to run this school any more,' said Genzhu. 'Your older son milked us of our blood, then he sold off our coffins. I hear he's selling coffins belonging to other villages now. And your younger son is no better: he's got the fever and he comes to this school and starts fooling around with another man's wife, his cousin's wife, no less. Ding Shuiyang, you were a teacher . . . don't you know that that's considered incest?'

'So, you tell me,' Genzhu continued, 'do you still think you deserve to be in charge of this school?'

Then he proclaimed: 'Starting today, you are no longer a teacher or caretaker at this school, so stop trying to tell everyone what to do.'

Grandpa stood silently in the centre of the room. He felt himself wilting, as if the muscle and bone had been stripped from his body. For a moment, it seemed as if he might collapse, but he dug in his heels and forced himself to stand his ground.

Later that evening, the lights in most of the classrooms were still burning, but the little building beside the school gate lay in darkness. The darkness was impenetrable, as if the two rooms were trapped beneath an avalanche of black stones. Grandpa and Uncle, caught between the crevices, hunkered in the inner room. Grandpa sat slumped, his face and hands wet with tears. Uncle lay on his bed, gazing out of the window at the night. He could feel the darkness bearing down upon him, pressing on his chest, making it difficult to breathe.

The atmosphere was oppressive, unbearably so.

'Son,' Grandpa said. 'You've got to go home.'

'Why?'

'You've got to go and see Tingting, and talk her out of leaving.'

Uncle thought it over for a while and decided Grandpa was right. He had to go home.

Even this late at night, there was a crowd of people at the school gate. Jia Genzhu, his brother Genbao and their cousins Jia Hongli and Jia Sangen were still loading school desks on to carts. The cook, Zhao Xiuqin, also seemed to be helping. Uncle couldn't hear what they were saying, but they seemed to be talking about Genbao's upcoming wedding. Their laughter and conversation swirled through the schoolyard like muddy water down a dry riverbed, after an unexpected rainstorm.

Uncle listened for a while before coughing to announce his presence. The talk and laughter died down, and Uncle stepped through the school gate and began walking home.

When he arrived at his house, he was alarmed to see the padlock hanging from the front gate. Frantically, he groped around the edges of the wooden gate until he found two keys hidden in a crack. He opened the padlock, raced through the courtyard, unlocked the door of the house and turned on the light. He found the main room little changed, but for a layer of dust on his mother's photograph and on the family's ancestral shrine. He spied a heap of his unwashed shirts and trousers on a bench against the wall. Moving into the bedroom, he threw open the red wooden wardrobe and saw that Tingting and Xiao Jun's clothes were missing. He fumbled around in a corner of the wardrobe for the money and the red bank-book that he usually kept hidden there. When he came

167

up empty-handed, Uncle realized that Tingting had left him for good. His family was broken, his wife and son gone.

If I die tomorrow, Uncle thought, they'll find me with two tears in my eyes: one for every good thing that I've lost.

CHAPTER THREE

1

It happened just like Jia Genzhu said it would: Uncle's marriage was ruined, his wife and child gone, his family destroyed. It was the latest in a series of calamities to hit Ding Village.

Ruin had come early this year, with the spring.

The plain was a thick carpet of green. In the fields, the new crop of wheat was raising its head, and the soil, which had lain dormant all winter, now turned its energy to growth. Rich or poor soil alike was fertile enough at this time of year to nourish the young wheat and allow it to thrive. It would be at least another fortnight, or perhaps another month, before the relative wealth or paucity of the soil began to show. By mid-spring, when the nutrients in the sandy topsoil had been exhausted, some of the plants would become emaciated, thin and pale. But now, in the first few weeks of spring, everything was lush and green.

Grasses and wild flowers lined the roadsides, sprouting from gaps between fields and invading plots of untilled land. They grew madly, uncontrollably . . . blooms of red and white, yellow and purple, sandwiched between rectangles of green like a calico print. Red stood out bold and strong against a blur of pale yellow and smudges of green. The plain was a patchwork of colour, a world in disarray, growing free and wild. Even the solitary trees had burst into life: new leaves budded from their branches, gently swaying in the breeze. It was like the whole plain was bursting into song.

Beyond the fields was the ancient path of the Yellow River, a silted, sand-strewn channel that had lain dry for centuries, perhaps millennia. A thousand yards wide at its broadest point, a hundred at its narrowest, it snaked across the Central Plain for miles and miles. No one knew its exact length: to the villagers, it seemed as boundless as the sky. A sandy swathe that lay several feet below the level of the plain, it was like a broad grey belt pulled tight around the midriff of the earth, an enduring reminder of a river defeated by time. Now that spring had turned the sandy belt to green, filling it with vegetation, the channel was indistinguishable from the landscape around it. The plain had turned into a level playing field, a vast flatness of green.

Green earth. Green sky. Green villages. All the world had become lush and green.

The wheels of industry, too, had awakened with the spring. The residents of Ding Village elementary school bustled around as if they had miraculously returned to full health, carting items from the school back to their homes. Jia Genzhu and Ding Yuejin had divided the school property among the residents: desks and chairs and blackboards, chests and wash-stands, beds and bedding once used in the teachers' quarters, crossbeams and rafters and scavenged planks of wood.

Uncle had returned to the village, to his own house. Tingting, who had gone back to her hometown to stay with her mother, sent word that she didn't want to see Uncle again as long as she lived. Or as long as he lived. The next time they met, she said, she hoped he'd be lying in a coffin. Once he was dead, she would come back to the village to sell the house and collect the furniture. And so Uncle had no choice but to leave the school and move back into his house, to keep an eye on the property and possessions that would be sold or taken after his death.

Grandpa was no longer the caretaker of the school. No longer did anyone regard him as a caretaker, or treat him as a teacher. He was just an old man from the village who happened to live in the school. Disconnected from the residents, he took no part in their meals or medicines, conversations or chess games, or the ups and downs of their disease. Nor did anyone show him much respect. Although he still lived beside the main gate, few residents passing through gave him so much as a nod. If they did deign to greet him, it was only because he had greeted them first. If someone did nod his way, he returned the greeting eagerly. As for what was being said or done inside the classrooms, as for what the several dozen residents said or did in their spare time, it had absolutely nothing to do with him. He was lucky that they let him live in the school at all.

Once, as one of the residents, a spotty young man in his early twenties, was coming through the gate, Grandpa asked him: 'Now that Genzhu's little brother is married, did he ever return those desks he borrowed?'

'You mean Chairman Jia? No one calls him Genzhu any more.'

Grandpa stared at the man, speechless.

'Didn't you know? Uncle Jia and Uncle Ding are our new chairmen.'

The young man continued into the schoolyard, leaving Grandpa speechless at the gate, gawping like a rejected traveller at a border crossing. The school was a different country, and Grandpa was no longer a citizen.

Then the next day, at dusk, as the sun faded from a brilliant yellow to a pale, washed-up pink, Zhao Xiuqin had returned from the village carrying a bamboo basket filled with cabbages, carrots, rice noodles, two fish, several pounds of meat and a bottle of liquor. The meat looked to be the freshest, finest cut of pork; the label on the bottle read 'Song River Sorghum', the best local sorghum whisky money could buy. Even unopened, the bottle gave off a powerful fragrance. As Zhao Xiuqin passed through the gate, Grandpa smiled benevolently and said: 'Aha . . . we're moving up in the world, I see.'

The cook beamed. 'Yes, I'm making dinner for Chairman Jia and Chairman Ding tonight.'

Grandpa was confused. 'So that meat isn't for everyone?'

'Chairman Jia and Chairman Ding managed to get us some government funding,' the cook explained, 'so we thought we'd all pitch in and make them a nice meal. You know, to thank them.'

It was only then that Grandpa realized Jia Genzhu and Ding Yuejin had been appointed co-chairmen of the Ding Village task torce on HIV and AIDS, thus the elevated titles. There was a new social order in the school, a new pecking order. It wasn't so different from the periodic political reshufflings in village, county, district or provincial government; there had been a changing of the guard, and nothing would be the same. Grandpa couldn't help but feel bitter, somehow impoverished. But since the lives of the sick villagers seemed to be less so, there was really nothing he could say. He had no authority, nothing to do and no one to lead.

He woke the next morning, still feeling useless and idle. After loitering at the gate for a while, he decided to take a walk around the outside of the school. He strolled along like a man making a circuit of his own property, admiring the early spring foliage that covered the exterior of the school wall. When he reached the gate again, Grandpa found a crowd of people busily carting things out of the school.

Some had two classroom desks hanging from either end of a shoulder pole, while others struggled under the weight of large blackboards. Some worked in pairs to carry away heavy crossbeams, while others worked in groups of three or four, pushing carts laden with beds taken from the teachers' quarters. Sweating from their exertions, faces beaming with excitement, the residents of the school were carrying their trophies back to their homes in the village. It was just like Grandpa had imagined in his dream: a flower-filled early spring, gold growing from the soil, a village hurrying its treasure home . . .

As they bustled around, the residents eyed one another's items and compared notes on who had got what:

'Your desk is better than mine . . . the wood's much thicker.'

'If you sell that plank of elm, it'll be worth a lot more than this paulownia.'

'You got a bed made of chestnut? All I got was one made of toon.'

The metal gates of the school opened like a sluice, releasing a flood of villagers. Grandpa, wondering what had happened, quickened his pace and caught up with Jia Hongli, a younger cousin of Jia Genzhu. Despite his illness, the young man was carrying a shoulder pole laden with three shiny classroom desks.

'What's going on here?' Grandpa demanded.

Jia Hongli gave Grandpa a sideways glance. 'If you want to know what's going on,' he huffed, 'why don't you go and ask your son Ding Hui?'

The young man stalked off with his cargo of desks, like a tiny mountain goat trying to drag a mountain home to graze. Still confused, Grandpa stood at the gate until he saw another resident approaching, struggling under the weight of an enormous blackboard. Grandpa couldn't see the man's face, but he recognized the blackboard by the nail sticking out of one corner. It was a favourite from his substitute-teaching days: a large chalkboard set in a fine-grained elm-wood frame, with a smooth glossy surface that chalk seemed to glide across. For convenience, Grandpa had placed a nail in the lower right-hand corner so that he could hang a piece of cloth for wiping the board. Now the blackboard was inching across the schoolyard, covering the man's back like the shell of a snail.

As the man reached the gate, Grandpa lifted the chalkboard from his back and forced it to the ground. Zhao Dequan emerged from underneath with a sheepish grin. 'Oh, Professor Ding . . .' he said nervously.

'So it's you!' Grandpa shook his head. 'Planning to teach classes in your house now, are you?'

Zhao Dequan glanced around in alarm to make sure no one was within earshot.

'I had no choice but to take it,' he explained. 'Chairman Jia and Chairman Ding gave us these things, and everyone has collected theirs. If I refused, it would look bad, and everyone would be offended, including the chairmen.'

Zhao Dequan turned to look behind him. Seeing that the schoolyard was empty, he told Grandpa: 'If you can't bear to part with this blackboard, I'll help you hide it in your room. Just don't tell anyone I gave it you.'

'What were you planning to do with it, anyway?' asked Grandpa, stroking the blackboard.

'Use it for my coffin, of course,' Zhao Dequan answered, a smile playing on his face. 'Everyone says your son Ding Hui has been selling off the free government coffins that were supposed to go to all the villages in these parts. Now the chairmen are making it up to us by giving everyone enough wood to build a coffin.'

Grandpa stared at Zhao Dequan, dumbstruck. Beneath his faint smile, Grandpa could discern a greyish tinge, the pallor of a man who didn't have much longer to live. If the colour of his skin were any indication, he'd probably be in need of the coffin very soon, maybe in a matter of days.

Zhao Dequan's comment about Ding Hui made Grandpa realize that, outside of his dreams, he hadn't seen his eldest son for more than two months. He remembered the dream he'd had of Ding Hui picking out caskets at the county coffin factory, and another one, just a few nights ago, about him travelling around the countryside, selling coffins . . .

2

At night, the moonlight shone as bright as the sun.

In the daytime, the sunlight was docile, as meek and mild as moonlight.

Spring began in earnest. The young wheat, having raised its head into the world, now stiffened and stood tall. The landscape was sprinkled with people weeding or watering the soil. Anyone well enough to work was out in the fields, even those with the fever. In Ding Village, Yellow Creek and Two-

Li Village, and in the more distant hamlets of Summerlin, Junction, Old Riverton and Ming Village, the spring planting season had begun. As the villagers bustled around shouldering hoes and shovels, my father travelled from village to village, peddling his black coffins.

As soon as he arrived in a new place, my father would set up a table at the entrance to the village and place a stack of forms, stamped with the official county seal, on the table. Then he would announce to the villagers that anyone who had the fever was entitled to one black government-manufactured coffin. All you had to do was fill out a form with your name, age, medical history, present symptoms, etc., have it stamped by the village party committee, sign your name at the bottom and affix your thumbprint to certify that you really did have the fever and might keel over in your field any day now. Then you would be entitled to purchase one black coffin, at cost price. If you purchased such a casket at market price, it would set you back 400 or 500 yuan, but by filling out this one simple form, you could get the same casket for the manufacturer's cost of only 200 yuan. Anyone who met the criteria, and had 200 in cash, was entitled to share in this generous government subsidy . . .

My father was a very welcome visitor, drawing queues of people everywhere he went. One day he was 'serving the people' in Old Riverton, the next he was doing his bit for the sick in Ming Village, a settlement on the east bank of the old Yellow River path, five or six miles from Ding Village. Ming Village had been hit hard by the fever, and its residents needed coffins as badly as they had needed grain during the famine years. After setting out from Ding Village early that morning, my father had made a stop in the county capital to turn in the forms he'd collected the day before, and had picked up two trucks carrying a consignment of eighty black coffins. Now he was on his way to Ming Village to sell them.

When the villagers saw the trucks rumbling up the road beside the old river path and coming to a stop at the gates of *the village, they rushed in from the fields to greet them. The whole of Ming Village gleamed beneath a golden sun. Rays of sunlight shone on the tiled rooftops of the neighbourhood's two-storey houses bought with blood. Light cascaded through glass doors and windows, and glinted from facades of spotless white porcelain tiles, making the village seem warm and bright. The large trucks, each with a cargo of forty black coffins, were parked outside the gates like two black mountain ranges. The overpowering stench of fresh black lacquer mingled with other odours: the soft perfume of wood shavings, sticky yellow glue and the metallic traces of coffin nails. The motley smell drifted into the fields, masking the scent of spring, and wafted through the lanes and alleyways, giving them a dark, funereal air.*

No longer did my father have to do all the work himself. He had a crew of young men to unload coffins from the trucks and help villagers fill out their paperwork, while he sat at a separate table, sipping water and calling up the villagers one by one to collect their completed forms and payments. After he had counted the cash and stuffed it in his black leather case, he would issue a receipt and direct the person to the trucks to collect his or her coffin.

Ming Village was wealthier than Ding Village – at least as wealthy as Cottonwood, the model blood-selling village my father and the others had toured so many years ago. But it had a higher incidence of the fever, and many more people had taken ill than in Ding Village. There was hardly a family untouched by the fever, and households with several sick family members were commonplace. Because Ming Village was a model blood-selling village that had grown rich during the boom, the villagers no longer wrapped their dead in straw mats or buried them in simple graves outside the gates. Black coffins were the fashion. But, after so many deaths, wood for coffins was in short supply. The villagers had chopped down all the usable trees in and around the village. Even the trees along the main road and in nearby villages had been lopped, leaving the landscape bare.

Then my father arrived with his cargo of coffins, like a shipment of coal before a big snowstorm. A timely visitor in their hour of need.

The villagers rushed in from their fields and queued up at the village gate, eager for a chance to buy a discounted coffin. The enormous line of people stretched 200 yards down the lane. To prevent any family from buying more coffins than they were entitled to, my father enlisted the help of the village mayor.

'Mr Mayor,' my father said, 'I wonder if you'd help me vet these application forms.'

The mayor thought it over. 'I don't know . . . if I don't tend to my family's land soon, our crops are going to die.'

'Does anyone in your family have the fever?' my father asked.

'No. None of us sold blood.'

'Do you have any elderly family members?'

'My father's eighty-four.'

'How about I sell you a coffin now, so you'll have it ready for him, just in case?'

After a long pause, the mayor asked: 'Can you give me a discount?'

My father did a quick calculation. 'I'll give it to you for one-fifty. That's fifty below cost.'

'Will you make sure it's a good one?'

'I've got three Grade-A coffins. You can take your pick.'

And so the mayor, official village seal in hand, agreed to help my dad vet the applicants. The first thing he did was to scan the queue for villagers who had no sick family members, and yank them out of line. Then he sat down next to my dad and looked through the pile of forms, weeding out applicants who had claimed their fever was full-blown when in fact it was only mild. When this was done, he got down to the business of selling coffins.

By midday, the villagers had made their purchases and were carrying home their coffins. The streets of Ming Village were thronged with people carrying shiny black caskets, singing the praises of the local task force on HIV and AIDS and talking about how lucky they were that the government had been so good to them. Upon reaching home, some of the villagers discovered that they didn't have room for a coffin, so they simply left them sitting in the middle of the courtyard or leaned them next to their doors, right on the street. Everywhere you looked there were shiny black caskets. Ming Village was a sea of coffins. The villagers were so thrilled by their cut-rate caskets that they forgot all about the fever, forgot all about their sick relatives lying on their deathbeds. Many walked around with cheerful, carefree smiles, while some shed actual tears of joy. Other families, whose sick relatives were not yet sick enough to merit a coffin, had managed to worm their way around the rules and purchase a casket anyway. Unable to flaunt their good fortune, they locked their casket inside the house where no one could see it, then stood outside exchanging pleasantries about the fine spring weather with passers-by.

The next day, my dad made a trip to Old Riverton, not far from Ming Village. This time, he brought three trucks filled with coffins. He instructed the drivers to stop the vehicles in a deserted area about a mile away, so that he could walk into the village alone and reconnoitre. As he strolled through Old Riverton, my dad noted the cement roads and multi-storey tiled houses, all built within the last decade. He could tell that the village was wealthy, and that the villagers must have sold a lot of blood back in the day. He knew they would now be suffering badly from the fever, but he also knew that most of them would have saved up enough money to afford a coffin. Having established these facts, my dad found his way to the home of the village party secretary, introduced himself as the vice-chairman of the county task force on HIV and AIDS, and produced a letter of introduction from the county government. As soon as the party secretary, a flustered young man, read the letter, he invited my dad to sit down for a glass of tea. After asking a few standard questions about the extent of the fever, village mortality rates, etc., my dad decided that it was time to test the waters.

'So, does anyone in your family have the fever?' he asked casually, sipping his tea.

The young party secretary lowered his head, tears streaming down his cheeks.

'How many?' My dad was all sympathy.

'My older brother died, my younger brother's bedridden, and now it seems like I've got it, too.'

Silently, Dad handed the young man a handkerchief so he could wipe away his tears. After a moment, he said resolutely: 'Mr Secretary, I probably shouldn't do this, but I'm going to make an executive decision: I'm sending our next shipment of coffins right here to Old Riverton, to take care of our sick folks here. But I'll need your help to keep an eye on things . . . we don't want people who aren't sick buying up all the cheap coffins and leaving none for the people who really need them, right? And because the government is selling them at cost, there won't be enough to go around. At market prices, one of these coffins will set you back at least 500 yuan, as I'm sure you know. But since it's up to me, no one in Old Riverton will pay a penny more than 200.'

'As for your family . . .' Dad paused, pretending to think. 'Since your younger brother's fever is already full-blown, I think I can manage to get him a coffin for 100 yuan, half the manufacturing cost.

The village party secretary gazed at my dad, tears of gratitude welling up in his eyes.

'Now, the regulations say you're not eligible for a coffin until you've been sick for at least three months, but you're the village party secretary after all, one of our grassroots officials. That ought to count for something. Tell you what . . . when I'm finished distributing the coffins, why don't you pick one out for yourself at the same price? Just don't let the folks in the village find out.'

The party secretary disappeared into another room. He emerged a moment later with 100-yuan notes, which he handed to my dad. Then, smiling, he went out to ring the bell, *summoning the villagers to gather in the square to buy their coffins.*

By noontime, Old Riverton was filled with shiny black caskets. Like its neighbour Ming Village, Old Riverton had become a coffin-town. The scent of wood and fresh lacquer rolled through the streets and alleyways, permeating every corner of the village. Now that they had their coffins, the inhabitants of Old Riverton, sick and well alike, could rest easy. At the very least, it was one less thing to worry about. Laughter and conversation, sounds that had all but died out over the last two years, were heard in the village once again.

3

Grandpa hadn't seen his eldest son for more than two months. He wanted to see my dad, wanted to visit the house and tell him a few things, but if he went there and found my mother alone, it would be awkward. It wasn't that Grandpa didn't like his daughter-in-law, he just never knew what to say to her.

All day long, Grandpa thought about paying a visit to his son. Just before dusk, my uncle showed up at Grandpa's door. The first words out of his mouth were: 'Dad, Hui wants you to come over to the house for dinner. He has something to tell you.'

Without a moment's hesitation, Grandpa accompanied Uncle to our family's house. The gentle mid-spring sunshine cast a pleasant yellow glow on the white porcelain-tiled walls, reminding Grandpa of the homes and courtyards of Ming Village and Old Riverton, the places he had seen in his dream. The only difference was a patch of spicy mustard greens on the south end of our courtyard, where the chicken coop and the pig pen used to be. The plants were a deep, rich shade of green, each about as tall as a chopstick standing on end. Their leaves were the same shape as the leaves of the scholar tree, only thicker and less glossy, covered with a network of tender veins. The plants jostled for space, spilling luxuriantly into half the courtyard and filling the air with their pungent, intoxicating fragrance. Spicy mustard greens gave off a scent not unlike peppermint, but theirs was a cruder sort of smell, not as delicate or refined as peppermint. It was precisely this crudeness that made the county deputy governor love them so. They suited his taste. Naturally, it was for the deputy governor that my parents had planted them.

As Uncle led the way into the courtyard, the first thing that caught Grandpa's eye was the enormous patch of spicy mustard greens. My mother, carrying a gourd filled with white flour, greeted Grandpa and Uncle on her way to the kitchen. 'Hi, Dad,' she said. 'We're having a treat for lunch today – noodles mixed with spicy mustard greens.'

My mother treated Grandpa as if nothing untoward had happened. It was just like it had been years ago, when she had first married into the family. My father also treated Grandpa as if there had never been any conflict between them. When he saw Grandpa at the door, he quickly composed his face into a smile, and pulled up a straight-backed chair with a comfortable cushion for Grandpa to sit on. The three men sat down together. Grandpa, Dad and Uncle: three corners of a triangle.

The kind reception unnerved Grandpa; he was uncomfortable at being treated so warmly by his son and daughter-in-law, when he felt so estranged from them. Flushing with embarrassment, he turned his head away and looked around the room. It was more or less as he remembered it. There were the same white-washed walls, a long red table along one wall, and a television and a sofa at opposite ends of the room. The television cabinet was red, its doors decorated with golden peonies.

Grandpa noticed a cobweb in one corner of the room. Usually my mother swept out cobwebs as soon as they appeared, but this one had fanned out from a corner of the ceiling to the top of the refrigerator. That one cobweb made the house seem different from before. For Grandpa, it was a sign that something had changed. Then he spied several large wooden trunks in a corner behind the door. He realized as soon as he saw them. His son really was moving away.

Grandpa couldn't take his eyes off the wooden trunks.

'I might as well tell you,' said my dad, taking a drag of his cigarette, 'we're getting ready to move.'

Grandpa turned to stare. 'Move where?'

Dad shifted his gaze uncomfortably. 'First to the county capital. Then, when I've saved a little more money, to Kaifeng.'

'Is it true you're vice-chairman of the county task force on HIV and AIDS?' Grandpa asked.

My dad looked pleased. 'Oh, so you've heard?'

'And is it true that you've been selling coffins in Ming Village and Old Riverton the last few days?'

Surprised, my dad removed the cigarette dangling from his mouth. 'Where did you hear that?'

'Never mind where I heard it. I'm asking you if it's true.'

My dad's expression hardened. He stared at Grandpa and said nothing.

'Did you or didn't you sell two truckloads of eighty coffins in Ming Village?' Grandpa pressed. 'And three truckloads of a hundred and ten coffins in Old Riverton?'

Astonishment was now thick upon my dad's face, like a layer of dried mud that could crumble at any moment. His features had frozen into a look of shock, an expression that might never thaw. Father and sons sat stiffly, three points of a triangle. The sound of my mother making noodles in the kitchen drifted through the courtyard and into the house. The soft thud of dough sounded like someone thumping a beefy hand on the wall behind them. My dad abruptly stubbed out his cigarette, grinding the long stub beneath his shoe until all that was left were shards of tobacco and confetti bits of paper. He glanced at my uncle, then turned to Grandpa, moving his gaze from Grandpa's face to his head of white hair.

'Dad,' he said. 'Now that you know everything you need to, there's no use talking about it any more. I just want to say one thing: no matter how badly you treat me, you'll always be my father and I'll always be your son. But there's no way I can let my family go on living in this village. I've talked it over with my wife, and we've decided to give the house and everything in it to Liang. All we're taking are our clothes. I know Liang hasn't got much time left, but I think his wife will come back to him if she knows he's got the house and the furniture. I can't believe she'd pass up a chance to inherit all the family property. As for you . . .' He paused. 'You can move with us to the city if you like, or you can stay here and look after Liang. When he's gone, you can join us in the city and I'll support you in your old age.'

That was all Dad had to say.

My uncle's face was wet with tears of gratitude.

4

Grandpa lay tossing and turning in his bed. Try as he might, he couldn't sleep. Since he'd left our family's house earlier that day, his mind had been overwhelmed by thoughts of my dad selling coffins and planning to move his wife and son out of the village. Just thinking about his son trading in coffins made Grandpa wish he'd killed his first-born when he'd had the chance. *Better that he were dead* was the thought that kept Grandpa awake, and made his head ache. He suddenly remembered how feuding families on the plain would bury sticks outside their enemies' houses as a curse. They'd take a twig from a willow or peach tree, sharpen one end and carve on it the name of the person they wished to die. Then, after smashing it against their enemy's door or the wall of their house, they'd bury it deep in the ground as a curse against that person. Even if they knew that the person wouldn't actually die, they still went through the motions. It might result in an early death, or an accident in which the cursed individual would break an arm or a leg, or lose a finger or toe.

Grandpa got out of bed, turned on the light and searched around until he found a willow twig. He whittled one end to a sharp point, wrote on a piece of paper *My son Ding Hui deserves to die,* and wrapped the paper around the twig. Under cover of darkness, he snuck into the village and buried the twig behind our house.

After returning to his rooms, Grandpa quickly undressed, got back into bed and fell fast asleep.

Despite Grandpa's willow-twig curse, my dad remained alive and well.

Zhao Dequan, however, was knocking on death's door. He wouldn't last the spring, the season when all living things prospered. Normally, if you had a serious illness, some life-threatening condition, all you had to do was make it through the cruel winter months and into spring. If you could hold out until then, you'd get a new lease of life, and maybe live to see another year.

But there wasn't much hope for Zhao Dequan. The day he'd carried the old blackboard with the heavy elm frame from the school into the village, he'd had to stop many times along the road to rest. When he'd reached the village, he'd got a lot of teasing questions from the villagers: 'Hey, Dequan, what's with the blackboard? You teaching classes now?' Some of them, like Grandpa, had been opposed to the sick removing the items from the school. 'Who'd have thought when all you sick people moved into the school, you'd start divvying up public property?' 'Good heavens, you're even taking the blackboards?'

Unable to answer these questions, Zhao Dequan increased his pace and hurried from the west end to the east end of the village without once stopping to rest. He turned into a narrow lane, entered his front gate, propped the blackboard up against a wall and collapsed right there in the middle of the courtyard.

Before Zhao Dequan got sick, he could easily lift 200lbs – a load of stones, say, or several sacks of rice – and carry it for miles without getting winded. But now, carrying a blackboard that couldn't have weighed more than 100lbs, probably a lot less, for several hundred yards across the village, he was exhausted. Drenched in sweat, wheezing like the wind through cracks, he lay paralysed on the ground, unable to get back up.

'Why on earth would you carry a blackboard all the way home?' asked his wife.

'Because they gave it to me . . . to make my coffin,' Zhao Dequan gasped, his face deathly pale. He tried to say something more, but his throat seemed to be blocked: he could hardly breathe, much less speak. As he coughed and gasped and tried to spit something up, his face flushed beet red. The spots on his face seemed to bulge from his skin, dark purple lumps in a blaze of red. His wife rushed over in alarm and began thumping him on the back. Zhao Dequan managed to spit something out, a ball of phlegm mixed with blood, before keeling over on the ground.

Zhao Dequan had carried his blackboard all the way home, but he would never again return to the school.

Several days later, his wife went to the school to speak to Jia Genzhu and Ding Yuejin. 'Chairman Jia. Chairman Ding. When my husband first came to this school, he was able to walk and move around without any trouble. Now he's lying in bed at home, breathing his last! You know the poor man is dying . . . why on earth would you give him a big heavy blackboard, when everyone else got desks and chairs? I've been in this village a long time, and I've seen other men beat and curse their women. But in all the years we've been married, my husband never raised a hand to me, never spoke an unkind word. Now he's dying, and I don't even have a coffin to bury him in. He sold his blood to support his family, and to build a nice house for me and the kids . . . the least we can do is make sure he has a decent coffin.'

Jia Genzhu and Ding Yuejin told Zhao's wife that she was free to go through the school and take any items she fancied, provided they could be used to make a coffin. Later, as they led her through the empty rooms and deserted classrooms, she saw that the school had been picked clean. All the desks and chairs were missing. The blackboards and blackboard stands, teachers' beds, footlockers and storage chests were all gone.

Even the mirrors had been stripped of their frames. The teachers' quarters were empty. Ransacked. The floor was strewn with old exam papers, homework books and tattered socks. The classrooms, too, were bare, littered with scraps of paper, dust and broken bits of chalk. Other than the personal belongings of the residents and the bags of food in the kitchen, there was nothing left in the school.

They'd given everything away. They'd robbed the place clean.

The metal basketball frame stood desolate in the schoolyard, its wooden backboard missing. The residents now used it for drying their laundry. As the sun dipped towards the west, Zhao Dequan's wife and the two chairmen stood forlorn in the schoolyard, trying to decide what to do. They had completed their tour of the school and come up empty-handed.

'I'll give you my chair, if you like,' Ding Yuejin offered.

'Forget it,' said Jia Genzhu. 'Let's go and talk to that hound Ding Hui, and see if he'll give her a coffin.'

Accompanied by a posse of other sick villagers, they paid a visit to my dad.

The scene at my family's front gate was not a friendly one. The crowd buzzed with anger, accusations and hearsay about my dad selling coffins in other villages. They shouted that they knew he'd been selling coffins that were meant for them, coffins that the government had provided free for people dying of the fever. My dad let them shout and argue and work themselves into a frenzy, while he said nothing. Finally, Jia Genzhu raised his voice: 'Would everyone shut up!'

As the villagers fell silent, Jia Genzhu pulled Ding Yuejin to the front of the crowd. 'We're the ones who helped you get those government coffins in the first place,' Jia Genzhu told my dad. 'So just answer us this: is it true you've been selling them?'

'Yeah,' Dad answered. 'So what?'

'Who have you been selling them to?'

'To whoever wants them. If you want coffins, I'll sell you some, too.'

Dad disappeared into the house and emerged with a brown paper envelope, from which he produced a small booklet identifying him as 'Comrade Ding Hui, vice-chairman of the Wei county task force on HIV and AIDS.' He then pulled out a sheaf of documents, all written on government letterhead and bearing official-looking red seals. There were letters from the party committees of Wei county and Henan province, as well as from various departments of city, county and provincial government. One document was titled 'An Urgent Memo Regarding the Prevention of Dissemination of Information Regarding "Fever Villages" (or "AIDS villages")'. It bore the large red seals of the provincial governor and the party committee of Henan province. Another, certified by the Henan Provincial Task Force on HIV and AIDS, read: 'A Notice Regarding Funeral Arrangements and Subsidized Low-Price Coffins for Fever Patients'. The city and county documents, marked with the seals of the city and county task forces on HIV and AIDS, were mainly memos about memos, notices about notices, all sent down from higher levels of government.

After my dad had showed the documents to Jia Genzhu and Ding Yuejin, he asked: 'Are you the co-chairmen of the Ding Village task force on HIV and AIDS?'

The two men stared at my dad and said nothing.

Taking their silence as an affirmative, my dad smiled and said: 'Well, I'm the vice-chairman of the county task force, which means I'm in charge of coffin sales and government subsidies for fever patients in this whole county. I'm the one who approved your request for ten pounds of grain, ten pounds of rice and a cash subsidy for everyone in Ding Village with the fever . . . Didn't you see my signature on the form?

'Now,' my dad continued. 'The regulations say that these government-subsidized coffins can't be sold for less than two hundred yuan each, but seeing as we're all from Ding Village, I think I can pull a few strings and get you coffins for only a hundred and eighty each. If you submit your requests right now, I'll have someone deliver the coffins tomorrow.'

As the sun sank in the west, a red glow settled over the village. The sweet scent of spring drifted in from the fields and dissipated through the village streets. Standing on the top step of his doorway like a political leader atop a rostrum, my dad scanned the crowd of villagers and addressed them in a loud voice:

'These coffins are not very cheap, actually. It would cost about the same to make your own. If they were such a great bargain, don't you think I'd have told you about it earlier?

'Honestly, I wouldn't sell one to my own brother, not if he asked. The wood is not even dry yet . . . In a couple of days, these coffins are going to start showing cracks as wide as your finger.

'You'd be better off buying wood and building a coffin yourself. Then you could make whatever kind you wanted.

'We're all friends and neighbours here . . . There's no need to get all worked up, or turn this into some kind of confrontation. Because if it comes to that . . .', pointing at Jia Genzhu and Ding Yuejin: 'You two might be in charge of the village task force, but I'm the guy in charge of the county . . . and who do you think wins? Who has the final say? If this turned into a fight or got ugly, one word from me and the higher-ups would have the police and public security here so fast it would make your head spin. But nobody wants that, am I right? What kind of a neighbour would I be – what kind of a *person* would I be – to do something like that?'

After that, nothing more was said.

After that, there was nothing more *to be* said.

The crowd of villagers dispersed and began heading back to the school. The setting sun hung red and heavy in the sky, like a ball of glowing red-vermilion ink. Like lead. It slowly sank towards the horizon, dragged to earth under its own leaden weight. The western border of the central plain appeared to be a swathe of fire; you could almost hear the flames, popping and crackling like a wildfire raging through a grove of cypress trees.

CHAPTER FOUR

1

Ding Village elementary was silent, sleeping the sleep of the dead. That day, the sky had been so clear it was as if you could see right through it, to a deep and bottomless blue heaven. But now, in the middle of the night, the sky was overcast, as damp and dark as a freshly dug grave. In the silence of the school, a deep well of silence, you could almost hear the clouds bumping against each other. Everyone was asleep. Even Grandpa was asleep.

Thump. Thump. Someone was knocking at Grandpa's window. The late-night visitor must have come in through the unlocked school gate. Since Genzhu and Yuejin had confiscated Grandpa's keys, no one bothered to lock up at night. People came and went at all hours, so the gate was always open. Anyone could walk right in and creep up to Grandpa's window, unheard. Thump, thump . . . The sound continued, steady as a drumbeat.

'Who's there?' Grandpa called.

'It's me, Professor,' the visitor wheezed. 'Open up.'

Grandpa opened the door to find Zhao Dequan standing on the threshold. In the few days since Grandpa had last seen him, Dequan had changed beyond recognition. Where he had been skin-and-bone before, now he was just bone. What flesh he had left hung limp from his skeletal frame, dark and discoloured, a patchwork of dry, hardened scabs; the sockets of his eyes, two deep, dark pits. One look at him and Grandpa could see that death was dancing in Zhao Dequan's body. His eyes were dull, bereft of light. He stood at Grandpa's door like a cadaver in shabby clothes. Under the electric lights, his shadow seemed more lifelike than his person, a dark silhouette flickering on the wall like a funeral shroud ruffled by the breeze.

When Grandpa opened the door, Zhao Dequan broke into a smile, a sickly grin that seemed to cost him a good deal of effort.

'Professor Ding,' he said. 'I've been thinking it over, and I decided that while I'm still well enough to walk, I ought to return the blackboard. I don't want to end my life by doing something so low. It's a blackboard, not a coffin. Once the fever is gone, the kids will be back in school, and their teachers will need something to write on. I'd rather be buried without a coffin,' he sighed, 'than leave those kids without a blackboard.'

Grandpa looked out and saw the blackboard loaded on a hand-cart parked beside the gate.

'I can't lift it myself,' said Zhao Dequan. 'Can you help me carry it inside?'

With a lot of clunking and clattering, Grandpa and Zhao Dequan managed to carry the blackboard into the room.

'Careful you don't hurt yourself,' Grandpa said, as they leaned the blackboard up against a wall.

'No matter. I'm going to be dead soon, anyway. If Genzhu and Yuejin see the blackboard, you can blame it on me . . . Tell them I'm the one who brought it back here.'

Zhao Dequan stood panting, trying to catch his breath. The same sickly smile was glued to his face like a sticking plaster. After he had helped Grandpa lean the blackboard against the wall and wiped the dust from his hands, Grandpa expected him to leave, but instead Dequan sat down on Grandpa's bed, still smiling his silent, cardboard-cutout smile.

Grandpa waited for him to say something, but it seemed the man had nothing to say. When Grandpa offered him a drink of water, he waved it away. When Grandpa poured him a basin of water so he could wash his hands, he ignored the basin and said: 'Professor, I'm fine. But if it's okay with you, I'd just like to sit here for a while.'

'Is something wrong?' Grandpa asked, taking a chair opposite the bed. 'If so, you can tell me.'

Zhao Dequan's smile faded. 'It's nothing, really.'

The two men sat quietly, as still as the night around them. Silence lay thick across the plain. Now and then, a chirp or a cry broke the stillness. Some tiny insect managing to make itself heard. Then there was silence, and after that, more silence.

'You ought to move back into the school,' said Grandpa awkwardly, trying to make conversation.

Zhao Dequan stared. 'Don't you see the state I'm in? I doubt I'll live more than a few days.'

'How can you say that?' Grandpa tried his best to be reassuring. 'You've made it through the winter and into spring. I bet you'll live at least another year.'

Zhao Dequan smiled wryly, unconvinced. As he shifted position on the bed, his shadow flickered over the walls like a black silk funeral shroud. It was clear that he was having trouble moving, but his shadow remained active. It was as if his spirit had already left his body and was hovering nearby.

Grandpa realized that Zhao Dequan was right: he really was going to die soon.

'Do you have a casket yet?' he asked, deciding he might as well be direct. 'Even if it's not the best quality, you've got to be buried in something.'

Zhao looked embarrassed. 'Jia Genzhu and Ding Yuejin gave my wife permission to cut down one of the paulownia trees to make my coffin.'

Zhao gripped the edge of the bed for support, as if he were getting ready to stand up and leave. But instead of leaving, he spoke again. 'Professor, that's really what I came here to tell you. Genzhu and Yuejin gave my wife special permission to cut down a tree for my coffin, but now everyone is jumping on the bandwagon, chopping down the paulownia and cotton-woods. And some of those people don't even need coffins.

They're cutting down all the trees in the village . . . I'm afraid that by morning, there won't be any left.

'You've got to do something, Professor. Once all the trees are gone, this village won't be the same. Even if I don't get my coffin, I don't care. The only thing I want to do before I die is give my wife the red silk jacket I promised her. Anyway, what use is a coffin when you're already dead? It's not worth cutting down every tree in the village.'

2

Grandpa stepped out of the school gate, hesitated for a moment, and began walking towards the village. Darkness blanketed the plain like a vast black lake. There was no moon or stars, only vague, flickering shadows. The road to the village was swallowed up by the darkness, making it easy to stumble over its uneven surface or stray into the fields on either side. Grandpa had to tread carefully, using the patches and points of light in the distance to gauge his direction. As he drew closer to the village, the dark night air was filled with the fresh scent of sawdust. At first, it was just a faint whiff coming from the direction of the light. Then the smell seemed to coalesce into something more solid: waves of it sweeping in from the west end of the village, rolling in from the north and south, washing in from the alleyways to the east. With it came a tide of sound: the buzz of saws slicing timber, the thud of axes chopping trees, the babble of human conversation. It reminded Grandpa of years long ago, when everyone in the village had laboured day and night smelting steel in backyard furnaces or constructing massive irrigation works.

Quickening his step, Grandpa walked in the direction of the nearest lights. He found Ding Sanzi and his father working at the edge of their wheat field, digging up the roots of a large cottonwood tree. By the light of their lanterns, Grandpa could see that they'd dug an enormous room-sized pit, exposing the root system of the tree. Ding Sanzi's father, stripped down to his underpants and covered in sweat, was using an axe to sever the last two connected roots, each the circumference of a large bowl. As he swung his axe, bits of dirt and wood flew through the air and stuck to his sweaty skin, making it look as if he'd been splattered in mud. Some distance away in the middle of the field, Ding Sanzi was trying to pull down the cottonwood by tugging on a heavy rope tied to a fork of the tree. Using all his strength, he yanked the rope, causing the tree to sway. There was a tremendous snapping and creaking of roots, and for a moment it seemed that the huge cottonwood might topple. When it refused to fall, Ding Sanzi shouted: 'Dad . . . come over here and help me pull!'

'Wait until I chop this last root, then it'll fall!'

As the older man raised his axe, Grandpa hurried over to block his way. 'Hey, who said you could chop down this tree?'

His axe frozen in mid-swing, Sanzi's father stared at Grandpa. After a moment, he laid down the axe and called to his son.

Sanzi came in from the field, took one look at Grandpa and snorted. Then he went over to a pile of clothes lying on the ground, took a folded letter from one of the pockets, and showed it to Grandpa.

The letter, written on Ding Village party committee stationery, was brief: 'Ding Sanzi has permission to cut down the big cottonwood next to his field west of the village.' Below this were the official village seal and the signatures of Jia Genzhu and Ding Yuejin.

Reading the letter in the light of the lanterns, Grandpa realized exactly what it meant: permission to fell the trees of Ding Village. He clutched the letter and stared at the two men, wondering whether or not he ought to stop them from cutting down the tree. As Grandpa was trying to make up his mind, Ding Sanzi snatched the letter from his hand and walked away. After he had folded the letter and put it back into the pocket of his clothes, he said calmly: 'Your son Ding Hui sold off our coffins, and now you won't even let us cut down a tree to make our own.'

Ding Sanzi, still strong despite being infected with the fever, walked back into his field, picked up the rope and continued trying to pull down the big cottonwood. Grandpa stood by helplessly for a while, then decided to go into the village and see what was happening there. He had not gone far when he heard a loud crack behind him, the splintering of wood. The sound reverberated through his chest, as if there were some acute ache in his heart. In that moment, Grandpa was once again consumed with the desire to strangle his eldest son with his bare hands. He could almost feel his palms sweating, and the ageing tendons in his hands flexing.

Grandpa entered the village and followed the glow of lanterns to a large willow tree. Plastered to the tree trunk was a notice nearly identical to the one Ding Sanzi had shown him. It was written on the same letterhead, and had the same two signatures and village seal. It read: 'Jia Hongli has permission to cut down the old willow tree at the northwest corner of the intersection on the west end of the village.'

Grandpa scrutinized the paper pasted to the tree trunk as if it were an official government poster on a bulletin board. He was speechless. Apparently, the chopping down of trees was now perfectly legal and above-board. Grandpa stood in a daze, staring up at the lantern hanging from a branch of the willow tree. In the pool of light, he could make out Jia Hongli perched high in the tree, hacking at the branches. After pondering for a few seconds, Grandpa shouted up at him.

'That looks dangerous, Hongli! Aren't you afraid you'll fall?'

Hongli paused and shouted back, 'So what? I won't live long, anyway.'

Grandpa tried appealing to Hongli's father, who was standing below the tree. 'Jia Jun, you're not going to let your son risk his life over a tree, are you?'

The older man smiled and pointed to the notice stuck to the tree trunk. 'It's all right. We've got permission to cut it down, see?'

Grandpa shook his head and continued on his way. As he walked through the village, he saw that every tree large enough to be used as timber had been marked for demolition: there were notices pasted to every elm, honey locust, paulownia, toon and scholar tree he passed. In every lane and alleyway, in every corner of the village, he found people chopping down trees by the light of lanterns, kerosene lamps or candles. Some of the trees and exterior walls were strung with electric lights connected to long grey extension leads (known in the village as 'rat-tail cords') that snaked into nearby houses. Nearly every other house was brightly lit, turning Ding Village into a blaze of light, as dazzling as the daytime sun. It looked as if every tree in the village had been served with an execution order. The night air filled with the ceaseless clamour of chopping and sawing, and the pungent scent of fresh-cut wood mingled with tree sap.

Ding Village seemed revived: the residents prowled the streets with hatchets and saws, searching for the trees they'd been given permission to chop down. The sick villagers had, of course, been given the trees most suitable for making coffins: the willows, cottonwoods and paulownia. But because the trees were public property and everyone was entitled to his or her share, even the healthy villagers were allowed to chop down trees. They had been given the toons, chinaberries and scholar trees, whose timber was prone to rot and insects, and so ill-suited for making coffins. But they were fine for making furniture, beds and tables and chairs that could be given to sons and daughters as wedding gifts.

Each family in the village, with the exception of ours, had been given one tree to use as timber. So it was that on this spring night, the whole of Ding Village was hard at work chopping down trees and dragging them back to their homes.

God only knows where they got so many hatchets and saws. It was as if the whole village had known in advance about the great tree-felling, and had bought in supplies of tools beforehand. The clash of metal rang through the night, punctuated by the snapping and cracking of tree branches.

Sounds from the east end of the village could be heard on the distant western plain, and noise from the west end of the village carried to the alleyways in the east. Ding Village was a hive of noise and activity, seething with rare excitement. There was the constant thud of footsteps, carts rumbling through the streets and the sound of voices, as villagers compared the quality of their timber with that of their neighbours. Looks of envy swirled around every pool of dazzling light, and followed in the wake of every glowing lantern being carried down the street.

Even the faces of villagers too sick to work glowed with the excitement of cutting down trees. The healthy villagers worked with enthusiasm, as if it were the big planting or harvest season. All night long, the village was filled with the sound of people working and the sweet scent of timber and sawdust. The conversation that accompanied all this coming and going and hustle and bustle followed more or less the same basic pattern:

'Wow, you got an elm!'

'Well, we needed a beam for the roof, so we asked for an elm.'

'Those pieces of wood look pretty short. What are you going to use them for?'

'Can't you tell? They're the perfect size for shelves.'

Another conversation went like this: 'Did you hear? Li Wang's family got the big toon tree at the west end of the village.'

'Li Wang? I can't believe it.'

'Would I lie? It's because his daughter's engaged to Ding Yuejin's cousin, that's why.'

And so it went. The speaker would whisper some mysterious bit of information, the listener would 'ooh' or 'aah' in understanding and the two would go their separate ways, eager to pass on the gossip to others.

Grandpa walked the streets dejectedly, pausing before this tree and that, as if paying his last respects before they were all chopped down. He couldn't help but be reminded of his dream of Ding Village: flowers on the surface, and gold beneath the soil. He wandered the village in a daze, peering around him in confusion. When he reached the village centre, he was surprised to see that even the venerable old scholar tree – so large that it would take three or four people to encircle its trunk – was also marked for demolition. Zhao Xiuqin and her husband Wang Baoshan stood by as her brothers, two stout young men from another village, removed the heavy bell that hung from one of the branches. After they had taken it down and hung it from a smaller tree nearby, one of the brothers scaled a ladder and began sawing at the branches, while the other began digging up the roots.

The last time Grandpa had passed the old scholar tree, it had been safe and sound. Now, in the short time it had taken him to make one circuit around the village, it was besieged by people hacking and sawing and trying to chop it down. Moving closer, Grandpa passed under an extension lead that stretched from a nearby house into the branches of the old tree. In the glow of a 200-watt light bulb, the area around the tree, once the site of village meetings, was as bright as day.

'Xiuqin, are they really letting you cut down this tree?' Grandpa called out.

Zhao Xiuqin, sitting in the circle of light beneath the scholar tree, raised her head and blushed uncomfortably. She seemed quite embarrassed that her family had been caught chopping down the oldest, largest and most venerable tree in the village.

'I never expected Chairman Jia and Chairman Ding to be so grateful,' she answered with a nervous laugh. 'I was just doing my job, cooking their favourite meals and making sure they had whatever food or liquor they wanted. But when I mentioned that all the big trees had already been cut down and that this was the only one left, they told me I could have it!'

Amidst the cacophony of trees being felled, Grandpa stood forlornly, remembering his dream of flowers on the plain and gold beneath the surface.

3

It happened just like Zhao Dequan said it would.

The trees of Ding Village disappeared overnight.

All the mature trees were gone. At first, it seems, there had been some discussion about only felling trees of a certain size, those with trunks as broad as a bucket, say. But when morning came, the villagers woke to find that even the smaller trees in and around the village were gone. Anything that had a trunk the size of the circumference of a bowl had been chopped down for timber. Discarded notices from the village party committee littered the streets like fallen leaves after a windy evening. The spring sun shone warm as usual, but without foliage or the shade of trees, the village felt scorching and unpleasant.

All the mature elms, scholar trees, paulownia, chinaberries, toons, cottonwoods and persimmon trees had been felled, leaving only saplings with trunks barely as thick as a man's arm. Even these were scarce, as rare as wheat seedlings in an abandoned field. From the moment the sun rose, it began beating down upon the village, scorching people's flesh.

In the days to come, the villagers would wake from their beds, stand at their doors and gaze with blank surprise at the world outside. They would gaze at the barren landscape and wonder what had happened.

'Good heavens, would you look at this place?'

'How did it come to this?'

'So it's finally come to this . . .'

4

The trees were gone. So was Zhao Dequan.

He passed away at about noon, on the day after the big tree-felling. The evening before he died, Grandpa asked Uncle: 'Do you think you could go to Lingling's parents' house and get her red silk jacket? I want to give it to Zhao Dequan.'

Uncle agreed to travel to Lingling's hometown, a distance of six or seven miles from Ding Village. He could have made the round trip that same evening, but he decided to stay overnight, and didn't return until the next day. When he got back to Ding Village at around noon, Zhao Dequan was still alive. As he watched Uncle hand his wife Lingling's red silk bridal jacket, Zhao Dequan smiled, closed his eyes, and quietly passed from this life.

He was still smiling when they put him in the coffin.

Zhao Dequan was buried with his red silken-jacket smile.

VOLUME 5

五

CHAPTER ONE

1

Uncle and Lingling moved in together.They lived as husband and wife, brazenly, in plain sight of everyone in the village.

They were like water and sand, seed and soil, yin and yang; like positive and negative magnetic poles. They were water flowing, being absorbed by sand; seed scattered by the wind, taking root in soil; yin and yang coming together as one; two magnets clinging to each other, unable to deny their attraction.

After the incident at the school, Lingling got a beating from her husband, a cursing from her in-laws, and was sent packing back to her mother's house. As soon as she was gone, Ding Xiaoming's family set about finding him a replacement wife. Everyone felt that the beating was justified, and that Lingling had deserved it: not only had she brought the fever into her husband's household, she had cheated on him with his own cousin. It was only fitting that Xiaoming, still in his mid-twenties and uninfected, should kick her out and start looking for a new wife. If he could find a suitable match, he could remarry after Lingling died, or ask her for a divorce and remarry even earlier. Lingling's parents were sensible people; when they came to Ding Village to pick up their daughter, they apologized to Xiaoming's parents: 'We're sorry we didn't do a better job of raising our daughter. It's probably best for everyone if Ding Xiaoming gets remarried. And if you need help paying for the dowry, we'll give back Lingling's wedding gifts.'

And so Xiaoming's parents began trying to find a new match for their son.

Lingling's parents, grumbling and cursing, brought their daughter home.

But spring had come early that year, and summer was right on its heels. The weather grew warm, then hot; padded winter coats were replaced by spring jackets, then by shirtsleeves. By the time it was warm enough for a single layer, Lingling returned to her husband's home in Ding Village to fetch her summer clothes. As she was walking out of the door with her bundle of belongings, her mother-in-law eyed the bulging bundle and asked: 'Are you sure you haven't taken anything that doesn't belong to you?'

'I'm sure,' Lingling answered.

'It's only a matter of time before Xiaoming finds a new wife,' her mother-in-law continued. 'If you're still alive when he does, you must come back and give him a divorce.'

Lingling said nothing. Once she was through the door, she turned back to gaze at the house, with its gleaming white porcelain-tiled walls. The seams between the tiles were as straight and black as if they'd been painted on with ink. After a few moments, she left the house and began walking out of the village.

She came to the concrete road outside the village. A straight line cutting through the fields, it was raised about half a foot above the surrounding soil, with drainage ditches on either side. The rows of cottonwood trees that had once lined the ditches were gone, chopped down by the villagers. The ditches were now filled with weeds and wild grass that rustled in the wind. At this time of year, the wheat plants – having raised their heads and steeled their spines – stood tall, and the fields were filled with people irrigating their plots.

Walking down the treeless main road under the blazing midday sun was like passing through a corridor of fire. The spots on Lingling's face started to itch in the heat, but she didn't want to scratch them, for fear of breaking the skin. She stroked her face with the tips of her fingers, softly, as if she were caressing the face of a newborn child. She walked along slowly, aimlessly, stroking her face, her eyes fixed on the pavement in front of her. Suddenly she heard her name being called: not loudly, not softly. The sound seemed to fall from up above.

'Lingling . . .' It was Uncle's voice.

She stopped and raised her head. Uncle was standing by the side of the road, only a few steps away. He looked just the same as she remembered. Slightly paler, perhaps; a bit closer to death. For a moment, they just stared at each other. Then Lingling, remembering where she was, looked behind her nervously.

'We're alone,' said Uncle. 'But even if we weren't, there's nothing to be scared of.'

'What are you doing here?' she asked.

Uncle sat down at the side of the road. 'I heard you were back, so I waited for you here.'

'What do you want?'

'Sit by me.'

Lingling seemed to hesitate.

'Tingting left me and went back to her hometown,' Uncle explained.

Lingling sat down beside him, shoulder to shoulder.

After an awkward silence, Uncle spoke. 'So you came back for your summer clothes?'

'Um-hum,' Lingling murmured, jiggling the bundle in her arms.

'How are you feeling?'

'About the same.'

'Me, too,' said Uncle. 'I made it through the winter and most of the spring, so I think I should be able to live through summer, maybe longer.'

Their conversation exhausted, the two were silent for a while. Then Uncle smiled and took Lingling's hand in his. It was not long after Zhao Dequan's death, not long after Uncle had visited Lingling at her parents' house to pick up her red silk jacket, but they acted like two people who hadn't met in years: hand in hand, gazing into one another's eyes, their silent thoughts unspoken. Uncle turned over Lingling's hand, examined the dried scabs on her wrists and hands, and then lightly, tenderly, scratched them. Lingling shrank back. Her eyes filled with tears and she pulled her hand away.

'Don't leave,' Uncle said. Linging looked up in surprise. 'Tingting wants a divorce, and so does Xiaoming. That means we can be together.'

Lingling was silent.

'Neither of us has much time left.' Uncle's eyes were moist. 'Everyone says that after this winter, the fever's going to explode. No matter what happens in this life, at least we can be together in death. They can bury us side by side, and we'll keep each other company.'

Lingling raised her head again, teardrops glistening in her eyes like big bright pearls.

'What is there to cry about?' Uncle asked, wiping away her tears. 'We're going to die anyway, so who gives a damn what other people say? We should move in together. I'd like to see them try to stop us. Let's move in together and show them all. Tingting, Xiaoming. The whole village . . . we'll show the lot of them.'

Uncle smiled through his tears. 'So Tingting and Xiaoming want to divorce us? Let's move in together and sue *them* for divorce.

'If you go back home, your parents and brother will feel sorry for you, but what about your sister-in-law? She knows you've got the fever, so you know she's going to give you the cold shoulder.

'You can move into my house. Or if you don't want to be around Tingting's stuff, we can live outside the village, in the building beside the threshing grounds. I'll bring some pots and pans and cookware, and it'll be just like home.'

And so Uncle and Lingling moved in together.

They lived together brazenly, like husband and wife. Like a pair of young lovers. Like a couple of fools.

*

206

Uncle and Lingling set about making the two-room building of mud brick and tile into a home. Uncle brought bowls, woks, sheets and blankets from his house so they could live in comfort. The fields around the village were divided into private plots, but the threshing grounds were communal, usually shared by about a dozen households. After the Communist government was established in 1949, the threshing grounds had been divided among 'mutual-aid teams'. Later, when the People's Communes were formed, they were shared by 'production brigades'. Now that the communes had been disbanded and the villagers had returned to farming private plots, the threshing grounds were divided informally among groups of households. When the thatched hut next to this threshing ground had collapsed, the villagers had pitched in to build a two-room building of mud brick and tile. During the busy harvest season, when the villagers took turns threshing wheat, the building was used as a place to rest or nap. During the rest of the year, it was used for storing farm equipment.

And now it was Uncle and Lingling's new home.

They set up a makeshift stove, and the outer room became a kitchen. They made a bed from planks of wood, and the inner room was transformed into a bedroom. They mounted shelves on the walls and heaped them with basins and bowls; they nailed baskets to the walls and filled them with chopsticks; they arranged the pots and pans and woks and crocks. When there was a place for everything and everything was in its place, the little mud-brick building felt just like home. A house that they could call a home, a place that made them *feel* at home.

At first, Uncle tried to be discreet about the move, waiting until it was dark to sneak back to his house and collect his things. But after a few days, when he realized that no amount of discretion could keep the villagers from finding out, he threw caution to the wind and ventured out in broad daylight. If the cat was already out of the bag, the water over the dam, the soy sauce spilled and the vase broken, what the hell did it matter, anyway? He was comfortable with his transgressions, resigned to his fate. And so he made no secret of the fact that he was carting food, fuel and furniture, the necessities of daily life, from his house to the threshing ground. If, on his way, he happened to run into one of the villagers, he was as guileless as glass.

'Hey, Ding Liang!' shouted one of the village men. 'Where are you going with that load of stuff?'

Ding Liang stopped in his tracks. 'It's not your stuff. Why should you care?'

That shut the man up. After a while, he mumbled: 'What the hell . . . I was just trying to be helpful.'

'If you want to be helpful, why not trade places? You take my fever, and I'll take your health in exchange. That will really lighten my load.'

'You're unbelievable.'

'Oh, yes? How so?'

'Just go, leave.'

But Ding Liang stood his ground. 'Why should I be the one to go? It's not like I'm standing in your living room.'

Seeing that Ding Liang wasn't going to budge, nor answer any questions about his relationship with Lingling, the other man left. But he didn't go directly home. Instead, he paid a visit to Lingling's husband and in-laws. Moments later, Lingling's mother-in-law emerged from the house, her face angry and her hair dishevelled. She stormed through the village, heading straight for the threshing ground. Clutching a stout wooden stick she had picked up somewhere along the way, she looked like a soldier armed for battle. A crowd of curiosity-seekers, women and children mostly, trailed along behind her.

As she reached the threshing ground, she let loose a torrent of abuse: 'Lingling, you slut! You're so loose you could drive a truck between your open legs! Come out here and face me, you whore!'

But it was Uncle, not Lingling, who emerged from the mud-brick house to face the angry mother-in-law. When he was standing a few metres away from her, he stopped, tucked his

208

hands into his pockets, and took up a defiant posture: one foot forward, one foot behind, so that his upper body slouched backwards. 'If you're going to curse anyone, Auntie,' he drawled, a smirk playing at the corners of his mouth, 'if you're going to beat anyone, it ought to be me. I'm the one who seduced Lingling, and talked her into moving in with me.'

The woman fixed Ding Liang with a stare. 'No, you tell her to come out here this instant!'

'She's my wife now, so if you've got a problem with her, you can take it up with me.'

'Your wife, you say?' Her eyes widened in disbelief. 'Until she and Xiaoming are divorced, she's still his wife, and my daughter-in-law! Look at you, you're a disgrace! Your cousin is a respectable man, and your father was a teacher . . . I honestly don't know how he ended up with sons like you. You boys are a disgrace to the family name.'

Uncle laughed. 'Call me a disgrace if you like, Auntie. You can call me names, beat me and curse me all you want, but it's not going to change the fact that Lingling belongs to me. She's mine.'

Lingling's mother-in-law was no longer angry – she was livid. Her face swept through the whole spectrum of anger: shocked white, thunderous grey, furious red, seething purple. It was as if Uncle had delivered her a personal humiliation, or spat right in her face. Her lips and hands trembled with rage. At this point, there was nothing for it but violence and curses. Nothing short of a good, round beating and tongue-lashing could set this straight. The scream that issued from Lingling's mother-in-law's lips was incomprehensible, but there was no mistaking her gesture: an arm raised high in the air, brandishing a big stick.

Uncle removed his hands from his pockets, took a few steps forward and squatted on the ground in front of her, penitent.

'Go ahead, Auntie. Hit me. Beat me to death, if that's what you want.'

Her arm remained raised, the stick frozen in mid-air. If she wanted to beat him, here he was, squatting on the ground in front of her. But was that really what she wanted, to beat her own nephew? Maybe her curses were just for show, a way to vent her anger and save face in front of the other villagers. If she hadn't cursed him out, she'd never be able to face people or hold her head high, at least not in this village. But no, she couldn't bring herself to beat her nephew, not after he'd squatted on the ground, offered himself up like that, and even called her 'auntie'.

The spring sun flooded the threshing ground with pale translucent light. All around, the wheat was moist and green. In someone's field, a lonely goat – goats were such a luxury these days, who had the energy or the means to raise them? – nibbled at the tender stalks of wheat.

Baaaaa . . . The goat's thin bleating floated through the air like a ribbon of sound.

Uncle crouched on the ground, arms crossed over his chest, waiting for the blow to fall. But the blow never came. Lingling's mother-in-law lowered her stick and turned to the villagers. 'You see that? I don't know how Ding Liang can still call himself a man, when he'll squat down in the dirt and take a beating for some filthy whore.'

Then, raising her voice: 'You saw it, didn't you? We all saw it. We ought to go to the school right now and bring them down here so they can see what kind of son Ding Shuiyang raised. The kind of man who would humiliate himself for a common slut.'

Still shouting and cursing, Lingling's mother-in-law turned and began walking towards the village. The crowd of onlookers followed her, throwing backward glances at my uncle, like a lynch mob going back to the village to fetch reinforcements. Uncle slowly rose to his feet and watched them leave.

When they were some distance away, he shouted: 'All right, Aunt! So you cursed me and made me lose face. But Lingling and I are going to live together, whether you like it or not. If you keep on like this, I won't be so nice next time!'

From then on, Lingling and Uncle didn't care what anyone said. Now and then, humming a happy tune, uncle returned to his house to cart odds and ends back to his love nest.

The older villagers, with an insight born of long experience, were openly sympathetic to the young couple. If they happened to meet Uncle on the road, they would gaze at him for a while, and then inquire how they might help. 'Liang,' said one elderly man. 'Is there anything you kids need? If so, I can lend you something from my house.'

Uncle, moved by this kindness, stopped and thanked him for his concern. 'That's kind of you, Uncle,' he said, tears welling up in his eyes. 'But we have everything we need. Besides, if you helped us, you'd be the laughingstock of the village.'

'Let them laugh. A lifetime is a lifetime, whether it's a long one or a short one. When you're this close to death, I say live and let live.'

Uncle, unable to hold back his tears, began to cry.

If one of the younger villagers happened to see Uncle on his way to the threshing ground, perspiring and struggling under a heavy load of food or furnishings, he would take the pole from Uncle's shoulders and transfer it to his own. 'You're not strong enough to be carting all these things around,' one young man chided him. 'If you need something carried, you just give me a shout.'

Uncle laughed. 'I can handle it. I'm not worthless yet.'

The man smiled and edged a bit closer. 'So, brother, be honest . . . has the fever stopped you and Lingling from, you know, doing it?'

'Not at all,' Uncle bragged. 'We do it twice a night.'

The man carrying the shoulder pole halted in surprise. 'Seriously?'

'Of course. Why else would Lingling be willing to ruin her reputation by moving in with me?'

The young man, taking Uncle at his word, shook his head in amazement.

The conversation ended when they reached the threshing ground, but the young man couldn't keep himself from staring at Lingling, eyeing her from behind when she wasn't looking. Sure enough, Lingling had a fantastic figure: narrow waist, shapely behind, a broad back and shiny jet-black hair that flowed over her shoulders like water. Noticing that his visitor was staring at Lingling's hair, Uncle sidled over and whispered in his ear: 'She lets me brush it.'

The young man took a deep breath and turned to stare at Uncle. 'You dog, you . . .'

Uncle laughed. Lingling heard the sound behind her, but continued bustling around hanging laundry and doing chores, her movements allowing the visitor to fully appreciate her beauty. In every way, Lingling was more than a match for Song Tingting, uncle's wife. Maybe her rounded face wasn't quite as easy on the eye as Tingting's slightly more oval face, but she was young, barely into her twenties, and nubile from head to toe. She had an irrepressible youthful energy that Tingting lacked. The youthful visitor stared at Lingling, lovestruck.

Uncle gave him a swift kick in the behind. The young man blushed, and so did Lingling. Then, remembering the shoulder pole he was carrying, he went into the house to unload Uncle's things. Lingling poured the visitor a glass of water, but after being caught staring so blatantly, he was too embarrassed to sit down for a drink. He made an excuse about having something to do, and with one last glance at Lingling, took his leave. Lingling escorted him as far as the door, and Uncle accompanied him to the edge of the threshing ground.

'You've got it good here, brother,' said the young man as they reached the edge of the threshing ground. 'If I had a woman like Lingling, I wouldn't care if I got the fever twice.'

'When you know you're going to die soon, you grab love while you can, right?' Uncle smiled.

'You ought to marry her,' said the young man earnestly. 'That way, you can move back into your house and live together properly.'

As Uncle watched his visitor walk off, his smile faded. He seemed lost in thought.

2

One day, as Grandpa was pottering around his rooms, Uncle came to visit. He had some news: he and Lingling wanted to get married. Uncle planned to divorce his wife, and Lingling planned to divorce her husband: two more bits of news. He had also come to ask a favour.

Uncle and Grandpa, it seemed, had a lot to talk about.

'Dad, I want to marry Lingling,' Uncle announced, grinning.

Grandpa stared at him in shock. 'You've got some nerve, coming here.'

It was the first time Uncle had visited Grandpa, or held a proper conversation with him, since he'd moved in with Lingling a fortnight earlier. Although he'd come to discuss a serious matter, Uncle wore the same lazy grin he always had. Even Grandpa's angry reaction wasn't enough to wipe the smile off his face.

'I want to marry Lingling,' Uncle repeated, leaning casually against the table.

'You're just like your brother.' Grandpa looked askance at his youngest son. 'You'd both be better off dead.'

Uncle straightened up, the smile fading from his face. 'Dad, I'm serious. We're going to get married.'

Grandpa stared in disbelief. After a few moments, he said through gritted teeth: 'Are you insane? How much time do you think you have left? Or Lingling, for that matter?'

'What's so insane about it? And who gives a damn how much time we have left?'

'You think you'll live through next winter?'

'Probably not. That's why I'm in a hurry to marry her. Every day counts.'

Grandpa's silence seemed to stretch for an eternity.

'How can you possibly marry her?' he asked, after a while.

213

'I'm going to go and see Tingting and ask her for a divorce.' As Uncle spoke, his face lit up with a smug grin, as if he'd just done something very clever or scored some sort of victory.

'This time it's me asking her for a divorce.' His grin widened. 'And not the other way around.'

Uncle's face grew serious. 'But Lingling's afraid to set foot in her in-laws' house, so you've got to talk Xiaoming and his parents into granting her a divorce.'

For a long time, a very long time, Grandpa said nothing. After a lifetime of silence, a lifetime and then some, Grandpa spoke again through gritted teeth. His words were cold and hard.

'I won't do it. I'm too ashamed.'

Uncle left Grandpa's rooms. On his way out, with a wink and a smile, he said: 'If you won't do it, I'll send Lingling to get down on her knees and beg you.'

3

Which is exactly what Lingling did.

She came to Grandpa's rooms and knelt on the ground in front of him.

'Please, Uncle,' she said. 'I'm begging you to help us. I don't think Ding Liang is going to live through the summer. Even if he does, I doubt he'll last the autumn or winter. He's got pus-filled sores all over his crotch. They're so infected, I have to spend hours every day wiping them down with a hot towel.

'I doubt I'll make it through the year, either. Xiaoming and his parents don't want me, and neither does my family. When I went home, my brother and his wife, even my own parents, avoided me like the plague. But until I'm dead, I have to go on living, right? Wouldn't you agree? Until the day I die, I have to find a reason to go on living.

'Tingting wants a divorce, and so does Xiaoming. Even Xiaoming's parents agree. Since that's what everybody wants, why not go ahead and do it? Then your son and I can get married. Even if it's only for a few months, at least we'll be legally married, and when we die, we can be buried together like decent, respectable people.

'Uncle, just once before I'm gone, I want to be able to call you "Dad". And when I'm dead, I want you to bury me next to your son. We love each other, and we should be buried as husband and wife, as family. With me to keep him company, you'll never have to worry. And if someday you pass away, after living to be a hundred years old, I promise to be a filial daughter-in-law in the afterlife, and take good care of you and your wife.

'Uncle, please . . . Talk to Xiaoming and his parents. As someone who loves your son, as your future daughter-in-law, I'm begging you . . . I'm willing to go down on my hands and knees, to kowtow as many times as I have to, if only you'll help us . . .'

With this, Lingling struck her head against the ground, in the ritual kowtow.

Once. Twice. A third time.

She wouldn't stop until Grandpa agreed to help.

CHAPTER TWO

1

A summer's evening, cool and pleasant. All across the plain, no one wanted to sleep. It seemed a pity to stay indoors and sleep away such a fine evening. In Ding Village, Willow Hamlet, Ferry Crossing and other villages on the plain, sick and well alike sat in doorways or outside, chatting about things past and present, gossiping about other people's lives, and generally rambling about this and that as they enjoyed the cool night air.

Uncle and Lingling, too, were enjoying the fine evening. They sat together outside their little mud-brick house on the threshing ground. The village lay in one direction; in the other, the school. The wheat-threshing ground was located about halfway between the two. Separated by less than a mile in either direction, it occupied the tranquil mid-point.

Distant lights in both directions gave off a faint yellow glow, a dusky gleam that seemed brighter, somehow, than the moon or stars. It was only during the wheat harvest that the threshing ground lived up to its name. The rest of the year, it was nothing more than a flat stretch of dirt, an empty yard that no one used.

That night, the moon appeared to be floating right over-head. To the villagers, it seemed to hang directly over their houses. But out on the threshing ground it hung above the plain, flooding the landscape with water-coloured light. Beneath that pale moon, the plain was a vast lake of invisible shores. Flat, tranquil and reflective. When a dog barked in the village, the noise rippled the silence of the plain like a fish leaping from the surface. From the surrounding fields came a faint rustling of wheat, like water trickling through sandy soil.

Uncle and Lingling sat outside enjoying the pleasant evening, the soft breeze and, even more, their own pleasant company.

'Come and sit over here, by me,' said Uncle.

Lingling moved her chair closer, so that she was sitting in front of him.

There, outside their little house in the centre of the threshing ground, they sat face to face, gazing at one another. They leaned forward in their chairs, so that their faces were almost touching. Their features were clearly visible; in the moonlight, their noses cast a faint shadow on their faces. Had either of them exhaled a long breath, the other would have felt it on his or her face.

'Did you like the noodles I made?' Lingling asked.

'They were great,' Uncle answered. 'A hundred times better than Tingting's.'

As he spoke, Uncle took off his shoes and rested his feet on Lingling's thighs. Sighing with pleasure, he tipped his head back and gazed up at the vast, starry sky. Playfully, flirtatiously, he began rubbing his feet over Lingling's body, pinching her skin between his toes. Then, with another sigh of pleasure he said: 'It would have been better if you and I had got married years ago.'

'Better how?'

'Better in every way.'

Uncle sat up straight and stared into Lingling's eyes, looking deeply into them, like a man searching for something at the bottom of a shadowy well. She sat very still, allowing him to gaze at her. With the moonlight illuminating her from one side, she looked like a woman posing for a portrait. Her features were composed, but her hands were busy massaging Uncle's legs, kneading his skin, giving him all the comfort she had to offer. Everything she had to offer. Although it was hard to tell in the moonlight, her face had a slight pink flush. She seemed bashful, as if she had been stripped naked by Uncle's gaze.

'It's lucky we both got the fever,' said Lingling.

'How so?'

'Otherwise, I'd still be married to Xiaoming and you'd be with Tingting. We'd never have had a chance to be together.'

Uncle pondered this. 'I suppose not.'

For a moment, both felt almost grateful for the fever that had brought them together. They pushed their chairs even closer, and Lingling continued massaging Uncle's feet and legs.

After she had finished, Lingling removed Uncle's feet from her lap and helped him put his shoes back on. Then she kicked off her shoes and swung her legs on to his lap, primly and properly, without any naughty games of footsie. He began to vigorously massage her calves, moving down to her ankles before slowly working his way back up again over her calves, knees and thighs.

Each time he increased the pressure, he would ask, 'Is that too hard?'

'A little,' she would answer.

'How's this?'

'Too soft.'

Gradually, Uncle got a feel for what Lingling meant by 'not too hard and not too soft', and a sense of where to apply more pressure and where to apply less. When he rolled up the legs of her trousers, her calves gleamed in the moonlight like two smooth, bright pillars of jade. Her legs were pale and supple, soft and moist, free of sores or any other marks of the fever. Ardently, clumsily, Uncle kneaded and stroked her legs, all the while inhaling the alluring perfume of her flesh.

'Does that feel good?' he asked.

Lingling smiled. 'Very good.'

Uncle's expression turned solemn. 'Lingling, I want to ask you something serious.'

Lingling raised her head. 'Go ahead,' she said, as their eyes met.

'But you have to tell the truth,' Uncle added.

'So ask me.'

Uncle thought for a moment. 'Do you think I'll live through the summer?'

Lingling gave a little start. 'What kind of a question is that?'

'I'm just asking.'

'But don't people in the village say that if you live through the winter, you can live through another year?'

Uncle resumed massaging her legs. 'The last few days, I've had dreams where I hear my mother calling me.'

Surprised, Lingling sat up a little straighter in her chair. She swung her legs off Uncle's lap, slipped on her shoes and peered at him intently, as if she were searching his face for clues. 'What did she say?'

'She said even though it's summer, she gets cold when she sleeps. She said since it's not my father's time yet, she wants me to come and sit by her bed and warm her feet.'

Lingling was silent, thinking about what Uncle had said.

Uncle was silent, thinking about what his mother had said to him in his dream.

The lonely silence seemed to stretch on and on. After a while, Lingling raised her eyes to look at Uncle.

'When did your mother die?'

'The year the blood-selling started.'

'Same as my father-in-law.'

'What did he die of?'

'Hepatitis.'

'Did he get it from selling blood?'

'I'm not sure.'

The two fell silent. It was a deathly silence, a silence of the dead. As if there were not a human being left on earth, not even themselves. As if everyone were dead and buried. As if all that remained were sand and soil, crops and trees, the chirping of insects on a summer's evening, and the moon that shone above. In the silvery light, the faint chirping of insects carried from the fields. The movement of worms and insects could be heard from underground, as if burrowing through the cracks in a coffin. It was a standing-at-a-graveside sound, a noise that sent a chill up your spine and seeped into your bones. Like a trickle of ice-cold wind, it got between the cracks and joints, worming its way into your bone marrow. Most people would have shivered at the sound, but Lingling and Uncle barely quivered: they had talked about death so much, they were no longer afraid of it.

They looked at one another.

'It's getting late.'

'Let's go to bed.'

They went into the house, into the bedroom, and closed the door.

Soon, the bedroom was warm with their scent. As cosy as starched, freshly washed sheets; as joyous as the bed of newlyweds.

It had been a pleasant early summer evening, crisp and cool. Lingling and Uncle had enjoyed the evening as much as anyone else in the village. As they were making love in the candlelit room, Lingling suddenly asked: 'Liang, am I the only person you're thinking of right now, the only one in your heart?'

'Of course you are.'

'I don't think I am.'

'I'd be a fool to think of anyone else.'

'I think I know a way to get your mind off your mother and your dreams of dying, so that you only think of me.'

'What is it?'

'Think of me as your mother, not as Lingling. If you call me "Mother", maybe you'll stop dreaming about her, and stop worrying about dying.'

Uncle stopped what he was doing and stared at her.

Lingling extricated her body from beneath his and sat up in bed.

'My dad died ten years ago,' she said, looking into his eyes, 'just like your mum. Both of us lost our parents. From now on, you be my daddy, and I'll be your mummy.' Lingling blushed a deep red. She wasn't bashful about what they'd been doing, but because she'd finally spoken her mind. It wasn't a blush of embarrassment, but of earnestness. Although Lingling was shy around other people and often spoke with lowered head, Uncle knew that her true character was different. When they were alone, her shyness disappeared, and was replaced by a wild, adventurous streak. At times, she was even wilder than Uncle.

Because she was still young, barely in her twenties.

Because she was going to die soon.

Because every day, every second, every bit of happiness mattered.

Lingling threw off the covers, exposing Uncle's naked body. She sat at the edge of the bed, smiling mischievously, like a child playing a game. 'From now on, Liang, you can call me "Mummy". I'll love you like a mummy would, and do anything you ask me to, even wash your feet. And I'll call you "Daddy", and you have to love me like a daddy and do anything I ask you, just like my daddy did when he was alive.'

Lingling leaned into Uncle and gazed up at him, like a pampered child begging for attention. There was a shade of a smile on her face, a hint of anticipation, as if she couldn't wait to call him 'Daddy', or for him to call her 'Mummy'. She began stroking his skin with her fingertips, licking his flesh with her tongue. Her touch was a moist wind blowing over his skin: tickling, tantalizing, tingling. Uncle squirmed, unable to endure the sensation. He was caught between wanting to laugh and wanting to pin her body beneath his.

'You temptress.'

'You demon.'

'Witch.'

'Warlock.'

'Mummy . . . I want to do it.'

Lingling froze, as if she hadn't expected Uncle to really use that word. Mummy. She seemed shocked that he'd said it, and maybe a little frightened. She raised her head to look at him, searching his face to see if he'd really meant it, or if his words were false. But Uncle wore the same easy smile he always had. The same lazy, foolish grin. Rascally, but with a touch of sincerity. Lingling wasn't certain she liked what she saw there; when Uncle reached out to touch her, she gently moved his hand away. Uncle couldn't stand it – he had to have her. His smile faded, and his expression grew serious. He gazed at her for a while, then opened his mouth and said it again.

'Mummy . . .'

At first, Lingling didn't respond. Her eyes filled with tears, but she wouldn't allow herself to cry. After a few moments, she reached silently for Uncle's hand, the hand she had just pushed away, and placed it softly on her breast. It was a reward of sorts.

For a long time after that, the room was silent, but for the sounds they made. Sighs and moans. The rhythmic creaking of the bed, and the wood groaning under their weight, as if the bed had broken a leg, or was about to collapse. Neither worried about the bed collapsing. They were each immersed in their own mad passion. Making love with abandon.

Covers got kicked off the bed; clothes got scattered to the floor. They didn't care, or even notice. By the time it was over, everything was on the floor.

When Lingling awoke, the sun was already high in the sky. It took her a moment to realize she hadn't died during the previous night's exertions, a frenzy that had driven her to the brink of exhaustion. It was like dying in a dream and waking up the next morning, shocked to find oneself still alive.

Lingling was awake before Uncle, who was still filling the room with his ragged snores. Thinking about the frenzied madness of the night before – how he had called her 'Mummy', and she had called him 'Daddy', and all the things they had done, the things they had shouted at each other – Lingling blushed a deep crimson. Lying next to Uncle's sleeping form, thinking back to the night before, Lingling blushed and smiled. She rose from the bed silently, tiptoed to the door and threw it open. The full force of sunlight hit her head-on, sent her reeling, so that she had to grab the door-frame for support. When she had regained her balance, she saw from the position of the sun in the sky that it must be nearly noon. In the surrounding fields, the wheat was growing tall and lush, filling the air with its rich golden scent.

As usual, Ding Village seemed silent and still. Lingling noticed a knot of people approaching from the opposite direction, a group of villagers carrying shovels, ropes and wooden poles. They seemed to be passing by the threshing ground on their way back to the village. Some were dressed in funeral caps or mourning clothes, their silent, wooden expressions betraying neither grief nor joy. Only a couple of the men laughed and chattered as they walked. Lingling could hear snippets of their conversation, carried on the wind: *Don't be fooled by the nice weather. Sure, the wheat is growing well now, but come autumn, there's going to be a drought . . . What makes you say that? . . . It's in the almanac. It says come the sixth lunar month, there's going to be a drought . . .*

As the group of villagers rounded the corner of the threshing ground, Lingling recognized some of them as Ding Xiaoming's neighbours. They had been her friends and neighbours, too, when she and Xiaoming had lived together. Standing at the door of the little mud-brick house, she hailed one of the older men.

'Hey, uncle!' she shouted. 'Who died?'

'Zhao Xiuqin,' the man answered.

Lingling was shocked. 'But I saw her just a few days ago, carrying a bag of rice from the school into the village!'

'Well, she got the fever more than a year ago, so she was lucky to make it this far. But that's why she died, you know, because she brought home that bag of rice. She set it outside the door, and the minute her back was turned, one of the family's pigs got into the bag and ate it all. You know Xiuqin's temper . . . she got so mad at that pig, she started chasing it around the yard and hitting it, beating it so bad she broke its spine. But it wore her out, it did. She started bleeding inside, coughing up a lot of blood, and the night before last, she died.'

Lingling turned a sickly shade of grey. She could almost feel herself bleeding internally, her own stomach filling with blood. Cautiously, tentatively, she ran her tongue over her lips and found no taste of blood. That was reassuring. But her heart was still racing, pounding in her chest, and she had to grab the wall for support.

'You haven't started making lunch yet?' the man asked her. 'I was just about to.'

The funeral procession continued on its way. Lingling was just about to turn and go back into the house when she spied her husband, Ding Xiaoming, at the back of the crowd. He carried a shovel, and seemed to be deliberately lagging behind the others. She wanted to rush indoors, but it was too late: he'd already seen her. She would have to say something.

'Did you come to help with the burial?' she called out.

Ding Xiaoming stared at her. 'Xiuqin's dead, and she had family and friends and people that cared about her. But you've got no one, you're living out here like an outcast. It should have been you!' He raised his voice. 'You should have been dead a long time ago!'

Xiaoming's angry words hit Lingling like a burst of gunfire. Before she could muster an answer, he had passed her and was rushing to catch up with the others.

Lingling stood in shock, watching him disappear in the direction of the village. After a few moments, she turned and slowly walked back into the house. She found Uncle awake, sitting on the edge of the bed getting dressed.

Lingling's eyes filled with tears. 'Let's really do it,' she said, a sob in her voice. 'Let's get married as soon as we can. And let's move back to the village, okay? Just once before we die, I want us to be a respectable couple. You have to promise me, Daddy.'

CHAPTER THREE

1

Not long after that, Uncle went to ask his wife for a divorce. Tingting was living in her hometown of Song Village, located five or six miles from Ding Village. Uncle and Lingling made the trip on foot, and brought with them a bag of snacks for Uncle's son, Little Jun. Uncle went into Song Village alone, while Lingling waited for him beneath a shady tree on the outskirts of the village.

When Uncle and his estranged wife were seated comfortably in the living room of her parents' house, he told her: 'I think we should get a divorce. To tell you the truth, I'd like to marry Lingling before I die. I just want to spend a few happy days with her before we're gone.'

Tingting paled. She seemed to be thinking something over. 'All right,' she answered after a moment. 'I'll give you a divorce if you ask your brother to get me two good coffins. But make sure they're good ones . . . I want the very best caskets, the kind with carvings all over the sides.'

'Who are they for?'

'That's none of your business.'

'I can guess who one of them is for,' said Uncle with a roguish grin. 'He's got the fever too, hasn't he?'

Tingting turned her head away and said nothing. There were tears in her eyes.

Uncle couldn't bring himself to say anything more, so he let the subject drop.

2

Grandpa went to talk to Xiaoming about the divorce.

When he arrived at the house and found no one home, he went out to the family's field. Along the way, he ran into his sister-in-law, Xiaoming's mother. Like a man asking a stranger for directions, he shouted brusquely: 'Hey, you there! Are you off to water the fields?'

It turns out she was on her way to water the wheat crop. Her family's field was located east of the village, near the ancient Yellow River path. While she was out there, it had occurred to her that if she mixed some chemical fertilizer into the irrigation water, it would save her the trouble of fertilizing the field by hand. She was just on her way home to fetch a bag of fertilizer when she'd run into Grandpa along the old river path. At first, she had no idea who he was shouting at. She glanced around to see who else was there, but seeing only the waist-high grass that grew along the roadside, realized that his question must have been meant for her.

'Yes,' she answered simply. 'It's that time again.'

Grandpa planted himself in the middle of the road, blocking her way. 'I tell you, I could just kill that son of mine.'

'I was afraid you were here as his matchmaker,' she said with an icy smile. 'To talk Xiaoming into giving that slut a divorce.'

Grandpa coloured slightly. 'The pair of them are a disgrace.'

Xiaoming's mother gave a snort of disbelief. For a few moments, she stared at Grandpa with disdain, her lip curled in a sneer. Then her expression softened. 'I'll tell you what,' she said, more kindly. 'Since you and I are in-laws, let me be honest with you. A divorce isn't out of the question. Xiaoming's got a fiancée now, a nice little girl – a virgin – never been married. But she's asked for five thousand yuan to buy bridal gifts. If we can come up with the five thousand, she'll agree to go ahead with the wedding.'

Xiaoming's mother glanced around, as if to confirm that no one was lurking in the tall grass, eavesdropping on their conversation. When she was certain they weren't being over-heard, she continued. 'Your son is in a hurry to get married and make an honest woman of Lingling before he dies, right? So why not ask the two of them to come up with the five thousand yuan? Then Xiaoming can afford to get married, and those two can make it official, and be buried together when they die.'

Grandpa stood dumbstruck. A gust of wind rushed by, leaving his face and clothes smelling strongly of mugwort. The wheat was high, the fields needed water, and the mugwort was in bloom. It was that time again.

'The thing is, my son and his girl are both healthy,' Xiaoming's mother continued. 'She even showed him a slip from the hospital proving she doesn't have the fever. But your son and that slut of his don't have much time left. There's no way they can out-wait Xiaoming. But if they can get their hands on five thousand yuan, he'll agree to the divorce in a heartbeat. Then your son can marry the slut, my boy can marry his girl, and everyone will be happy.'

Grandpa remained rooted to his spot. Xiaoming's mother brushed past him and continued on her way, hobbling off in the direction of the village. As he watched her leave, Grandpa shouted after her: 'All the books say it's a bad idea to put fertilizer in the irrigation water. Half of it evaporates, or ends up fertilizing the weeds, or flows into someone else's field!'

Xiaoming's mother walked a bit further before she turned and shouted back. 'Brother-in-law, you used to be a teacher! You ought to be ashamed of yourself, acting as a matchmaker for those two!'

Grandpa stood tethered to the ground, like a useless wooden signpost along an ancient, dried-up river. A gnarled and withered stump surrounded by lush new fields of green.

It was nearly dusk by the time Grandpa located his nephew. Ding Xiaoming had finished irrigating his fields and was lounging along the old river path, relaxing after a hard day's work. His mother had gone home to make dinner. The sunset stained the plain a deep violet, the colour that happens when red sun, blue sky and green fields collide. A hazy violet light hung over the landscape like steam rising from the soil. When Grandpa arrived, he found his nephew smoking a cigarette beneath a scholar tree on the embankment, exhaling plumes of smoke that turned golden in the rays of the setting sun.

'Where did you pick up that nasty habit, Xiaoming?' Grandpa chided. 'You never used to smoke.'

Xiaoming threw Grandpa a look and turned away his head.

Ignoring the insult, Grandpa squatted down on his heels. 'Don't you know that smoking is bad for you?'

Xiaoming took another long drag from his cigarette, as if to prove he knew smoking was bad for him but didn't care less. 'Too bad I'm not a bigwig county cadre like your son Ding Hui,' he said. 'I bet people give him all kinds of fancy liquor and cigarettes, more than he could ever drink or smoke. So I enjoy a pack of cheap smokes now and then. What do you care?'

Grandpa laughed and sat down next to Xiaoming. 'I know my boys are good-for-nothings,' he said with a rueful smile. 'They'd be better off if someone ran them down with a car. But since that doesn't seem likely, what can you do? It's not like I'm allowed to strangle them. Besides, I'm too old for that. I haven't got the strength.'

Xiaoming smiled. A mocking, thin-lipped smile that seemed tethered to the corners of his mouth by two golden threads. 'So you just let them go on living the good life, huh? Ding Hui's life is paradise, and he's not even sick. Ding Liang's got his paradise, too, at least until he croaks.'

Grandpa gazed at his nephew in silence. His cheeks were flushed, as if Xiaoming had slapped his face and left two angry red marks. Grandpa lowered his head for a moment, then raised it again, offering it up for another slap.

'Xiaoming, if you want to take out your anger on someone, take it out on me. Go ahead, hit me. Slap me on both cheeks.'

Xiaoming laughed bitterly. 'That's very noble of you, Uncle Ding. Professor Ding. But if I ever laid a finger on you, Ding

Hui would probably send his cronies to arrest me, and Ding Liang would pour his blood into my family's rice cooker and give us all AIDS.'

'I'd sooner kill myself than let Hui lay a hand on you,' Grandpa vowed. 'And if Liang ever dared raise his voice in your presence, I'd chop his head off.'

This time, Xiaoming didn't laugh or smile. His face was no longer mocking or bitter, but hard and angry, flushed as dark as congealed blood. 'You certainly know how to talk, Uncle,' he said quietly. 'I suppose it comes from all those years of reading books and being a teacher. I always thought you were a reasonable man. But when Liang stole my woman, why didn't you say something? Why didn't you try to stop him? You should have given him a good thrashing, or at least a good cursing, instead of letting them move in together like that.'

'Xiaoming. Be honest with your old uncle.' Grandpa's tone was gentle. 'Deep in your heart, do you really want Lingling back? Do you want to spend the rest of your life with her?'

Xiaoming snorted. 'I wouldn't touch that piece of trash again, no matter how desperate I was.'

'Then why not divorce her and let them be together?'

'Uncle, since you asked me to be honest, I might as well tell you the truth. I'm engaged to someone. She's younger than Lingling, prettier and taller, and with lighter skin. She's educated and classy, and she doesn't want a penny of my money. All she wants me to do is go to the hospital and take an AIDS test to prove I don't have the fever, to prove I never sold my blood. She's going to take one, too. That's our wedding present to each other. Blood tests. We were supposed to get married this month, but now Lingling and Ding Liang are shacked up together, and everyone in the village knows about it. I even hear they want to get married, make it official and all that, so they can be buried together when they die. Now I don't feel like getting married right away, because I don't want to give Lingling a divorce. If she and Ding Liang want to get married, they can wait – they can wait until they're dead!'

Listening to Xiaoming's angry, wounded talk, his smug and vengeful words, Grandpa realized that the situation was hopeless. When Xiaoming had finished speaking, Grandpa clambered down the embankment and began walking back towards the school.

The sunset reflected off the sandy soil, flooding the landscape with red. The cries of the season's first cicadas rose from the plain, a collective buzzing like a chorus of tiny cracked bells off somewhere in the distance. After Grandpa had taken a few slow steps, he turned around and saw Xiaoming rise from the embankment as if he, too, were heading home. Their eyes met, and Grandpa halted. From the way Xiaoming was staring at him, it seemed the young man had something left to say. Grandpa stood and waited for him to speak.

'Let Liang and Lingling wait,' Xiaoming shouted. 'Let them wait until they're dead! Because that's the day I'll get married. When they're both good and dead!'

Grandpa turned and continued on his way.

Further along, on a sandy shoal that had once been surrounded by water, a stand of mugwort grew as tall as pines. Grandpa was reminded of the pagoda pines and cypresses he'd seen in the city of Kaifeng. Mugwort grew wild all across the plain. In some of the other villages, they called it wormwood. Here was a small forest of it, a cluster of wormwood pagodas covered in a profusion of pale green and yellow leaves.

Grandpa followed the narrow path through the mugwort, displacing clouds of grasshoppers that clung to his shoes, trousers and shirt. He walked slowly, silently, through the last rays of the setting sun. The light had nearly faded, and he was about to turn from the path in the direction of the school, when he heard footsteps behind him. He turned to see Xiaoming a few dozen paces away, running to catch up. Xiaoming was sweating and gasping for breath, his face streaked with sand and dirt that he'd kicked up along the way. When he saw Grandpa turn around, he stopped in his tracks.

'Hey there, Uncle!' he shouted.

'Xiaoming? What are you doing here?'

'I came to say I'll give her a divorce. I'll let them be together, on one condition. You have to agree to it, and so does Ding Liang.'

'What is it?'

'First you have to promise.'

'First tell me what it is.'

'Well, I've thought it over, and I'm willing to give Lingling a divorce, right now, and let her marry Ding Liang. They want to make it official before they're dead, right? Well, I can agree to that if Liang promises to write a will saying I'll get the house and all his property when he's dead. Once your other son leaves the village, he won't be coming back, and his house will be empty. His house is nicer than Liang's, anyway. You can stay in Hui's house, so you'll have a place to live in your old age, and Liang can leave his house and property to me.'

On one side of the path was a clump of mugwort; on the other, a deep ditch. Grandpa stood between the two, staring at his nephew, his eyes narrowed to a squint.

'So what do you say, Uncle? If you agree, I'll go into town tomorrow and file the divorce papers, and they can go into town the day after and apply for a marriage licence.'

Caught between a ditch and the wormwood, Grandpa continued squinting at his nephew.

'Did you hear what I said, Uncle? You know the old saying: don't let your fertilizer flow into a stranger's field. Keep the wealth in the family, right? It's better for Ding Liang to will his property to me, his own cousin, than let it go to an outsider like Song Tingting. Or worse, let the government get their hands on it.'

Ditch. Wormwood. Nephew. Grandpa caught between them, squinting.

'When you think about it, Uncle, it makes perfect sense. What does Hui need with his stuff once he's dead? He can't take it with him. That's what you should tell him. Besides, it's not like I'm going to be using it while he's still alive. I won't move into the house until he and Lingling are both gone. But he's got to promise to put it in his will. Otherwise, I won't give

Lingling a divorce, and they'll never be able to get married. If he dies without making an honest woman of her, that's something he's going to take to his grave.'

In that moment, Grandpa's vision blurred, turning what was left of the sunset – a sheet of red and gold – into a haze of blood and fog. Grass and trees, wormwood and brush, mugwort and sedge swam before his eyes, swirled around his feet and spun off into the distance. Even his nephew seemed to have receded, and was now a tiny spinning blur . . .

'I've got to go.' The voice sounded far away. 'But you tell Liang about what I said, and tell him to think it over. After all, how many happy days do any of us have? You come into this world with nothing, and you leave the same way. You can't take it with you. All you can do is enjoy it while you can. Happiness . . . that's the only thing that's real.'

With these words of wisdom, Xiaoming took his leave. He sauntered down the road and disappeared into the setting sun, leaving the wormwood and the ditch far behind him.

3

On the far reaches of the plain, along the western horizon, trees and villages seemed immobilized against the sunset, as static as drawings on a sheet of paper. The banks of the ancient Yellow River, now just worn-down sand dunes, were covered with patchy vegetation. Where they faced the sun, the grass grew tall, but where they lay in shadow, the surface was bare, the sandy soil encrusted like a scab over an old wound. The tops of the embankments were uniformly bald, their sand-strewn pates reflecting sunlight like gold. The thick, sweet stench of sun-baked soil and wild grass spread like molasses over the plain. At dusk, the plain was like a vast lake of salt-sweet warmth, a body of water stretching endlessly and giving off a moist, sweet stink.

A lonely goat wandered towards the village from the direction of the school, its thin bleating causing ripples in the silence like a reed floating on the surface of a lake. A man led his cattle in single file back to the village after having taken them out to graze. Their mooing echoed through the fields, their bodies like a field of mud advancing slowly across the plain and into the dusk.

A man stood on the outskirts of the village and shouted to his neighbour working in the fields.

'Hey there! Are you busy tomorrow?'

'Not really. Why?'

'My dad died, and I was hoping you could help me bury him.'

There was a moment of silence. Then the man in the fields asked: 'When did he die?'

'Earlier today.'

'Have you got a coffin?'

'Yes, Yuejin and Genzhu gave us one of the willow trees.'

'What about the funeral clothes?'

'My mother has had them ready for a while.'

'All right, then. I'll come over early tomorrow morning.'

And the plain fell silent again, as still as a lake on a windless day.

4

I, Ding Liang, being of sound mind and body, agree to give Ding Xiaoming all my property after Xia Lingling and I have passed away. Ding Xiaoming is to inherit the house, courtyard, trees and all the items in the house, as well as the half-acre of irrigated farmland located north of the old river path between the Zhang and Wang family fields. The main property consists of one three-room house of brick and tile, two adjacent buildings (a kitchen and a storeroom), and a courtyard with three paulownia trees and two cottonwoods, which Xia Lingling and I promise not to cut down or sell during our lifetimes. Household items and furnishings include one standing wardrobe, one long table, two wooden trunks, one coat rack, one washstand, four red-lacquered chairs, five stools, two benches, one double bed, one single bed, two large water vats and four clay storage jars. Xia Lingling and I pledge not to sell, give away, destroy, damage or remove any of these items from the premises.

As my verbal agreement with Ding Xiaoming is not legally binding, I have written down the terms of our agreement in this letter, which should be considered my last will and testament. I entrust this document to my younger cousin Ding Xiaoming, until such time as it becomes effective after my and Lingling's deaths. My father, Ding Shuiyang, is not to contest this will or otherwise lay claim to any of my property.

Signed: Ding Liang
On the *th day of the *th month of the year 19**

5

When Uncle went to Ding Xiaoming's house to deliver the letter, his last will and testament, they met at the courtyard gate. Uncle stood outside, unwilling to set foot in an enemy courtyard; his cousin stood just inside the gate, unwilling to step outside, into unprotected territory.

'There! Take it!' said Uncle, flinging the letter in Xiaoming's face.

It fluttered to the ground and Xiaoming bent down to pick it up. After he had scanned the contents, he said: 'Cousin, you're the one who stole my wife.' He sounded wounded. 'You've got no call to treat me like this.'

CHAPTER FOUR

1

Uncle and Lingling got married. They had made it official: they were husband and wife. Now, finally, they could move into Uncle's house.

On the day of the move, they borrowed a cart, and in two trips, managed to move everything from the threshing ground back to the village. By the time they arrived at Uncle's house, Lingling was perspiring heavily. But there was still work to be done: there were quilts and kitchenware and furniture and boxes to be unloaded and arranged in the house. By the time they had put everything in order, Lingling was drenched in sweat. She stripped off some of her clothes and went outside to take the air. Her sweating subsided, but by evening she began to feel parched and feverish again, as if her whole body were burning up. Thinking she was coming down with a cold, Lingling took some medicine and a draught of ginger tea, but neither brought down her fever.

A fortnight later, she realized what was happening.

It wasn't a fever, but *the* fever. Her disease was full-blown. She was dying.

She hadn't a bit of strength left in her body. She didn't have the energy to eat, or even to lift a bowl. One day, Uncle made her some ginger tea to help bring down her fever, but when he raised the bowl to her lips, she refused to drink it. She stared in alarm at his gaunt face and the several new spots that had appeared on his forehead.

'When did you get those spots on your face?' she asked.

'Don't worry, I'm fine.'

'Take off your clothes.'

'I'm fine,' said Uncle, with his usual careless grin.

'If that's true,' Lingling raised her voice, 'then take off your clothes and show me!'

As Uncle removed his shirt and loosened his trousers, Lingling saw the angry rash of red bumps that stretched around his midriff. The blisters were fierce and shiny, as if they were bursting with blood. Uncle had stopped wearing his leather belt because it chafed the rash, and had instead replaced it with a long, cloth sash threaded through the belt loops of his trousers. Lingling hadn't noticed the sash before, because Uncle had always been careful to cover it with his shirt. Now, with the ends of the sash dangling from his waist, Uncle looked like one of those old-time peasant-farmers who tied their trousers with whatever bit of cloth they could find.

As she gazed at the rash on Uncle's waist, Lingling's eyes filled with tears. Then, despite her tears, she began to laugh.

'It's probably better this way,' she said, chuckling. 'That both of our fevers have flared up at the same time. Just a few days ago, I was worried that I'd die first, and you'd end up getting back together with Tingting.'

Uncle, too, began to laugh. 'I was afraid to tell you, but my fever flared up first. The day I stopped wearing my belt, I thought, "Oh God, please let Lingling's fever get worse, too. Don't let me drop dead and leave her here, alive and well."'

Uncle smiled, a wicked smile. Lingling reached out and gave him a little pinch.

'I haven't touched you in weeks,' said Uncle, setting the bowl of ginger tea on the bedside table. 'It's been weeks since we did anything in bed. Didn't you notice, and think my fever was getting worse?'

Lingling shook her head and smiled. After that, they had a lot to talk about.

'Well, isn't this great?' said Lingling. 'The minute we move into the house, we both get sick.'

'If we have to die soon, at least we'll die together.'

'I hope I'm the first to go, so you can give me a nice funeral. But you have to promise to buy me some decent clothes. I don't want to be buried in one of those horrible black funeral outfits. I want a dress – no, two dresses, one bright red. Ever since I was small, I've loved bright red. As for the other one – something plain, a lighter colour. That way, I'll have a change of clothes in the afterlife.'

'And I'll buy you a pair of red high heels, the sexy kind, like the ones city girls wear.'

For a long time, Lingling was silent. She scrutinized Uncle's face, as if she were unsure about something.

'Forget it. It's better if you die first. Otherwise, I'd worry too much,' said Lingling.

'But I'd give you a great funeral. I've got my dad and brother to take care of mine. But if I'm not around when you die, who's going to make sure you get a proper burial?'

'You say that now,' said Lingling, with tears in her eyes, 'but I'd still worry about you.'

'What, don't you trust me?'

'That's not what I meant.'

After a few more complaints about what Uncle might do if left to his own devices, Lingling said: 'I think it's best if we die together.'

'No, let's not. If I die first, you should be free to enjoy the time you have left. And if you die first, I should be able to do the same.'

'You're not thinking about me, you're thinking about yourself.' Lingling pouted. 'What you really mean is that *you* should be free to enjoy the time you have left.'

'That's not what I meant.'

'That's exactly what you meant.'

They continued to argue, like two children playing at being angry, until Uncle turned around and accidentally knocked the bowl of ginger tea from the bedside table. It fell to the floor with a crack and shattered into pieces.

The fighting stopped.

Lingling and Uncle stared at the broken bowl. Both knew that breaking a bowl of medicine was a bad omen. It meant that a person was going to die soon – so taking medicine was pointless. They stared at each other in silence. The room grew still, the atmosphere oppressive. They could feel themselves beginning to sweat, like buns in a bamboo steamer, or peas boiling in a pot. Both of them had grown thin, so very gaunt and thin. Lingling's once-voluptuous bosom seemed to have collapsed. The breasts that Uncle had adored now hung from her chest like two sacks of withered flesh. Her moist and rosy skin, which had maintained its glow despite the many rashes and spots, had turned ashen, marred with discolouration like patches of rust.

Her eyes were sunken, the hollows as large as hen's eggs. Her cheekbones jutted out like the poles of a funeral tent. Her person was so shrunken, so diminished, that she seemed hardly a person at all. Her dry, dull hair, which hadn't been combed in days, lay on her pillowcase like a tangle of rust, a clump of wormwood that had sprouted from the pillow. As for Uncle, he still managed to put away as much food as ever, but Lord only knows where it went. His square face had become hatchet-like, his cheekbones sharp as knife-blades. His eyes held none of their former light: the pupils had shrunken, leaving too much white.

After breaking the bowl, he stared for a long time at the ceramic shards that littered the floor.

'Lingling, when I said I wanted you to die first, I wasn't being selfish. I was only thinking of what's best for you. If you don't believe me, I'll kill myself right now.'

'Kill yourself how?'

'I'll hang myself.'

'Go ahead, then.' Lingling sat up in bed and ran her fingers through her tangled hair. Her expression was calm and composed. 'We're both going to die soon, anyway. Go get some rope. When I see you stand on a stool and put your head in the noose, I'll put my head in another noose and we'll both kick the stools away at the same time. If we can't live together, at least we can die together.'

Uncle stared at Lingling, unsure if she was serious.

'Go get some rope,' she repeated.

Uncle didn't move.

'Go on. I think there's some under the bed.'

Backed into a corner, Uncle stared at Lingling for a long time before he bent down and began rummaging under the bed. He found the rope, fashioned two nooses, stood on a bench and hung them from the rafter above. When he had finished this task, he turned to look at Lingling. It was as if he were sizing her up, testing to see who was more courageous. It was a tender look, a teasing challenge. Uncle was surprised to find that Lingling – so gentle in life, so wild in bed – would be so steadfast in the face of death. After Uncle had secured the nooses, Lingling stood up calmly, washed her face, ran a comb through her hair and went out to lock the courtyard gate. When she returned, she stepped up on to the wooden stool and looked at Uncle.

'If we die together,' she declared, 'it will prove that our love was not in vain. That we have no regrets.'

It was barely noon, and the sun hung in the eastern sky, its fiery rays streaming through the window and on to the bed. The quilt was neatly folded, the clothes in their cupboards, and the chairs and tables lined up against the walls. Everything they had moved from the threshing ground had been unpacked, and the room was in perfect order. Lingling had even laundered the curtain that hung from the door, washing it until it was sparkling clean. She had made this house her own, washing and scrubbing until every last trace of Song Tingting was gone. It was her house now. She had even removed Tingting's mattress and replaced it with one that she and Uncle had slept on. Time and again, she had wiped down the boxes and trunks that Tingting had used, to rid them of the other woman's smell. She had collected the bowls that Tingting had eaten from and taken them out to the coop to use for chicken feed. This was her and Uncle's home now, and Lingling would die happier knowing that her house was in perfect order. She had even taken the shovels and hoes from behind the doors and stored them beneath the eaves of the courtyard. Lingling glanced around the four corners of the room and saw that everything was neat and tidy. Four square walls of a tomb. There was nothing left to unpack, nothing to tidy up, nothing left to do but die. Satisfied that the room was perfect, Lingling picked up a damp towel from the washstand and wiped her face. Then she stepped calmly on to the stool that Uncle had prepared for her, grasped the noose dangling from the rafters and turned to look at him.

At this point, there was no retreat. No moving forward and no turning back. The only choice was to stick one's neck into the noose. Uncle took the circle of rope in both hands. Lingling did the same. She stared hard at Uncle, her gaze compelling him to put his head into the noose, so that she could follow suit. They were boxed into a corner now, at a dead end, and the only thing left to do was die. But at that moment, Uncle broke into a grin, a wicked, devil-may-care sort of grin, and said: 'Still, I'll take every day I can. If you want to die, you go ahead, but I want to go on living.'

With this, Uncle stepped off the stool, sat down on the bed and looked up at his wife, still clutching the noose in her hands.

'Lingling, come down from there. If you do, I promise to be your servant, and wait on you hand and foot.'

Uncle stood up, took Lingling in his arms and lifted her down from the stool, then laid her gently on the bed and began removing her clothes. He gazed at her nude body, at the skin that had once been so fair but was now as dry and dull as withered grass after a long winter. Her face was pitiful to look at, wretched and gaunt, streaked with resentful tears.

'Let's do it,' she begged. 'Let's just hang ourselves.'

'No, let's not. Each day we're alive is better than being dead. And just think about how much we have to live for. We've got food to eat, a place to live, and we've got each other. If we're hungry, we can fry up some cakes in the kitchen. If we're thirsty, we can drink sugar-water. And if we get lonely, we can go out into the street and talk to people. I want you so much,

Lingling. I want to stroke your face and kiss your lips . . . the only thing I worry about is not being able to make love to you.'

But that is exactly what Uncle did, summon all of his strength and make love to his wife.

Uncle always was a rascal.

Afterwards, Lingling thought of something. 'Liang, we didn't even apply in person. Do you think your brother will come through with our official marriage licence?'

'Don't worry about that,' Uncle answered smugly. 'I hear they're promoting him to head of the county AIDS task force. Getting a marriage licence should be a piece of cake.'

2

As it happened, my father did take care of everything. He handled two divorces and one marriage without Tingting, Lingling, Xiaoming or Uncle ever having to set foot in a government office. Uncle and his wife got a divorce, Lingling and her husband got a divorce, and Uncle and Lingling got two bright-red booklets embossed with an official seal from the civil-affairs department of the local district government.

When my father went to the house to give Uncle and Lingling their little red marriage certificates, most of the villagers were taking their midday nap. The sun was a bright poison hanging overhead, the air was filled with the buzzing of cicadas, and summer heat flowed through the streets like scalding water. The village was very, very still. Trampling the silence, my father left his house and walked through the village. He had some business to attend to in the county, but first he made a stop at my uncle's house.

Uncle's courtyard gate was unlatched, but instead of walking in or shouting to see if anyone was home, my father pounded on the wooden gate with his fist. When no one answered, he knocked more loudly.

'Who's there?' my uncle called from inside the house.

'Liang, it's me. Come outside for a minute.'

Dressed in a pair of white cotton underpants, Uncle went out and opened the gate. He seemed surprised to find his brother standing there. 'Oh, it's you,' he mumbled groggily.

'I got those coffins Tingting asked for,' my father said coldly. 'Two Grade-A coffins with carvings of houses, buildings and appliances. I'll wager no one in her family has ever had such a fancy, expensive casket.'

Still only half-awake, Uncle stared at his brother in silence.

'Is it true what I'm hearing? That you willed this house and courtyard to Ding Xiaoming?'

Uncle was suddenly wide awake. Without answering, he turned his head away, darting sideways glances at his brother and at the courtyard.

From his pocket, my father produced the marriage certificates, printed on shiny red paper. He flung them at my uncle through the open courtyard gate. They hit Uncle in the chest, clinging to his naked skin for just a moment before fluttering to the ground like falling leaves.

'You ought to be ashamed of yourself,' my father hissed. 'You could die any day now, and here you are, signing away the family property and raising all kinds of hell over a woman. You're going to die without descendants, and there'll be no one to make offerings at your grave. You've got nothing to live for, so why don't you just die now?'

My father spun on his heel and began to walk away. After he had taken a few steps, he glanced back at Uncle. 'Four divorce certificates plus two marriage licences. Do you know what those six pieces of paper cost me? I had to promise the official one of my most expensive coffins, for free!'

This time the words were not hissed, but shouted. My father stalked off without looking back. He was the same father I'd always known, a skinny man, lean as a sheet, but now that he could afford to buy his clothes in the city, he dressed a little better. He wore an unlined blue jacket with upturned collar and contrasting red stitching, and a pair of grey cotton trousers, neatly creased. My mother must have laid out the jacket and folded the trousers very carefully to get them to look like that, because she didn't own an iron.

My father's clothes set him apart from the other villagers. He looked like a city man now, a county cadre who worked in the city. Then there were his shoes, his shiny black leather shoes. A lot of the village men wore shiny black shoes, but they were mostly imitation leather. If they were real leather, they were probably pigskin. But my father's shoes were made from real cowhide, the genuine article. They were a gift from someone for whom he'd helped procure coffins. The black patent leather had been polished until it shone like a mirror. As my father strode through the streets, the trees and houses of Ding Village were reflected in his shoes. Although, of course by then, there weren't many trees left, so the trees reflected in his shoes were mostly tiny ones.

After he had watched my father turn the corner, Uncle seemed to regain his senses. He bent down and picked up the marriage booklets. Flipping through their pages, he found nothing new. They were nearly identical to the ones he and Song Tingting had received so many years ago. Only the date and one of the names had changed. The differences were so minor that Uncle began to feel like remarriage was a bit of an anti-climax, a futile exercise. For a few moments, he stood in the courtyard, feeling disappointed. When he turned around, he saw Lingling standing behind him, looking very pale. Uncle realized that she must have heard everything his brother had said, and seen him throw the marriage certificates. She looked like she'd been slapped across the face.

'If I'd known it was such a hassle, I wouldn't have bothered,' Uncle groused.

Lingling stared at him but said nothing.

'I mean, fucking hell, who cares if we shack up or get buried together without a marriage licence? What are they going to do, chop our heads off? Dig up our graves?'

'You think they'd bury us together if we weren't married?' Lingling asked. 'Your dad and brother would never allow it.'

Lingling took the booklets from Uncle's hand and scrutinized them closely. After she had looked through all of the words and pictures, she wiped the dirt off carefully, as if she were washing her own face.

3

Oddly enough, as soon as she and Uncle had their marriage certificates in hand, Lingling's temperature retreated. Her fever went down and her strength returned. It was as if she were cured, as if she were well again. Although she was still far too thin, she had regained her spirit, and some of her former glow.

After my father left, Lingling and Uncle went in for a nap. Uncle fell asleep quickly, and awoke to find Lingling sitting on the edge of the bed, waiting for him to wake up. While he had been napping, she had wiped down the furniture, laundered their clothes and given the floor another sweeping. She had even found time to go out into the village and buy a few packets of cigarettes and several pounds of festively wrapped fruit candy.

When Uncle saw Lingling sitting on the edge of the bed and smiling, he asked: 'What's with you?'

Lingling laughed. 'I'm better. My fever's gone.' She took his hand and placed it on her forehead so he could feel. 'Now I want to go out and tell everyone in the village we're married!'

Uncle put his hand to her forehead again, wondering if she was delirious.

Lingling grabbed the bag of candy and plopped it down on the bed.

'Liang, Daddy, I swear I'm much better. Let's go into the village and tell everyone we're married. Because of the fever, I know we can't have a big celebration, but the least we can do is pass out candy and cigarettes and tell everyone the good news!

'Even though it's a second marriage for both of us, I'm only twenty-four, so it's kind of like a first marriage for me,' she enthused. 'Come on, let's make the rounds and tell everyone! When we come back, I promise to call you Daddy a hundred times, as many times as you want.

'Hurry up, Daddy,' she tugged at his hand. 'Don't you want to come back home tonight and hear me call you Daddy again?'

Taking Uncle by the hand, she led him to the washstand, moistened a towel and began washing his face. She was careful to wipe the corners of his eyes and the sides of his nose, and to scrub the palms and backs of his hands. When this was finished, she picked out a pair of trousers and a shirt and helped him to get dressed. After she had buttoned Uncle's shirt, she grabbed the bag of candies, took him by the hand and led him out of the door, like a mother taking her child out to play.

Uncle and Lingling went from house to house, announcing their marriage and showing their certificates. They were husband and wife now, and had the booklets to prove it. From house to house they went, spreading the joyous news and passing out candy and cigarettes. At the first house they visited, a woman in her late sixties opened the door, their elderly neighbour. Lingling thrust a handful of festively wrapped candies at the woman, saying: 'Hello granny, we brought you some wedding candy. Ding Liang and I are married – we just got the certificates. With everyone so sick these days, we can't have a banquet, but we wanted to come over and tell you the good news.'

At the second house, a middle-aged woman in her forties opened the door. 'Hello, auntie,' Lingling greeted her. 'Liang and I just got married! Because of the fever, we're not having a banquet, but we wanted to come and tell you the news, and bring you some wedding candy.' After she had stuffed the woman's pockets full of candies, Lingling pulled out her marriage certificate and held it up for the woman's approval.

At the fifth house, a young woman known around the village as Little Green came to greet them. Little Green was a newlywed herself, but she had recently moved back in with her mother. She and her husband, a man from another village, seemed to have had some sort of falling-out, but the details were sketchy. Almost as soon as she opened the door, Lingling handed her one of the red booklets and said: 'Little Green, can you take a look at this and tell me if it looks the same as yours? I don't know why, but it looks fake to me, like the red's too red or something.'

'Isn't it just like the one you and Ding Xiaoming got?' Little Green asked.

Lingling blushed. 'I've compared them a hundred times, but they still look different. It's like the red on this one is brighter.'

Little Green stood in the doorway, turning over the booklet in her hands and examining it from every angle. She even held it up to the sunlight, as if it were a suspected counterfeit bill. Unable to find anything wrong with it, she said as much to Lingling. 'I can't see anything different. It's the same size as mine, the same colour, with the same words and the same seal.'

'Well, that's a relief.' Her worries laid to rest, Lingling turned and began to walk away. Then, realizing that she had forgotten to give Little Green any wedding candy, she raced back to the house and stuffed several handfuls of sweets into Little Green's cupped hands.

After they had rounded the corner and were about to knock at the first door on the next street, Lingling suddenly realized that, so far, she was the one doing all the work. While she had been knocking on doors, delivering the happy news, passing out cigarettes and sweets, accepting congratulations and trading small talk, Uncle had been standing behind her, grinning his lazy grin and chomping on wedding candy. She paused at the door, lowered her hand and turned to Uncle. 'It's your turn,' she told him. 'This family's mostly men, so it'll probably be a man who comes to the door. You should be the one to knock.'

Uncle tried to shrink away, but Lingling grabbed his hand and dragged him to the door.

'All right,' he said. 'But remember what you promised. You have to call me Daddy at least a hundred times tonight.'

Lingling's cheeks coloured, but she nodded her head.

Uncle grinned. 'Maybe just once, right now.'

'Daddy.'

'Say it louder.'

'Daddy!'

Smiling, Uncle stepped forward and knocked on the door.

'Who is it?' A man's voice rang out from the courtyard.

'It's me, Uncle. I wonder if I might borrow something of yours.'

When the door swung open, Uncle grinned, passed the man a cigarette and lit it for him. 'So, what did you want to borrow?' the man asked.

'I was just joking. Actually, Lingling and I are married. We just got the papers today, and she insisted we come over and give you some cigarettes and wedding candy.'

At this, the man broke into a broad smile. 'Congratulations, kids. That's great news. I'm really happy for you.'

After Uncle and Lingling had said goodbye, they moved on to the next house, which was Ding Xiaoming's. Having mustered up his courage, Uncle was about to knock on the door when Lingling grabbed him by the arm and dragged him away.

After Uncle and Lingling had made the rounds of the village and handed out all their candy and cigarettes, they went home to get some money so they could buy more candy and cigarettes for the residents of the school. They planned to visit the school to tell Grandpa and the others their good news. But along the way something happened: a minor incident that would have major consequences.

As Uncle was walking into his own courtyard, he stumbled over the wooden threshold and took a tumble. His thin summer clothes were torn, his elbows and knees scraped and bloodied. It was nothing serious, some minor scrapes and a bit of blood, but the pain from his injuries was nothing compared to the pain Uncle felt in the rest of his body. The fall triggered a cold, piercing pain that radiated from his spine and caused him to break out into a sweat. Uncle felt it as soon as he sat up from the ground and began wiping the blood from his hands.

'Lingling,' he moaned. 'It hurts all over.'

Lingling hurried him into bed and helped him get cleaned up, mopping the sweat and blood from his face, arms and legs. Uncle knelt on the bed, shrimp-like, his head bowed and his body curled up into a ball. Beads of sweat dripped from his forehead on to the bedclothes. His lips were pale and contorted, his whole body shivering with pain. He clutched Lingling's hand so tightly that his fingernails dug into her flesh. 'Mummy,' he said. 'I'm scared that I won't have the strength to get past this.'

'You'll be fine, Daddy. Just think of all the other people who got the fever when you did. They're all dead now, but you're still alive, right? You always make it through.'

Uncle's eyes filled with tears. 'Not this time. It's like the pain's tearing through my bones.'

Lingling gave him an herbal pain remedy and fed him half a bowl of soup. When the pain had subsided a bit, she sat beside him and they talked for a long time, about many things.

'Do you really think you won't get past this?' she asked.

'I don't think I can,' Uncle answered grimly.

'What am I going to do if you die?'

'Go on living. Take every day you can get. And keep an eye on my dad and brother to make sure they dig us a big grave, roomy enough for both of us. I want it to be big and deep and wide, like a house or a courtyard.'

'What about the coffin?'

'My brother promised to get nice coffins for us. The good kind, made of cedar or tung, at least three inches thick.'

'What if he doesn't?'

'He's still my brother. No matter what, he and I are family. Why wouldn't he?'

'Didn't you see the way he threw our marriage licences on the ground? And then he yelled that you were raising all kinds of hell and signing away the family property on my account.

He hates that you married me. If you die first and he doesn't give me a coffin, or dig a big enough grave for both of us, what am I supposed to do?

'And another thing, coffin prices have skyrocketed. You used to be able to get a decent coffin for four or five hundred yuan, but now they sell for seven or eight. If your brother were to give us both nice coffins, it would come to about one thousand five hundred yuan. Do you really think he's willing to part with that kind of money?

'Seriously Liang, if your brother decides not to give me a coffin, there's not a thing I can do about it. If anyone has to die first, it should be me. That way, you can make sure they dig the grave big enough for both of us, and give us two fancy coffins, as nice as houses. So you've got to go on living, Daddy, okay? If one of us has to go first, let it be me.'

They talked without stopping, hardly pausing for breath. They talked long into the night, until the pain was nearly forgotten. Tonight was supposed to be the night when Lingling called him Daddy, again and again, a hundred times over. She'd promised to wait on him, to serve him any way he liked, to let him sit back and enjoy. But now the fever had taken hold of him. Pain had grown roots. If it weren't for Lingling's voice, he wouldn't have been able to stand it. What had begun as a flesh wound, just broken skin, now went deeper, because of his body's inability to fight back. Having lost his ability to resist pain, the tiniest twinge became an agony in his joints and in his bones. A pain that seeped into the marrow like hot knives plunging into his joints, digging and gouging. Like metal rods prying his bones apart, or a rusty needle, threaded with twine, passing up through his spine. The pain was inhuman. Uncle clenched his jaw until his teeth ached and sweat poured down his face like rivulets.

The night was as endless as a path across the plain. Pale, milky moonlight seeped through the curtains; crickets chirped outside the window. It was stifling. The pain made Uncle feel as if his soul were on fire, a heap of burning coals. Like an iron forge, hot enough to smelt metal. It was impossible to find a comfortable position. First he knelt, shrimp-like, in the middle of the bed, with his backside sticking up into the air. Then he tumbled sideways on to the sheets and lay in a foetal position, like a dead shrimp curled up into a ball. Or he tried lying prostrate, hugging his knees to his chest, like a dead shrimp lying on its back. Like a shrimp that had been dead for some time. It was the only position that took away some of the pain. Some of the pain, but not all of it. Not enough to stop him from crying out.

'God, I can't stand it any more. Lingling, I'm dying. Mummy, give me something to stop the pain.'

He screamed and cried and clutched the sheets until they were wadded up into a ball. He was drenched in perspiration, sticking to the sheets. Lingling tried to wipe away his sweat, keeping up a steady stream of conversation, a collection of things she knew he loved to hear. Anything to try to ease his pain; anything that might get through to him. If he didn't like what he was hearing, he would beat the pillow with his fists and cry: 'The pain is killing me, and you say that to me?'

And Lingling would mop up his sweat with a damp towel and change the subject.

'Daddy, don't get mad, but I want to ask you something.'

Uncle turned his head to look at her. Sweat glistened on his forehead.

'Who would you guess Tingting's new boyfriend is, back in her hometown?'

'Come on, Mummy, aren't I in enough pain already?'

Lingling smiled. 'Well, no matter who he is, there's no way they're happier than us.'

Uncle's gaze softened.

'I'll bet Tingting doesn't call her man Daddy, like I do. And I'm sure he's never once called her Mummy.

'I'm your real wife now, Daddy. But even before that, I was your wife anytime you wanted. In and out of the school, out in the wheat fields or in our little house at the threshing ground. Anytime, day or night, whenever you wanted. All you had to do was ask, and I never once told you no. I always gave you what you wanted.

'If you wanted something sweet, I made you something sweet. If you wanted something salty, I made you something salty. I never let you near the stove, and never made you get your hands wet doing laundry. I've been good to you, haven't I?'

Before he could answer, Lingling said: 'Yes, I did all those things as your wife.'

It was as if she had not expected him to answer, as if she had posed the question to herself. 'But when you wanted me to be your mummy, I hugged you and rocked you, put my breast in your mouth and patted you on the back, like putting a little baby to sleep. And when you wanted me to be your daughter, I called you Daddy at least ten times a day, just like you were my real dad. I didn't tell you, but one day I counted how many times I called you Daddy, and it was at least fifty times. But you only called me Mummy once that day, and that was just because you wanted me to wash your feet. But that was enough for me. I was happy to wash your feet and empty out the water afterwards. And once you even woke me up in the middle of the night to give you a bath. So you tell me, Liang, was I really good to you, or was it all fake?'

Lingling stared at Uncle as if he'd wronged her somehow.

'You tell me, Daddy . . . was I really good to you, or was I faking it?'

Uncle knew she'd been good to him. He thought he'd been good to her as well, but from the way she talked, he could tell that he must have done something to upset her, or to hurt her in some way. He couldn't think what it might be. Or maybe it was several things. All he could do was try to look apologetic, like a man facing an angry wife, a complaining mother or a grumbling sister.

Lingling, wearing only shorts and a thin cotton gown, sat on the edge of the bed, holding Uncle's hand. She spread his fingers apart, pinching them one by one as if she were counting. She seemed almost unaware of what she was doing. As she gazed at him, colour flooded into her cheeks. Although she had grown very thin, a rosy glow was thick upon her skin. She looked like a bashful young girl, sitting close to a boy for the very first time, sharing her first intimate conversation. The lights were low, giving the room a soft, gentle glow. Earlier that evening, mosquitoes had buzzed around the room, but now they were perched, invisible, listening to the sound of Lingling's voice. Their absence made the room feel soft and quiet.

A gentle stillness, warm and soft, had settled over them.

Uncle was no longer huddled, foetal or curled up like a shrimp. He lay on his side, legs outstretched, head resting on his pillow, not complaining about the pain or about the room being too hot, but listening to Lingling talk. He was like a child listening to his mother tell a story, or a boy hearing tales about things he had done long ago and forgotten.

'I've been so good to you, Daddy. So why do you keep saying you're not going to make it? Why do you keep telling me you're not going to survive? Of course you're going to survive. Think about all the people who've died from the fever. It's always the ones with liver problems who die first, then the ones with bad lungs or stomach trouble. If all you have is a fever, it takes a long time to die, and with bone pain, it takes even longer. Your lungs and stomach are fine, and I've never heard you complain about your liver. So what makes you think you're going to die soon?

'I know you're in pain, but everyone says bone pain takes the longest to kill you. So when you yell that you're dying, does that mean you don't want to live? I mean, isn't that just asking for death, hurrying it along? You shouldn't call death to your bedside. Why would you do that? Is it because I haven't been good enough, is that why you want to leave me so soon? Or do you just think that since you have the fever, living is pointless?

'Just look at me, Daddy. The minute we got our marriage licences, the fever I'd had for two weeks disappeared. It went away, and now I'm as good as new. And do you know why? Because I love you. I love being married to you. It's like we're on our honeymoon. I mean, we just got our licences, so this is our first day of really being married. We haven't even slept together yet, at least not officially. So how can you talk to me about dying?

'Liang, don't you love me any more? Because if you do, Daddy, if you still care about me like you used to, please stop talking about dying. Stop saying you're not going to make it. Just keep thinking about me, and calling me your mummy, and letting me take care of you. I'll do anything you want – feed you and dress you, and even help you in bed.

'Now that we're married, we're officially a family. I've called you Daddy so many times, but I still haven't had the chance to call my own father-in-law Dad. Professor Ding is my dad now, too. Tomorrow, I want to go to the school and invite him to live with us. I can take care of you both. I'll cook and clean and wash your clothes, and when I've got my strength back, I'll knit sweaters and woollen pants for both of you. You've never seen how well I can knit. Back home, all the neighbours used to come and ask me to make them sweaters.'

Lingling noticed that Uncle's eyes were closed.

'Did you doze off, Daddy?'

'My eyelids feel heavy.'

'Is the pain any better?'

'Yes, it's like it's gone. Doesn't hurt at all.'

'Then close your eyes again and go to sleep, and everything will be better in the morning. Tomorrow we'll have a lie-in, maybe stay in bed all day. We'll sleep until the sun is shining on our backs, and then we'll have breakfast for lunch.'

As she was talking, Uncle's eyes fell shut again, as if they were weighted down with bricks. She thought he might be asleep, until he mumbled: 'It doesn't hurt, but I feel hot all over, like my chest is on fire.'

'What should I do?'

'Maybe you could wipe me down with a wet towel.'

Lingling dipped a towel in a basin of tepid water and used it to wipe Uncle's chest and back. 'Is that any better?' she asked when she was finished.

'My chest is still burning,' Uncle answered, without opening his eyes. 'Maybe you could get me some icicles.'

Although it was the middle of the night, Lingling went out to the village well and drew some icy cold water. When she came back, she soaked the towel in the cold water and used it to moisten Uncle's skin. 'Feeling any better?' she asked.

'A little,' answered Uncle, opening his eyes. But soon the towel grew warm, heated by the contact with his skin. Uncle rolled over peevishly and curled up into a ball again.

'I'm burning up. Please, get me some icicles.'

Lingling thought for a moment, then stripped off her light summer clothes, hung them from the bedpost and went outside with the damp towel. It was well after midnight, and the chill was rising from the ground, seeping in from the fields. A bitter wind swirled through the courtyard, turning it as cold as a deep, dark well. The moon was nowhere to be seen, leaving only the stars overhead and a distant haze that hung over the western plain. The chill silence of the village seeped into the courtyard, piling up against the walls. Standing stark naked in the centre of the courtyard next to the bucket of water, Lingling began to ladle water over her body. Again and again, she poured the cool water over her skin, until she was drenched and shivering with cold. Shaking uncontrollably, she towelled herself dry, stepped back into her slippers and raced into the house. She got into bed next to Uncle and pressed her cold flesh to his burning flesh, like a human icicle.

'Does this feel better, Daddy?'

'You're so nice and cool.'

Lingling held Uncle as he slept, allowing his heat to be absorbed into her cool flesh, siphoning away his fever. When the heat from his body had been transferred to hers, he began to complain that he was burning up again. Lingling ran into the courtyard, doused herself with cold water until she was coughing and shivering, towelled off and rushed back to the bedroom to press her body against Uncle, taking in all his heat and fire. Again and again, she hopped out of bed, raced into the courtyard, doused herself with water and got back into bed, shivering and coughing. By the sixth time, the fever seemed to have left Uncle's body and he fell into a peaceful slumber, snoring loudly.

4

Uncle was snoring like a bellows. His snores muddied the room like run-off from a farmer's field. It was late morning, and the sun had been up for hours. When Uncle awoke from his dreams, his fever was gone and his body felt limp and tender, as if he'd just emerged from a hot shower after a long day's work in the fields. He opened his eyes and saw that Lingling was not sleeping next to him. The last thing he remembered, she'd been lying close to him, her nude body as smooth and pleasantly cool as a pillar of jade. He'd fallen asleep embracing her coolness, but when he awoke, she wasn't in bed.

She wasn't in bed because she hadn't slept in the bed. She was lying, fully dressed, on a straw mat on the floor.

The night before, after Uncle had dozed off, Lingling had spread a brand-new straw mat on the floor and selected a nice outfit to wear: a pale blue skirt, a light pink cotton blouse and, although it was midsummer, a pair of silk stockings. She had got dressed and combed her hair neatly, as if she were getting ready to go out. The flesh-coloured stockings, moon-coloured skirt, and her blouse the shade of a winter sunset were well-chosen and well-matched, fresh and cool and pleasing to the eye. Pleasing to Uncle's eyes, which is why she had chosen them.

Fully dressed, Lingling had lay down on the straw mat and fallen asleep. She had died in her sleep. Even in death, she looked as if she were sleeping. Her features were contorted, but only slightly, as if she'd suffered only a little bit. For the most part, her face looked serene and peaceful.

When Uncle sat up in bed and saw Lingling lying on the floor, he called her name. When she didn't respond, he called her 'Mummy'. When she still didn't respond, he leaped out of bed, kneeled beside her and began shouting for her to wake up. His heart skipped a beat when he realized she couldn't hear him. Fearing that she was already dead, he tugged at her hand, cradled her head in his arms and howled. 'Mummy . . . Mummy . . .'

When Uncle took Lingling in his arms, she did not stir. Her head remained slumped against his chest. She was like a girl who couldn't wake up. Although there was still a bit of pink in her cheeks, her lips were dry and cracked, as scaly as the wings of a dragonfly. He realized that she must have been running a very high fever when she died, a fever brought on by dousing herself in freezing water so many times the night before.

As one fever raged, another even worse fever had rushed in and claimed her, taken her from this world against her will. Taken her from Ding Village and from Uncle. Knowing she was going to die, but not wanting to disturb Uncle from his sleep, she'd got out of bed, put on her nicest clothes, lain down on the floor and let the fever claim her.

The fever had burned her alive. Her parched lips looked as if they'd been charred. And yet they were frozen in a faint smile, one of satisfaction for what she'd done for Uncle, and for what she'd done in life. A smile with no regrets.

CHAPTER FIVE

1

By the time Grandpa arrived at the house, Uncle had already plunged the knife into his thigh, releasing a fountain of blood. The day before, after he'd fallen in the courtyard, the pain had nearly killed him. But the gash in his leg would finish the job. It was his turn to die. Lingling was lying on the ground, waiting for him to join her, and Uncle was eager to catch up.

Grandpa showed up like the wind at the door, like a character out of a dream. He had struggled out of his dream and somehow made his way to Uncle's house. When he arrived, his son was already dead. Uncle had won his race with death, and caught up with Lingling.

He died at about noon. The village was as warm and silent as it had been the day before, and the villagers were taking their midday nap. Inside the school, the sick residents searched for a bit of shade where they could lie down and rest. Grandpa was napping in his dream. In his half-muddled state, he imagined he heard Lingling's voice shouting: '*Daddy . . . Daddy . . . Daddy . . .*', her cries slicing through the air like bright shiny razors. Thinking she was calling to him, Grandpa sat up in bed and looked around the room, but Lingling was nowhere to be found. He lay down again and let the cicadas buzzing outside his window lull him to sleep. Again he heard the piercing cries, a confusion of sound ringing in his ears. Grandpa knew that he was dreaming, but he allowed the dream to wash over him, let himself be carried on the tide,

257

moving past the school, across the plain, into the village and towards Lingling's voice . . .

Grandpa saw Uncle step out of the house and into the courtyard. Lingling was on the ground behind him, clinging to his leg and crying. 'Daddy, you can't do this! You don't want to end up like me . . .' Grandpa couldn't understand why Lingling was calling her husband Daddy, instead of by his name.

Mystified, Grandpa stood in the courtyard and observed them shouting and struggling, as if he were watching a performance on stage. He saw Lingling clutching Uncle's leg, trying to prevent him from leaving, but she was too weak and frail to hold him back. Uncle began crossing the courtyard, dragging Lingling along behind him.

The courtyard was the same as it had been before Uncle and Lingling had moved in. There were the paulownia trees, with their thick canopies of green. Dazzling sunlight streamed through gaps in the leaves, leaving scattered pools of light on the cool, shady ground. There was the same washing-line strung between two trees, their trunks deeply scarred by the metal wire wrapped around them. There were rusted shovels and hoes propped against the outside wall, and a pig trough right outside the kitchen door. Tingting and her pigs were gone, but the disused trough remained. Hardly anything had changed. The only difference was an aluminum bucket, half-full of water, which someone had carelessly left in the middle of the courtyard, where anyone might stumble over it. When the bucket wasn't being used, it was always kept in the kitchen. Grandpa guessed that someone had used it to wash on a hot summer day and had neglected to return it to the kitchen.

As Uncle passed through the courtyard, he stopped and stared at the bucket for a few seconds before limping into the kitchen. Lingling was still clinging to his leg. When Uncle picked up a knife from the cutting board and raised it over his head, Grandpa assumed that he meant to stab Lingling. He was about to rush forward and stop him when he saw his son raise his left leg, place his foot on the cutting board and plunge the knife into his thigh.

As the knife entered his flesh, Uncle screamed: 'You fucking bastard, your wife's dead – why are you still alive?'

At Uncle's cry, Grandpa froze. He saw a flash of something white, sunlight glinting from the blade, and then a stream of blood as Uncle pulled the knife from his leg. Blood spurted from the wound like water from a public fountain, a mushroom-shaped projection that spattered the ground with droplets of blood, shining red pearls. A ray of sunlight pierced the kitchen window, transforming the fountain into a translucent pillar of blood, a shaft of clear red glass stuck sideways into Uncle's leg. The blood rose at an angle and arched through the air before splashing to the ground, or streaming down Uncle's leg. Droplets of blood littered the ground like grains on a threshing-room floor.

Lingling, who had been kneeling on the floor and weeping, suddenly fell silent. Her skin was ghastly pale, her face wet with tears.

'Oh Daddy,' she moaned. 'How could you be so stupid? You're the one who's always saying we should take every day we can get. Why are you in such a hurry to join me?'

Uncle smiled down at Lingling. It was a weak and sickly sort of smile, as if he didn't have the strength. It didn't stay on his face for long. A sudden burst of pain rocketed through his body, causing him to drop the knife and clutch his leg, wrapping both hands around the gash that went through his flesh and down to the bone. Doubled over, he crouched next to the cutting board, his forehead covered with pellet-sized beads of perspiration . . .

Wrenching himself from his dream, Grandpa leaped out of bed and raced towards Uncle's house, taking every shortcut he knew. When he burst through the gate, he saw the shiny white aluminum bucket standing in the middle of the courtyard, just as it had been in his dream. The bucket was half-filled with water, and a ladle bobbed on its surface like a tiny boat. Cicadas buzzed in the paulownia trees, their cries dropping from branches like pieces of overripe fruit. Among the pools of sunlight, Grandpa saw a trail of blood leading from the kitchen into the house, a long red string snaking across the courtyard. The air was filled with the stench of blood. Grandpa stared around him in a daze, then raced into the house and burst through the bedroom door. As soon as he saw Uncle lying on the ground beside Lingling, Grandpa knew that his boy was dead, that both of them were dead. Ding Liang and his new bride lay face-up, side by side on a straw mat. The hem of her skirt, soaked with his blood, bloomed with bright-red flowers.

2

Funerals were all about keeping up appearances. Sometimes they were a way of rehabilitating one's reputation, or settling old scores.

As it happened, the bodies were piling up. Ding Yuejin's younger brother, Ding Xiaoyue, passed away on the same day as Uncle; and Jia Genzhu lost his little brother, Jia Genbao, on the same day that Uncle lost Lingling. Four deaths in less than two days. Four bodies to bury, but not enough hands to go around. When Grandpa went into the village to ask for help digging the grave, he found that Ding Yuejin and Jia Genzhu were a step ahead of him. Everyone Grandpa approached gave variations on the same answer:

'Sorry, but I already promised Director Jia [or Director Ding] I'd help him.'

'If you can wait a few days until we've buried Xiaoyue and Genzhu, I'll be glad to help.'

'Maybe you can set the bodies aside until we've got time to bury them.'

'Genbao died before Lingling, and Xiaoyue beat Liang by a few hours. You know how burials are . . . first-come, first-served.'

When Grandpa went to Jia Genzhu's house to ask if he could spare a few men, Genzhu stared at him for a long time without speaking. 'Why don't you ask your son?' he said at last. 'I hear the higher-ups are giving nice coffins to the heads of all the village task forces, to reward them for their hard work. Yuejin and I are directors of the Ding Village task force. Why don't you go and ask your son where our coffins are?'

When Grandpa went to ask his nephew Ding Yuejin for help, the young man raised his chin and stared at the sky. 'You tell me, Uncle . . . all the other village cadres got free coffins from the higher-ups. How come Hui hasn't given us ours?'

Grandpa trudged back to Uncle's house in disappointment. He sat beside the bodies of his son and his wife, gazing at the sky, staring at the floor, and waiting for his son Hui to return from his business in the city.

It was after dusk by the time Hui arrived at the house. When he saw the bodies lying side by side on two wooden doors in the living room, he shook his head and sighed. For a long time, he and Grandpa sat in the moonlit courtyard, heads bowed, each immersed in his own thoughts. The night was silent and still, as if there were not a living soul left in the village. Some time after midnight, they heard footsteps. The men who had gone to dig graves for Yuejin and Genzhu had returned to the village and were passing by the front gate. Grandpa raised his head and looked at his son.

'We can't wait. We have to bury them. Another day, and the bodies will start to stink.

'You see how it is, Hui,' he continued. 'It's not that there aren't enough people to help. It's that the villagers hate us. You should have listened to me when you had the chance. If you'd have got down on your knees and apologized, we wouldn't be in this mess.'

Ding Hui slowly rose to his feet. He looked at his father, then at the bodies of his brother and Lingling, and gave a derisive little snort.

'Don't worry, Dad. I'll give them a funeral like no one has ever seen, and I'll do it without asking anyone in Ding Village for help. I won't even borrow one of their shovels. Just watch me.'

With this, Ding Hui stomped out of the courtyard and headed for home. He walked quickly and angrily, his feet pounding the streets with enough force to loosen cobblestones, or send bits of rock and brick hurling through the village and over the plain.

Grandpa was left alone to watch over the two corpses.

3

The night passed silently and uneventfully. But the next morning at daybreak, a group of strangers appeared in Ding Village: a dozen or so stout, strong men from neighbouring villages, all between the ages of thirty and forty, with years of experience digging foundations and constructing tombs. They arrived with an elderly man whom the villagers later learned was a seventy-year-old master engraver. It took them one day and one night to dig Lingling and Uncle's grave. In our family plot, south-west of the village, they dug an open trench next to my mother's grave, cut an entrance into one side, and proceeded to hollow out a large underground burial chamber. It was as spacious as a small house, vastly bigger than a typical grave. By then, the fever had swept across the plain and people were dying in droves, dropping like autumn leaves. With so many bodies to bury, graves had shrunk to about half their former size. But Uncle's was a king-sized grave, a tomb built for two, and it dwarfed even the his-and-hers graves that people had dug before the fever. Uncle's tomb was bigger: a lot bigger.

More important than the size of the tomb was the care that went into its construction. Working with a knife, shovel and miniature spade, the elderly engraver covered one wall of the tomb with an elaborately carved map of Dongjing, the capital city of the ancient Song dynasty (now the modern city of Kaifeng). His depiction of Dongjing's famed pavilions and pagodas, gardens and lakes, temples and ancestral halls was like a painting in the palace of an emperor. It lent the tomb a classical air, a whiff of elegance and antiquity.

On the opposite wall, he engraved a landscape of modern-day Kaifeng that included high-rises and landmark buildings, fountains and public squares, the city hall and municipal communist party committee offices, thriving commercial districts and crowded shopping streets lined with vendors' booths. Bold calligraphy above the classical landscape identified it as 'Song Dynasty Capital'. The modern depiction was entitled 'New Kaifeng'. Although the landscapes were a bit rough – not as fine as if they had been painted on a scroll, say – they were still an artistic marvel, a rarity in these parts. It was as if all the wonders under the sun had converged on Ding Village, to live in vivid detail on the walls of a tomb. The news spread quickly through the village, and people began flocking to see it.

They came in droves. They arrived in groups, like travellers on a package tour.

Everyone who climbed into the tomb emerged singing its praises. What exquisite craftsmanship, what elaborate carvings, what lifelike detail! The dragons and phoenixes on the Dragon Pavilion . . . so real that you could reach out and touch them. And the crowds of people . . . it was as if you could hear their voices. As the wondrous tales passed from person to person and spread through the village, the tomb drew even more curiosity-seekers. Young and old alike came to gawp at Uncle and Lingling's grave. It was as if an imperial palace had suddenly sprung from the soil, or a long-lost city been unearthed on the plain.

The day that Uncle and Lingling were to be buried, people flocked to their grave like sightseers at an imperial tomb. It was just after sunrise, and the eastern horizon was a crimson lake, a sea of fire. The fields were brilliant with light, and shining golden stalks of wheat that now stood nearly knee-high. Around the fields there were clumps of grass in shades ranging from jade green to dull yellow. Uncle and Lingling's twin grave was located at the far end of our family's plot. Two

263

mounds of soil stood on either side of the trench marking the entrance to their tomb. Even though the feet of many visitors had trampled the earth, the smell of freshly turned soil was still thick and fragrant in the air.

Villagers climbed down into the trench and emerged chattering and clicking their tongues in amazement. When others emerged from the trench after inspecting the tomb, they would ask: 'Can you believe it?' And the newcomer would say something like: 'It's almost worth dying for.' Or 'I wish someone would build me a tomb like that.' Or 'If I could be buried in there, I'd take the fever a hundred times over.'

Soon, the men who were helping to bury Jia Genbao and Ding Xiaoyue arrived to see the tomb. They were Ding Village's most experienced excavators, gravediggers and bricklayers. The other villagers made way for them, so that they could see for themselves. As they descended into the tomb, the men seemed sceptical, but they emerged smiling and thoroughly convinced. One of them, a middle-aged grave-digger, asked the young man who was sitting outside the tomb, guarding the tools: 'Did you do those carvings?'

'No, my uncle did.'

'Where'd he learn to carve like that?'

'It's a family tradition.'

'You think he'd be willing to do some carvings in the two graves we're digging?'

'This is an imperial-style tomb,' the young man answered. 'Back in the old days, you'd have to be an official of the fourth rank to get a tomb like this. Of course, nowadays things are different, but even my uncle still needs permission from the higher-ups to do these carvings. Without a signed and sealed order from a government official, he can't do it. You can't go around carving this stuff on any old tomb.'

'So how did Ding Liang manage it?'

'His brother Ding Hui is chairman of the county task force.'

That ended the conversation. The local craftsmen and gravediggers went back to the village. It was nearly time for the other villagers, who had promised to help bury Genbao and Xiaoyue, to begin preparing the bodies and placing them in the coffins that waited outside their families' front gates. The two coffins had been constructed some time before, after the big tree-felling. Both were made of four-inch-thick planks of paulownia wood, with three-inch-thick planks of cedar on either end. The ends of the caskets, engraved with large funeral ideographs touched up with gold or silver paint, glittered like metallic flowers. The coffins were nice enough, but the graves Jia Genzhu and Ding Yuejin had dug for their younger brothers were nothing compared to the tomb my father had built for his younger brother. Uncle's was an imperial-style tomb, befitting a high-ranking official. And my father had filled it with engravings of Kaifeng's glorious past and present, so that Uncle might be laid to rest in the company of that inspiring scenery.

Jia Genzhu and Ding Yuejin thought the only pity was that the village adulterers should occupy such an elaborate tomb. They couldn't help but take it personally, as a loss of face. Fortunately, their younger brothers had fine coffins, the sort usually reserved for the oldest and most venerable villagers. The sort of coffins usually afforded only by well-to-do families with a certain amount of power and influence. Caskets that reflected the wealth and status of their occupants, or their occupants' relatives.

The two families lived on the same lane, just a few doors away from each other. As the villagers milled around the coffins at the two front gates, they talked about how nice the caskets looked, and how Jia Genzhu and Ding Yuejin had done their brothers proud, and although their graves weren't nearly as fancy as the one Ding Hui had built for his brother, wasn't it nice that they'd managed to come up with two such lovely coffins . . .

In that instant, two trucks drove into the village and parked in front of Uncle's house. Each truck contained a coffin wrapped in several layers of cloth and heavy paper. When the coffins had been unloaded, they were placed on long wooden benches and carefully unwrapped.

By now, the trucks had attracted a crowd of curious villagers. They clustered around Uncle's front gate, eager to get a look at the coffins. What they saw were a pair of his-and-her caskets. Both were made of gingko, an extremely rare and expensive timber.

With the spread of the fever, death had become common-place on the plain. People died like falling leaves, like lamps being extinguished. Timber was in short supply, and the dead needed coffins as badly as the living needed houses. Paulownia trees were as scarce as silver, and cedar as precious as gold. But the coffins my father had delivered were not made from paulownia or cedar, but from the finest gingko. Uncle's coffin was slightly larger, and it even had a name: the Golden Casket. It was made from three-inch-thick planks cut from a 1,000-year-old gingko tree. The grain was flawless, the wood soft to the touch but very solid, perfect for carving or painting on. With the exception of the base of the coffin, the side that would rest against the soil, every surface was engraved with extravagant scenes and famous landscapes. There were classical landscapes with mountains, rivers and heavenly clouds. Big-city scenes with broad avenues and narrow streets, streams of cars and pedestrians, bridges and interchanges that looped like intestines. There were tree-filled parks peopled with tiny figures flying kites or boating on lakes.

In the past, his-and-her coffins had been engraved with classical scenes such as images of piety from *The Twenty-Four Filial Exemplars*; the legend of Meng Jiangnu, the loyal wife who cried down a section of the Great Wall while mourning her husband; and the legend of Liang and Zhu, the 'Butterfly Lovers', a Chinese Romeo and Juliet. But the engravings on Uncle and Lingling's caskets were mostly big-city scenes depicting famous landmarks: Beijing's Tiananmen Square, Shanghai's Oriental Pearl television tower, Guangzhou's high-rise hotels, and various bustling commercial districts, department stores, suspension bridges, fountains, parks and public squares. Needless to say, whoever had done the engravings must have been well travelled, in order to depict these cosmopolitan scenes so realistically. He had brought to life the wealth and splendour, the bustle and excitement of the modern Chinese metropolises of Beijing, Shanghai and Guangzhou. Every scene was in vivid colours, highlighted with red, gold and silver paint.

The villagers crowded around the coffins, gasping at their splendour.

'Good heavens,' exclaimed one woman. 'Can you believe this thing? I'll bet even emperors never got caskets this nice.'

Gingerly, she reached out to touch the engravings. 'Come here, you've got to feel this. It's smoother than a baby's bottom!'

The villagers clustered around, touching the engravings and running their fingers over miniature high-rises, overpasses crowded with cars, street lamps lining public squares and people sitting beside lakes. Another woman, noticing that the cover of the casket was ajar, peeked inside and saw that the interior was also engraved. Gingerly, she raised the lid, revealing more engravings and an enlarged photograph of Ding Liang pasted at the head of the casket. The engravings presented an idyllic portrait of big-city life: a flat with refrigerator, washing machine, television set, home-entertainment centre, microphone, speakers and karaoke machine. A sumptuous banquet waited on a table: mouth-watering platters of chicken and duck, meat and fish, bottles of expensive wine, cups and wineglasses and festive red chopsticks. There were high-rises and office buildings, cinemas and theatres, all clearly the property of the Ding clan. Signs over the entrances to the buildings read 'Ding Family Theatre', 'Ding Family Cinema' and 'Ding Family Towers'. Even the appliances and electronics were labelled with Ding Liang's name.

But perhaps most important of all was the building engraved at the foot of Uncle's coffin. A sign above the entrance to the building identified it as the 'People's Bank of China'. In this way, the accumulated wealth of an entire nation, the fruit of decades of Chinese economic development, would accompany Uncle into the afterlife. All the power and glory and prosperity of the world, stuffed into one casket.

The villagers turned to Lingling's coffin. Although her 'Silver Casket' was a shade smaller than Uncle's, it was made from the same material, the rare and expensive timber of the gingko tree, and the exterior was engraved with the same big-city scenes. Inside, at the head of the casket, was a photograph of Lingling smiling. Engravings on the inside of the casket showed silks and satins, clothing and jewellery, dressing tables, make-up boxes and other feminine items. There was also a handy assortment of kitchen items that no woman should be without: sideboards filled with bowls and plates, cups and glasses, modern cooking ranges with exhaust fans, aprons and bamboo steamers. There were potted plants and flowering bushes, grapevines and a pomegranate tree, a symbol of fertility. The engraving even included a miniature Lingling, hanging Uncle's freshly washed shirts and trousers to dry under the pomegranate tree.

As the villagers were marvelling over Lingling and Uncle's coffins, Grandpa emerged from Uncle's house, beaming and looking years younger than he had just a few days before.

'Professor Ding, these coffins are incredible,' said one villager. 'Liang and Lingling are very lucky.'

'I don't know about lucky,' Grandpa said, standing beside the coffins. 'But at least they will be buried with respect.'

'What kind of coffins are these?' asked another.

'The old-timers used to call them "gold and silver caskets", but these are more modern versions. You probably noticed all the city scenes.'

It was nearly time to place the bodies in the caskets. With the exception of Jia Genzhu and Ding Yuejin, everyone in the village seemed to be gathered outside Uncle's house. Ding Yuejin's own mother was there, as were Jia Genzhu's wife and son. Crowds of people, some from neighbouring villages, milled outside the house and overflowed into the streets. The atmosphere was lively, as if Ding Village were putting on a performance and everyone had come out to see it. There was a crowd of laughing, chattering, jostling people: men and women, elderly folk and children, locals and visitors. Some of the kids were perched in trees or on the tops of brick walls, as if they were waiting for the show to begin.

The sun had risen, and was nearly overhead. Bright streaks of sunshine animated the crowd, turning a mournful event into a celebration. Turning a funeral into a public performance. My father was still at our house, talking to the men who had delivered the caskets from the city. My mother was at Uncle's house, serving tea and passing out cigarettes to out-of-town guests who had come for the funeral. My little sister was running around in the crowd, squeezing through a forest of adult legs and generally getting underfoot.

At last, my father set out for Uncle's house, trailed by a crowd of locals and visitors from the city and surrounding villages. When the mob outside Uncle's gate saw him approaching, someone shouted: 'Are you going to put the bodies in the coffins?'

'Yes,' my father answered. 'It's time.'

The time had come to dress the bodies and place them in their coffins with the items they would be buried with: brand-name liquor and cigarettes for Uncle, and a change of clothes and costume jewellery – that looked just like the real thing – for Lingling. As the villagers surged into the house, eager to help carry the bodies and funeral items, my father noticed that among them were a few of the gravediggers, bricklayers and others who were supposed to be helping with Jia Genbao and Ding Xiaoyue's funerals.

Although my father was gratified by all the attention, he didn't want to be thought rude for stealing people away from Genbao and Xiaoyue's funerals.

'Hey, you there!' he shouted. 'Why don't you go and help Genbao and Xiaoyue's families? They'd be embarrassed if no one showed up.'

'We dug their graves first,' answered one man. 'So it's only fair that these two get buried first.'

Grandpa was also uncomfortable with the situation.'I don't know,' he said. 'That doesn't seem right, does it?'

Ding Yuejin's mother piped up. 'Oh, I don't mind if these kids get buried first. After all, we're one big family, right?'

'Exactly,' said Jia Genzhu's wife. 'We're all friends and neighbours here. What does it matter who gets buried first?'

And so it was that Genbao and Xiaoyue's funerals were pushed aside, temporarily forgotten as the whole village pitched in to help bury Uncle and Lingling.

Uncle and Lingling's funeral was very well attended. A crowd of nearly two hundred mourners watched as their coffins were placed in the burial chamber and the entrance sealed with brick. My father had paid for a fancy tombstone, an imposing granite monument with the following inscription:

Here lie Ding Liang and Xia Lingling,
star-crossed Butterfly Lovers

When the monument was raised, the crowd broke into applause as loud as spring thunder. The thunderclap that heralds the passage of winter and the coming of spring. The rumbling that can be heard when the insects awake, and the sleeping dragon raises its head.

VOLUME 6

CHAPTER ONE

1

Uncle and Lingling were buried.

Ding Xiaoyue and Jia Genbao were in the ground.

The funerals were over, and my family was leaving town.

The day he buried his brother, my dad moved his family to the city. They were leaving Ding Village for ever, and they had no intention of ever coming back. They blew out of town faster than fallen leaves carried on an autumn wind. As for the chances of my family ever returning to Ding Village, it was about as likely as a pile of leaves hopping back on to the tree they had fallen from. There was no going back to the tree.

The whole family, *my* whole family, hitched a lift on one of the trucks that had delivered Uncle and Lingling's coffins. They took only their most precious possessions: the television set and refrigerator, some boxes tied with string and a few suitcases filled with clothes. In the rush to leave, belongings were tossed willy-nilly into the back of the truck, to be sat on by the army of gravediggers, bricklayers, engravers and others who had come to help with the funeral and were now heading back to the city. The workers rode in the back, and my parents and sister sat in the cab of the truck.

They left just after midday, after the funeral was over and the golden sun was beating down on the plain, burning up the soil. Waves of shimmering heat swept across the plain like a fast-moving blaze. Before they left, my father stood beside his brother and Lingling's freshly dug grave, rich with the scent of fragrant soil. He called my grandfather over and asked: 'So, are we finished here?'

Grandpa glanced around, slightly confused by the question. 'Uh, yes, I suppose we're finished.'

'In that case, I'd better be going.' My father turned to his crew of helpers and shouted that it was time to go. After the men had set off in the direction of the village, he turned back to see Grandpa still standing by the grave, staring at the headstone. On the surface, Grandpa seemed calm, as if nothing unusual had happened. Then again, he seemed dazed, as if he knew that something had happened but he wasn't quite sure what it was, or what it meant. He appeared lost, caught halfway between confusion and understanding. He stared at the words on the tombstone as if they were some ancient calligraphy he couldn't read.

His thoughts were interrupted by my father walking over to stand beside him.

'So, did I do right by my brother?' my father asked. 'I think Liang would have been proud. I gave him a tomb fit for an emperor, and two fancy caskets. The question is: did he deserve it?'

Grandpa said nothing.

'You tell me, Dad . . . what did those two ever do for anyone?'

Grandpa remained silent.

'I've done enough for them to last a lifetime, but what did they ever do for me? I've done my duty to my brother, and now I expect him to do something in return.' My father spoke softly, emphasizing each word carefully. 'I want you to remember this, Dad . . . if anyone ever brings up the blood-selling, I want you to tell them it was Liang who was responsible, and that I had nothing to do with it. Ding Liang was the bloodhead, not me. I never touched a drop of blood in my life.'

Grandpa stared at his son for a very long time before he spoke.

'Hui, I want you to be honest with me. Is it true that the higher-ups are giving coffins to all the local village cadres? And if it's true, why haven't you given Jia Genzhu and Ding Yuejin theirs?'

'I spent the money on Liang and Lingling's funeral,' my father answered matter-of-factly. 'Do you think fancy caskets made from gingko trees just fall from the sky? I had to trade a hundred paulownia coffins to get those, not to mention what it cost to dig the grave.'

My father turned away. Without looking at Grandpa, he said: 'I've got to go, but I'll come back to see you.'

He said it casually, as if he were taking a trip, not moving out of the village permanently.

My father walked away, leaving Grandpa standing by Uncle's grave.

Before he disappeared, he turned back and shouted: 'Don't forget, Dad! If anyone brings up the subject of blood-selling, tell them Ding Liang was the rich bloodhead, not me. And if they don't believe you, they can dig him up and ask him!'

Leaving Grandpa with those instructions, my father ran to catch up with the others. His feet pounded the sunlit ground, kicking up the soil and leaving his shiny black leather shoes covered in dirt.

2

For some time now, the inhabitants of the plain had been dying, falling like autumn leaves, never to return to the tree. With so many dead, burials had become perfunctory. Burying a dead relative was like going to the outskirts of the village with a shovel, digging a hole and burying your dead pet dog or cat. There was no grief, no tears. Cemeteries were silent. Tears were like raindrops on a blazing summer's day, evaporating before they hit the ground.

So it was that Lingling, Uncle, Jia Genbao and Ding Xiaoyue's funerals were just four more bodies, four more coffins to put into the ground. When the funerals were over, my parents and sister left Ding Village and moved to the big city. They were city people now.

They left Uncle and Lingling lying in their sealed grave, with their tombstone that read: *Here lie Ding Liang and Xia Lingling, star-crossed Butterfly Lovers.* Everyone in the village agreed that it was a fitting inscription.

But three days later, not quite three days after their burial, the grave was broken into and robbed. Uncle and Lingling's caskets were gone, stolen by grave robbers, and the walls of their tomb defaced. Someone had stolen the carvings – those big-city scenes and dragons and mythical beasts – right off the walls.

The night the tomb was robbed, Grandpa had a dream:

The sky was filled with bright-red suns. There were five, six, seven, eight, nine of them, crowding the sky and scorching the plain below. Drought had left the soil parched and cracked. Across the plain and well beyond, crops had died, wells run dry and rivers vanished. In an effort to banish the suns from the sky, to rid the sky of all the suns but one, strong young men had been chosen from each village, one man for every ten villagers. Armed with pitchforks, spades and scythes, they chased the suns across the plain, trying to drive them to the ends of the earth, topple them from the sky, and toss them into the ocean. Because surely one sun in the sky was enough.

As the men drove the suns towards the horizon, their women and children and old people stood outside the village gates, banging on drums and gongs and washbasins to spur the men on and boost their morale. The suns raced across the sky, pursued by gangs of armed men on the plain below. Everywhere they went, the earth trembled and the air was filled with fire and smoke and the sound of their killing cries. Smoke rose from the grass and soil, trees and houses went up in flames, consumed by the heat of too many suns. There was fire and smoke and ashes, ashes everywhere . . . the mob had caught up with one of the suns and were just about to bring it down, to topple it from the sky, when Grandpa heard someone pounding on his door.

*

One of the village men had run into the schoolyard and was shouting and pounding on his door.

'Professor Ding, Professor Ding, come quick! Someone broke into your son's grave!'

Grandpa awoke from his dream to find sunlight streaming through his window, warming his bed in its fire. He leaped out of bed and raced towards the cemetery with the man from the village. When they arrived, a crowd was milling around the entrance to Uncle's tomb, inspecting the broken bricks and toppled headstone. All the soil used to fill the entrance to the grave had been dug up, leaving a gaping pit and mounds of dirt on either side. Grandpa took off his shoes, climbed down into the pit barefoot and peeked into the burial chamber. He saw that Uncle and Lingling's corpses had been pulled from their coffins and tossed on the ground. The coffins and the items inside them – brand-name liquor and cigarettes, expensive clothes and jewellery – were gone. The thieves had apparently brought tools, because some of the engravings were missing from the walls. A large chunk had been gouged from the left-hand wall of the tomb, leaving a small pile of debris beside Uncle's head, and bits of soil clinging to his hair and skin. The big-city scene on the right-hand wall looked like it had been hit by an earthquake: houses and buildings toppled, bridges and overpasses collapsed, and the ground around Lingling's body littered with clods of dirt and chunks of debris. The tomb had been ransacked. Grave robbers had taken everything.

A cold, dark stench of decay hung in the air.

As Grandpa stood at the entrance to the burial chamber, he remembered a bit of doggerel he'd heard as a child. It was an old folk saying here on the plain, a truism passed from generation to generation:

> *When graves are robbed of treasure,*
> *there's not enough treasure to go around.*
> *When graves are robbed of coffins,*
> *there are too many coffins to be found.*

VOLUME 7

七

CHAPTER ONE

1

It was a summer of drought. Drought swept across the plain like fire. The heat of too many suns in the sky.

By late August, the height of summer, the plain hadn't seen a drop of rain in nearly five months. The last rainfall had been in early April. At first, the farmers, unaware of the drought, had diverted water to their fields any way they could. They dug deep irrigation wells and used diesel engines from tractors to pump even more water from the earth. By June and July, the wheat was in ear, the cottonwoods were in bloom, and there was no moisture left in the ground. With no nearby rivers to draw from, the soil was parched.

The wheat had grown knee-high, but as the drought wore on, it turned brittle and dry. In the early days of the drought, the young plants woke refreshed and green, nourished by the moist night air. Now morning found them looking soggy, as if their leaves and spines had wilted overnight. When the sun burst from the eastern horizon and roared into the sky, the plants were dry, their leaves brittle under the burning sun, and their heads drooped, crumbling at the slightest touch. With each gust of wind, chalky dust rose from the scorched earth and swirled across the plain. A stench of something burning filled the air.

The plain was as pale as ashes, as far as the eye could see.

The leaves on the trees withered and curled. The scholar trees, whose shallow roots couldn't absorb enough moisture from the soil, began shedding yellow leaves, as if autumn had come early. The deep-rooted elms remained green, but they attracted legions of insects. The whole insect kingdom converged on their branches and leaves. Small green worms, spotted ladybirds and yellow beetles turned the elms into private fiefdoms, marching up and down the branches, munching on the stems and leaves.

Insects that hung from branches were liable to drop. If you passed below an elm, you could feel them plopping on your head.

The trees that once shaded the village were gone. Now, if you stood beneath a tree, you could feel sunlight on your face. The village, once green, was barren. It blended into the landscape.

Crops died in the fields. Grass withered on the plain. The soil was bleached, as far as the eye could see.

The last survivors stood out, pale yellow patches in a sea of bleach.

Some of the trees, still alive but unable to support so many leaves, had thinned their foliage so that only the trunk and roots remained. The drought-resistant cicadas, however, were thriving, multiplying, buzzing day and night. By day, their cries were everywhere, like chilli peppers spread out to dry in the sun. By night, their cries were sparser, hanging from the branches like grapevines on an arbour.

When the sun rose every morning, the branches of trees gleamed with cicadas, their wings and bodies glinting golden yellow in the sunlight. All day long, a burnt stench hung over the plain. Dark plumes of smoke rose from the ground. At sunset, the smoke vanished, and the plain turned to fire. By nightfall, everything was ashes.

You looked forward to the end of each day, but the next one always came too soon. The sun rushed in while you were still slumbering in your bed, exhausted from the night before. The early evening was too hot for sleep, so it was only after midnight that you found some rest. But as soon as your head hit the pillow, the sun was up again, crawling through the doors and windows, warming your blankets, stroking your body and tickling your face. If you tried to ignore it, if you tried to roll over and go back to sleep, you were sure to be awakened by a disturbance of a different kind: footsteps ringing through the streets, sounds outside your window, a knock on your door and a voice telling you that someone else in the village had died.

'Uncle, you've got to come and help. My mother's gone. She died early this morning.'

'Sorry, brother, but I need to call in that favour. When your family needed help, I came and worked for three days. Now we need your help, but it's only for one day.'

And so another day began, another day of scorched earth.

Fire rolled across the plain.

A hundred thousand suns, burning up the sky.

2

It was a summer of fever. Fever swept the plain, just like everyone said it would.

Winter and summer had always been seasons of death, when freezing-cold temperatures or sweltering heat claimed the most sick and elderly lives. Old-timers on the plain said that all the Qing dynasty emperors had died either in the depths of winter or the height of summer. But for those in Ding Village, those already sick with the fever, this would be the summer that they died. Having lived through the winter, they had expected to survive another year, but the drought proved too much for them. The heat was too extreme. The sun cremated the earth, raising purple smoke from the soil. The air scalded people's throats and raised blisters on their lungs.

Wheat died and grass withered. The last remaining leaves curled up and died.

On the east side of Ding Village, the Zhao family lost their daughter-in-law. She died at the age of twenty-nine, just a few days after coming down with a fever. Burned alive and parched to death, she left behind a three-year-old son.

On the west side of Ding Village, forty-year-old Mr Jia had always been careful about his health. He knew that he had the fever, and that his body had lost its ability to fight back, so he was always on guard against colds and flu, cuts and bruises. He was meticulous about what he ate, and avoided anything that might make him ill or upset his stomach. But it was a trip to the latrine that did him in. He had walked through the blazing sun and squatted in the cool shade of the latrine, but the combination of extreme temperatures caused him to catch cold. For a few days, he had a runny nose and a slight headache. Then his nose stopped running, but his fever flared up, and left him with a raging headache. Unable to stand the pain, he smashed his head against a wall and died.

They found him lying in a pool of blood, with his brains bashed in.

In the village centre, a pretty young girl who had married outside the village was visiting her family. Little Min had been feeling fine, but a few days into her visit, her whole body broke out in an itchy, angry rash. Without a tear or a word of complaint, she told her parents she'd stayed long enough, and that it was time to go back to her husband's house. Then she packed up her things and left. She was halfway home when she hung herself from the branch of a persimmon tree.

Ding Zuizui, known to everyone as 'the Mouth', died because of a story. One day, as he was standing at the crossroads talking to another villager, a man who also had the fever, the Mouth started telling this story:

'Once there was a minor official who got a big promotion, so he went home to his wife and told her to make him a feast to celebrate. After she'd warmed the wine, cooked the food and laid it on the table, she asked her husband: "Now that you're a big official, does that mean your thing is bigger, too?" "Sure," he said. "I'm bigger all over." But later that night, when they were in bed, she noticed that his thing was as tiny as ever. "If you're such a big official, how come it feels so small?" she asked. So the man explained that when an official gets a promotion, so does his wife. "My thing's a lot bigger now," he told her, "but so is yours, which is probably why you couldn't tell . . . Your thing's too huge!"'

When the Mouth had finished, he threw his head back and roared with laughter. It was an old joke, one of his favourites. But the other man didn't even smile. He went home, grabbed a kitchen cleaver, and came back to confront the Mouth.

'Everyone is fucking dying and you're still making jokes?' the man shouted. 'What the hell are you so happy about all the time? If you want to laugh, go laugh in your grave!'

The man attacked the Mouth with the cleaver, chopping until he was dead.

People were dying in droves. They were dying like dogs, or chickens, or ants crushed underfoot. There was no wailing or crying or pasting up of funeral scrolls. People were buried the same day they died. Coffins were prepared in advance, and graves were dug while a person was still alive. With the weather so hot, if you waited a day to dig the grave, the body would start to rot, so coffins and graves were kept on standby for speedy burials.

By the time the fever erupted, the sick villagers weren't living in the elementary school. They had left the school and gone back to their homes.

The reason they left had nothing to do with the fever, and everything to do with a decision by the higher-ups to cancel their food subsidy. Their monthly subsidies of grain and cooking oil had been revoked. They found out about it only after a few of the younger residents went into the county to pick up the goods and returned at noon, empty-handed.

'Ding Village isn't getting any more help from the government,' one of the young men announced. 'They said we're not getting anything from now on, not even a pound of flour.'

Jia Genzhu, Ding Yuejin and the other residents were outside relaxing in the shade, clustered around a television set they had rigged up in the schoolyard. When they heard the news, they stopped watching television and turned to stare.

'Why would they do that?' someone asked.

'Because they think we're the ones who broke into Ding Liang and Lingling's tomb and stole their coffins. That's why they're pulling the plug.'

All eyes turned to Jia Genzhu and Ding Yuejin. Everyone knew that the order must have come from my father, because he suspected the pair of robbing his brother's grave. The residents of the school were counting on their two chairmen to go and talk to my father and straighten things out, to tell him that they had nothing to do with the grave-robbing and coffin-filching. But the two men exchanged a guilty look and said nothing.

Several days later, everyone moved out of the school and returned to their homes.

On the day of the move, Grandpa was working in his vegetable patch near the school gate. It was a tiny plot, the size of a few straw mats, behind the back wall of his house, right next to my grave. Using two buckets on a shoulder pole, he drew water from the school well and brought it back to the plot where he grew leeks, chives and miniature cabbage. The water was quickly swallowed up by the thirsty soil. It was like pouring water into a ravine, or into the sand dunes of the dried-up Yellow River path. Before the drought, four trips to the well had been enough to water his tiny garden, but now it needed seven trips, carrying fourteen buckets of water.

He had just finished watering his plot when he noticed Jia Genzhu and about a dozen residents of the school standing by the gate, watching him. They carried bedrolls and suitcases, bowls and chopsticks, fans and straw mats and assorted belongings. All of them were staring at him as if he were the man personally responsible for taking away their food subsidy and driving them from the school. All eyes were on Grandpa, accusing him.

But as he stood in the vegetable patch with his empty buckets, staring back into that sea of faces, Grandpa seemed less intimidated than before. Maybe he'd let them down in the past, but they'd let him down, too. He'd once been in their debt, but now he owed them nothing. Maybe they'd once been friends, but now they were like strangers from another village, and he had nothing to say to them. Grandpa knew that some of the residents – not just one or two of them, but many – had broken into his son's grave. They'd destroyed a tomb and stolen two coffins, the likes of which hadn't been seen around here for 100 years, and wouldn't been seen for another 100. But that was fine with him, because it meant that they were even. The debt he owed Ding Village had been repaid in full.

Now he could face the villagers. He could view them as they viewed him. With cold, silent stares.

Jia Genzhu ended the standoff by spitting on the ground, like he was trying to dislodge something from his throat. Then he led his people away.

As they walked towards the village, they kept turning around to throw dirty looks at Grandpa. Their looks seemed to say that Grandpa owed them, that he was still in their debt, and that a plundering of his son's grave wasn't enough to set the accounts straight. They had something coming to them, and they wanted payback. Grandpa stood in his vegetable plot, thinking about those dirty looks and wondering what they meant. What more did they want from him? What else could he do? After they'd desecrated his son's grave, he hadn't complained or accused or said a single nasty word. Wasn't that enough for them? What more did they want?

Grandpa was about to head back to the well for more water when he saw Ding Yuejin, the last to leave, trudging through the gate with his luggage.

'Hi, Uncle. Watering your garden?'

Grandpa decided to skip the small talk. 'When your cousin Liang's grave was robbed, I didn't raise a fuss in the village. I never said a single word. What more do you people want from me? Are you trying to drive me to my death?'

Ding Yuejin, now standing face to face with Grandpa, set down his luggage and thought for a moment.

'Ding Liang was a good man,' he said slowly. 'But that brother of his is another story. First he steals our coffins, then he cancels our food subsidy. What makes him think we had anything to do with robbing his brother's grave? But even if we did, that doesn't change a thing. It doesn't mean Ding Hui is a good man.'

Ding Yuejin squinted at Grandpa through the bright sunshine. 'Do you know what he's doing now? He's arranging marriages for people who died of the fever. First they put him in charge of coffins and food subsidies, and now he's the matchmaker for every dead person in the county! I hear he gets 200 yuan for every match he makes. Just think about all the people who have the fever, and about all the boys and girls who'll die before they can get married. Can you imagine how much money he stands to make, before this is all over? It should have been Ding Hui who died, not his brother.'

Ding Yuejin picked up his luggage, brushed past Grandpa and began walking towards the village. As Grandpa watched him leave, it dawned on him why the residents of the school had been so hostile, and why they had given him such dirty looks. Dropping his buckets and shoulder pole, Grandpa raced after his nephew, shouting: 'Yuejin! Yuejin! Was it true, what you said?'

Ding Yuejin turned around. 'If you don't believe me, go and ask him yourself!'

He continued on his way, leaving Grandpa standing in the middle of the road beneath the blazing sunshine, like a small clay figure of a man that someone had left to dry in the sun. Like an old wooden hitching post bleached by the sunshine, a piece of rotting wood that no one wanted any more.

3

Although Grandpa kept meaning to go into the city and visit my parents and sister, he never did. He couldn't seem to bring himself to make the trip. Then again, maybe he just didn't want to face my dad.

Instead, he spent his days in the elementary school. The school was deserted now, and the classrooms were bare.

288

The desks, chairs and blackboards were gone. The tables and wooden planks that had served as beds were also missing, carted off by the former residents. Every tree in the schoolyard, from the biggest to the smallest, had been chopped down. The villagers had even taken the windowpanes.

Not a day went by without someone showing up with a letter authorizing them to remove certain items from the school. The letters always bore the official village seal and the signatures of Jia Genzhu and Ding Yuejin. When everything had been taken, Grandpa found himself the caretaker of an empty schoolhouse, a deserted schoolyard and his own two small rooms. With nothing to watch over and nothing left to do, Grandpa got bored. He talked about visiting my dad in the city, but somehow, he never did. The days were as empty as his heart, which seemed to have left his body, in the same way that his youngest son had left this life. It felt like everything he'd ever loved had died. Although my dad was still alive and well and living comfortably in the big city, it made no difference to Grandpa. In his mind, his eldest son was already dead.

He felt the same way about Ding Village.

For him, the village had ceased to exist.

With no desire to see any of the villagers, Grandpa spent his days in the elementary school. The school was as empty and silent as it had been a year ago. All the people were gone. There were no teachers or students or sick residents. The two-acre campus held but one living soul. Now that Grandpa was alone, he could go to bed as early as he liked and sleep as late as he wanted. He could eat when he was hungry, drink when he was thirsty, empty his bowl or leave leftovers, to stretch one meal into two. And if he didn't bother to wash the pot he'd cooked in, who cared? No one would ever know. What did it matter if his face was unwashed? No one would ever see it.

The idleness began to weigh on him. Grandpa felt as if he were living on the fringes of the world, rather than inside it. Every so often, cries and wailing from the village informed him that someone else had died, but he never bothered to find out who it might be. What concern was it of his, if another person vanished from this world?

When he saw a funeral procession leaving the village or passing by the school, he would stand and watch for a few moments before returning to whatever he'd been doing.

Not that there was anything to do but weed and water his garden, or stand and watch it grow. When he had rid his tiny plot of weeds and pests, the only thing left was to wait for more to appear.

Although drought had reduced the plain to ashes, turning the soil a feathery grey, here was a small oasis of green. Grandpa guarded his vegetable patch as carefully as he would his own life. Uncle and Lingling were dead. Tingting and Little Jun had left. My dad had moved to the city, taking his wife and daughter with him. Grandpa had no family left in Ding Village. But when he thought about his broken family, he didn't feel particularly sad. He felt cleaner somehow, lighter, as if a burden he'd borne for decades had been lifted from his shoulders.

The days went by, each one much the same. As summer reached its peak and the trees shed their remaining leaves, Jia Genzhu showed up at the school gate. He stood silently, watching Grandpa catch insects in his garden, and then said, in a small voice: 'Hello, Uncle.'

Grandpa wheeled around, startled. What he saw was even more startling. It had been more than a fortnight since Grandpa had gone into the village, and a little more than three weeks since the sick villagers had moved out of the school. That was the last time he had seen Jia Genzhu, on the day he and the others had left. But the man squatting by Grandpa's garden was not the Jia Genzhu he had known. This person was so emaciated he hardly seemed human. His face was sickly, and there were dark circles under his eyes. His eyes were so shrunken you could place an egg, or maybe a fist, in each socket. Crouched in the shade of the schoolyard wall, not far from my grave, he looked like a phantom, a spirit risen

290

from the ground. His skin was desiccated, like he'd been left out in the sun and wind too long.

Genzhu, who had never called my grandpa 'uncle' in his life, seemed embarrassed by the endearment. His face cracked into an awkward smile.

'What's wrong with you?' Grandpa asked.

'I'm dying.' Genzhu's smile grew as thick as tree bark. It seemed too heavy for his face, like it might peel away at any moment. 'I doubt I'll live more than a few days. Since I've got no future anyway, I thought I might as well come and have a talk with you.'

Grandpa left his vegetable patch and sat down at the foot of my grave. When he was settled on the ground, six feet above where I lay, he turned to Genzhu with a serious let's-have-that-talk expression. It was just before sunset, and the heat was rolling off the plain. The evening humidity was seeping in. Sitting in the shade of the schoolyard wall, with a slight breeze cooling their skin, Grandpa and Genzhu felt almost comfortable.

A concert of cicadas buzzing in the distance made Grandpa think of Ma Xianglin playing on his fiddle. It had been almost a year since the musician had died, a year since his performance the previous autumn.

'I'm going to die soon.' Genzhu pushed his face close to Grandpa's. 'You can see it in my face, can't you?'

Up close, Genzhu's face looked even more ghastly.

'It's nothing to worry about,' Grandpa assured him. 'As soon as you get through this hot spell, you'll be fine.'

'You don't have to lie to me, Uncle. But there's something I need to tell you before I die. If I didn't, I'd never rest in peace.'

'So tell me.'

'I will.'

'Tell me.'

'I'm going to.'

Grandpa smiled. 'Just spit it out, son.'

'Uncle, I can't stop thinking about killing Ding Hui. All day long, I think about ways to kill him. At night, I dream about watching him die.'

Genzhu peered intently at Grandpa, trying to gauge his reaction. It was like he was a thief, trying to steal something in plain sight, and wondering whether or not anyone would stop him. He kept his eyes fixed on Grandpa's face.

Grandpa stared back in shock. Genzhu's words had hit him like a rock to the side of the head, leaving him dazed and speechless. He felt like the young man had asked to touch his cheek, then slapped him across the face. Grandpa's face was as pale as a late-December moon, his mind as empty as the schoolyard, as barren as the plain. He looked at Genzhu searchingly, wondering whether his words were true or false, or if he'd just blurted out the first thing that came into his head. Although Genzhu talked of killing, his expression seemed kinder, his eyes gentler than they'd been on the day he left the school. It was as if he was simply asking Grandpa to borrow one of his things, or asking him to help search for something he'd lost.

The sun was burning towards the west now. A sharp blade of sunlight flashed around the corner of the schoolyard wall, leaving a neat rectangle of light on the ground.

'Did you rob Liang's tomb?' Grandpa asked.

'You really think I'd do that?'

'Well, someone broke into the tomb and stole those coffins. Someone will have to answer for that.'

Genzhu thought for a moment. 'I agree. Someone has to answer for that. But do you know what's been happening in the village? Over the last two weeks, they've been digging up the bodies of girls who died of the fever, and marrying them off to dead boys in other villages. They're selling our girls, digging up their bones and giving them to outsiders. My cousin Hongli was supposed to be married to Zhao Xiuqin's niece Jade after he died, but yesterday we heard she'd been promised to some family from Willow Hamlet, the Ma family. When they came to dig up her body yesterday, they told us it was Ding Hui who arranged the match, and that he's making money on both ends. He charged both families a fee of one hundred yuan, and Jade's family got 3,000 for the dowry.'

Genzhu's voice hardened. 'I'm not the only one who wants to kill Ding Hui. There are a lot of people around here who'd be glad to see him dead. That's why you need to tell him to stay away from Ding Village, or I might not be able to stop myself from bashing his head in. You're a good man, Uncle. That's why I'm telling you this. If you weren't, I'd have let Ding Hui come back here and get beaten to death.

'You know, I was only sixteen when I started selling my blood. One day, I ran into Ding Hui on my way home from school, and he tried to buy a pint of my blood. When I asked if it hurt, he said it was no worse than an ant bite. When I asked if it was dangerous, he said: "Don't you want to get married someday, kid? If you're not even willing to sell a pint of blood, how do you expect to afford a wife?"

'That was how I got started selling blood. So you see, uncle, I'm not being unfair. I've got my reasons for wanting him dead, and so do a lot of other people. So you tell your son that if he doesn't want his brains bashed in, he'd better stay away. If he shows up here, there's no telling what we might do.'

At this point, Jia Genzhu stood up as if to leave. Grandpa assumed this meant the conversation was over, and that Genzhu had no other agenda. Apparently, he had come all this way to tell Grandpa he wanted to kill his son, and to pass on a warning to Ding Hui not to return to the village. The sun had set while they were talking, turning the plain into a great thick lake of blood. Genzhu was just about to leave, to walk into the sticky red sunset, when he stopped.

'Oh, uncle?' His words came out quickly. 'I have just one more thing to ask, a favour. I don't have long to live, so I swear this will be the last favour I ever ask you. You know your nephew and I are local cadres, so we share the village seal. He's in pretty bad shape these days, just like me, and I doubt either of us will make it through the month. Anyway, the day before yesterday, he and I had a talk about which one of us should be buried with the seal. It turned into an argument because, of course, we both wanted it. So we finally decided to draw lots. He won the draw, which means he gets to be buried with the seal. But since then, I haven't been able to get any sleep. I keep tossing and turning, thinking about how much I want that seal in my casket when I die. I know I've done some unfair things to you and your family in the past, but I'm a dying man, and I'm begging you to go to Ding Yuejin and reason with him. You and he are family, and I know how much he's always respected you. If you ask him to give up the seal, I know he'll listen.'

Genzhu stood between the vegetable patch and the school gate, gazing at Grandpa imploringly. The setting sun behind him was like a lake of blood, soaking into his clothes.

Grandpa, still sitting in the shade of the schoolyard wall, stood up. The upper half of his body emerged into the fading sunlight, while the lower half stayed in shadow.

'Is it that important to be buried with the seal?' Grandpa asked, squinting into the sunshine.

'Maybe not, but I've got my heart set on it.'

'Why not just carve a new seal?'

'Then the new one would be fake. Let Ding Yuejin have the new seal, and I'll take the old one. If you can convince him to give up the seal, I promise to stop thinking about ways to kill Ding Hui.'

Genzhu gazed at Grandpa for a few moments, then mumbled something under his breath, turned and walked away. Although there wasn't much wind that day, Genzhu moved slowly and unsteadily, like he was afraid that a sudden gust might blow him over.

As Grandpa watched him stagger away, a thin reed being carried on the wind, he decided to stay out of this business about the seal. But as long as Jia Genzhu was still alive and able to walk, he decided he had better go into the city and tell my dad to stay away from the village, at least for a while.

Or maybe he'd tell him to stay away from the village for ever.

Either way, he decided to go to bed early, so he could get an early start the next morning.

CHAPTER TWO

1

Grandpa finally caught up with his son, but it wasn't easy.

After a long and difficult journey, he tracked him down to a village called Cottonwood. It was the same model blood-selling village that the people of Ding Village had toured ten years earlier. This time, my dad was in Cottonwood gathering statistics on how many people had died of the fever, and how many among those were single. He made a list of all the dead unmarried men, women, boys and girls of Cottonwood, and then started taking applications from their families for his matchmaking service. The families had to provide a photo, or at least a physical description, of their dead relative. A team of helpers, university students that my dad had brought from the city, took notes on each person's age, height, weight, face shape, skin tone and appearance. They set up a row of tables in the village centre and sat sifting through statistics and photos, and sorting the dead into categories. My dad paced back and forth along the row of tables, sometimes stopping to sit down and ask a question, or to give the students instructions.

My dad was a city person now, but he went out into the countryside every day, the same way that people in the countryside went out to their fields each morning. Knowing this, Grandpa went from village to village searching for my dad, until he caught up with him in Cottonwood. Ten years before, during the blood boom, Cottonwood had been a prosperous village. The tall buildings and white porcelain-tiled houses were still there, but they had become dilapidated. Grandpa stood sadly at the entrance to the village, staring at the ruin it had become. Big chunks of white tiles were missing from the walls of buildings, and what tiles remained were yellowed and weathered. The once-smooth tiles were as rough as sandpaper. Weeds sprouted between the cracks of tiled roofs and brick archways. Because of the drought, the weeds were as pale and withered as the grass that grew along the old Yellow River path.

As Grandpa walked along Cottonwood's grand-sounding streets – Sunshine Boulevard, Harmony Avenue, Prosperity Lane and Happiness Road – he noticed that their surfaces were cracked and crumbling, littered with potholes and chunks of concrete. The houses lining the streets were exactly the same as in Ding Village: most had padlocks hanging from their metal gates, or white funeral scrolls pasted on the lintels. There were old and new scrolls with various poetic couplets, some of them poignant: 'Grey-hairs bury their black-haired young / Saplings die, while old trees stay green.' Others were resigned: 'The dead are in a better place / but for the living, nothing's changed.' A few displayed a sense of gallows humour: 'In hell you roast, in heaven you feast / but the food on earth is bittersweet.' Some of the scrolls were plain white, while others had large circles where each ideograph would be. These new-style 'blank couplets' were made by inking the round base of a ceramic bowl, then pressing it against the paper. The vertical scrolls to the left and right of each door had seven large circles, and the horizontal scrolls above each door had four circles in a line. Everywhere Grandpa looked, the circles stared forth from doorways, like empty eyes.

Grandpa continued walking towards the centre of the village. When he came to Longevity Boulevard, he saw that the door of the social club was wide open. The place where the villagers had once watched television and played ping-pong, chess and mahjong seemed to have been abandoned. One of the door panels was missing, maybe stolen, and the other had two gaping holes. The courtyard was a shambles. It looked like a battle had taken place there. Doors and windowpanes were smashed, the dirt was littered with broken glass and piles of rubble, and the ground was overgrown with weeds. In the moist shade of the courtyard, the weeds grew tall and green, offering shelter to grasshoppers, frogs, moths and flying insects. The setting reminded Grandpa of a grave-yard in an old ancestral shrine.

Further down the street, Grandpa came to an abandoned flour mill. Severed power lines hung like vines from the ceiling, and rats scampered across rows of disused machinery. The machines for grinding, milling and rolling oats had once been painted bright green, but now they were covered with a thick layer of rust.

Next to the mill was a structure that looked like it had been either a stable or a cowshed. Now that the villagers had stopped raising horses and cows, the structure was empty. Its thatched roof was gone, replaced by a weathered straw mat nailed to the wooden frame. Inside, there was a battered wooden feeding trough with a wide crack running down the centre. An old man and a little boy, probably his grandson, were playing near the trough and catching crickets.

Grandpa greeted the man like a long lost friend. 'How's your family? Are they well?'

'His dad died,' the man answered, pointing at the little boy. 'And his mother remarried, but other than that, the family's fine.'

Saddened by this news, Grandpa shook his head and sighed.

'I'm looking for someone,' Grandpa told the man, 'and I wonder if you've seen him. Do you know a cadre named Ding, visiting from Wei county?'

'Are you talking about Ding Hui, the chairman of the county task force?' the old man asked.

'Yes, yes, that's him. He's the one I'm looking for.'

'Oh, Ding Hui is a great man, a wonderful man!'

The old man began telling Grandpa about all the wonderful things my dad had done for Cai county and for the village of Cottonwood. No matter that my dad was a Wei county cadre, *he had provided low-cost coffins to the people of Cotton-wood, which meant the dead had one less thing to worry about. Now he was giving solace to the living with his matchmaking service for the dead. The families of Cotton-wood would never again have to worry about their unmarried relatives being lonely in the afterworld. My father had even found a match for the village idiot, a man who had sold a lot of blood while he was alive but never managed to hook a wife. Now that he was in his grave, my father had paired him with an eighteen-year-old city girl who had died in a car accident. For a dowry of only 5,000 yuan, the man's mother was able to bury her son with a fever-free, virgin bride.*

There was another village girl, a student at the best university in Beijing, who found out she had the fever, came home to Cottonwood and died a few weeks later. Although she was educated and pretty, when her parents began searching for a posthumous match, they didn't ask for a penny of dowry money. All they wanted was to find a scholarly young man, someone who was their daughter's intellectual equal, to keep her company in the afterworld. When a search of all the villages within a thirty-mile radius failed to turn up an appropriate match, they began to fret that they had let their daughter down. Then my dad arrived in Cottonwood with his stack of photos and files. He showed them a photo of a handsome young man who'd died of the fever while studying at a university down south. Within minutes, the two families had agreed to the match. They even held a big, fancy wedding banquet to celebrate the marriage of their dead children.

'And it's cheap!' the man exclaimed. 'The government only charges 200 yuan for each match, and it's a huge relief for the families.'

Grandpa stared at the man for a few moments. 'Do you know where this Ding fellow is now?'

'Oh, sure,' the man answered. 'He's doing business in Red Star Square. Just go up the street until you reach the crossroads.'

Grandpa said goodbye and continued walking along Longevity Boulevard. Ten years ago, the paved concrete boulevard had been smooth, but now its surface was cracked and pitted. There were gaping potholes filled with dirt and weeds, and dry grass sprouting from the cracks in the pavement. Even the smooth sections were covered with a thick layer of dirt, raising clouds of dust as you passed. The restaurants, food stalls, clothing shops and kiosks lining the boulevard were shuttered, their owners gone to who knows where. Longevity Boulevard, like the other streets of Cottonwood, was deserted. You rarely saw any passers-by, and when you did, they were either very young or very old. All the villagers in their thirties and forties seemed to have disappeared. The few that Grandpa saw reminded him of Jia Genzhu: skeletally thin, covered with blisters and sores, with the shadow of death on their faces.

Grandpa knew that Cottonwood had prospered during the blood boom, but like Ding Village, it had been destroyed by blood, sold into ruin. People were dying, and villages were turning into ghost towns. Pretty soon, children and old people would be the only ones left.

Grandpa followed the dead, silent boulevard until he came to the crossroads marking Red Star Square, where the village blood station used to be. There had been a large, circular flower bed in the square, but the flowers were gone and the soil was trampled flat. This was where my dad and his helpers had set up shop, arranging marriages for the young, unmarried dead of Cottonwood. There were a few dozen villagers crowded around the tables, asking questions about this and that. Some were there to sign up dead sons, daughters, brothers or sisters for the matchmaking service, while others had come to check if there was any news on a suitable match.

A middle-aged man handed my dad a photograph of a smiling, handsome teenage boy. After scrutinizing the photo, my dad looked up at the man, taking in his tattered, dirty undershirt and mildewed, sun-bleached straw farmer's hat.

'Handsome boy. Was he your son?'

The farmer, gratified, nodded and smiled.

'How old was he?'

'Sixteen.'

'When did he die?'

'Three years ago.'

'Did he go to school?'

'Until junior high.'

'Was he ever engaged?'

'Yes, but when she found out he had the fever, she married someone else.'

'Are you looking for any particular type of girl?'

'No, just someone close to his age.'

My dad passed the photo to one of his assistants, a slightly effeminate young man, with the cryptic comment, 'Mid-range.'

The young man flipped through a stack of several dozen photos until he came to one of an average-looking girl. After reading the biographical information printed on the back of the photo, he looked up at the farmer.

'How about this one? Twenty years old, grade-school education, and no special requirements, just a dowry of 4,000 yuan.'

'Four thousand?' The farmer sounded shocked.

'That's about as cheap as it gets.'

'Maybe you could look again,' the farmer forced a smile, 'and find us something under 2,000 yuan. That's all my family can afford.'

Embarrassed, the young man began flicking through a larger stack of photos. He pulled out a photo of a woman holding a baby, and showed it to the farmer. 'This one's only 2,000 yuan.'

The farmer glanced at the photo. 'But my son was just a boy,' he said with the same forced smile. 'She looks too old for him.'

After a bit more searching, the young man came up with a photo of a wide-eyed girl, slightly on the chubby side.

'How about her? The family says they'll settle for 3,000 yuan.'

She wasn't a bad-looking girl, the farmer thought, and if he could borrow another 1,000 yuan, the price was within reach.

After a few more questions about the girl's age, name, home-town and family situation, he nodded in agreement and handed over 200 yuan for the matchmaking fee.

'How soon can we do the wedding?' the farmer asked.

'You'll have an answer within three days.'

'When you talk to the girl's family, can you tell them my son was a high-school graduate?'

'Not unless you have a diploma proving he was.'

'But he's so much better-looking than her. If they were alive, he'd be out of her league.'

'But her family owns a brickworks, and their business is booming. They've got more money than they can spend.'

'If they're so rich, why do they need a 3,000 yuan dowry?'

'That's not the point!' The young man lost his patience. 'It's about return on investment. They didn't spend all that money raising a daughter, just to give her away for free.'

The farmer thought for a moment. 'My son was such a sweet-tempered boy. If you ever met him, you'd know. He'll treat that girl like a princess, every day of her life.'

The farmer was so earnest that the young man had to smile. 'Don't you worry, sir. We'll present a strong case to the family, and do everything we can to talk them down on the price.'

Grinning happily, the farmer stepped away from the table. The next customer was a middle-aged woman looking for a match for her daughter. After my dad had introduced the woman to his young assistant, he handed him a picture of the daughter and told him to find a photo of a man about twenty-five years old.

At this point Grandpa, who had been watching some distance away, stepped forward, coughed and said, 'Hui?'

When my father heard his name, he turned around in surprise. 'Dad! What are you doing here?'

Grandpa pulled my father to one side so that they could talk privately. They stood at the edge of the trampled flower bed, near the entrance to a building that had once been the village blood bank. Grandpa noticed that the bright-red cross above the doorway looked new, as if it had been painted yesterday. He could almost smell the fresh red paint, and the thick red stench of blood.

Standing under that red cross, Grandpa told my dad about his meeting with Jia Genzhu, and about how the man had threatened to kill him if he ever came into the village again.

'That's why I think it's best if you don't come back to Ding Village,' Grandpa said.

When my dad heard this, a smile blossomed on his face. His lips curled back like flower petals. 'Jia Genzhu is a nobody,' he told Grandpa. 'I've got so much clout in the city now, that if I so much as stamp my foot, I can bring down the rafters of his house!'

'But son, now that he's dying, he's got nothing to lose. He's not afraid of anything.'

'You go back to Ding Village' – my dad was still smiling – 'and ask him if he wants a posthumous marriage for his cousin Hongli. You ask him if he wants his parents to go on living happily after he dies. Because if he does, he'd better mind his own business and keep his nose out of mine.'

At this point, somebody called my dad's name. He turned and walked back to the crowd, leaving my grandpa alone outside the abandoned blood bank.

2

Grandpa didn't return to Ding Village that night. He drove back into the city with my dad, and went out for dinner with my parents and sister. At a four-storey restaurant strung with colourful lights, my dad treated the family to a first-class meal of roasted chicken, Peking duck, and a kind of soup my grandpa had never heard of before. The thick soup, served in very small bowls, was made of transparent slices of something that might have been shark fin, and garnished with coriander leaves and shredded ginger. It had an odd fishy odour, and seemed to have a cooling effect. After Grandpa drank it, he felt a slight chill pass through his body, as if he had just given blood. The second their bowls were emptied, they were cleared away by one of the gorgeous waitresses. My father looked at Grandpa expectantly.

'Did you like the soup?'

'It seemed very fresh.'

'It costs 220 yuan per bowl, about the same as a coffin.' My father watched to see how Grandpa would react.

When he heard the price, Grandpa's jaw dropped and his face went pale. He wanted to say something, but he couldn't seem to get the words out. After they finished dinner, my parents and sister decided to take Grandpa on a tour of the city. As they left the brightly lit restaurant, Grandpa kept asking my dad how much the meal had cost, but my dad refused to say. 'Don't worry about the price,' he told Grandpa. 'I can afford it. That's all you need to know.'

Instead of splurging on a fancy meal, Grandpa thought they'd have been better off having noodles or turnip and vermicelli stew at home, but of course he didn't say it out loud.

When they turned from the narrow lane on to a broad boulevard, Grandpa was shocked by what he saw. In the year since he had last visited the county seat, it had grown into a big city to rival the metropolis of Kaifeng. Forests of high-rise buildings and apartment blocks towered over a boulevard broad enough for seven or eight large trucks to pass abreast. Although it was night, the boulevard was as bright as day, illuminated by bunches of tiny white lights that hung like grapes from lampposts. Flashing green and red lights winked from lampposts and the trunks of trees. The city seemed unaffected by water shortages or dry spells. While drought had turned the countryside pale, here the grass, trees, flowers and shrubs were the colours they were meant to be. The trees lining the boulevard were so lush and green that they looked almost fake. The men and women Grandpa passed looked different, too. Not long ago, they had seemed a bit rustic, as if soil from the fields still clung to their skin. Compared to someone from Ding Village, they were city folk, but if you put them next to someone from a big city like Kaifeng, they would still look like villagers. But now you'd never know the difference: there wasn't a trace of the countryside to be seen.

Despite the hot weather, all the young men seemed to be sporting thick-soled white trainers and had long, bleached hair. Female hairstyles, on the other hand, had got shorter. Some of the girls even wore crew cuts, which made it easy to mistake them for boys. But their short shirts and blouses were a reminder that they were girls, the kind of girls who weren't embarrassed to bare their bellies to male passers-by, or show their navels to the world. Grandpa saw bellies decorated with brightly coloured tattoos of butterflies, dragonflies and birds. Some of the girls had piercings, too: sparkly gold and diamond jewellery that winked from their navels.

Although it had only been a year since Grandpa's last visit to the county seat, it seemed like decades. The city had changed so much. As he trailed along behind my father, staring at the bright lights and tall buildings, he felt as if he'd stepped into a different world. Music blared from every shop and restaurant, making his heart race. Grandpa began to feel dizzy, so he asked my dad if they could go home. My dad led them away from the brightly lit boulevard and down a long, narrow alleyway hemmed in by high-rise buildings and paved with slabs of grey stone. After a while, they came to a large grove of trees. There were cypresses with thick trunks that a grown man couldn't have put his arms around, and several gingko trees surrounded by protective metal railings. The gingkos were so enormous that it would have taken several people with outstretched arms to encircle them. Suddenly, through the trees, Grandpa saw a row of single-storey courtyard homes with grey brick walls and tiled roofs. All the homes were identical, and looked to be at least several hundred years old. The elaborately tiled rooftops had soaring eaves decorated with stone figures of lions, dragons and mythical beasts. When they came to the last house, they stopped and my mother unlocked the gate.

'You live here?' Grandpa asked, surprised.

'This is where all the county cadres live,' my dad answered.

Grandpa saw that my dad was smiling broadly, grinning from ear to ear. It was the same smile he had worn on his wedding day, the same smile he'd worn when his blood bank first turned a profit. As Grandpa stepped into the courtyard, he felt a rush of cool, moist air and the fresh damp scent of plants and trees. It was a scent that had all but disappeared from Ding Village, one that had been missing from the plain for months. In the centre of the courtyard was a large gingko tree with a thick crown of leaves that shone green under the moonlight. Judging by the size of the courtyard, Grandpa guessed that the house must sit on one mu of land, more than 5,000 square feet. The courtyard was paved with slabs of dark stone, and the rooms around it were fashioned from brick, with rooftops of glazed ceramic tiles. Although the house had an antique air about it, the scent of freshly baked tiles straight from the kiln made Grandpa realize that it had been built only recently. It was not a Ming or Qing dynasty courtyard home, but a cleverly wrought reproduction. Looking up at the gingko tree that shaded most of the courtyard, Grandpa couldn't help but think of Uncle and Lingling's coffins, which had been made of the same rare type of wood.

Grandpa followed my dad into the house, and was surprised by the understated decor. There was none of the sumptuous tackiness of the restaurant they had been to, nor anything remotely modern or flashy. Rather, it looked like a grand old family home of centuries past. All the furnishings were Ming or Qing dynasty pieces made from expensive red sandalwood or yellow pear. Richly grained tables, chairs, chaises and bookcases gleamed deep red or muted yellow in the light of frosted glass lamps, and the air was thick with the fragrance of wood. Standing in the spacious main room, Grandpa felt as if he'd stepped into some sort of temple. After my mother had served the tea, and my sister had left to do her homework, father and son sat down for a long, face-to-face chat.

My father motioned to a chair. 'Have a seat, Dad.'

*But Grandpa remained standing, staring at the walls of
the room. While the exterior walls were grey brick designed
to look old, the interior walls were newly painted, white as
snow.*

'Did you build this house yourself?' Grandpa asked.

'Not just this house,' my dad answered proudly. 'I paid for
the whole complex.'

*Grandpa sat down. He no longer seemed surprised. With
the air of a man confirming a long-held suspicion, he asked:*
'Did you pay for it with the money you earned selling coffins?'

Dad shot Grandpa a look. 'That was about helping people.
Those coffins were a once-in-a-lifetime opportunity.'

'And did the money go to you, or to the government?'

'If it all went to me,' *my dad grinned,* 'I'd own half this city
by now.'

'What about this new matchmaking scheme? Do the fees go
to you, or to the higher-ups?'

The smile faded. 'Like I said, it's about helping people. The
county pays me a salary, and I arrange matches for people
who need them.'

*After that, there was no more conversation. Darkness began
to seep in from the courtyard, bringing with it a hint of rain.
Grandpa went to the door and raised his head to the sky.
Through the leaves of the gingko tree, he saw that the sky was
crowded with stars: tomorrow would be another sweltering
day. What Grandpa had mistaken for rain was nothing more
than the night scent of the gingko.*

*It was after midnight, and time for bed. Dad led Grandpa
to a bedroom in the south wing of the courtyard. It was
smaller than the main room, but besides a large wooden bed,
the decor and furniture were exactly the same.*

*As Grandpa was getting ready for bed, my dad surprised
him by asking:* 'Dad, you're not going to try to strangle me
again, are you?'

*Grandpa, caught off guard by this question, wasn't sure
how to answer. The hand that had been unbuttoning his shirt
froze, and a blush rose to his cheeks.*

Noting Grandpa's embarrassment, my dad laughed. 'I'm happy to let you stay in my house, as long as you don't try to strangle me in my sleep. After all, it's just one night. It's the least I can do, as a filial son.'

My dad walked past Grandpa to a wooden door, painted the same stark shade of white as the walls. Grandpa hadn't noticed the door before, because it blended in with the wall and was half-covered by an ink-brush portrait of the god of wealth. My dad pressed a latch, hidden beneath the portrait, and the door slid back, revealing a small inner room. He flipped on the light switch, and the room was suddenly as bright as day, as dazzling as a big-city street. To Grandpa, it was as dazzling as a dream, because the entire room was filled with cash. There was a large table heaped with something and covered with a white sheet. My dad pulled aside the sheet, revealing a tabletop piled with cash, 100-yuan bills bundled into 10,000-yuan stacks and secured with red rubber bands. These had been bundled into medium-sized bricks of 100,000 yuan, then into larger bricks of a million yuan, each neatly secured with a length of red silk ribbon tied into an elaborate butterfly knot. All the bills seemed to be brand new, and gave off a pungent scent of ink. Red silk ribbons and red, green, yellow and orange bills littered the table like brightly coloured pressed flowers. Grandpa couldn't imagine why his son hadn't put the money away somewhere safe, instead of leaving it lying around on a table. He was just about to ask, when my dad walked over to a chest of drawers and opened it. Every drawer was stuffed with cash. He threw open the cabinets and drawers, revealing even more stacks of cash. Everywhere you looked, there were bricks and stacks and piles of cash. Mountains of money in every colour of the rainbow.

The smell of ink was so strong you could choke on it. All that money made it hard to breathe. Between the bundles and bricks of money, my dad had stuffed mothballs and cloths to absorb moisture and prevent rot. The needle-sharp stench of lime, naphthalene and camphor irritated the nostrils, and *mingled with the musty smell of the room that hadn't been aired in days.*

The clash of smells and colours made the room seem monstrous and bizarre. Being inside it was as unpleasant as standing at the edge of a septic pit before sunrise. My dad seemed used to it, as if he had been born and raised in just such a room, but Grandpa felt his throat growing tight, making it hard to breathe. He forced himself to breathe through his nostrils, and rubbed his nose to rid himself of the stench. Gazing around the room again, Grandpa wondered if he were dreaming. He knew he was prone to dreaming, so he tried pinching himself on the thigh, a method he had used before to wake up from his dreams. Usually he'd find himself in bed in his room at the school, but this time when he pinched himself, all he felt was a searing pain. Instead of waking up in his bed, Grandpa found himself still standing with my father in a tiny space more like a bank vault or a national treasury than the annexe of a guest bedroom. He felt as if he were drowning in a sea of cash, being suffocated by mountains of money. In addition to the smells he had noticed before, there was also a hint of rain wafting in from the courtyard, a scent he now recognized as gingko leaves. Maybe he wasn't dreaming at all. Maybe he was awake and standing with his son amidst piles of ill-gained cash.

'How much is there?' Grandpa asked.

Dad smiled. 'I'm not sure.'

'What do you need with all this money? It's more than you could spend in a lifetime.'

My dad seemed embarrassed. 'Is it my fault this fever never ends? If it keeps on like this, I don't know what I'm going to do. I just opened five new factories for the county, and we still can't make enough coffins to keep up with demand. All the trees on the plain are gone, so I have to ship timber in from the north-west. And this month, I sent a dozen matchmaking teams into the villages to gather statistics and arrange posthumous matches. It's been two weeks, and we've only managed to find matches for a third of the families who signed up.'

'And this matchmaking business is more of your philanthropy?'

'I've spent my whole life doing philanthropy,' my dad smiled.

Grandpa turned away and was silent for a moment. 'And the other cadres who live here, do they all have vaults like this?'

Dad nodded.

'Filled with this much money?'

'I don't know,' my dad shook his head. 'We just do our jobs, and stay out of each other's business.'

Grandpa didn't say anything more. He gazed around at the piles of money, and then at his son, who was beginning to look sleepy.

'Take my advice, Hui,' he urged quietly. 'And keep your family away from Ding Village. It's not worth risking your life.'

My dad snorted. 'I'm not worried. They can't touch me now. Besides, Ding Village is my home. Not only am I planning to go back, in a few days I'll be there to to exhume my son's grave. I found him a wife, and we're holding a big ceremony to celebrate. They won't dare try to hurt me, especially when they see how much money I'm splashing out.'

Dad rubbed his bleary eyes and looked up at Grandpa with a smile, the smile of a filial son.

'Get some sleep, Dad. You can sleep in here tonight, and dream sweet dreams. It's the least I can do for my father.'

3

That night, lying asleep next to my dad's cash-filled room, Grandpa did have dreams, although they weren't the kind he expected. Before falling asleep, he was sure he would have visions of money, but he didn't see a penny in his dreams. All he saw was me, stretching out my arms to him, and calling for him to save me.

My dad had found me a wife. Her name was Lingzi, and she was several years older than me. Her leg was a bit deformed. I suppose it was something she was born with. She also had epilepsy, which meant she suffered fits every couple of days. During one of her fits, she fell into a river and drowned. Of all the unmarried dead girls looking for husbands, she was the ugliest. But my dad agreed to the match anyway. Not only did my dad agree to the match, he jumped at the chance.

Lingzi's dad was a very powerful man.

My dad came to Ding Village with a group of people, dug up my bones and put them in a new coffin. The coffin was made of gold, and it was even fancier than my uncle's. They dug me up so they could take me to Kaifeng and bury me next to my dead wife. Lingzi's dad gave us a nice plot in a funeral park overlooking the Yellow River. It was a good piece of land, the sort you see advertised in estate agents' brochures: excellent location, southern exposure, river view, just steps away from the water, cool in summer and warm in winter. Someone had offered more than two million yuan for the land, because he wanted to turn it into a plot for one of his relatives, but Lingzi's dad decided to set it aside for us, instead.

The day they dug me up, my dad showed up in Ding Village with twenty or so people. They lit incense at my grave, burned paper offerings, set off firecrackers, dug up my plain wood coffin and put my bones into another, fancier, golden coffin so they could take it to the funeral park in Kaifeng. But what my dad didn't know was that I didn't want to leave Ding Village in the first place. I didn't want to leave Grandpa or my grave behind the school, and I was scared of going to a strange place. As soon as they lifted my golden coffin, I started thrashing around inside and screaming for my grandpa. Not screaming for my father. Screaming for dear life.

'Grandpa! Don't let them take me!'

My cries shook the heavens.

'I don't want to leave here! Don't let them take me!'

My screams ripped a hole in the sky.

'Save me, Grandpa, save me . . .'

Grandpa woke up. He sat on the edge of the bed in a daze, staring at the pale sunlight seeping through the curtains like milk.

CHAPTER THREE

1

It was a lucky coincidence.

The morning Grandpa was packing his things and getting ready to visit my dad in the city, my dad came to him. Dad happened to be passing through Ding Village with his team of matchmakers and decided to stop by the school. He ran into Grandpa as he was walking out of the school gate.

My dad was wearing grey uniform shorts, leather sandals, a white short-sleeved shirt and a straw hat that made him look like a farmer from somewhere down south. He was more tanned than when he'd left Ding Village, his face ruddy and healthy from the sun. When they met at the school gate, my dad handed Grandpa a paper bundle tied with string.

'What's this?' Grandpa asked.

'Wild ginseng,' my dad answered. 'It's the best kind.'

The package felt heavy, too heavy, in Grandpa's hands.

The sun was not yet overhead. It shone from the east like a burning haystack, scorching the plain below. The landscape was barren; everything had withered. Grass, wheat, people and villages were dying. Everything had dried up, and the plain was as pale as sand – the same colour as Grandpa's face when he saw my dad standing at the school gate.

'You didn't run into Jia Genzhu in the village, did you?' Grandpa asked, alarmed.

'No, but I'm not scared of him. He can't do anything to me.' My dad seemed to know what Genzhu was planning, and about his conversation with Grandpa. 'The villagers already warned me, Dad. They told me not to come back, but I came anyway, to show them I'm not afraid. And in a few days, I'm going to hold a big ceremony to celebrate my son's wedding. When they see what I've got planned, Genzhu won't dare lay a finger on me.'

Now even more alarmed, Grandpa stared at his son as if he were a stranger at the gate.

'Qiang was only twelve. Are you really going to marry him off?'

'I've already arranged it with the girl's family.'

'Where are her people from?'

'They're from the city. She's a wealthy man's little princess,' said my dad, grinning. 'Not long after her dad got promoted to governor and started organizing the county blood drive, she got some strange disease, fell into a river and drowned. She's a few years older than Qiang, but what does age matter?'

'How much older?' Grandpa asked.

'Five or six years.'

'And you think that's a suitable match?'

'Her dad's the county governor! If he thinks it's suitable, who are we to disagree?'

'When's the wedding?'

'That's what I came to tell you. I'll be back in a few days to remove his bones. We're taking them to a funeral park in Kaifeng, where he'll be buried with the girl. Their grave is on a very nice plot of land.'

My dad then told Grandpa that he couldn't stay long because his helpers were waiting for him on the main road, south of the village. He asked a few questions about Grandpa's health: was he eating okay? Did he have decent clothing? Was he able to draw water from the school well, or had it dried up in the drought? As my dad was about to leave, he remembered that he had wanted to visit the house on New Street, which had been vacant for many months. Instead of walking along the road, he and Grandpa cut through the dried-up wheat fields on the outskirts of the village. They walked single-file along the ridges that divided the fields until they came to the south end of the village, and to our house on New Street.

What they saw made them stop in shock.

Someone had smashed the padlock on the gate and left it lying on the ground. Both the wooden gate and the front door were gone. The wooden window frames were intact, but the panes were smashed and the courtyard was littered with broken glass. Every piece of furniture inside the house, from the chairs and tables to the curtains and washstands, was missing.

They'd robbed the house, just like they'd robbed my uncle's grave. And the courtyard smelled of urine.

His face mottled with anger, my dad stood on the front stoop, peering into the empty house. He turned to Grandpa. 'Who did this?'

Grandpa shook his head.

My dad kicked the wall. 'Damn those sons of bitches! It was Genzhu and Yuejin, I know it!'

My dad's face was pale, twitching with anger. Grandpa, afraid his son might do something rash, suddenly dropped to his knees and began pleading with him.

'Hui, if you want to blame anyone, blame me, okay? Let's just say I'm the one who stole the doors and furniture and urinated in the courtyard. If you have to punish someone, punish me.'

Grandpa looked up at his son like a little boy pleading with his father. My dad looked down at Grandpa with disdain, like a father who has lost patience with a misbehaving child.

After a few moments, my dad turned on his heel and left without a word. He didn't look back.

2

My dad could easily have taken a shortcut, but instead he marched proudly through the centre of Ding Village, his head held high. Some of the villagers were sitting around the crossroads that marked the village centre. The weather was hot, but not so unbearable that you couldn't go outdoors, so they had gathered at the crossroads to eat breakfast and socialize. Most of them had already finished eating when my dad arrived. He had been walking quickly, taking long strides, but as he neared the crowd, he paused for a moment to wipe off his shoes.

One of the men, Wang Baoshan, caught sight of him and shouted, 'Ding Hui! What are you doing here, so early in the morning?'

My dad smiled and approached the crowd. 'I was passing by the village, and thought I'd come and have a look.'

He pulled out a packet of expensive, filter-tip cigarettes, handed one to Wang Baoshan, then began passing out cigarettes to the other men in the crowd.

'You've got to try these,' my dad boasted. 'A whole pack will set you back half the price of a coffin. Each one costs as much as a ten pound bag of salt, a bottle of liquor or one pound of pork.' The villagers gasped in astonishment.

'Are you serious?' Wang Baoshan asked.

'Smoke one and you'll see,' my dad answered, taking his lighter out of his pocket.

After he had lit Wang's cigarette, he went down the line, lighting cigarettes for each of the men. But when he came to Jia Genzhu, sitting with a group of villagers on the right, he skipped right over him. My dad took one look at Genzhu and passed him by, then handed a cigarette to the next man. Genzhu's face was discoloured and covered with dried scabs, and he was so thin and sickly that one push might have sent him sprawling on the ground. His eyes were dull and clouded, and filled with desperation. It was as if the fever had stolen not just his strength but his spirit, leaving him helpless. He had no choice but to endure the insult and try to get along with my dad as best he could. When my dad had first started passing out cigarettes, his eyes had lit up, but when my dad passed him by without a glance and handed a cigarette to the man behind him, his face had flushed deep red. Deep purplish red, the colour of liver.

After my dad had given away all his cigarettes, he said goodbye to the villagers and headed back to the main road, where his team of matchmakers was waiting for him. As he sauntered off, his head held high, my dad turned back for one last look. Genzhu was staring at him with undisguised fury. Impotent, helpless fury. The two men locked eyes. My dad narrowed his, and looked daggers at the man who had recently threatened to kill him.

With that look, my dad drew blood. One last twist of the knife.

3

Grandpa knew everything now. It was as if everything my dad had ever done had been laid out before his eyes. While my dad was leaving the village, Grandpa was hurrying back to it. His first stop was Ding Yuejin's house.

Yuejin and his family were gathered around the table, eating a sumptuous breakfast of stir-fried golden pumpkin, scrambled eggs with dark green leeks, piping-hot rice porridge and fried cakes. They were enjoying this feast behind closed doors when Grandpa burst into their courtyard. Yuejin, who seemed surprised to see him, motioned Grandpa to take a seat. Now that he was so sick, he told Grandpa, his family felt that he deserved to eat whatever he wanted. The cakes were supposed to be a special treat just for him, but he had insisted they make more so everyone could share them.

'Don't stop eating on my account,' Grandpa said as he sat down. 'I don't want to interrupt your breakfast.'

Grandpa knew that since everyone had moved out of the school, Yuejin had been receiving regular food subsidies from the county government. Because he had the official village seal, he was able to get the best-quality rice and flour for free. His family ate very well, behind closed doors where no one could see. Grandpa glanced around the courtyard and saw piles of brand-new desks and chairs from the school stacked beneath the eaves. There were also several logs, sawed into six-foot lengths, that Grandpa knew had come from the big paulownia tree that once stood in the schoolyard. Also a dozen or so wooden nameplates, still marked with class numbers, which had once hung above the classroom doors. The sight of all these things, so clearly stolen from the school, embarrassed Grandpa, but he didn't want them to think he was snooping, so he quickly averted his eyes.

Yuejin's family lived comfortably. Their house had a tiled roof and a courtyard of poured concrete, and the rafters were hung with ears of corn from last winter's crop. Everyone was rosy-cheeked and healthy. Even their pigs seemed exceptionally plump. When one of the pigs came snuffling around the table, looking for scraps, Yuejin shooed it off.

As the pig scampered away, Yuejin turned to Grandpa. 'So, Uncle, what brings you here so early?'

Grandpa unwrapped the paper package my dad had given him, revealing three large ginseng roots. With round knobs at the top, and tendrils branching out from the sides like arms and legs, they looked like little dolls. The skin was pale yellow, almost translucent, and gave off a strong medicinal smell. Yuejin's family, none of whom had ever seen wild ginseng before, gathered around for a closer look. 'Ooh, it's true what they say,' said one of the women. 'They look just like little people.'

Grandpa picked up one of the roots and offered it to Yuejin. 'This one's for you. You can boil it to make ginseng tea. This is wild ginseng from the north-west. It takes decades for the roots to grow this thick. It's supposed to be a good tonic for strengthening the body, and will probably fight the fever better than any medicine.'

Ding Yuejin, who knew that wild ginseng was incredibly expensive, refused to accept the gift. When Grandpa insisted, he backed away, blushing and stammering. 'No, no, Uncle. I can't take that. Ding Hui meant it as a gift for you.'

But Grandpa pressed it into his hand. 'Your cousin was very specific. He asked me to give this piece to you.'

Yuejin relented. After he had carefully wrapped the ginseng in paper and set it on the table, he said suddenly: 'Uncle, you should tell Ding Hui to stay away from the village. Genzhu and some of the others are planning to hurt him.'

'Genzhu promised me he wouldn't,' said Grandpa. 'If you'd be willing to give up the seal.'

Yuejin thought for a moment. 'All right,' he said with a smile. 'Tell Genzhu that if I die before him, I'll leave him the seal. I don't care about being buried with it. It's not like it's going to do me any good once I'm dead.'

He glanced at the breakfast table, laden with dishes of food, and seemed embarrassed. 'But I have a feeling he'll die first. Other than the rashes and itching, I don't have any other symptoms. That's a good sign. If he dies before me, I've got to go on living. I need that seal to collect my food subsidies from the county cadres.'

The package of ginseng was still lying on the table, where Yuejin had left it. Eyeing it suspiciously, he asked: 'Uncle, you didn't come here to speak up for Jia Genzhu, did you? After all, you and I are family. We Dings have to stick together.'

Now it was Grandpa's turn to look embarrassed.

'Of course not, of course not,' he assured his nephew. He stayed for a while longer, made some small talk, then left.

Grandpa's next stop was Jia Genzhu's house.

4

As Grandpa walked through the courtyard and into Genzhu's living room, he noticed that the house looked a lot like Ding Yuejin's. The dozen or so desks and chairs stacked beneath the eaves were brand new, taken from the school. A pile of logs was all that was left of the cottonwood and paulownia trees that had once stood outside the school kitchen. Genzhu had even taken the basketball hoop and frame. It had been dismantled, and was lying in a twisted heap in the middle of the courtyard. Inside the house, the rafters were stacked with wooden frames ripped from the windows of the school. There were other odds and ends that Grandpa recognized, piled in corners or scattered about the room: pots, woks, a bamboo steamer, a metal bucket, a high-backed chair, a large blackboard, piles of blank homework notebooks and bags of unused chalk and pencils.

Jia Genzhu's living room looked like a school supply warehouse.

Grandpa spied a rusted sheet of metal propped behind the living room door. It was the same piece of metal that had served for so long as the school bell. He couldn't imagine why Genzhu had taken it, or how he planned to use it. Maybe he thought the metal would be worth something. But to Grandpa, it wasn't just a piece of metal to be sold for scrap, but the school bell he'd been ringing for decades. He felt like it belonged to him, not to the school, and that Genzhu had stolen something personal.

Grandpa couldn't take his eyes off it.

Genzhu noticed Grandpa staring. 'You didn't come here looking for that bell, did you?' he asked.

Grandpa smiled sheepishly and shifted his gaze. After he'd assured Genzhu that of course he hadn't come to snoop, that he'd never do such a thing, he showed him the piece of ginseng he'd brought. 'My son Hui asked me to give you this. It's genuine wild ginseng. He said if you let it steep for a while in boiling water, then drink the tea, you'll get some of your strength back.'

Grandpa pushed the ginseng towards Genzhu, inviting him to take it. 'You really ought to try it, son. People have been taking ginseng since ancient times. Why, even the emperors used it to treat illnesses that their doctors couldn't cure. It will relieve your symptoms, and if you keep taking it, you might even get cured.'

Genzhu looked down at the ginseng in Grandpa's hand, then raised his head and said coldly, 'Ding Hui came into the village this morning and passed out cigarettes to everyone but me.'

'Oh, surely not!' Grandpa gave an unconvincing laugh. 'Not after he went out of his way to bring you the ginseng. Even the best cigarette can't compare with a tiny piece of this.'

'Isn't he afraid that if I start taking ginseng,' Genzhu sneered, 'I'll get my strength back and bash him over the head when he's not looking?'

Grandpa went pale. For a moment, his smile froze, but he quickly managed to regain his composure. 'Son, just take the ginseng,' he said with a reassuring smile. 'Once you've got your strength back, I think you'll feel differently. Hui's coming back to the village in a few days to exhume his son's grave, so if you still want to bash his head in, you'll have your chance then.'

5

At sunrise, my dad arrived in Ding Village with a big group of people and a gilded coffin. The coffin, made of five-inch-thick planks of gingko, was engraved with scenes of Beijing, Shanghai, Guangzhou and other rich, modern Chinese cities. There were scenes of foreign cities, too, places that no one would have recognized if they hadn't been labelled as Paris, New York or London. I didn't know where New York or Paris were, and I didn't care. All I knew what that my home was Ding Village, and that Ding Village was on the East Henan plain. I didn't care how fancy my casket was, or if the gold paint on it was real, or if it was worth as much as all the land in the village.

The sunlight glinting off my coffin was blinding. It was like the sun had fallen from the sky and turned into an oblong square. My dad and the others paraded my coffin through the village, attracting a lot of attention. Everyone who was still alive came out to see it, to gape at the golden casket with carvings of places they'd never seen before, and never would. Right there, on my coffin, was the modernity and excitement of China's big cities, and the wealth and grandeur of all the cities in the world.

They set the coffin beside my grave, burned incense, made paper offerings and set off firecrackers. Then they dug up my grave, transferred my bones from the plain wood coffin to the golden one, and carried it away with great ceremony.

When they lifted that golden coffin, I started thrashing around inside it, screaming for my grandpa. Not screaming for my father. Screaming for dear life.

'Grandpa! Don't let them take me!'

My cries shook the heavens.

'I don't want to leave here! Don't let them take me!'

My screams ripped a hole in the sky.

'Save me, Grandpa, save me . . .'

My voice filled the schoolyard and echoed through the village and across the plain. My cries rose to the heavens, and fell like raindrops on to the parched and blighted earth.

6

The day I got married, there was a slight breeze, the weather almost cool. My mother and sister set out early to fetch my bride, or in this case, her remains. Her bones. My dad came to Ding Village to dig up my remains and take them to Kaifeng, to be buried with Lingzi. What was left of me would be travelling to my bride's hometown, not the other way round.

The sun hung low in the sky, a brilliant ball of light against a backdrop of clear blue sky. Luckily for the villagers, there was a breeze that day, and Ding Village was pleasantly cool. Luckily for the crops and plants, the previous night had provided a little moisture to their pale, withered stems. Little bits of green had begun to appear, pushing up through sandy soil.

Several dozen people were standing around my grave near the school gate. Among them were the same men who had built Uncle and Lingling's tomb. They had brought picks and shovels, bags bulging with fireworks and funeral offerings, and a top-of-the-range casket covered with engravings and gilded with gold. All the engravings were scenes of rich modern cities, one big city after another, like pictures from paradise. The cities were crowded with tall buildings and wide streets, parks and squares, shops and restaurants. There were engravings of diners seated in swanky restaurants, with uniformed security guards and well-dressed hostesses to greet them at the doors. In a public square, there was a garden and a children's amusement park filled with games and rides I'd never seen: a roller-coaster twisted like a dragon; a spinning ferris wheel with tiny seats; bumper cars crashing into one another. The scene was as fresh and intoxicating as a grove of trees on an early spring morning, but instead of chirping birds there were well-dressed adults and children. So lifelike, you could almost hear their laughter and conversation, as if their voices had been carved into the wood.

Although the casket was a size smaller than an adult coffin, the interior was also richly decorated with engravings. One was a landscape of trees, flowers, bridges and a lake surrounded by wooded hills. There were even tiny boats floating on the surface of the lake. Among the trees stood an old-fashioned two-storey brick-built house with a roof of glazed yellow tiles. There was a gingko tree and a large cypress in the courtyard, which was surrounded by a stone wall. Although the two red scrolls on either side of the gate were no wider than the flat edge of a chopstick, the tiny writing was still clear enough to read: 'In Paradise, the days stretch on and on / but the trees stay green all year long.' A scroll above the gate identified the house as the 'Ding Family Residence'. A cobblestone path led from the gate to the main rooms, corridors and wings of the house. If you followed the path through the courtyard and peeked through the doors and windows, you could see that each room was crammed with furniture, appliances and home electronics. Landscape paintings, calligraphy scrolls and traditional musical instruments hung from the walls. My father had been careful to include a well-stocked bookshelf filled with storybooks for me to read, and heaps of snacks and beverages, in case I got

322

hungry or thirsty. This was the house my parents had made for me, the property they had bequeathed me. It was a place where my teenage wife and I could settle down and live happily for all eternity.

On the bottom panel of the coffin, where my bones would lie, there were engravings of a dozen or so buildings of various sizes, shapes and styles. Each of the buildings was labelled with the name of a famous Chinese bank: Bank of China, the Central Bank of China, People's Bank of China, Industrial & Commercial Bank of China, Agricultural Bank of China, China Everbright Bank, and so on. It was as if every major bank in the country had set up their headquarters on the floor of my coffin. I would be laid to rest with all the money in China, and my bones would sleep upon the wealth of the world.

My father stood beside my grave, admiring the gilded coffin and the world he'd made for me. It was a world of cities, villages and dramatic landscapes, all the wealth and splendour of the plain, a kingdom of wealth and entertainments. My dad said a few quick words to his crew, who were standing around with shovels, spades and pickaxes – decorated with red ribbons to celebrate the happy occasion. The ceremony began with fireworks. My father's helpers set off long strings of firecrackers and several boxes of large fireworks, and burned a red paper effigy of a bridal sedan chair. Then they made six circuits around my grave, three clockwise and three anti-clockwise, before scattering more firecrackers on the ground for the guests to pick up and light themselves.

Ding Village hadn't celebrated like this in years. The villagers couldn't remember the last time they had seen a ceremony so exciting and lavish. There were tiny firecrackers that exploded with a pop, and great strings of them that popped and crackled for minutes on end. There were fireworks that exploded with a bang or a boom, and rockets that whizzed up into the air, sending down showers of sparks. It was a display to light up the sky and dazzle the senses. The noise of fireworks mingled with the babble of voices; smoke

323

*and charred bits of red paper floated through the air. Then
there was the golden gingko coffin that waited beside my
grave, the incense and paper offerings and plates heaped with
cakes, deep-fried treats and enormous apples and pears that
my father had brought from the city. The acrid stench of
gunpowder and burned paper competed with the scents of
incense, human sweat and apples.*

*Once the festivities were over, my dad and the others began
the solemn task of exhuming my grave.*

*The sound of firecrackers had brought a surge of villagers
to my graveside. They flooded into the schoolyard like visitors
to a temple fair. Some came to gawk, some to help, and others,
just to join in the fun. Everyone talked about how lucky I was
to have such a grand wedding ceremony. Even though the
bride and groom were dead, it was better than most weddings
in which both parties were still alive.*

*Although Ding Village had lost a lot of people recently, the
ceremony drew a big crowd. It seemed as if half the village
were there. Some of the people sitting or standing around my
grave wore broad straw hats to block the burning sun, while
others were bare-headed. Sunlight and perspiration glinted
from several bald heads, making them look like freshly washed
melons bobbing in a sea of human heads. At a signal from my
father, the gravediggers dug their red-ribboned shovels and
spades into the ground. Before long, there were two heaps of
dirt on either side of my grave. As this was happening, the
middle-aged master of ceremonies began making the rounds,
doling out cigarettes and treats, as if he were presiding over a
celebration rather than an exhumation. There were brand-
name cigarettes for the men in the crowd, and candies, cakes
and sweets for the women and children.*

*Rarely had there been so much activity at the school gate.
Ding Yuejin and several other young men walked around
stomping on spent firecrackers to make sure that they were
extinguished. Because the weather was so dry, he explained
to my dad, it would be easy for a pile of kindling to catch fire,
and he wouldn't want to see me burned in my grave.*

When Ding Xiaoming arrived, he walked up to my dad, all smiles, and asked if he needed help with anything. Seeing that my father had the situation under control, he picked up a shovel and joined the crew of men who were digging up my grave.

There was also a woman named Fen, who had been a cook at the school and a good friend of my mother's. Fen was now horribly thin and frail, and didn't look as if she would live more than a few days, but she still made a point of asking after my mother. She told my dad how much she missed my mum, and said that she would never forget her kindness. When Fen was a new bride, it had been my mother who went to her hometown to meet her and escort her to her in-laws' house in Ding Village.

Then there was 'Woody' Zhao, a young man who had refused to leave his house for days after finding out that he had the fever. But today he had joined the celebration and seemed to be in a better mood. When he noticed that the gravediggers were getting dirt on the plates of food near my grave, he moved them out of the way and asked my dad what he should do with them. Dad waved his hand and said, 'Take them, if you want.' Woody stuffed a couple of steamed buns into his pockets and divided the deep-fried sweets among the children who were playing in the crowd.

The schoolyard was a sea of bobbing heads, like an audience at a concert. Nearly 100 people had turned out to watch the fireworks, or to offer help, or to see how the elderly man who was the senior master of ceremonies would conduct the ritual. At each step in the process of exhuming my grave, he set off a string of firecrackers to frighten off evil spirits. He lit the first string of firecrackers when they broke the soil and began digging, and the second string when the helpers climbed down into my open grave. After they had wiped the dirt from my coffin and were preparing to open the lid, he set off a third string of firecrackers, draped a large red cloth over the grave and asked the crowd to move back a few steps, ensuring that no one would be able to see what state my body was in. Then *he lowered a red tunic and trousers into the grave so that the helpers could begin dressing my remains.*

When this was done, it was time to raise my remains. This was the most solemn part of the ceremony. Everyone seemed to be holding their breath, waiting for my red-clad bones to appear. At this point, the elderly master of ceremonies pulled my dad aside and told him to go and get Grandpa, and then find somewhere far away from my grave to watch from. If Dad and Grandpa saw my remains and started crying, they might scare my ghost away. He also told Dad to talk to Grandpa about whether or not there would be a wedding banquet in the village, and whether they would be needing his services. Dad promised they would talk about it, and went off to find Grandpa.

In fact, my dad had already made up his mind about the banquet. He was planning to hold it in the city, rather than in Ding Village, because what was the point of treating a bunch of sick people and their families to a big, expensive meal? Instead, he had reserved three floors of the largest restaurant in the city, and invited all his closest friends, acquaintances and influential colleagues to join the feast. Lingzi's dad, my new father-in-law, was the highest-ranking official in the county, so no one refused the invitation. Everyone who was anyone would be there, and they were all looking forward to rubbing elbows with the county governor.

My dad searched the whole school and couldn't find Grandpa anywhere. He went back to the gate and searched through the crowd, but Grandpa wasn't there. At this point, my dad realized that he hadn't seen Grandpa since they'd started digging up my grave. No one else had, either.

My dad organized a search party.

They found Grandpa sitting alone by the side of the road leading to the village. He was hunched beneath the branches of a small elm, smoking a cigarette and looking out at the village and the withered, yellowed plain. He seemed to be lost in thought. Maybe he was thinking about important things like grief and loss, death and dissolution. Feelings that were miles wide and fathoms deep. Then again, maybe he was just tired and wanted a quiet place where he could sit down and rest. A place where he could be alone. He gazed at the dead crops and dried-up plain with a melancholy and worried expression. The little elm had more branches than leaves, and didn't offer much in the way of shade. Grandpa might as well be sitting in the blazing sun. As my dad approached, he saw that the back of Grandpa's white cotton shirt was stained with perspiration.

'Dad,' he said cautiously. 'What are you doing? It's too hot to be sitting out here.'

Grandpa slowly turned around. 'I suppose Qiang's been moved from his grave?'

'Uh-huh.'

My dad squatted down next to Grandpa. 'What are you doing out here?'

Grandpa stared at my dad for a long time before asking the question that had been on his mind. 'Exactly how much older is this Lingzi girl?'

My dad grinned. 'You didn't come out here to watch for Jia Genzhu, did you? Are you afraid he'll show up at the grave and make a scene?'

Grandpa ignored the question. 'I want to know, Hui. How much older is she?'

'Qiang needs someone older to take care of him.' My dad sat down on the ground. 'And I wouldn't worry about Genzhu, if I were you. I was actually hoping he'd show up today. I'd like to see him try to lay a finger on me.'

'Is it true Lingzi had a crippled leg?'

Grandpa looked into his son's eyes, but my dad averted his gaze.

'Yes, but it wasn't obvious. They say you'd never notice unless you looked really close.'

Then, changing the subject: 'If Genzhu does cause any trouble today, I'll make him wish he'd never been born.'

Grandpa ignored the comment. He was more interested in me. 'And her dad is the county governor?'

Dad just smiled.

'I also hear the girl had epilepsy.'

My dad stared at Grandpa, wide-eyed, wondering where he could have got this information.

Grandpa knew from my dad's reaction that the things he'd dreamed were true. With a deep sigh, he turned back to the road and continued watching Jia Genzhu's house, which was visible in the distance. Although the wooden gates were unlocked, no one had come in or out of them in a long time. Just as Grandpa was beginning to think the house was empty, a man emerged from the gate carrying a strip of white cloth tied to a bamboo pole. After he had hung it from a tree, the man calmly went back inside. In Ding Village, this was the traditional way of signalling that someone had died. When Grandpa saw that strip of white cloth hanging outside Genzhu's gate like a flag of surrender, he felt his heart skip a beat. He turned to my dad with a look of regret and relief.

'Hui, I've seen the way you put on airs, but really, did you have to marry off your son to a girl like that?'

'How could I have possibly found a better match?' My dad seemed puzzled. 'Don't you know her father is moving up in the world? They just promoted him to mayor of Kaifeng!'

Grandpa snorted derisively and gave my dad a look of disgust. Without a word, he stood up, wiped the sweat from his face and the dirt from the seat of his trousers, and turned to the crowd of people at the school gate. The red cloth that had been spread over my grave was now draped over my golden coffin. Grandpa knew that meant the exhumation was finished, and that my remains were inside the new coffin. My leg bones were wrapped in the pair of red trousers, my ribs and arms in the red tunic, and the bones of my feet in a pair of red cloth shoes. In transferring my remains to the golden casket, the exhumation had been made a celebration, and a sorrowful event into a joyous one. When Grandpa began walking back to the school, my dad followed him.

'Dad, you're too old for this. Why don't you come and live with me in the city?'

Grandpa glanced at his son and kept trudging towards the school.

'Life is good in the city, and there's nothing left for you here. All your relatives are gone. Why not leave this place and never come back?'

This time, Grandpa didn't even bother to turn around.

At the school gate, eight young pallbearers lifted my golden coffin on to their shoulders and prepared to carry me from the school. The master of ceremonies lit another long string of firecrackers, and amid much noise, the procession began. Because I had died so young, there were no sons or daughters dressed in mourning to walk beside my coffin. But because I was getting married, the head of my coffin was decorated with the red cloth, which had been twisted into the shape of a flower. This was how I would leave Ding Village.

This was how they would carry me away.

They were taking me away from my grandpa and my school and my home.

They were taking me to a strange place where I'd be married to a crippled, epileptic girl who was six years too old for me.

They were taking me away.

There was the pop-popping of firecrackers and the babble of voices, fountains of sparks rising into the air and bits of burnt paper fluttering down. My father, walking behind my coffin, glanced around at the villagers who had come to join in this rare celebration.

He instructed the pallbearers to stop for a moment, then stood atop a little sand dune and announced loudly:

'People of Ding Village, brothers and sisters, friends and neighbours, thank you for coming out today. In the future, if you ever need help with anything, anything at all, you can find me in the city. But I was born right here, and as a native son of Ding Village, you know I'll always be truthful with you. So I may as well tell you about my latest venture: the county governor and I are planning to buy nearly 1,000 acres of land on the banks of the Yellow River, halfway between Kaifeng and the county seat, and turn it into a funeral park. It will be

a burial site fit for an emperor, with the best location, steps away from the water, and feng shui to rival the imperial tombs of the Mang mountain range in Luoyang.

'I know you've all heard the saying,' my father continued in a booming voice, 'that it's best to be born in Suzhou or Hangzhou, and best to be buried in the mountains of Mang. But how many people are lucky enough to be born in those cities, or buried in those mountains? I can't do anything about where you were born, but now that I'm a county cadre, the least I can do is see that you're buried in style. Fellow villagers, friends and neighbours, I give you my pledge: anyone from Ding Village who wants to be buried in my funeral park will receive the finest plot of land on the banks of the Yellow River, right next to my son Ding Qiang. I guarantee that you'll be able to purchase one of these fine burial sites for the lowest possible price. You'll be getting a final resting place with a river view and auspicious feng shui practically for free.'

When my father had finished his sales pitch, he looked up at the blazing sun, which was nearly overhead, and swept his eyes over the crowd. Then he stepped down from the sand dune and signalled to the pallbearers that it was time to continue the procession.

The villagers trailed after my coffin, chattering excitedly about the planned funeral park. Grandpa stayed behind for a few last words with my father.

'It's safe to leave the village now,' said Grandpa. 'Jia Genzhu is dead. He won't be bothering you any more.'

My father laughed. 'Dad, as long as you don't plan on killing me, I'll always be safe. There's not a person in any village on this plain who would dare to mess with me now.'

My father rejoined the funeral procession into the village, leaving Grandpa standing at my empty grave, next to the space where my golden coffin had been. Grandpa's face had turned pale, his features rigid. My father's words seemed to have triggered something in him, brought back some long-forgotten memory. He could feel his heart thundering in his chest, the perspiration oozing from his pores, the palms of his hands growing slick with sweat. He shifted his gaze from my father's retreating back to the crowd of villagers and the golden coffin, draped with red silk, being carried into the village like a bridal sedan chair. Like a flame being held aloft. The midday sun was dazzling, and a layer of haze hung over the plain like a luminous veil. The silence in all directions was absolute. Willow Hamlet, Two-Li Village and Yellow Creek lay hushed beneath the sunlight. Even the cattle and sheep grazing among the dunes nibbled their dry grass in silence. The only living sounds came from the cicadas, crying lustily from the branches of the few remaining trees. Their buzzing, and the distant explosions of fireworks, echoed in Grandpa's ears. As he turned to look at my empty grave, the grave they had opened and not bothered to fill in, realization came crashing down upon him: they were taking me away. My father and the others were carrying me away, taking me away from him for ever. Grandpa was alone in the school, friendless in the village, and abandoned by his family. I don't know how I hadn't noticed it before, but there wasn't a single black hair left on Grandpa's head. His silvery-white hair stuck up in tufts, making him look like a sacrificial lamb that had been hoisted into the air, waiting to be dashed upon the ground. The wrinkles on his weathered, ancient face were as numerous as cracks upon the arid plain, and the eyes that followed my funeral procession held no sorrow, or anger, or tears. All that was left was an indescribable hopelessness. His eyes were twin pools of despair, wells that had dried up long, long ago.

They were carrying me away, farther and farther away. Grandpa was now just a blur in the distance. From inside my coffin, I began to scream.

'Grandpa! Don't let them take me!'

My cries shook the heavens.

'I don't want to leave here! Don't let them take me!'

My screams ripped holes in the sky.

'Save me, Grandpa, save me . . .'

The idea struck Grandpa like a thunderclap, draining the colour from his face and making his hands shake. Trembling, *he bent down and picked up a stick, a stout piece of chestnut that someone had left lying on the ground. He began walking towards the crowd, following the funeral procession. In a few quick strides, he caught up with my father, who was lagging at the edge of the crowd. Grandpa raised the stick over his head and brought it down on my father's head, smashing in the back of his skull. The blow fell so quickly that my father didn't have time to turn around, or to cry out. He swayed for a second, then fell with a soft thud, like a sack of flour.*

A puddle of blood bloomed on the ground, as red as a blossom in spring.

CHAPTER FOUR

After he killed my dad, Grandpa acted like he had done the village a tremendous service. Ignoring my dad's body lying on the ground, he ran off to spread the good news in the village and to everyone he met along the way.

'Did you hear? I killed Ding Hui.'

'Hey, you there! Ding Hui's dead. I bashed him over the head with a stick.'

'Hi, just thought I'd let you know . . . you don't have to worry about Ding Hui any more. I killed him.'

As Grandpa raced towards the village, he seemed sprightlier, as if he was suddenly ten years younger. Starting at the west end of the village, he went from house to house opening doors, walking into people's courtyards and announcing his news.

'Hi, have you heard?' he called, pushing open the gate of the first house he came to. 'I killed my son, Ding Hui. Smashed his head in.'

At the second house: 'Are your parents home? Well, when they come back, tell them that Ding Hui is dead and that I killed him. I bashed him in the back of the head with a stick of chestnut, this long and this thick.' Grandpa illustrated his words with a gesture. 'Killed him with the first blow.'

At the third house: 'So you're back here, visiting? That's just as well. You can burn offerings at your brother and parents' graves and tell them that Ding Hui is finally dead. I killed him with one blow to the skull.'

At the seventh house he came to, Grandpa walked into the courtyard and saw that all the rooms were shuttered and locked. There were weathered funeral scrolls pasted to the

333

lintels of every door. He knelt in the middle of the courtyard, clasped his hands together and bowed three times. Then, although there was no one alive to hear his announcement, he said: 'Brothers, you brothers and your wives, I came to give you some good news. My son Ding Hui is dead, and I killed him.'

When Grandpa arrived at Jia Genzhu's house and saw the black coffin in the courtyard, he fell to his knees and touched his head to the ground. 'Genzhu, you were always like a nephew to me. I wanted to tell you the good news in person, and I hope you'll rest easier knowing that Ding Hui is dead. I killed him myself, bashed his head in with a stick.'

Later, Grandpa knelt in front of a cluster of new graves outside the village gate and cried: 'Listen, everyone . . . I've got some good news! Today I killed Ding Hui, my first-born son. I came up behind him and bashed his brains in. Ding Hui is dead . . .'

VOLUME 8

Summer was over, and autumn was here again.

Summer had passed without a drop of rain. Now it was midway through autumn, and there hadn't been a rainstorm for more than six months. The dry spell had lasted for 180 days. It was the worst drought seen on this plain in nearly a century. All the grasses and crops had died.

The trees were gone, too. Unable to resist the drought, the paulownia, scholar trees, chinaberries, elms, toons and rare honey locusts quietly passed away.

The big trees had all been chopped down, and the smaller ones had been lost to drought. There were no more trees.

Ponds congealed. Rivers stopped. Wells ran dry.

When the water disappeared, so did the mosquitoes.

Cicadas shed their skin and left before it was time. Their golden yellow corpses littered the trunks, branches and forks of dead trees, and clung to the shady side of walls and fences.

But the sun survived. The wind lived on. The sun and moon, stars and planets were alive and well.

A few days after my father's funeral, they came to arrest Grandpa. He was a murderer, a man who had murdered his son, so they had to take him away. Three months after his arrest, in the second month of autumn, it rained for seven days and seven nights without stopping. And when the rain was over, they let my grandpa go. It was like the rain had been his salvation. They took him away at the height of the drought, when all the grasses and trees were dying, and asked him a lot of questions. They asked him about Ding Village and blood-selling and coffins and matchmaking the dead. When he had answered all their questions and the rains had ended, when the wells and ponds and rivers and ditches were no longer dry, they let him go.

They sent him home and spared his life.

When Grandpa came back to Ding Village, it was already late autumn. The dusk of a late-autumn day. The sun above the plain was a blood-red ball, making red of the earth and sky. Laughing on the horizon, cackling from the western plain. All across the silent land, there were sounds of life. Chirps and squeaks and tiny insect sounds. Normally, at this time of year, the trees would be shedding their leaves, but most of the trees were gone. The grass had all but been killed off. Almost, but not quite. In the fields and in the spaces in between, along the sand dunes of the ancient Yellow River path, there were spots of green, pale-green patches of something still alive. Mingled with the autumn's rotting grass was a smell as fresh as spring. The scent of something new and clean.

Against the bright red sky, an occasional bird took flight. Crows and sparrows; an eagle. Their shadows flitted across the ground like wisps of smoke.

It was to this that Grandpa had returned.

He hadn't changed much. Grandpa was as thin as ever, and his face was pale, ashen grey. Wearing an old straw hat and carrying his bedroll, he looked like a traveller returning home after a long journey. What struck him first about Ding Village was the silence, the intensity of the silence. In the three months that he had been gone, in those 100 days from mid-summer to mid-autumn, Ding Village had become a different place.

No, it was still the same place, but all the people were gone. The streets were as silent as death, empty of man or beast. There were no chickens, pigs, ducks, cats or dogs. Now and then, the call of a sparrow shattered the quiet, like a stone hurled through a pane of glass. Grandpa met only one living thing, a stray dog so skinny you could see its ribs. It came out of Zhao Qiuqin's gate and stood in the middle of the road, staring at Grandpa. Then, without barking, it slunk away with its tail between its legs.

Grandpa stood in the centre of the village, gazing around him in confusion, wondering if he'd taken a wrong turn. Then he saw a structure he recognized: a decrepit cowshed. It hadn't changed much since he'd last seen it; it was still on the verge of collapse. A fallen rafter lay atop its crumbling brick walls like a chopstick resting on the cracked rim of a bowl.

The concrete roads, built years earlier with blood money, were now covered with a layer of dirt so thick you could plant crops in it. There were cracks and fissures, as crooked as national boundaries on a map.

Ma Xianglin's house at the village crossroads was more or less the same. Grandpa recognized the faded white funeral scrolls pasted to the lintels of the door. Finding the gate ajar, Grandpa went into the courtyard and called out, 'Is anybody home?'

There was no answer. The house was deathly silent.

Grandpa moved on to the next house, which belonged to Wang Baoshan. He shouted the man's name, but again, there was no answer. This house, too, was deathly still. The only occupants seemed to be a pair of mice. Disturbed by Grandpa's voice, they skittered through the courtyard and into the house.

The next house, too, was deserted. The whole village seemed deserted. Everywhere Grandpa looked, he found no sign of life.

When the fever had exploded, it had destroyed Ding Village. Most of those who hadn't died had moved away. Then came the drought, which swept away the last inhabitants as if they were leaves on a breeze. Ding Village had been snuffed out like a candle.

Grandpa went from house to house, door to door, shouting until his voice was hoarse. The only living creatures to answer his call were a few stray dogs following behind him, wagging their tails.

There was a fine red silken sunset, like the cloth they'd draped over my golden coffin so many months earlier. It settled over the houses and streets with only the faintest sound, like a feather floating through the air.

Grandpa walked until he came to my uncle's house on New Street. Ding Xiaoming and his family had taken possession of the house after Uncle died, but now they seemed to have moved away, too. A padlock hung sadly from the door.

Further down the street, our three-storey house was still standing, but all the doors and windows were gone. Someone had even removed the courtyard gate. The villagers had stripped the house bare. The courtyard was in slightly better shape. Mustard greens had taken over the entire courtyard. The air was thick with their crude, numbing scent.

Grandpa decided to visit the school. As he crossed the village, he felt as if he were passing through an endless ravine, or trudging through a barren desert. The road to the school was as deserted as the ancient Yellow River path. The sunset was a dazzling, silent hush of red. A cool breeze carried the mingled scents of rotting plants and newly sprouted grass across the plain. They swirled through the air, blending into one another like the clean and muddy currents of a river. The sand dunes along the ancient Yellow River path seemed somehow smaller than before. Then again, maybe they'd grown in size. At this distance, it was hard to tell.

The school hadn't changed too much. There were a few more weeds in the schoolyard, and a lot more grasshoppers, dragonflies and moths flitting through the air.

Grandpa was exhausted. He couldn't remember ever feeling so tired. He walked into his rooms, took one look at the teaching awards gathering dust on the walls, and collapsed on his bed. He never wanted to get up again. Grandpa fell asleep. As always, he dreamed.

In his dream, Grandpa passed through all the places he had known: Willow Hamlet, Yellow Creek, Two-Li Village, Old Riverton, Ming Village, Cottonwood, and so many, many others. He must have walked for hundreds of miles across the plain, visiting hundreds of villages and market towns, every one of them the same. In every place he went, he found no people or animals or trees. Only the buildings and houses remained. The people had died or moved away, and the animals had been slaughtered or starved. The trees, of course, had been chopped down to make coffins.

The houses were still standing, but their wooden parts were gone.

Doors, crossbeams, cabinets and window frames had been salvaged and made into coffins.

Even in the most distant counties, it was rare to see a single soul.

People and animals had been obliterated, and the plain was barren.

That night there was a rainstorm, a torrential downpour that transformed the plain into a vast expanse of mud. Grandpa dreamed of a woman, digging in the mud with the branch of a willow tree. With each flick of the branch, each stroke of the willow, she raised a small army of tiny mud people from the soil. Soon there were hundreds upon thousands of them, thousands upon millions, millions upon millions of tiny mud people leaping from the soil, dancing on the earth, blistering the plain like so many raindrops from the sky.

Grandpa found himself gazing at a new and teeming plain. A new world danced before his eyes.